SMOKE SCREEN

STEELE RIDGE: THE BLACKWELLS

ADRIENNE GIORDANO

STEELE RIDGE
www.SteeleRidgeSeries.com

TEAM STEELE RIDGE
Edited by Kristen Weber
Copyedited by Martha Trachtenberg
Cover Design by Stuart Bache, Books Covered
Author Photo by Debora Giordano

Print Edition, June 2022, ISBN: 978-1-948075-85-5
Digital Edition, June 2022, ISBN: 978-1-948075-84-8
For more information contact: adrienne@steeleridgepublishing.com

DISCOVER MORE STEELE RIDGE

STEELE RIDGE: THE BLACKWELLS

Flash Point, Book 1

Smoke Screen, Book 2

STEELE RIDGE: THE STEELES

The BEGINNING, A Novella

Going HARD, Book 1

Living FAST, Book 2

Loving DEEP, Book 3

Breaking FREE, Book 4

Roaming WILD, Book 5

Stripping BARE, Book 6

Enduring LOVE, A Novella, Book 7

Vowing LOVE, A Novella, Book 8

STEELE RIDGE: THE KINGSTONS

Craving HEAT, Book 1

Tasting FIRE, Book 2

Searing NEED, Book 3

Striking EDGE, Book 4

Burning ACHE, Book 5

STEELE RIDGE CHRISTMAS CAPERS

The Most Wonderful Gift of All, Caper 1

A Sign of the Season, Caper 2

His Holiday Miracle, Caper 3

A Holly Jolly Homecoming, Caper 4

Hope for the Holidays, Caper 5

All She Wants for Christmas, Caper 6

Jingle Bell Rock Tonight, Caper 7

Not So Silent Night, Caper 8

A Rogue Santa, Caper 9

The Puppy Present, Caper 10

For the Love of Santa, Caper 11

Beneath the Mistletoe, Caper 12

ALSO BY ADRIENNE GIORDANO

DEEP COVER SERIES

Crossing Lines

PRIVATE PROTECTORS SERIES

Risking Trust

Man Law

Negotiating Point

A Just Deception

Relentless Pursuit

Opposing Forces

THE LUCIE RIZZO MYSTERY SERIES

Dog Collar Crime

Knocked Off

Limbo (novella)

Boosted

Whacked

Cooked

Incognito

The Lucie Rizzo Mystery Series Box Set 1

The Lucie Rizzo Mystery Series Box Set 2

THE ROSE TRUDEAU MYSTERY SERIES

Into The Fire

HARLEQUIN INTRIGUES

The Prosecutor

The Defender

The Marshal

The Detective

The Rebel

JUSTIFIABLE CAUSE SERIES

The Chase

The Evasion

The Capture

CASINO FORTUNA SERIES

Deadly Odds

JUSTICE SERIES w/MISTY EVANS

Stealing Justice

Cheating Justice

Holiday Justice

Exposing Justice

Undercover Justice

Protecting Justice

Missing Justice

Defending Justice

SCHOCK SISTERS MYSTERY SERIES w/MISTY EVANS

1st Shock

2nd Strike

3rd Tango

SMOKE SCREEN

STEELE RIDGE: THE BLACKWELLS

ADRIENNE GIORDANO

STEELE RIDGE
www.SteeleRidgeSeries.com

1

"So, you're a repo guy."

Phin stood smack in the middle of Kayla Krowne's living room—the one inside her massive twelve-thousand-square-foot home—peering out over her small private beach and the still waters of Lake Norman.

He'd expected more boat traffic. Particularly with the streaks of purple and orange lighting up a summer sky. Who wouldn't want to be floating around watching that spectacular sunset?

He supposed Tuesday nights in June weren't big boating nights. He didn't mind so much.

The entire scene gave him a sense of peace. And quiet.

At least on the lake.

Inside Kayla's house?

Les Blakely, the Senate majority leader from Charlotte, put his finger on Phin's hot button and pressed that fucker hard enough to break it.

Phin dragged his gaze from the lake, looking down at Blakely, who—eh-hem—happened to be a good six inches shorter.

"Asset recovery," Phin said.

The senator shrugged a bony shoulder and ... snorted.

Seriously?

Phin cocked his head and hit the guy with the flashing, toothy smile his brothers said caused men to shit themselves and women to lose their clothes. Either way, Phin had perfected it, learned to use it in a variety of ways.

A tool in his arsenal.

At times, like now, it kept him from pounding men like Les Blakely into the ground. And that was something because Phin still burned, a damned month later, about Blakely vaporizing a domestic violence bill that Kayla had lobbied hard for. Shelters around the country needed that funding and Blakely had managed to bury the bill for probably another year.

Fucker.

"Asset recovery," Blakely said. "Is that what we're calling it these days?"

Phin focused on keeping his face neutral. No hard stare, no clenched jaw or pressed lips. He stood there, shoulders back, doing his Mr. Smooth thing, while a hot knife carved up his intestines.

Fucker, fucker, fucker.

"Gentlemen." A hand clamped on Phin's forearm, dragging him from the near-homicidal rage brewing inside him.

He glanced down at the hand squeezing his arm, then at its owner.

Kayla—thank you, sweet baby Jesus—stood beside him. He'd known her for years now and, as usual, her timing couldn't be better.

Accompanying Kayla was an exceptionally noticeable, not-quite-petite woman with a mane of dark curly hair and deep blue eyes. And who might this lovely creature be?

Maybe she was what Phin needed to relieve his now-pissy mood. Female company. Never a bad thing. Especially if it led to Phin's hands rifling through those wild curls.

"Kayla," Blakely drawled. "Lovely party."

"It is," Kayla agreed. "Senator, could I pull you from my good friend Phin? I have an important matter to discuss that requires a bit of privacy."

Ha. Privacy his ass. Clearly, Kayla had overheard the exchange and wanted to keep Phin from getting blood on her marble floors.

As one of the country's premier lobbyists, Kayla had power. Not the kind Blakely had. Hers was subtle. Backroom influence where she'd wheel and deal senators and congressmembers on behalf of her clients.

A world Phin had left behind three years ago.

"Of course," Blakely said.

The weasel nodded. "Blackwell, good to see you."

Not in this lifetime.

"Kayla," Phin said, "maybe you can talk him into reviving that domestic violence bill."

Kayla drilled him with a look that should have blown him clear through the floor-to-ceiling windows.

Tomorrow, she'd call and ream him. Today? He'd gotten his jab in. After all, she couldn't expect Phin to stand there and listen while the man insulted his family.

"Later," she told Phin. "Now, I want to bend his ear about the appointment of our next Secretary of State."

Oh, boy. Kayla ushered the senator away, leaving Phin thinking he'd like to be a fly on the wall for *that* conversation.

"Hello."

The brunette.

He banished thoughts of Blakely-the-weasel and flashed *the* smile again, offering his hand. "I'm Phin Blackwell."

She accepted his hand. "I know."

Interesting. This chick with her soulful blue eyes didn't seem the panty-dropping type. But, dang, that mane of curly hair combined with the black dress that managed to hug her body while revealing absolutely nothing made for a fascinating sexy-librarian package.

He made quick work of the handshake, making sure not to grip too hard or linger too long. He didn't need those slimeball tactics. His mother had taught him better.

Inside though? His brain filled with visions of lowering that little side zipper on her dress and peeling it off.

With his teeth.

He let the fantasy play out while his body hummed. Things might be looking up after the Blakely incident. "And you are?"

"Madison—Maddy—Carmichael."

Phin ran through his mental contact list. Carmichael. If he knew Kayla at all, chances were she'd brought this woman to him for a reason. A reason that probably included a job.

And wasn't that why Blackwell Asset Recovery Services, aka BARS, paid up to ten grand a plate to send him to these political shindigs?

"A pleasure, Maddy Carmichael," Phin said. "Why do I feel like Kayla engineered this meeting?"

"Because she did. I need your help."

Interesting indeed.

A woman about his mom's age—Congressman Jenkins's wife—squeezed beside Phin, eyeing him with the hunger of a Bengal tiger.

The things he put up with for his job.

Ignoring the tiger, he focused on Maddy. "Always happy to oblige a woman in distress."

At that, she rolled her eyes. Definitely not the panty-dropping type.

"Easy, Charlie Charm."

Charlie Charm?

Phin laughed. An honest-to-God ripple that flew right up his throat. How he loved a woman capable of verbal swordplay. "Is that why my friends call me CC for short?"

This time, Maddy laughed. "Good one. But this is serious."

"Whatever *this* is."

She leaned in. His cue to dip his head in anticipation of whatever apparently naughty secret she'd like to share. He had a few of his own, if she'd be willing to play.

"I'm the acquisitions manager at the Thompson Center," she said, her breath warm on his neck.

And oooh-eeee. Phin concentrated on staying in character. Mr. Smooth. Mr. I-see-this-all-the-time-and-am-not-completely-fucking-stunned.

"As in President Thompson?" he asked.

"Exactly."

Phin straightened and considered her words.

After two terms that ended three years ago, former United States President Gerald Thompson shook things up in Washington by forgoing a traditional presidential library. Instead, he'd opted to spend the twenty months before leaving office fundraising for a presidential *center*. One housing memorabilia, clothing he and his wife had worn, exhibits, a theater. A gym to get kids off the street.

Thompson's vision? To revive the Charlotte area he'd grown up in, which now suffered from the killer combo of economic decline and rising crime.

Phin cocked his head, his curiosity exciting him for reasons that suddenly had nothing to do with Maddy's hair. "What can I help you with?"

Please let it be what I think it is.

"I'll assume you've heard about the robbery at the Center?"

"Priceless jewels designed by a former president's father? You bet I have."

She leaned in again and he dipped his head, letting her get right next to his ear. "Can we talk in private?"

They sure could.

MADDY FOLLOWED PHIN BLACKWELL DOWN A LONG HALLWAY lined with eclectic art she never would have comingled, but somehow worked. The Warhol to her left slowed her steps. On the way back, she'd stop and savor it.

She kept moving and, ooohhh, stopped cold in front of an oil painting.

A *Titian.*

In front of her, Phin looked back. "Titian," he said. "I know. Who puts a Warhol next to Italian Renaissance? That's Kayla."

"It's ... stunning."

And darn it, she had soooo many questions. The first being how the heck much did Kayla make as a lobbyist that she could afford a Titian?

Phin pointed to a staircase leading to the lower level of the enormous house. "This way."

The man knew his way around. What that little factoid had to do with anything, she wasn't sure, but she took a second to ponder it because what single woman wouldn't?

A man like Phin, tall and fit with his movie-star good looks, electric smile, and slick suit?

Dangerous.

Before she'd even been introduced, from a good five feet away he'd managed to get into her space, all that insane hotness and male energy sending tiny shocks shooting along her skin.

At the staircase, Phin paused, holding his hand out. She moved past him and he set his hand on her lower back. A simple gesture that probably didn't mean one teeny thing to him, but ignited a fresh wave of tingles over her and, well, hardened her nipples.

What am I doing?

The same thing she always did, that's what.

Step one: Meet a gorgeous man.

Step two: Fall hard for said man.

Step three: Dream of a wedding.

Step four: Get her heart broken.

Every time, the fairy tale seemed just ... out ... of her ... reach.

At this point, she'd become convinced it had something to do with losing her father so young. Daddy issues, one of her friends claimed.

Whatever the problem, when it came to Phin Blackwell, she needed to steer clear. Far, far away.

This guy had to be a total player. Way out of her league.

Kayla on the other hand? Beautiful, successful Kayla would be his perfect match.

A woman unafraid to disrupt established rules. When Kayla Krowne entered a room, her confidence came with her. Something Good Girl Maddy admired and maybe even craved.

Yeah. Good luck. She was too worried about pissing people off to become such a dynamo.

Kayla and Phin? That would be a power couple.

With the way Phin filled out a suit, Maddy wouldn't mind being the female dynamo in that power couple instead of Kayla.

Kayla, a board member and major donor for the Thompson Center, had said they were friends. Whether that included sex, Maddy didn't know. What she did know was the *friendship* had garnered this meeting.

The bottom of the stairs welcomed them to a finished basement painted a muted gray bordering on white. Subtle lighting warmed the space and, *whoopsie,* Maddy averted her eyes from a couple on a large sectional, their bodies close as they peered out another set of floor-to-ceiling windows.

From the sofa, the man, clearly irritated by the interruption, shot Phin a look.

"Apologies," he said.

He leaned down, getting close to Maddy's ear where his warm breath tickled her skin and, well, other parts that Good Girl Maddy had been ignoring lately. Parts that reminded her she hadn't been touched by a man since that last blind date four months ago when the guy continually ran his foot up her calf under the table.

"There's a guest suite with a sitting area," Phin said. "It's private. Are you comfortable with that?"

Meaning, was she comfortable going into a bedroom with a strange man who made her nipples hard and whom she'd like to see without a shirt?

Typically, no.

Never.

But this was Kayla's friend, and she trusted Kayla.

"It's all right," Maddy said. "Good thing you know the house."

And yikes. Had she really said that?

"I do. She invites me to a lot of her parties." He paused at a door, meeting Maddy's eye. "I interned for her and another lobbyist my junior year in college. She's a friend who knows I have a long ride home and lets me stay in this room when the parties run late."

The hot sting of humiliation crawled up Maddy's throat. "I wasn't ..."

Who was she kidding? Of course she was. "I'm sorry. I shouldn't have jumped to conclusions."

Phin shrugged. "Most people do."

"That must be hard."

"People constantly judging me? Forming opinions when they don't know me?" He laughed. "You get used to it."

When he shifted to open the door, she reached out, touched his arm. "I really am sorry. It won't happen again."

"Okay," he said in a clipped tone that let her know he didn't believe her.

That, yes, it would most definitely happen again. What, in this man's life, would lead him to be so cynical?

Not my problem.

He opened the door to a bedroom larger than Maddy's apartment. More floor-to-ceiling windows served as outer walls and all Maddy wanted was to sit up in that bed one morning, look out the window, and take in the lake's beauty, the wash of bold pinks and purples of a dawn cotton candy sky.

"Amazing," Phin said. "Isn't it?"

"It sure is."

He gestured to the two upholstered chairs positioned in front of the glass. "Let's sit."

She lowered herself to the chair, set her purse on the floor, and smoothed her dress while aligning her thoughts. President Thompson had sent her here. Well, President Thompson via her boss, Frank Silvain. Now, she had a job to do and wanted to make her employer happy.

Finally, she shifted to face him. "I'm way out of my lane here."

He hit her with the Charlie Charm smile again. She totally didn't trust that smile.

"That's where the fun is," he said.

Maddy let out a low whistle and zinged him with her best no-nonsense look. "Look, you're a nice guy, but I need you to back off on the slick. And, frankly, if you don't want people judging you as a player, don't give them reason to."

Again, Phin laughed, but even as he tried to sell his amusement, his eyes narrowed a fraction.

Insulted?

Maybe.

"Lady," he said, "you're a pisser."

"Whatever. All I know is Kayla seems to think your family can help recover the jewels stolen from the Thompson Center."

There. She'd said it. Just blurted it out. As if it was someone else's crazy idea. As if she hadn't been the one to go to her boss and suggest they speak to a company that specialized in this type of thing. A company that Kayla Krowne, one of their board members, had a connection to. A company like Blackwell Asset Recovery Services, that Maddy had heard, was really—really—good at locating insanely expensive stolen items.

Rumor amongst the museum management crowd had it that the last item BARS successfully retrieved was a five-hundred-thousand-dollar bottle of brandy.

And who cared enough about liquor to spend half a million dollars on it? Collectors. Curious bunch.

Phin's eyebrows rose, but other than that, no body language. Zero.

"What are you thinking?" she asked.

"I'm thinking a lot of things. There hasn't been much on the news about the heist. My brother, Ash— Cameron— is on the FBI's art crime team. I'm assuming you know that. *He* won't even give us details. All I know is that there was a robbery and pieces made by the president's father were taken."

"Do you know the story about his biological father? Why he doesn't have the same last name?"

Phin nodded. "Louis Pierre, world-renowned jeweler. He and the president's mother had an affair. She never told Pierre she was pregnant."

"Correct. She married a man who adopted the president as a toddler. The president didn't find out about his biological father until he was a teenager. Out of respect for the man who raised him, he chose not to change his last name to Pierre, but he did meet his biological family. As Thompson's political career took off, Louis Pierre designed countless items for his daughter-in-law, the soon-to-be First Lady."

"Who also happens to be granddaughter to none other than the Queen of England."

"Skip ahead to a few months ago," Maddy said. "I proposed the idea for a thirty-day exhibit featuring the clothing and jewelry worn by the First Lady during election week. A bold request on my part, considering the value and personal nature of the pieces. I hounded my boss, the Center's director, to take it to the board. I'm sure he got sick of me asking and thought the board would deny me and that would be the end."

"You're persistent."

"I am. He arranged for me to present the idea to the board. I asked an artist friend to help with a rendition of what the exhibit would look like. My presentation lasted twenty minutes, where I ticked off all the points about how the public would enjoy items most would never, ever, get a chance to see up close. I left there with a promise that they'd speak to the president and First Lady."

"I guess it got approved."

Maddy couldn't even summon a smile. At this point, she regretted the entire proposition. "The following morning, President and Mrs. Thompson called me themselves. They told me I had impressed the board with my passion for the project and they loved the idea. That's the kind of people they are. They're all about sharing their experiences."

He smiled at her again, this one not so much the CC one. This one, softer and ... genuine. And, oh boy, that smile might be more devastating than the CC one because her nipples waved a white flag.

"That's amazing," he said.

Maddy cleared her throat. "At the time, maybe. Now? Nightmare. I feel responsible."

He drew his eyebrows together. "For what?"

"If I hadn't talked everyone into it, the jewels wouldn't be missing."

"That's crap. You didn't break into that building."

"I created the target."

Phin considered that a moment. "They marketed the hell out of that exhibit. Everywhere I went there was an ad, a news clip, or social media post. That kind of press draws criminal attention. Typically, someone knows someone who knows someone at the target location. My guess is that's how the thieves got around the security system."

An inside job? If that was meant to make her feel better, it didn't. President Thompson and his wife ran a meticulous operation. The idea of one of their carefully vetted employees stealing? Sickening.

"How many pieces are gone?"

"Seven. The FBI is investigating. It's moving slowly."

"It's only been a few days."

She put up a hand. "I know it sounds unreasonable to be critical after so short a time, but ..."

"What?"

"Kayla thinks, at the very least, you might ask around and get information for us. Your fee, whatever it is, won't be a problem. The board wants these items recovered."

"I can see why. Louis Pierre's jewels are priceless. We recovered a thirty-five-carat emerald last year. Stolen from a private collection. It was originally a necklace, but by the time we found it, the gems had been removed from the setting and the gold melted down. We got to the stone before it could be recut."

"That's what I'm terrified of."

"Not to be flip, but even if the pieces are broken up and melted down, his father created them. He could remake them if we find the stones."

Maddy shook her head. "It's not just the Pierre items that are missing. It's literally an international incident."

Phin studied her for a few seconds. "I'm not following."

Of course he wasn't. "There were seven pieces stolen. Three were Pierre's work."

"And the other four?"

"Jewels borrowed from the personal collection of the First Lady's grandmother. The Queen of England."

2

IF EVER THERE WAS A TIME FOR PHIN TO SOIL HIMSELF, THIS was it.

He sat back, stared out at the darkening sky while his head went to war with his body. Between his slamming pulse and the thoughts bombing his brain, he needed to get hold of himself.

Focus.

A job like this would put BARS on another level. A seriously big level.

And he wanted it. To come out of the shadows and maybe, for once, get credit for doing something meaningful. To look at men like Blakely, who considered the Blackwells nothing but glorified thieves, and flip those fuckers off.

"Jesus," he said, "I should have brought a drink with me."

"You and I both."

He faced Maddy again. "Who knows the queen's jewels are gone?"

"The Center's board, my boss, the director of security, President and Mrs. Thompson, the FBI agents working the case, and the two of us. Baltimore police responded to the initial call, but as far as I know, they weren't briefed on the exact items stolen. The FBI took over the scene within minutes. By now, some of our employees may know."

What the hell did that mean? They either knew or they didn't? "May know?"

"We boarded up the exhibit space as soon as the FBI processed it, but someone could have seen it before it was sealed. The security director may have told his staff. They're a tight group."

"But, as far as you know, the media doesn't know about the queen's pieces?"

"No. We've told the press that the queen's jewels were safe. We lied. For obvious reasons, we need to get the pieces back quickly."

Talk about an international incident. And, hell, from what Phin knew about the queen's personal collection, which wasn't a lot, the historical and monetary value made the pieces difficult to insure.

"What kind of loss are we talking about?"

"For both the Pierres and the queen's collection? A lot. Among the missing items are three tiaras. One of them is valued at one point two million. The second tiara has forty-seven vertical diamond strands. The diamonds alone are worth over a million dollars. We're estimating the third tiara at nearly a million. Then there are two brooches, a diamond bracelet, and a triple-strand diamond necklace."

"Did the Thompson Center insure them?"

Maddy let out a soft grunt. "I didn't know it until yesterday, but no. It was a calculated risk that came down to paying enormous insurance fees the Center couldn't afford."

"The board gambled and lost."

"Yes. As crazy as this will sound, the money wouldn't matter. It's the historical value that's impossible to measure."

Phin shook his head. "My mother would call this a humdinger."

"Will you help us?"

BARS was good, but were they *this* good? It'd sure be fun to find out. "Let me take it back to my family. I'll also reach out to my brother at the FBI. I'll fall through the floor if he's willing to give us any intel. But now that we've been approached by the Thompsons, and given the high profile, the feds may want all hands on deck."

And wouldn't that be interesting? Big brother, who'd walked away from all things BARS to be a straitlaced FBI agent, might want their help. Again.

"I highly doubt that," Maddy said. "They haven't exactly been forthcoming."

Phin glanced over at her. "I guess it depends on how bad they want to find the queen's stash."

Phin rolled out of bed at 7:15, a minor miracle since he'd arrived home after two and then stared at his bedroom ceiling for ninety minutes, thinking about the tremendous opportunity laid at his feet.

It took every argument he could conjure not to walk down that long hallway in the middle of the night to Zeke's door and bang on it.

Sometimes, living with his family in the mammoth Friary they'd converted to a multiunit home, gave him hives.

And, hello? His mother in residence didn't offer a ton of privacy when it came to bringing women home. He'd gotten used to either going to the woman's place or making use of the condo BARS leased in Charlotte.

There were times, though, like now, when having his family close made life easier.

This Thompson deal, if Zeke agreed, would be a total freaking win for BARS.

Before hopping in the shower, he put on coffee and texted Zeke, requesting a meeting. Mom tried to keep track of all their schedules, but with five men to wrangle, that was an epic failure.

If they needed a meeting, Zeke would group text them and bam, everyone showed up. New business meant making money, and they all liked their toys.

Phin's recent acquisition of an Audi RS 5 proved the point. Schmoozing slimeballs all night drained him and he needed time to decompress. Lately, the closest thing to heaven he'd experienced was opening the Audi up on a quiet highway.

He enjoyed the steep, winding mountain roads leading to their home in Steele Ridge, the town he, along with his cousins on his mom's side, grew up in and watched fall into bankruptcy before his billionaire cousin, Jonah Steele, bought it. Literally bought the damned town to save it from economic ruin.

Over the years, Phin hadn't gotten to know the Steele bunch as well as he'd have liked. Probably his own fault because Mom and Dad had insisted on secrecy regarding Dad's repo business. Those secrets led to assumptions by outsiders that criminal activity might be involved. Which seriously sucked. There wasn't a ton Phin could do about it, other than keep his head up.

After the family had bought the Friary and the massive acreage around it, Zeke had gone nuts installing security. The security alone sent the Steele Ridge gossips to delirium.

Who could blame them? Without information, curious minds created alternate realities.

Bon Jovi's "Wanted Dead or Alive" blared from Phin's phone just as he slid into his T-shirt.

He scooped the phone from the bedside table. A 9:00 meeting with Zeke. Phin checked his watch, an old Timex that had belonged to his dad.

An hour to kill.

He finished dressing, opting for a pair of drawstring cotton shorts to go with his T-shirt. He never minded wearing what his brothers called his James Bond suits, but after a night with limited sleep, he needed casual. It didn't keep the guys from roasting him about his pressed T-shirts.

When did neat clothing become a crime?

Whatever. Phone in hand, he walked to his suite's galley kitchen, keeping his steps light in case Cruz might still be asleep below him.

The aroma of the maple coffee Mom had picked up at the farmer's market the weekend before ignited his senses. In the five days since she'd bought it, the stuff had become an all-out obsession. Maybe that's what he'd do after the meeting with Zeke. Instead of the Audi, he'd take the jeep. Put the top down and go in search of the address on the coffee bag. He'd buy a case of the stuff. Maybe he'd even take Mom with him. Get her out of the office some.

He stuck his phone in the front pocket of his shorts, poured coffee, black no sugar, and headed to the French doors leading to the small balcony that overlooked the back end of the property. Morning sunshine and tweeting birds greeted him. He dropped into the cushioned chair and sat for a second, sucking in the thick, humid air. Summer in North Carolina. No joke.

Certain days, he didn't mind giving up his political aspirations to work for BARS. That career meant an office job that prohibited lazy mornings on his balcony.

The bonus today was he hadn't crawled out of a stranger's bed in the middle of the night and schlepped home.

"Phinny, Phinny, Phinny," he muttered. "What the hell are you doing?"

Thinking never served him. Made him get too far inside his mind and sent him spiraling down a hole he had no business going down. Like the one where he mourned the opportunity to effect positive change in the world. That would have been fun.

Sipping his coffee, he checked the headlines on his phone. Nothing about the Thompson Center heist.

A bird, an eastern phoebe, let out a call and he peered up, searching the trees while his thoughts tripped back to the night before and the fascinating Maddy Carmichael.

He liked her spunk, not to mention her curves. Her quick wit. Smart women did that to him. Fired his engines. Challenged him intellectually.

Hopefully, he'd be seeing more of her.

He checked the time. Forty more minutes.

While waiting, Phin could put a call in to Ash. Try to pry intel from big brother.

A second of thought nixed that idea. Wasn't worth the ass-frying from Zeke for contacting Ash first. Lately, navigating the tension between those two made prison sound like a day spa. And Phin had found himself the target of both their wraths enough to have learned a lesson or two.

The first being *not* to speak to Ash before Zeke about BARS business. Even if, in the next—he checked his watch—thirty-seven minutes, his curiosity might drive him to madness.

. . .

PHIN WALKED INTO ZEKE'S OFFICE AND FOUND HIS BROTHER AT his desk, cursing his laptop screen.

He wore a loose gray T-shirt and a Charlotte Knights baseball cap. Probably a bad hair day, since big brother had complained the day before about needing a haircut.

"Hey," Phin said, dropping into one of the guest chairs.

"Morning."

Zeke shut the laptop, something that had nothing to do with privacy and everything to do with avoiding distraction. He ran his fingers over his morning scruff. "Mom is killing me with spreadsheets. Have I mentioned how much I hate spreadsheets?"

Phin smiled. "Maybe a time or two."

BARS hadn't necessarily been the career of choice for Zeke, but Ash's decision to follow his dream left Zeke in charge. Someone had to do it and he was next in line. He'd taken on the role, nearly driving them all insane trying to control every damned thing until barely six weeks ago when he'd realized he needed a life and figured out how to delegate.

On their last big job, the FBI had recruited BARS to assist on a case and Zeke had managed to fall in love with the case agent. And thank God, because their brother had been a whole lot less of a dickhead since Olivia Westcott came on the scene and moved into the Friary with her young son, Brodie.

Zeke had even gone so far as to hire Liv as their full-time art expert. She now worked for BARS, but still had spies within the Bureau.

Speaking of ... Phin hadn't seen Liv around the last few days.

"Where's Liv been?"

"She's staying at her bungalow in Asheville for the next few days to help the UNC professor finish cataloging the warehouse full of O'Fallon's pilfered goods."

"Is that the case where the politician stole priceless antiquities for decades in order to provide his kids with an inheritance?"

"That's the one. Brodie is staying with her parents. I miss the little bugger. It's too quiet around here."

"Well," Phin said, "at least you have spreadsheets to keep you busy."

His brother laughed and flipped him off before rocking back in his chair. "How'd last night go?"

Ha. He'd love this. "As you know, Kayla's events are like a who's who in Charlotte politics. That weasel Blakely was there."

Zeke groaned. "Better you than me."

"I'd like to pound the fucker into the ground. He has the personality of a rock. How the hell does he keep getting elected?"

"Money. He can outdistance the pack with his war chest. Who else was there?"

"Kayla introduced me to a woman named Maddy Carmichael."

"Carmichael. Why do I know that name?"

"She's the acquisitions manager for the Thompson Presidential Center."

Zeke snapped his fingers. "Yes. She was quoted in an article after the heist."

"That's what she wanted to talk to me about."

That got big brother's attention, and he sat forward again, resting his forearms on his desk. "Interesting."

"Yes, sir. Hold on to your shorts. The Pierre pieces

weren't the only ones boosted. Four pieces the first lady's granny—none other than the Queen of fucking England—loaned her are in the wind. The feds are keeping it quiet." Phin offered a cheery grin. "International incident."

"Ya think?"

"I'm surprised Liv didn't tell you about it."

Zeke shook his head. "She may not know about it if the feds have that tight of a lid on it."

"Maddy—Ms. Carmichael—got approval from President and Mrs. Thompson to inquire about us helping."

Zeke's mouth fell open, then closed again.

Phin had to laugh. "Guessing that look is a good one?"

"It's a we-have-a-lot-to-consider-before-taking-this-job one. What pieces are we talking about?"

Phin dragged his phone from his front pocket and checked his notes from the night before. "Three tiaras, two brooches, a diamond necklace and bracelet. The bracelet, one of the brooches and two tiaras are the queen's. The tiaras alone are worth millions. Forget about the historical value."

"Does the queen know?"

"Nope. The Thompson's lied. Said the queen's pieces were safe. That's why the feds are keeping it quiet. The Thompsons want to recover the items before word gets out."

Zeke blew air through his lips. "Good luck with that. The black market is probably already active. It's only a matter of time."

"Which is why we should move on it. Phenomenal opportunity."

"I agree. But even if we take the job and recover everything, the FBI will never give us credit. What's in it for us?"

"Besides the payday?"

"Obviously."

Phin set his phone on his thigh and held his hands wide. "Ye of little faith. We may not publicly get credit, but I'll make sure everyone who's anyone in DC and Charlotte knows we did it. The jobs will come rolling in. Can we handle a sudden influx of work?"

"We can handle it."

The half second it took for Zeke to respond didn't bolster Phin's confidence. "You sure?"

"Between all of us, we have enough connections and know the market and the players. From the beginning, I thought this was a highly synchronized job. I mean, you just don't decide to put a ladder up to a window and break in to what amounts to a presidential museum. They had to have gathered intel on security, run scenarios. Practiced. It's a pro wanting it to look amateurish." His brother eyed him. "Did you call Ash about this?"

"Figured it'd be better if we called him together. It doesn't sound like the feds have much. There's a reason the Thompsons came to us."

Zeke hit the speaker button on his desk phone. "Let's call him. We'll make like we're checking in. Casually get around to asking about the heist. Wink, wink."

On the second ring, Ash picked up. "Hey."

"You're on speaker. I got Phin here."

"Good. I was gonna call him. How was Kayla's fundraiser?"

Ash checking in wasn't a surprise. He loved his job, but part of him, the natural-born schmoozer part, missed the $10,000-a-plate events.

"It was good. Food was amazing. The view even better. The woman knows how to throw a party. How'd you know I was there?"

"Sources."

Zeke snorted. "Translation: Mom told him."

Ash laughed. "Of course she did. Rumor has it Kayla raised a boatload of cash for the new wing in the children's hospital."

She'd done more than that. With a simple introduction, she'd potentially brought BARS a ton of clout. "She definitely did that. Packed house."

"Senator Blakely there?"

"You bet."

"Did he insult you?"

"Affirmative."

"He's such an asshole."

He and Ash were of the same mind there. Phin considered sharing how Kayla lured Blakely away, but ... Nah. Regarding politics and Kayla, his brother had an issue. What that issue was, Phin didn't know, but more times than not, Kayla's machinations irritated Ash. Still, the woman was Phin's friend, and he had no intention of stoking the ready-to-burn fire between her and big brother.

"What else is going on?" Ash asked.

"With?"

"Anything. How's business?"

"Good."

Phin glanced at Zeke and let out a silent chuckle over Zeke's refusal to give Ash any deets. A toddler-esque, but entertaining move.

"Zeke, you're an ass," Ash said, his tone lacking any heat.

At that, Phin cracked up. His brothers. Had to love 'em.

"Mom said it's been busy," Ash continued. "Any new clients?"

Zeke met Phin's eye and Phin knew exactly where this would go.

"You show me yours," Zeke said, "and I'll show you mine."

Toddler.

Phin shook his head. Somehow he'd entered the death-trap known as the relationship between his two oldest brothers.

"Uh, no," Ash said.

"*I* met an interesting woman last night," Phin offered. "The insanely attractive Maddy Carmichael."

"The Thompson Center's Maddy Carmichael?"

"Yep."

"Why was she there?"

Ever so slowly, Zeke inched his head back and forth. As if Phin would blurt it after the whole I'll-show-you-mine nonsense.

"Beats me," Phin said. "Kayla introduced us. If nothing else, she's a great contact."

"Did she say anything about the heist?"

"Just that the FBI was on it. Shame about those Pierre pieces."

"The goal is to recover them before they're dismantled."

"Yes," Zeke said. "The historical value alone makes them priceless. Good thing only the Pierres are missing."

A long pause came from the other end of the line, and Zeke flashed a smile.

As much as Zeke enjoyed it, this was *not* fun. Phin hated hiding things from his family. Secrets gave him a damned rash.

But this was the tone Ash had set early on. The boundary between his job and family.

The hard truth of it was, Phin didn't blame him for not sharing intel. Sharing meant risking his cases. If nothing else, Phin admired Ash's loyalty to Lady Justice.

Even if it alienated his family.

The silence dragged on, sucking the oxygen from the room. Time to end this little chat. "Okay," Phin said. "Gotta go. Work to do."

"Me too," Ash said. "I'm up to my nuts here, but I told Mom I'd get out there this weekend."

"It'll be good to see you."

This from Zeke. Well, look at his brothers being all cuddly.

"Yeah," Ash said. "I actually miss you assholes."

"Whatever. We're out."

Phin reached across and poked the disconnect button.

Zeke double-checked the phone, making sure the line was dead before meeting Phin's gaze again. "He's not sharing."

"Which puts us in a pickle because if we take this job and don't tell him, he'll lose his mind."

"Not our problem. He has a code of confidentiality, so do we."

"Even if it embarrasses our brother?"

Zeke gave him a hard look. "I don't know what you want me to do."

Ash wasn't the only one dealing with the line between job and family. All Phin knew was that he hated the secrecy. And people like that weasel Senator Blakely looking at him like he was trash because they were in the repo business.

Sure, his family liked to call it asset recovery, but make no mistake, Dad started with repossessing cars. Phin wasn't ashamed of that. Never.

The business had grown, though, thanks to Ash and more-so Zeke, who'd upgraded them to expensive art, jewelry, and whatever the hell else rich people got robbed of. But ...

Blakely.

People like him crawled right under Phin's skin, judging him.

"What's your problem?"

Zeke's voice pulled Phin from his thoughts. "Sorry. What?"

"You're ... weird ... today. What's your problem? Don't tell me you let Blakely get to you. You *know* that guy. Total Napoleon complex."

Phin did know. And yet ...

"It still sucks."

"You let him get to you. Dammit, Phin."

Phin sat forward, propping his elbow on the arm of his chair. "You never wanted to run BARS. You enjoyed letting Ash deal with the administrative headaches. And here you are. Taking over."

"What's your point?"

No idea. All he knew was that the conversation with Blakely had taken root inside of him and festered. "I don't know."

"You're thinking too much. I've told you a hundred, maybe a thousand times, you can't worry about what people think or say."

"Doesn't it piss you off that people think we're shady?"

"No."

Well, *that* was bullshit. "Liar."

"People like Blakely think we're shady until they need us. Then we're saviors because we found their Rembrandt or half-million-dollar bottle of brandy. I don't care what they think. They're clients. It's not personal."

"They don't have the right to judge us."

"Jesus, Phin." Zeke shook his head, stared up at the ceiling for a second before coming back to Phin. "As long as you know who you are and you're satisfied, people like Blakely shouldn't even be on your radar."

"What if I'm *not* satisfied?"

And, oh crap. He said that. For a second, his mind went berserk. *Take it back. Talk your way around it. Explain yourself. Say something.*

But Phin had nothing. The master schmoozer silenced.

"Whoa." Zeke put a hand up. "What specifically are we talking about? The job? Or you as an individual?"

Phin slouched back, scrubbed his hands over his face. Fatigue. That's all this was. Between having to play his role last night, the constant living behind a smokescreen and the townspeople gossiping about those shady Blackwells, he was zonked. Add the lack of sleep and his body hadn't just protested, it lobbed grenades.

"Forget it," Phin said. "I'm tired."

"I can tell. Take the morning to decompress. It's a nice day. Hop in the jeep and go for a drive. Do whatever it is you need to do to get rid of the sewage floating in your mind."

Good advice. Advice he'd thought of himself an hour ago. "I planned on it. What about Maddy Carmichael's offer? I told her I'd talk to you and call her ASAP with an answer."

"I'm intrigued. I'd like to see the scene. Get a handle from inside on how this happened. Call her and ask if we can come by this afternoon for a look. That'll give me the morning to run numbers with Mom. Until then, get some rest. I need you sharp."

3

Maddy strode from the Thompson Center cafeteria, stopping to drop off a couple of trays she'd collected from a coffee table near the lounge area windows. She never minded helping out when necessary.

The Thompsons had a vision for the Center. That vision included patrons spending the day wandering exhibits, grabbing a brick-oven pizza or freshly made salad and dining at a pristine table.

After lunch, folks could move to the interactive parts of the Center. Maybe the indoor basketball court President Thompson occasionally dropped in on for a game of HORSE. Other options included ping-pong and pool. Not interested in games? No problem. The library contained the president's favorite books and research papers. Magazines and trade publications. Law journals.

All of it designed to give visitors a taste of the president's life, but more importantly as a refuge for children and teenagers struggling with poverty and the lure of crime.

Having come from modest means, President Thompson

understood that if they, everyone at the Center, could get kids off the street, dreams might come true.

Maddy rode the escalators from the basement level to the first floor where she'd walk the exhibits, scouring each floor until she made it back to the executive suite on level four.

Part of her job meant checking on exhibits, talking to patrons, getting their reactions to certain pieces. What they loved. What moved them. What left them feeling "meh."

Did the college exhibits need to be moved? Did anyone really care that President Thompson worked his way through Yale as a janitor?

On floor two, she spoke with a teacher leading her fifth-grade class through the exhibits, letting her know the basketball court and ping-pong tables were available if the kids had energy to burn.

Maddy continued to the third floor, stepping off the escalator where Percy, one of the security guards, stood at the entrance to the Congress years exhibit. His kind face and white beard had earned Percy the nickname of Santa.

"Hello, Ms. Maddy."

"Hi, Percy. How's everything today? Any complaints?"

"We have a toilet paper shortage in the second-floor bathroom. I let maintenance know about that. One kid said the middle-school projects exhibit was boring."

Kids. Such a challenge. "No shock there."

What kid enjoyed seeing school projects? They wanted excitement and adventure. Navy SEALs. Covert missions, the photos of Air Force One. Still, they needed to know, to *see,* that becoming president didn't magically happen. It required hard work. Basic learning taken to higher and higher levels until dreams came true.

If they could dream, they could achieve.

That was the message.

Maddy clearly had work to do on the middle-school exhibits because the message wasn't clear.

Sigh.

"Also," Percy said, "a retired librarian came through and suggested the president should read Vikram Seth's *A Suitable Boy*. She felt strongly it would make a,"—he made air quotes—"positively enormous contribution to the classic literature exhibit."

Oh my. As part of a challenge offered by her English professor, Maddy had read the book in college. At 1,488 pages, *A Suitable Boy* held the dubious honor of being one of the longest single volume books published in the English language. Her professor had basically dared the class to read it for extra credit.

A-plus in that class, thank you very much.

"I'll suggest it to President Thompson," Maddy said. "With the size of that book, it's a good thing he's retired."

Percy laughed, then shifted his gaze to a twenty-something couple stepping off the escalator.

"Good afternoon," he called. "Welcome."

Maddy nodded. "Hello. I'm Maddy Carmichael, the acquisitions manager. Do you have questions?"

The man gave Maddy a once-over, his gaze lingering on her boobs.

Men.

His girlfriend followed his gaze, noting his fascination with Maddy's knockers. At which point, the girlfriend grabbed the guy's arm and led him into the exhibits entrance.

Alrighty then.

Maddy went back to Percy. "I'll see you later. Thank you, Percy."

"Of course, ma'am."

After completing her walk-through, she made her way to the executive suite, where a wall of spotless floor-to-ceiling windows framed double glass doors.

The glass wasn't a coincidence. Nothing about this building's design was. Windows conveyed transparency, and until the robbery, that's what the Thompsons wanted.

No secrets.

Maddy lifted her left hand. Most wore their keycards on a lanyard around their necks. Not Maddy. She wore a stretchy bracelet with her keycard attached.

She swiped her way into the executive suite and nodded at the Secret Service agents standing in reception. Both President and Mrs. Thompson were still entitled to protection and the agents had become a routine sighting for employees.

Seated at her desk was Aileen, their full-time wonder-girl of an assistant.

"Hey, Maddy. How was lunch?"

"Good. They have a pecan salad today you might like."

A die-hard foodie, Aileen enjoyed sampling the new menu items and reporting back on the flavors and textures. She'd become the litmus test for the food and beverage manager because if Aileen found a dish lacking, most others did as well. Which nixed the item from the menu. All part of the attention to detail the Thompsons demanded.

"President Thompson is here and wants to see you. They're in the conference room."

"They're?"

"Louis and Frank."

Frank was the Center's director and Maddy's immediate supervisor. Louis would be Louis Pierre Junior, President Thompson's half brother and the CEO of Pierre Ltd, the world-renowned jewelry company started by his and President Thompson's father.

During the robbery, three of their most famous—and expensive—pieces were stolen.

Whatever this meeting was, it had to have been impromptu because Maddy had nothing on her schedule.

She hustled down the hall, stopping at her office to toss her purse and keycard on her desk. While there, she grabbed her portfolio, a leather one with her father's initials embossed on it. Mom had surprised Maddy with it on her college graduation day, ten years after a car accident took her father from them.

Now, Maddy used it constantly, taking it to meetings or important events. All the time, somehow feeling as if her father were with her.

Her very own shield of protection.

Before leaving her office, she straightened her blouse, smoothed her skirt, and drew a breath. Typically, she was the only woman in the room, an especially intimidating situation with a former leader of the free world.

Even if he'd always been personable with her.

She strode to the conference room and knocked.

"Come in."

The president's voice. Maddy opened the door, sticking her head in. "Hi. Aileen said you were looking for me?"

From his spot at the head of the table, President Thompson waved her in. Since leaving office, he'd opted for a more business casual look of dress shirts with the top button undone and slacks. No ties or suits unless the situation absolutely demanded it.

Here, in the Center, despite the Secret Service detail that accompanied him everywhere, he wanted to be seen as an everyman. It was, he often said, the thing that got him elected.

"How was your walk-through?" he asked.

The men liked to tease her about her obsessive routine. She never minded. That obsessing had saved their butts on countless occasions. Whenever a museum, library, or whoever wanted to borrow an exhibit item, Maddy knew exactly where to find it.

"Informative," Maddy said. "Percy told me a retired librarian suggested you might enjoy Vikram Seth's *A Suitable Boy.*"

The president made a humming noise. Clearly, he hadn't read it. Well, she'd happily enlighten him.

"Being a Dickens fan, you might like it. It's set in post-independence India and is about four families connected by marriage. I read it in college and enjoyed it."

"I'll add it to my list."

"It's nearly fifteen hundred pages."

He craned his neck. "You read the entire thing?"

"I did. It earned me an A-plus in my classic literature class."

"I'd expect no less after fifteen hundred pages."

Everyone laughed.

"Maddy," Frank pointed to the open seat beside him, "have a seat. We wanted to get an update on the Kayla Krowne event last night."

Meaning, they wanted to know if she'd spoken to Mr. Sexy, Phin Blackwell. Maddy let out a silent breath. She wasn't in trouble. Why she would be, she'd had no idea, but when her bosses called her into an unscheduled meeting, what was a girl to think?

She set her portfolio on the table and lowered herself

into the chair. "Of course. I spoke to Phin Blackwell about hiring his company."

"And?" This from Louis, who sat at the opposite end of the table and seemed to have grown a few more frown lines in the last week. "Please tell us he agreed to help."

"He told me he'd speak to his brothers—it's a family-run business—and get back to me ASAP. I haven't heard from him yet, but he said it intrigued him. I thought that was a good sign."

Louis nudged his chin at President Thompson. "Should you put a call in to them? Maybe grease it? Dad is worried we won't find these pieces. And I'll reiterate, we're willing to offer a reward."

"We'll find them," President Thompson said.

She wished she had his confidence. Then again, the man was a career politician and knew how to work an audience.

"With a reward," Louis said, "we might find them faster. I have a ton of interview requests from local media about Dad's pieces. I could go on one of the morning shows and announce it."

President Thompson shook his head. "The FBI says no media. I'm sorry, Louis. We can't risk it." He brought his gaze back to Maddy. "Do you think you'll hear from the Blackwells today?"

"Sir, I have to believe we will. It's not every day we present a company like theirs such an exceptional opportunity. If you'd like, I can call him."

A hardship, that wouldn't be.

"Let's give him until the end of the day."

"Gerry," Louis said, "Dad is devastated. You should get on this."

Nobody moved. Well, nobody except Maddy, who turned her attention to a large print of the White House on the wall across from her because, my goodness, she'd never heard anyone, not even the First Lady, tell President Thompson what to do.

"And you don't think I am?"

The president's voice had lowered an octave, the words coming out slow. Controlled.

Scary voice. The one that, thankfully, he had never used with Maddy, but still made her suddenly need to pee.

"My wife," he continued, "convinced her grandmother to let us borrow priceless jewels belonging to the royal family. They were stolen on my watch. You don't think *that* stirs a sense of immediacy?"

Louis sat back.

The reminder delivered of who was king in this building.

President Thompson folded his hands on top of the table. "If we don't hear anything from the Blackwell camp by tomorrow morning, I'll call them. As soon as we're done here, you and I will call Dad and explain the situation. Believe me, we'll find these pieces. I don't care what it takes."

PHIN LED THE CHARGE INTO THE LOBBY OF THE THOMPSON Center and found Maddy standing in front of a large U-shaped reception desk where she chatted up the uniformed security guard sitting behind it.

As with the night before, her hair fell over her shoulders, the wild curls bouncing and charming him all over again.

Dang, those curls.

She wore a fitted cotton blouse tucked into a slim skirt with high-heeled pumps. Something about the professional attire mixed with the wild mane of hair sent his mind places. Really naughty places his mother would scold him for.

He was a man. Sue him.

The guard made eye contact, then quickly scanned the four men following Phin. They must've looked like an interesting lot. Phin, in dress slacks and a sport coat, Zeke in jeans and a Henley with the BARS logo on the sleeve. Cruz had dressed up, at least in his mind, by wearing khakis and an ironed T-shirt, and Rohan had opted for jeans with a loose button-down.

Maddy turned, meeting Phin's eye. "Good afternoon. Thank you for coming."

"Thank you for accommodating us," Phin said.

Phin made the introductions and gave Cruz, a guy who slayed women without even trying, the mother of all I-will-kill-you looks when his gaze held Maddy's for what Phin considered beyond the line of professionalism. Then again, his brother was also a man. *Sue him.*

Maddy led them to a set of escalators and Cruz whispered, "What's that look for?"

"You were staring."

"I wasn't *staring*. Even if I was, so what? She's damned fine to look at."

Point there.

Before stepping onto the escalator, Zeke shot them his version of the I-will-kill-you-look. "Knock it off, fuckers," he muttered.

Phin and Cruz followed directions, riding the escalator in silence behind Rohan and Zeke while Phin conjured images of Maddy's curls tumbling over a pillow.

He didn't need *that* distraction right now and fought to focus on the professional opportunity afforded them.

At the top, Maddy turned right where the mouth of the
exhibits entrance yawned large. Discreet signage pointed
patrons in various directions, but they blew right on by,
winding their way through a replica of the diner where
Thompson had announced his presidency.

Recently, Phin had eaten at that diner with an event
planner he'd met at a costume ball. He'd figured her to be a
good contact. They wound up hitting it off and landed in the
sack for a fun night.

All in a day's work, he supposed.

What did that say about him? Other than his being
willing to prostitute himself in case his sexual partners
spewed intel while in the midst of an orgasm.

He brought his attention back to the various memorabilia from campaign stops. A photo of the Thompsons in
front of the "Welcome to Iowa" sign was a nice touch, since
the citizens of that fine state sealed the deal on his
presidency.

A few feet ahead, Cruz let out a low whistle when they
reached a glass-encased wax replica of Thompson and the
First Lady. Thompson wore a navy tuxedo with velvet lapels
and the First Lady a floor-length gown with a diamond
necklace that must have weighed ten pounds.

The necklace, no doubt, instigated his brother's whistle.

"Stunning," Maddy said, "isn't it?"

"Beyond stunning. It's a Pierre?"

Maddy halted, smiling at Cruz. "You recognized it?"

He shrugged. "It's what we do. A Pierre has a certain
look to it."

"The president's father designed it. This was the day
after the election at one of the balls."

Phin studied it. How did the thieves leave that piece?

No time to grab it, that's how.

When the media first reported the theft of the Pierre pieces, Phin had read that the thieves broke a window, crawled through, and grabbed whatever they could before the guards showed up. They'd been in and out in under a minute. Given that limited time, they wouldn't have detoured, run down the hallway to grab the necklace, and then come back to the queen's exhibit.

Maddy continued through one helluva replica of the Oval office and halted in front of an area blocked by temporary walls and a cheap door.

"Once the FBI finished processing the scene," Maddy said, "we closed off this area. The repairs should begin in the next few days."

Beside Phin, Zeke peered back at the opening to the Oval Office replica they'd just walked through. "Was anything taken from any of the other exhibits?"

Maddy unlocked the cheap door and pushed it open. "No. They were in and out in just under a minute."

"Two men?" Phin asked.

"Inside the building, yes. There was one outside. He helped them get the ladder up and stood watch. We have security video we can share with you. President Thompson has signed off on it."

Ash and his fed buddies would love that. Phin met Zeke's eye and held his gaze. Big brother obviously had the same thought. They couldn't get hung up on it.

Pausing near the door, Phin let his brothers enter first. Some things, he supposed, never changed. As "the baby" he always went last.

He followed Cruz into the wrecked exhibit. To Phin's right, the lone window had been boarded up, leaving the overhead recessed lights to do the work. The lack of natural light gave the place an antiseptic feel compared to the warmth and immersive experience of the other exhibits.

Zeke did a slow 360 turn, taking in the broken glass still littering the floor, the mannequins dressed in formal attire.

The knocked-over jewelry stands.

Phin imagined it. A hammer coming through the window, the security system blaring, glass around the window edges being cleared, a blanket thrown over the sill. Two guys plowing through, tearing up the space, grabbing whatever they could before guards showed up.

"Trashed it," Rohan said, already at work snapping pics.

"They sure did," Maddy agreed.

Zeke finished his perusal and faced Maddy. "The windows weren't shatterproof?"

"Only the first floor. A calculated risk to save money."

Add that calculated risk to the lack of insurance Maddy had told him about the night before and it added up to a major loss.

Zeke wandered to the boarded-up window. "Can you walk us through it after they came in?"

She pointed to a wall mural of Thompson's swearing-in. In the background, the Capitol Building loomed large. "This area obviously represented the swearing-in. The female mannequin is wearing the First Lady's dress. Reinforced glass protected everything in the displays. The FBI thinks they smashed it with an ax. This mannequin wore a diamond bracelet and a pink diamond brooch from the queen's collection. Both stolen."

She ran her high-heeled shoe over scattered pieces of glass, pushing them into a pile. "So many people put work into this exhibit. The loss is devastating."

Maddy moved to her right, where another wall mural showed the National Statuary Hall, a chamber within the

Capitol building containing sculptures of prominent Americans. Inaugural luncheons took place in the chamber.

While interning for the lobbying firm where he'd met Kayla, Phin had had the privilege of touring the Capitol building, something the then-hopeful politician in him had been energized by. He'd wandered through the building, imagining himself taking meetings, running to a vote, rising in the ranks of Congress, and making positive contributions to his country.

That was idealist-Phin.

Another time.

An old dream.

Maddy pointed to a round banquet table, the top set with formal china. A wineglass and water glass lay on their sides, unbroken. In the middle sat a display case, its glass top shattered.

"We set the table to replicate the inaugural luncheon. The First Lady wore a Pierre brooch that was in that destroyed case."

Maddy continued on, walking them through the abused exhibit, pointing out where the other boosted items had been.

"Seconds." She sighed. "That was all it took for them to break in and steal priceless historical treasures."

Phin turned, took in the room again, and faced Maddy. "Can we get photos and video from before the break-in?"

"Of course. Do you have any initial thoughts?"

Zeke looked at Rohan, the two of them exchanging some kind of voodoo magic that meant they were reading each other's minds.

"I'd have to see the video," Rohan said, "but there's no way this wasn't highly organized. They made it look impromptu with the broken window and lack of finesse, but these guys were pros. They knew they'd only have a minute, maybe two."

Cruz gestured to the room at large. "They knew what they were looking for."

"You're saying they'd been here before?"

"I'd bet on it," Zeke said. "A heist this big? Takes planning. You probably have video of them walking through."

"My gosh," she said. "Everything is saved. It's all digital. We have every day since the Center opened."

Phin nodded. "Then we have work to do."

"Does that mean you're taking the job?"

Zeke met Phin's gaze, then moved on to Cruz and Rohan, all of them offering a barely perceptible nod.

"Oh," Zeke said, "we're taking the job."

4
———

MADDY PUSHED THROUGH THE EXECUTIVE SUITE DOORS WITH hearthrob Phin trailing behind. The rest of the BARS team had gone back to the office, leaving Phin to collect whatever data they'd need to start their recovery attempt.

Aileen peered up, her single-woman radar locking on the insanely handsome man entering her orbit. Phin Blackwell had that way about him. His long, easy strides and chin-high posture created an oxygen-consuming confidence that announced his presence before he'd even said hello. The broad shoulders and sparkling blue eyes didn't hurt.

"Aileen," Maddy said, "this is Phin Blackwell. Phin, meet Aileen. She keeps this place running, so if you ever need anything, she's the one to call."

Hellos were exchanged, and Aileen did her best to tear her attention from Phin while handing Maddy a note.

"Maintenance called. They fixed the burned-out light bulb you found on your walk-through yesterday."

Maddy took the note, held it up. "Excellent. Thank you."

Phin in tow, she made her way to her office and gestured to one of the guest chairs. "Have a seat."

After cornering her desk, she sat in her chair, opened her desk drawer, shoved her keys aside, and grabbed her dad's portfolio. "I'd like to make a list of what you need from me and then I'll pull it all together."

"Ah," he said, "a list-maker."

"And proud of it. Lists keep me organized."

He hit her with the Charlie Charm smile. Oh, that smile. All wicked and cool and enough to make her want to explore the edges of his mouth. Maybe drag her fingertips over his skin, drop kisses there while her body did that tingly thing she'd experienced at Kayla's.

Alrighty then.

Clearly, she was in need of male attention, but this was business. And nothing messed up a woman's career like mixing in pleasure with the wrong guy.

And yet, despite all that heat, the Charlie Charm smile still struck her as somehow ... hmmm. Fabricated? Practiced?

"Okay, CC." She laughed and held up her pen. "What do you need from me?"

"CC? Should I be insulted?"

"No. That smile is a gift I wish I had."

"Why?"

Maddy cocked her head. "Who wouldn't want it? It's a fabulous melding of destabilizing and endearing. And please don't take this the wrong way. You're smart enough to have mastered how to use it."

Phin's gaze locked on the wall behind Maddy, where her MFA and bachelor's degrees hung amongst various photos. Maddy at events with President Thompson—some with the First Lady— the ribbon-cutting on the Thompson Presidential Center, Maddy standing in the replica of the Oval Office.

Beside that, she and President and Mrs. Thompson in the actual Oval Office, a completely surreal experience offered by her grateful bosses as a reward for her hard work.

Phin pointed to the wall. "What would the smile do for you that your brain wouldn't?"

She supposed he had a point. Her mother always said that brains went further than good looks. "I guess I didn't think about it that way. You're right."

"Sure, I'm right. You should be proud."

At that, she let out a snort. He couldn't have been more off base on that one.

"What? If you're not proud, why do you have the wall of Maddy?"

Holy cow, the man could be blunt. Her own damned fault for leading the conversation from professional to personal.

Not good, Maddy. Not good.

She dropped her pen and sat back. "The second I step into my office, I see the photos and the degrees and it reminds me how hard I've worked and need to *keep* working. In the next few years, I'm going to add a PhD to this wall. I need a good two years to complete my studies and haven't been able to start yet. Too busy here and I didn't want to get distracted. President Thompson knew from the beginning what he wanted. He gave me a shot to help him build it. The least I can do is work hard."

"From what I saw today, you're an exceptional visual storyteller. The Middle East crisis exhibit? All those photos of the men lost? The kids rescued? That was something. Touring that exhibit was like a movie unfolding. I don't think many people have that talent. Talk about a gift."

"That was a difficult exhibit to put together. President

Thompson didn't want to sugarcoat it. People died, and he wanted to honor the victims. We owed it to their families, and I wanted them—the families and the Thompsons —satisfied."

He studied her with narrowed eyes for a few long seconds, so she playfully mirrored the look. "Phin, are you trying to analyze me?"

He laughed. "I guess I am. Are you a middle child?"

Oh, he was dangerous. Way too attentive. And probably why he was good at his job.

"I am. Classic middle. I have two older siblings—we call them the elders—and two younger. The littles. I was the mediator."

"Coming from a family with five kids, I bet your parents appreciated that."

"My mom did. My dad died when I was twelve."

"Ah, jeez. I'm sorry. I lost my dad when I was sixteen. It sucked."

Wasn't that the truth? And why, why, why, was she allowing this conversation to go places that would ruin her day?

Thinking about Dad wasn't the problem. She loved the memories of their trips to museums and galleries. He'd hated it. She sensed it even then, but he'd indulged her. *Encouraged* her love of art and history when Mom was too busy wrangling the elders and the littles.

And then Dad, along with all their amazing adventures, was gone.

A sharp stick plunged into her chest. Memories. So tough.

She lifted her chin. Conjured a smile. "You and your brothers must work well together. I've heard great things."

"Kayla?"

Maddy nodded. "She's in your corner, for sure."

"We know how to get a job done."

She picked up her pen. "Speaking of, let's get that list started."

Taking her not-so-subtle hint, Phin straightened in his chair and leaned forward. "Security footage. Usually the thieves do a dry run or visit a few times to get the workings of the place."

Maddy gawked. "A dry run? You mean they could have practiced?"

"Could be. At the very least, they were probably here during the day, checking doors and windows for entry points. They needed to know the setup. Typically, they try to get in as close to the job date as they can, in case security measures change."

"This was also a temporary exhibit," Maddy said. "Their timeline would be even tighter."

"Exactly. I bet they were here in the last two weeks."

Maddy added a note to her list, her stomach shriveling at the thought of the thieves casually walking through the exhibits.

"We'll also need a list of employees and volunteers. How many of each are there?"

"Sixty full-time and thirty part-time. Three hundred volunteers. We're definitely not the biggest staff. President Thompson did that purposely. He wanted a tighter-knit group. When he's here, he attempts to speak to everyone."

"Nice. I'm assuming they do background checks on new hires."

"Yes. There's no hard-and-fast rule about hiring folks with a criminal record. The Thompsons see the Center as a place for refuge and growth. If someone has been involved with theft, that's a tough one because of our acquisitions. But we have several employees who've had issues with drugs and are now clean. I actually don't have access to those files. I'll refer you to HR." She made a note. "What else?"

"Aileen mentioned something about you doing a walk-through? What's that?"

Maddy set her pen down and relaxed back in her chair. "I take my lunch from noon to one every day. It's usually in the cafeteria, but sometimes I'll go out. Before returning to my office, I do a walk-through of all the exhibits. Checking on things, making sure everything is in order. I talk with visitors about what they like versus what they don't. Yesterday, I found a burned-out light bulb in the campaign trail exhibit. I called maintenance to let them know."

"You know every inch of this place, don't you?"

She sure did. "I could rebuild it in my sleep."

"That may come in handy." He pointed to her list, and she sat forward again. "We'll need building blueprints and schematics of exhibits. And security team schedules for the last few weeks."

Maddy noted all of it. They'd provided it to the FBI, but she hadn't been the one to do it and would speak to Frank. "I'll work on it and hopefully have it by tomorrow morning. Is there anything else?"

"Not that I can think of. Tomorrow works. We can't take possession of anything until the contracts are signed, anyway. That probably won't happen until tomorrow."

Maddy slid her pen into the sleeve and gently closed her portfolio before returning her gaze to Phin and his sparkly blue eyes. Total killer, this guy. "Thank you for getting here so fast."

"No need to thank us. It's not every day a bunch of guys

get to help a former president. It's an honor. We'll do whatever we can to make sure we don't let the president down."

PHIN ARRIVED HOME, PARKING THE AUDI IN FRONT OF THE Annex, where he knew he'd find his brothers already scouring the dark web and working their contacts to see what they might scrape up about the Thompson heist.

Later, he'd drive the car around to the garage in case it rained and walk back to the house.

As he'd suspected, he found the crew at the conference table in the large, open area in the center of the building. Zeke referred to it as the Theater. As in the place where all the drama happened. Still dressed in the same clothing they'd worn to the meeting with Maddy, they all stood in a row at the end of the oversized table, studying the far wall where they'd hung photos of the destroyed exhibit on the giant whiteboard.

"Hey." Phin eased into the open space beside Cruz.

At the end of the row, Zeke leaned in for a better look at Phin. "How'd it go?"

"She's working on security footage and the employee list. Should have it tomorrow."

"Good. Mom is on the contract."

Phin waved a hand at the wall. "Any initial thoughts?"

"Other than this being a seriously ballsy heist?" Cruz asked.

"Yeah. Other than that."

"Whoever it was," Rohan said, "will have to break the pieces up and melt down the metal. No legit collector would even consider buying all the pieces intact. Too high-profile."

Cruz cocked his head. "It's screaming Vera brothers."

Two brothers born in Europe and now U.S. citizens, the

Veras posed as wealthy business executives investing in start-up tech companies. Their actual jobs? Running a criminal organization responsible for seemingly impossible heists. The most recent included four men walking into a hotel in the middle of a high-stakes poker tournament, pepper-spraying the guards, and making off with millions.

When it came to crimes involving art, they gave no reverence to historical value. They aimed for the big score and if pieces had to be broken up to be moved, so be it.

For them, it all came down to the payday.

"I thought the same," Zeke said. "It's almost ridiculous how easy they made this look. Since Armand went away, little brother Xavier has been upping their game."

Three years earlier, Armand, the family patriarch, had found a new home in prison for financial fraud. The government, unable to gather enough evidence to convict the group of art theft, exacted their pound of flesh by busting Armand for money laundering.

In his absence, his younger and bolder brother, Xavier, had taken the helm.

"No shit." Cruz said. "Their heists are riskier and happening more often."

"Xavier," Rohan said, "has a taste for money. It's never enough. They keep bringing more people in, growing the organization. Word is Armand is blowing a gasket."

Zeke pointed to the screen on the far wall. "Let's bring them up. See what we can find."

Cruz took his normal spot at the center of the table and fired up his laptop. Seconds later, lists of articles appeared on the big screen. "Rohan got started and sent me these to look at."

As BARS grew, Rohan, the resident computer geek, found himself buried in Internet research with no time to get it all done. Cruz, their gearhead and pilot for plane repos, became his backup, jumping in as needed. Especially when something involved kids. Rohan couldn't take any nastiness involving kids.

Phin stepped closer to the monitor, perusing the descriptions. "Click the second one."

The article from one of the local outlets popped up, along with photos of Xavier and Armand. Farther down the page, a chart showed various members of the Veras' criminal organization. Armand sat at the top, with Xavier in the second spot. Below Xavier sat six more boxes with an absolute spiderweb of lines showing subordinates.

"I guess Rohan is right about them bringing on more soldiers."

"Armand likes control," Zeke said. "With all these people, he had to run a tight ship or risk someone skimming. Armand would never have approved this job. He likes to fly under the radar." Zeke pointed at the photos they'd stuck on the whiteboard. "This is Xavier. If *we're* thinking it's them, the feds are already on it. They're days ahead of us."

"But," Cruz said, "they have a pesky thing called the law. We can play outside the lines. I'll make some calls, see who's heard what."

"I'll call Rory Emlynson," Phin said.

A financial planner by day, Rory moonlighted by hooking up unscrupulous collectors with stolen goods. He liked to call himself a facilitator because he never actually took possession of said goods. He connected people and collected a commission once the deals were complete.

Rohan turned from the images on the wall and swung his gaze between Zeke and Phin. "Has anyone talked to Ash?"

"This morning," Zeke said. "I put another call in to him when we got back. Voice mail."

This time, it was Phin's turn to lean in and grab his brothers' attention. "We should tell him, right?"

"I vote yes," Cruz said. "No freaking drama. Please."

Ha. Cruz. The guy had the body of a gladiator and, when it came to family, the mind of a yogi. He couldn't stomach infighting.

Zeke peered at Rohan. "What's your vote?"

"It's not worth a battle. Once we get a signed agreement, we let him know."

"If we're straight with him," Phin added, "we can help each other. They've probably gone through the security footage. Maybe he can give us something we can move on."

The true suckfest would be that if BARS recovered the jewels, the feds would, no doubt, take credit.

"It chaps my ass that we could recover this stuff, and the feds will get the glory."

"Man," Cruz said, "you got to quit worrying about shit you can't control."

Zeke sighed. "Literally just had this conversation with him."

Not one to let an opportunity slip by, Phin raised both his hands toward each brother and flipped them off.

"Hello, my boys."

Phin dropped his hands and spun to where Mom entered. She wore her typical uniform of Levi's, loafers, and a cotton button-down shirt. Her work uniform, she called it. She'd tucked her wavy brown hair behind her ears, the silver streaks illuminated by the overhead lights.

She walked toward them and held up a piece of paper.

"I have something to show you."

"Good news?" Zeke asked.

"*I* think so."

She passed the document to Zeke, who perused it before handing it back to her. "You should tell them."

A wide smile took over her face—was that a twinkle in her eyes?—and a sudden warmth lit inside Phin. Was there anything better than making their mom happy?

"Boys," she held the document up for them to see, "this is a contract signed by Gerald Thompson. BARS has officially been hired by a former President of the United States. Your father would be amazed and I ..." Her voice took on a gravelly tone, like pebbles clogging her throat.

Hang on. Was their hard-ass career military mother choked up?

She stopped, cleared her throat while Phin imagined his body plummeting through the floor. She made eye contact with each of them, then nodded. "I could not be more proud of you. Thank you."

Silence hung in the room. A sort of shocked awe that held Phin, and apparently his brothers, speechless. That alone might be a miracle.

Sure, they'd known the contract was coming, but seeing it? Seeing their mother's reaction to it? Whole other level.

As much as Phin hated giving up his dream of a political career and possibly impacting a life with proper healthcare and the myriad of other things that made being an American a privilege, this moment with his mother?

Not trading it.

Ever.

Sacrificing his own dreams might damned well be worth it.

"So," Phin said, smacking his hands together. "I guess we better get hold of Ash before he hears we took this job."

· · ·

At 7:30 on the nose. Maddy strode into the executive suite and paused for a second to take in the warm glow of morning sunlight through the windows.

Normally the first to arrive, she enjoyed settling into the day with quiet and coffee. That hour alone? No phones, no people chattering, no printers whirring.

Heaven.

In his endless generous spirit, President Thompson had gifted them with a commercial espresso machine Maddy had mastered and then taught her coworkers how to use, in hopes they wouldn't drive her insane by constantly asking for help. She'd even created a how-to video and sent it to each of them. It helped reduce the questions, but there was still the occasional outcry when the frothing spout ran amok.

She entered her office, tucked her tote bag in the normal spot behind her desk and dropped her keys in the top drawer before heading to the kitchen.

Two steps from her office, murmuring voices behind the conference room door drew her attention.

Someone. Several someones.

Not that she was eavesdropping.

Perhaps President Thompson had an early meeting. She cleared her throat loudly enough to alert the entire block they had company. Seconds later, before she made the turn into the kitchen, the ka-chunk of a door latch sounded. She swung back and found her boss standing in the conference room doorway.

"Morning," Frank said in his normal cool voice. "After you get coffee, would you join us? The FBI is here. They'd like to speak with you."

The FBI.

Maybe a break in the case? Forget coffee.

"Coffee can wait," she said.

Frank stepped back into the room, opening the door wider for her to enter. A clean-cut man in his thirties with short dark hair and a woman, maybe a few years older, sat at the table with President Thompson.

"Maddy," Frank said, "this is Special Agent Cameron Blackwell and Special Agent Renee Walker."

Cameron Blackwell, Phin's brother. She'd heard the name over the course of the investigation, but had never spoken to him directly.

Maddy shook hands with both agents, her mind ticking back to her meeting with Phin and his brothers the day before. Did Special Agent Blackwell know they'd hired BARS?

At the head of the table, President Thompson greeted her with his usual smile. "Good morning, Maddy."

"Good morning, sir."

She took the open seat next to Frank, across from the two agents.

"Ms. Carmichael," Special Agent Blackwell said, "thank you for joining us. We have some security footage to show you."

"Of course. Happy to help."

He pointed to the white screen on the far wall, then nodded to his partner, who tapped her iPad. A second later, the wall screen filled with a paused video frame showing knocked over mannequins and shattered glass. Maddy flicked her gaze to the date stamp. The night of the robbery.

"We've cued this," Special Agent Walker said, "at the point where the unknown subjects take the queen's tiaras."

Walker tapped the screen, and the video rolled. Like the first time Maddy had seen it, the footage hit her like a gut punch. From the time those pieces came into the Center's possession, she'd been the only one to handle them. They'd promised the Thompsons, who then promised the queen, Maddy would be the only one. She'd purchased the softest cotton gloves on the market, climbed into the enormous, specially treated museum-quality case and gingerly placed each piece. Adjusting and readjusting, climbing out of the case, checking the light for glares, making sure the seams were straight on the mannequin's clothing, then climbing back in, over and over, until she'd perfected the display.

Now, she watched men shatter cases, roughly snatch her carefully placed pieces off stands, and rip the triple-strand diamond necklace from the mannequin. Maddy's stomach knotted, the rage and disappointment shooting straight from her chest.

"It's horrible," she said.

Special Agent Walker paused the video and zoomed in. "Please look at the man on the right."

Maddy shifted her gaze. A red arrow appeared, pointing to a spot where the man's ski mask cinched up, revealing two inches of tattooed skin between his shirt collar and mask.

Beside that image, Walker brought up another video. This one of Maddy, in the exhibit, talking to three men. Well, speaking to two men, the third had turned and appeared to be reading one of the plaques.

"This footage is from two weeks ago. Is this you?"

Maddy checked the timestamp; 1:15. "Yes. This was right after the exhibit opened. I walk the building each day after my lunch. I like to get feedback from visitors."

"Uh-*huh*," Special Agent Walker said, emphasizing the last syllable enough that it dripped with disbelief.

And... *whoa*.

What was *that* about? She met Special Agent Walker's

gaze, but the woman gestured to the screen. "The man on the left."

Another arrow appeared. This one pointing to the man's neck.

And the tattoo peeking out over the top of his hoodie.

5

"OH MY GOD," MADDY GASPED. "IS THAT THE SAME MAN?"

"Appears so," Special Agent Blackwell said. "We haven't been able to get a match on facial recognition, but based on the location and image of the tattoo, our working theory is it's the same man. Do you remember speaking with these gentlemen?"

And, holy cow, Phin had told her about this. About how thieves did a dry run right before a robbery.

She thought back to the last couple of weeks. Each day, her routine had been the same. Lunch, walk-through, back to her office. Every day.

In the last few weeks, given the excitement over the collection, they'd had a variety of tours, talks, and other scheduled events, including a wedding in the ballroom. She'd spoken to hundreds of people.

She continued to stare at the screen, her mind spinning, spinning, spinning, replaying each day since the exhibit opened. The people. So many people.

The tattoo. Being an art lover, all art, how could she not remember?

Maybe because tats had become commonplace. Every-where she looked, including on her brother's body, she saw tattoos.

"I'm sorry." She shook her head. "I don't remember him."

"Ms. *Carmichael*," Special Agent Walker drawled, once again emphasizing syllables until they dripped like blood. "Forgive me, but I find that hard to believe. Look at these men. I can't imagine you regularly get three twenty-some-thing-year-old men waltzing through here dressed in ratty jeans looking, to my eye anyway, suspicious. You really don't remember them?"

Special Agent Blackwell cleared his throat but said noth-ing. Was that a warning to Special Agent Walker to check her tone?

Maddy pushed her shoulders back and met the agent's gaze straight on. "Special Agent *Walker*," she mimicked the condescending tone. Why not? The woman had no idea who came through here. What? Guys in jeans weren't allowed to visit? "Two days ago, we had a community activist, a former gang leader who's found the Lord, parading a dozen teenaged gang members dressed in *ratty jeans* through this building. Part of our mission is to provide a safe, educational environment for at-risk kids." She swung to President Thompson. "Sir, I've heard you say many times you wanted this to be a haven. A welcoming space with an opportunity to change lives."

"She's right." He gestured to the screen. "I've seen count-less people who look like this visiting the Center."

The two agents exchanged a look.

"All right," Special Agent Walker said. "Let's move on."

She tapped the iPad again, cueing up another video.

"This is security footage from your condo's parking lot and breezeway. Is this the front of your building?"

My building? Maddy's gaze fixed on the screen, her body somehow frozen. What the hell was going on? Why were they watching her building?

"Ms. Carmichael?"

Maddy turned, found Walker studying her. Watching. Did they think ...?

Panic banged around inside Maddy's brain, making her temples throb.

Hold it together here. She swallowed, fought to get her tongue moving in the desert that had become her mouth. "I'm confused."

"About whether this is your building?"

"About why you have this. Have you been *watching* me?"

"Please answer the question. Is this your building?"

Maddy forced her head to move again, to look at the video. "It appears to be, yes."

"You don't know what your own building looks like?"

Breathe. That's all she needed to do. Just take in air, let it out. *Look her in the eye.* That's all she had to do. Nothing to hide.

She brought her gaze back to Walker. "Of course, I do. But the exterior of the development looks the same no matter what unit we're looking at. Without seeing the building number, I can't confirm."

"Fine," Special Agent Walker said. She zoomed in on the building. On the sign in front of a row of low shrubs. "Can you read this sign?"

She sure could. A nagging thought—*lawyer, lawyer, lawyer*—hammered away, beating in time with her already throbbing temples. How could this be happening?

"Building Two."

"Is that your building?"

"It is."

"Excellent. Now, we've confirmed it's your building. You live in unit Two C, correct?"

"Correct." She held up a hand. "Excuse me, but I'm not sure what's going on here. What does where I live have to do with any of this?"

"We're getting to that," Walker said. She tapped the iPad, then pointed to the wall. "Please direct your attention to the screen. You'll see a man walk up the stairs and stop in front of what I have confirmed is unit 2C."

The video started and a man in jeans and a T-shirt walked into the frame. *Oh no.*

No, no, no. It couldn't be the same guy. The one with the tat.

Maddy checked the date. Fifteen days earlier. Before the robbery. Could this guy be going to her door? According to Walker, yes, but Maddy didn't know him. Why would he be going to her apartment?

"I don't know who that is."

"Keep watching, please."

The man climbed the steps and halted in front of Maddy's door. Stopped right there and turned, lifted his hand to knock and there it was.

The tattoo.

What in God's name?

She forced herself to not react. To stay completely erect, not shake her head, not breathe deeply even though—God help her—her lungs strained for oxygen.

She checked the timestamp; 5:02.

Okay. *That's good.* She spun her chair and faced the two agents.

"This was—" she looked at the date again, did quick

math. "A Tuesday. I don't get home until six o'clock. Everyone here will confirm that. Why would I invite someone to my house at five? It's a mistake, or he was up to no good. Either way, I don't know him."

Special Agent Walker tapped the iPad again. "Let's look at another piece of footage."

Her mind reeling, Maddy turned back to the screen. To her left, Frank and President Thompson remained silent. What could they be thinking right now?

She couldn't worry about that. Not when something wild and completely unexpected was happening. Was she a suspect? Did the FBI somehow think she was involved?

No. Couldn't be.

Lawyer, lawyer, lawyer.

More video footage from the Center appeared on the screen. The first floor. The campaign trail exhibit. A man dressed in khakis and a golf shirt stood in front of a mural of President Thompson's grammar school. The mural depicted the day then-candidate Thompson announced his presidency.

She focused on the man's profile, but he stood too far from the camera and the quality was a bit grainy. She checked the date. The day after the other man had visited her apartment.

Three seconds in, Maddy entered the frame and did what she'd done every day for the last two years since the Center opened.

She stopped to speak with a visitor.

The video froze.

So did she.

She focused on the images, forced herself to focus, to shut down her mind's chaos and zoom in on the video of the man pointing to the mural and her nodding, apparently agreeing with whatever he'd said.

Him. The one who'd been with the other two men she'd spoken to on the other video, who had his back to her.

He looked different this time. More ... refined.

Probably done purposely to somewhat disguise himself.

Did she remember him? *The smile.* A good one, like Phin Blackwell's, always made her a sucker.

The man onscreen had been cute. More rugged than handsome and when he lifted his hand, she noted the lack of a wedding ring. What single, ready-to-settle-down woman wouldn't?

"Wait." The word rushed out, her panic finally bursting free. "I remember. He told me he went to the same school as the president. That's why he was pointing."

Yes! That was it.

"Did he say anything else?" This from Special Agent Blackwell.

Maddy thought back on the encounter. On her disappointment when the man moved on without extending their conversation or making any attempt to engage her further.

A spurt of anger erupted over her constant tendency to analyze what *she'd* done wrong, what was lacking in *her* when, really? She should be analyzing everyone else. Particularly this guy. She'd wondered why he didn't find her attractive. She'd even thought about the three pounds she'd gained recently.

Damned exhausting, all this self-berating.

How dumb it all seemed now, considering the guy was a thief casing the place.

She shook her head. "No. He didn't say anything else. He walked away." She pointed. "If you start the video again, you'll see that."

The footage rolled. The man nodded at Maddy, hit her with his cute smile, and moved on.

The room fell silent for a few seconds while the video rolled. She knew little about legalities, but she'd watched enough true-crime shows to know she might be a suspect.

Lawyer, lawyer, lawyer.

She spun her chair, facing the agents. "Do I need a lawyer?"

Special Agent Walker shrugged. "You tell us."

Ohmygod.

They thought she had stolen priceless jewelry. How could that be? After everything, what was it about her that let them believe that?

At the end of the table, Maddy somehow felt President Thompson's gaze on her. Head high, she turned to him. "Sir. I'm not sure what's going on here, but whatever it is, I'm ..."

What?

Innocent?

The president remained seated, his posture straight, his features relaxed. All the cool confidence that helped him get elected.

"Maddy," he said, "take a breath. The FBI has been studying this footage for days. When they came upon these images, they thought it best to ask you about them. That's all."

She shook her head so hard it should have whirled from her body like a top. "I don't know these men. I swear to you. I don't."

How could they think, after how hard she'd worked, she'd be involved? That she'd *steal* from the Thompsons, from the Center?

No. She wouldn't get ahead of herself. If the roles were

reversed, she'd at least explore the possibility. *She'd* think she was involved.

"I'm not naïve," she told Walker. "I know what you're thinking, but I did nothing wrong. That exhibit was my baby." She pointed at the still black screen. "I don't know those men and I *really* don't know why the one with the tattoo would come to my home, or even know where I live."

Which, hello? *That* was terrifying. Had they been following her? She'd have to pay more attention. See if she could find them and turn them in.

"Ms. Carmichael," Special Agent Blackwell said, "we'd like to continue this conversation at our office. Would you be willing to do that?"

And there it was.

Maddy's body collapsed back against the chair, all the oxygen leaving her. They wanted to drag her downtown. Such a cliché. If it wasn't happening, she'd laugh.

She sat up again, pushing her shoulders back. *I can do this.* She looked Phin's brother in the eye. "Not without a lawyer, I won't."

PHIN SAT IN HIS OFFICE, FINGERS FLYING ACROSS HIS LAPTOP'S keyboard. Research had never been his idea of fun, but if he could find jewelry heists similar to the Thompson Center's, it might be a lead.

At this stage, all ideas were open to discussion.

His cell phone rattled against the desk, and he slid a glance at it. Ash.

He poked the speaker button. "What's up?"

"Hey," his brother said, the word coming quick. "I'm walking back to my desk. Zeke called me yesterday. I just tried him, but he's not picking up. I'm in the middle of something. Is he by you?"

"Zeke!" Phin yelled, hoping his brother was still in earshot.

"What?" came an irritated yell back.

"Hang on." Phin told Ash. "Sounds like he's in his office."

Grabbing the phone, he hustled to the other side of the Annex, stepped into Zeke's office, where his brother was nose-in on his computer.

Phin held up his phone.

"It's Ash. Returning your call." Phin gave him some hard eye contact and set the phone on the desk. This was it. The call telling Ash they'd taken the Thompson case. "He doesn't have a lot of time."

Zeke nodded. "Ash, hey. Thanks for calling back. I put my phone on do-not-disturb. Mom's killing me with spreadsheets."

"No prob. What's up?"

"I'll make this quick. We took on a new case. Thought you should know."

A long sigh came through the phone line. "Why do I think this'll wreck my day?"

Oh, the drama. Phin rolled his eyes. "Relax. It's not that bad. We're keeping you in the loop." Phin circled a hand. "You know, in the whole vein of open communication."

"Yeah. Okay. What case is it?"

"The Thompson Center heist," Zeke said. "The Thompsons have hired us."

When silence cluttered the room, Phin stared at the phone wondering if his brother had, perhaps, fallen mute.

Phin leaned in. "You still there?"

"I'm here. Picking myself up off the goddamn floor. Hold

on." A rustling sound came from the other end, then a few seconds later, the telltale click of a door closing.

"Dude," Zeke said, "where are you?"

"I came into the conference room. I don't need my coworkers hearing this. Is that why you called me yesterday? Pumping me for information."

Phin winced because, yeah, it probably looked that way. "We were *not* pumping you for information. Well, not totally."

Ash made a strangling noise and before he could launch into a lecture, Phin bulldozed right over that. "It was more like a warning shot."

"What the hell does that even mean?"

"Don't get pissy," Zeke said, his voice holding zero heat. "We weren't sure if the job would pan out."

"You can't take this job."

Hey, now, *that's* not happening.

Before Phin could speak, Zeke held up a hand. "Not your call," he told Ash. "We've taken the job. This is a courtesy call."

Another few seconds of silence ensued. Probably, if Phin knew his brother at all, Ash was getting his thoughts together while absorbing the fact that chasing his dream meant his say in BARS went buh-bye.

"Okay." He let out a hard breath. "How much do you know?"

"All of it," Zeke said. "The Pierre pieces. The queen's jewels. We're still collecting intel, but we got a dump of security footage this morning. Cruz and Rohan are on that. If you have anything, you can save us time."

"Ash," Phin said, "we all know if we don't find this stuff ASAP, they'll get broken up and melted down. Let's work together."

"This is a federal investigation."

Zeke laughed. "What's your point?"

His brothers. Pissers.

"My *point* is there are laws regarding a suspect's rights. Anything I tell you could jeopardize our case. You want me to do that?"

"Hell no," Zeke said. "*But* it seems to me we'd be better off working together. Although, you don't know how to do that. You only know how to manipulate situations to fit your needs."

Already knowing where this was going, Phin groaned. A month ago, BARS and the FBI had worked together on a case. A rocky case that put Ash and Zeke at odds.

"*My* needs?" Ash said. "If this is about the Lederman case, I was protecting your ass."

"I didn't need your protection. I needed honesty and trust."

When Ash went quiet again, Phin and Zeke exchanged a look. Regarding his job, Ash could be a wild card. Phin admired his dedication, his determination to separate right from wrong, but sometimes playing outside the lines got things done.

Phin dropped into one of Zeke's guest chairs and slouched. "More dead air. Excellent."

"Thinking," Ash said, his tone sharper than a straight razor.

Okey-dokey then. Zeke held his hands wide, his frustration with their brother clearly mounting because, yes, they were supposed to wait while Ash's moral compass dictated a path.

"We're following up on something we saw in the footage," Ash finally said.

Phin perked up. "What's on the footage?"

"Could be something. Could be nothing. We're trying to get a handle on it."

"For fuck's sake," Phin said, "tell us what you've got."

"We've got Maddy Carmichael at the Center talking to the unsubs the week before the heist. Probably doing recon."

Phin's head snapped back, the jolt reminding him of when they were kids, and randomly took swings at each other.

"One of them," Ash continued, "has a distinctive tattoo on his neck. It shows up again on the footage from the night of the heist."

"Hold up." Phin raised his hand as if Ash could see him. "You guys think *Maddy Carmichael* is involved? When it comes to her job, she's freaking Mary Poppins. Total pleaser. There's no way."

"Is that your expert opinion? Given you've known her for two days."

Scored one there.

"Point taken, but have you *been* in her office? The wall is a shrine to the Thompsons. Plus, she's smart. Too smart to be seen on video with your *unsubs*."

"That's what I thought at first, too. But there's more."

More, in Phin's not-so-expert opinion, was always bad.

"What's that?"

"There's the footage of her talking to guys at the Center. Then there's more of the dude with the tattoo. At her apartment."

Phin whirled a finger in the air. "Whoopdie-fucking-doo. In case you missed it, she's an attractive woman. Dude was probably hitting on her. Are you surveilling her?"

"No. When we saw the video from the Center, we got a warrant for the security footage from her condo building.

Just to see what kind of activity might be happening. A guy walked to her door. We checked that footage against what we have at the Thompson Center, and it's the same guy."

"This is why you think she's involved?"

"Jesus, Phin. What's with you?"

Yeah. What *was* with him?

Besides the fact that he had fantasies about Maddy on top of him, riding like a rodeo queen.

Yeah, he had a thing for this woman.

"I'll tell you what's with me. From what I can tell, she lives for her job. Thrives on it. And the feds are accusing her of theft? Of stealing from a guy who gave her the opportunity of a lifetime. Hate to tell you, big brother, she's smarter than that. You kids are way off."

"We're not accus—"

"*Fine.* You're suspicious. Either way, you're *judging* her *character* based on what you perceive—with extremely weak evidence—to be true. That sucks."

And, yeah, maybe Phin was getting a little loud because Zeke pulled a what-the-fuck face.

"Now I get it," Ash said. "This isn't about Madison Carmichael. This is about you."

"*Me?*"

"Senator Blakely pissed you off the other night. He judged *your* character. Jesus, Phin. Get focused."

What the hell? Before Phin could tear into—absolutely shred—Ash, Zeke put up a hand. "Both of you, relax. We don't have time for this. Ash, can you give us timestamps of when this happened? We'll take a look from our end."

"Yeah. But I can't give you the footage from her building. It's the same guy. No doubt."

"Did you ask Maddy about this?"

"She denies knowing him."

"Of course," Phin said. "You know she walks the Center every day, right? She's regimented. She likes to interact with the visitors. Get their reactions so they can improve the place."

"Yeah. And?"

Fucker. Phin looked at Zeke, held his hands wide, frustration frying his fingertips. "She *talks* to people!"

"Easy, bro" Zeke said.

Phin pinched the bridge of his nose. Damned pressure. Zeke was right. He needed to get hold of himself. He shook his head, eased out a silent breath. "Look, Ash, maybe they met at the Center. He liked her and followed her home to see where she lives. Who the hell knows what he could have been up to?"

"Oh-kay. I'll play. Your theory works except for one problem."

Ash's dripping sarcasm didn't bode well. "What's that?"

"He was at her house *before* he shows up on the Thompson Center footage."

Uh-oh. *That* was unexpected. "How—"

"We ran facial recognition on three months of footage from the Thompson Center. The guy only shows up that one time before the heist."

"You're saying she knew him prior?"

This from Zeke, while Phin envisioned his brains scattering over the pristine office.

"That's our working theory."

"Your theory sucks," Phin blurted.

"It might. But it's worth exploring. We've asked her to come to headquarters for an interview."

"Did she agree?" Zeke asked.

"Yes. She's getting a lawyer. Interesting, no?"

Who could blame her with such a big case? "No. *Not*

interesting. Why would she agree to have y'all interrogate her without a lawyer? I'd do the same thing."

"He's right," Zeke said.

"I gotta get back. I'll send you the timestamps. Keep me updated on anything from your end. And, Phin, look, I'm not sure what's going on with you regarding this woman, but we're following up on anything and everything. If she's clean, we'll lay off."

Phin made a *pfftting* noise. Made a show of his shocked disgust. "There's nothing going on with me other than she seems like a decent person who has a passion for her work."

"I guess we'll see."

"We sure will."

Phin punched the screen, then boosted out of the chair, wandering to the side wall. "None of this makes sense. If she's involved, she's one hell of an actress."

Zeke rocked back in his chair, propped his feet on the desk. "I'm not feeling it. Someone on staff could have told the unsubs her habits."

Phin snapped his fingers. "I'll call HR. Maddy CC'd me on an e-mail to them this morning regarding their employee list. Aside from the employees, they have three hundred volunteers."

"See if you can get start dates for employees and volunteers. And let's get a screenshot of this guy with the tattoo. See if we can find him."

"I'm on the employee and volunteer lists. You get the screenshot, and I'll start calling some shady jewelers I know. Maybe one of them knows the guy from a previous heist." Phin strode to the door. "And, full disclosure, I'm sending Priscilla Randolph's number to Maddy."

Phin, during one of his many schmoozing assignments, had met Priscilla, a thirty-five-year-old Charlotte defense attorney known among prosecutors as the princess of darkness. She'd given him her card in case he ever needed anything. Say a talented lawyer to get him out of a jam.

Over time, he'd run into her here and there. They'd struck up a friendship. Even met for lunch once in a while to talk politics and criminal cases. Interesting woman.

Zeke gave him a look. The narrowed-eyed be-careful-little-brother one.

"Don't say it," Phin told him. "If the feds think Maddy is involved, she needs a good lawyer. Cilla is a shark."

6

AT 3:00 FRIDAY AFTERNOON, MADDY STOOD IN FRONT OF THE main entrance to the Charlotte FBI headquarters waiting for the defense attorney Phin had referred her to.

According to online chatter, Priscilla Randolph was a badass.

As in, a badass times ten.

And now she was Maddy's badass.

A man in a gray suit strode by, throwing some serious rotten energy her way. That was the third person giving her nasty looks. Whether they were employees or visitors, she didn't know, but they were most definitely suspicious with the way they eyeballed her.

Did she look like a radical? She peered down at her navy slacks, white blouse, and heels. She'd even added a gold necklace for some I-am-a-professional oomph.

Obviously, it wasn't working. And that didn't help her already crackling nerves. She gripped her purse handle, squeezing hard enough to pop a knuckle.

This whole flipping thing exhausted her. Mental bedlam did that. And the meeting hadn't even started yet.

Sigh.

"Ms. Carmichael?"

A woman with poker straight black hair cut into a razor-sharp bob approached. She wore a skinny black pantsuit tailored to long legs and a trim body.

This, also according to online photos, was Cilla Shark, the nickname the press had given her several years back when she'd devoured the prosecution in a high-profile murder case involving a professional athlete.

At thirty-five, the shark looked more like a supermodel than a ferocious lawyer.

Maybe that was part of her plan. Lure investigators in with her looks and then shred their case.

Maddy took a few steps, meeting her new attorney halfway, and held out her hand. "Ms. Randolph, hi. Thanks so much for meeting me."

Swinging her briefcase to her other shoulder, Ms. Randolph shook Maddy's hand. "Call me Priscilla. Or Cilla. I'm happy to help." She offered a crooked smile. "I *love* eating the feds for a midafternoon snack. Especially on a Friday."

Oh.

Boy.

"Um." Maddy held up a fist. "Yay?"

Cilla laughed. "Definitely yay. Phin said you're a friend. Coming from him, that means something. I know we talked on the phone about your previous conversation with the FBI. Is there anything else you've thought of, before we head in?"

They'd spent an hour on the phone that morning, reviewing the points from the previous day's meeting with Special Agents Blackwell and Walker.

"No," Maddy said. "I told you everything."

She'd made sure of it. The minute she'd left the conference room the day before, she'd jotted notes, painstakingly recording every detail she could remember.

Just in case.

It turned out to be a good move when Cilla began peppering her with questions.

"Good." Cilla gestured to the door. "Let's get in there and see what the hell they want. Then we can both get on with our day."

Maddy double-timed her steps to keep up with Cilla's much longer strides. "How does this work?"

"Once we get in there, I'll do my thing. Let them know you intend to cooperate fully, yada, yada. If I don't like a question, I'll tell you not to answer." Cilla halted before opening the building's door. "One thing."

Maddy stepped aside, letting a woman exiting pass. "Yes?"

"When I say we're done, we're done. We're meeting with Cameron Blackwell and Renee Walker. I don't know Walker, but I've met Cam, and he's a wily one."

"You don't trust him?"

"Not as far as I can throw him. It's not his fault. He has a job to do. So do I. Also, if I say we're leaving, stop talking. I can't have you expounding on things you shouldn't be expounding on. The feds have liberties. Legally, they can lie to you. Tell you things to trip you up. And that can get you thrown in a cell. Which is why I will tell you not to answer certain questions. Now, when we get in there, they may or may not read Miranda rights. I've seen it both ways, but don't panic if they do. Got it?"

A sense of calm, of having a plan, eased over her.

Maddy gave Cilla one solid nod. "You're the boss. I'll do whatever you say. I'm just thankful you're here."

Cilla reached out and squeezed Maddy's arm. "Deep breath. I've got you. Now, let's have some fun."

FIFTEEN MINUTES LATER, AFTER CLEARING SECURITY AND being escorted to an interview room on the third floor, Cilla and Maddy sat squared off with special agents Blackwell and Walker.

"Ladies," Special Agent Blackwell said, setting a tablet and notepad on the table in front of him, "thank you for coming in."

"Of course." Cilla sat ramrod straight, her voice all business. "My client is happy to be of service." She gave a faux cheery grin. "Even though you've kept us waiting five minutes when *she's* paying my outrageous hourly fee. If I were you, I'd skip the pleasantries and get to it."

Lord, they hadn't even discussed the fee. Maddy put it out of her mind.

Across from her, Special Agent Walker rolled her eyes so hard she should have levitated from her chair.

"Understood." Special Agent Blackwell met Maddy's gaze. "Ms. Carmichael, you're aware the motion detectors are turned off when the guards do their rounds?"

"Oh, *come on,*" Cilla said, heavy on the sarcasm. "Half the employees probably know that."

"We're simply confirming."

Cilla looked over at Maddy and nodded.

"Yes," Maddy said. "There's one guard at night. In order to do his rounds, he has to turn off the motion detectors, or he'd set the alarm off."

"And how did you learn this? I can't imagine the security folks share details of their procedures with all the employees."

How *did* she know that? Much of what she knew about the Center came through osmosis. By being among executives, overhearing conversations happening in the conference room or hall or an office doorway.

"I'm actually not sure. It probably came up in a meeting. It's not unusual for me to be invited to a meeting that includes the head of security."

Special Agent Blackwell jotted a note. "I see. And have you ever told anyone outside the organization about this?"

"Never."

"You stated there is only one guard on duty at night," Special Agent Walker said.

"Yes. That came up in a meeting. I'm more intimately involved with the acquisition costs, so I sometimes sit in on budget meetings."

"I see. And who attended that meeting?"

"All department heads."

"Including security?"

Beside her, Cilla did an Emmy-worthy sigh. "She just said all department heads."

"Once again," Special Agent Walker said, "we're confirming."

"Confirm all you'd like. However, my client's time is important and you're wasting it. So, please, tell us what we're doing here so we can all get back to our lives."

"Getting to it, Ms. Randolph." Special Agent Walker brought her attention back to Maddy. "During this meeting, they discussed the number of guards?"

"Yes. Someone—I don't remember who—asked if we should add to the security staff."

"And what was the decision?"

"The Thompsons didn't feel it was necessary. The Center is privately funded and the Thompsons are careful with money. They want it to be a place for people to find joy. The bulk of the funds go to acquisitions and ways to improve a visitor's experience. During the day, there are multiple guards. Since the building is empty at night, they made the decision to save money by having only one guard."

"And since there's only one guard, when he's on rounds, no one is manning the monitors in the security office?"

Maddy shrugged. "I suppose."

"You don't know?"

"Not specifically, no. I mean, there are cameras. Someone off-site could be monitoring."

"All right. Let's go with the idea that no one is watching while the lone guard is on rounds. In which case, no one saw when two men climbed a ladder to the second floor and smashed the window. Is that true?"

"Don't answer that," Cilla said. "It's ridiculous. First, she wasn't there. There's no way for her to know who saw what. Second, if there's only one guard, unless he can instantly clone himself or, as Ms. Carmichael said, someone off-site is monitoring, there's no one watching the monitors while the guard is on rounds."

Special Agent Blackwell made another note and Maddy's pulse kicked up. The randomness of his note-taking unnerved her.

Maybe that was the point.

To trip her up, just as Cilla had said.

Special Agent Walker tapped her index finger on the table. *Tap-tap. Tap-tap. Tap-tap.* "Does security do rounds at the same time each night?"

"I don't know."

Special Agent Walker stared at her for a few long seconds. In terms of body language, there wasn't much of it. No raised eyebrows or cocked head.

Then she tapped her finger again. Three times. *Tap-tap. Tap-tap. Tap-tap.*

In the quiet room, that tapping might as well have been a gong vibrating off the walls.

"So," Walker said, "you don't know what time they do rounds? Or if they do them at the same time each night?"

"Asked and answered," Cilla said. "Move on."

Special Agent Walker sat back. "All right. Ms. Carmichael, the second-floor window was shattered, allowing the perpetrators access to the building."

"And?" Cilla said. "What's your question?"

"Getting to it, counselor. The first-floor windows have reinforced glass, but the second and third-floor windows don't. Were you aware of that?"

Maddy nodded. "Yes. The Thompsons hadn't realized the cost of reinforced windows. Knowing there would be motion detectors and guards on duty 24/7, they saved money by only reinforcing the first floor and basement windows. The executive suite doors are shatterproof as well. We can also lock those doors via an app."

"An app?"

"Yes. The Secret Service recommended it in case of an active shooter. We can barricade ourselves in."

Special Agent Walker met Special Agent Blackwell's eye, then came back to Maddy. Her smug smile loosened Maddy's intestines. Was this some kind of trap?

"So," Special Agent Walker said, "you knew the building could be breached at the second-floor level."

"For God's sake," Cilla tilted her head up, looking around the room. "Is there a sound problem in here?"

"It's okay," Maddy said. "I have nothing to hide. Yes. I knew that. When the opportunity arose to have the queen's collection in-house for a limited time, we—"

"Who's we?"

"Upper management, board members, the Pierres, Derek Vanmaster, the head of security. Anyone who'd be involved with the exhibit attended logistics meetings. I don't remember which meeting it was, but Derek raised the concern about the windows and placement of the exhibit. They didn't expect someone to put a ladder up to the building and smash a window."

"Why would they?" Walker shrugged. "They had security measures in place. Except, of course, if someone on staff shared the details of those security measures."

Maddy fought the blood rush destroying her focus. Were they implying ...

"Maddy," Cilla said, keeping her gaze on Walker, "I didn't hear a question, so no need to respond. Speaking of, are there any other questions, Special Agents? Or can we all get back to something meaningful?"

"Oh, there's more," Walker said.

Special Agent Blackwell slid the tablet he'd placed in front of him to Maddy. A video was cued up.

"Hit play," he said.

She did as she was told, rolling the video. Cilla angled sideways for a better view.

On screen, a man—was that the neck tattoo guy?—climbed a set of exterior stairs that looked like the ones leading to Maddy's apartment.

No way. Not again. Could it ...

Oh, God. Gaze fixed on the screen, Maddy drew a silent breath, taking in the stale, antiseptic air that suddenly burned her throat. Her eyes teared up and she blinked. The smell. That's all it was. The nasty, dank smell of a room where hundreds of criminals had sat.

The man climbed and climbed and climbed. *Step, step, step.*

Deliberate.

Please don't stop at my condo. Please.

He stopped—of course he did—and pulled something out of his front pocket.

Keys.

What?

Beside her, Cilla sat stock-still, all that lack of movement sending a giant warning flare because the woman struck her as someone rarely still.

Cilla created activity. Controlled chaos that disrupted peace.

All this stillness made Maddy's skin itch.

She focused on the tablet, where the man shoved a key in her door. Her gut twisted. A wave of nausea assailed her and panic blurred her vision. She pointed to the screen. "If that's my condo, I have no idea how he has a key."

Cilla touched her arm. The not-so-subtle message to close her mouth.

"Special Agents," Cilla said, her tone syrupy sweet, "please tell me you hauled us down here for more than this little screening? The least you could have done was provide popcorn."

Special Agent Walker gave Cilla a smug smile and leaned in. "This *little screening,* Ms. Randolph, is of your client's apartment. The man with the key, if you don't recognize him from the neck tattoo, is the same one on the Thompson Center security video the night of the heist."

"I'm aware."

Maddy checked the date and time stamp. "This is the Monday after the robbery. And it's the middle of the afternoon. I was at work. You can check that."

Special Agent Blackwell jotted a note. "We've already confirmed that. Why does he have a key to your apartment?"

"I don't know. Believe me, I am completely freaked out right now. This man, this creepy stranger, has my *key*. He could've walked in on me in the middle of the night. Or when I was in the shower."

Cilla reached over, set a hand on Maddy's arm and patted. The shut-your-mouth pat. "It's all right," Cilla said, her voice a purr that instantly brought Maddy back to focus.

Calm. She needed to remain calm. Not react. That's what they wanted. Hysteria that created mental chaos and loose lips.

"Ms. Carmichael," Special Agent Walker drawled, "we have you talking to this person at work. We have prior visits to your home, and now he has a key. You expect us to believe you don't know him?"

"I don't," Maddy said, her voice catching. "I swear to you."

Darn it. Why did she sound ... weak? *Emotional*. Of her siblings, she'd always been the rational one. Except for today. Today, when strange men had keys to her apartment and everyone thought she'd pulled off a major jewelry heist.

A whooshing filled her head. *Focus*. One thing at a time.

"Maddy, are your keys ever out of your control?"

Keys. Control. What? She swiveled to Cilla. Had she said something? She blinked, fought the roaring in her mind. Falling apart in front of FBI agents, one of whom was Phin's brother, wouldn't help.

Concentrate.

Keys. Out of her control.

Beside her, Cilla sat back, casually crossing her legs and flicking at a piece of lint on her sleeve like this whole encounter was nothing but a bother.

Later, Maddy might laugh at the sign of rebellion. Now, it gave her the push she needed to get her mind straight.

Were her keys ever out of her control? She faced the special agents again. "I don't carry my keys all day. When I get to work, I put them in my desk drawer."

Done picking lint, Cilla brought her attention back to Walker. "This is when the fun starts. *Maddy,*" she said, "do you lock your office, or your desk, when you step out?"

"No. I've never needed to."

"There you have it," Cilla said. "In the last thirty seconds, I've come up with at least ten—make that eleven—scenarios on how someone copied her keys." Clearly enjoying herself, Cilla sat forward, filling the space between them and the agents on the other side of the table. "I will destroy you on these keys."

Special Agent Walker chuckled, adding an eye-roll kicker.

Yikes. Scary women.

Maddy dared not look at Phin's brother. What must he be thinking right now?

How humiliating.

"You're saying," Special Agent Blackwell began, forcing Maddy to look at him, "someone entered the suite during business hours, walked past the receptionist, entered your office when you were coincidentally not there, stole your keys, left the building to copy them, and then returned them to your desk. All with no one noticing. You don't think that's a reach?"

When he put it that way, it sounded bad. Really bad. But it could happen. "Actually," she said, "it isn't. The other day I was out of my office for hours while giving a tour."

"A tour takes hours?"

"Sometimes, yes. There's a thirty-minute video for

students to watch. So, there's the tour, then the video and sometimes President Thompson pops in and does a Q and A with the kids. Then they have lunch in the cafeteria. I'm present for all of it."

Cilla flipped her portfolio closed, then stood. "Make that twelve scenarios." She glanced down at Maddy. "We're through here."

Maddy stood, gathered her purse from the back of the chair and followed Cilla to the door.

"Ms. Carmichael," Special Agent Blackwell said. "Please stay in the area."

"Not a problem." Cilla opened the door for Maddy. "Just make sure you've got something I won't have a ball ripping apart. Y'all have a great day."

"We'll be in touch," Special Agent Walker said.

Cilla flashed a winning smile. "Oh, goody. Something to look forward to. Just so we're clear, any communication with Ms. Carmichael goes through me."

Ohmygod. The woman was insane, talking to the FBI that way. Still, something about all that smart-ass bravado pushed Maddy's shoulders back, let her lift her chin a little higher, because Cilla Shark was Team Maddy.

What it would cost, she had no clue, but ...

Payment plan?

They strode past rows of cubicles with staffers talking on phones or huddled in deep conversation while their gazes drifted to Maddy. Did they know? Did they think she was involved in the theft of priceless jewels? Some of which belonged to the Queen of England?

Random people passed them and Cilla offered hellos and smiles as if this were the social event of the season.

Maddy's beheading perhaps.

Once the corridor was clear of people, Cilla held up a

hand. "There are cameras. No talking about the case until we get outside."

Good point. Who knew if the hallway had audio recording?

As she walked, she reached into her purse and fired up her cell phone. Cilla did the same. A few seconds later, her voice mail notification chimed. Then a slew of text notifications. Good God. Had everyone she knew called her?

She checked the screen. Three missed calls and a text from Phin Blackwell. Texts from her mother and the littles. And the elders. Two calls from Mom. The notifications went on and on and Maddy finally gave up counting. Beside her, Cilla's phone let out a series of beeps.

"We're popular," Cilla said.

Maddy checked Phin's text and almost lost the coffee she'd had on the way over. "Oh, no."

"We're fine," Cilla said, still staring at her phone.

Fine? The press swarming outside was *fine*?

"Someone leaked that you're here talking about the Pierre pieces. Leaks aren't unusual."

Cilla reached over, squeezed Maddy's arm. Her go-to move, Maddy supposed, when clients nearly pee themselves.

"I've got this, Maddy. We'll walk out the front door like this was nothing. That we are *happy* to help. And then we move on. No comment from you. Try not to look freaked out."

Easy for her to say. She had experience and wasn't the one a mob wanted to pounce on.

At the elevator bank, Cilla paused and tapped her phone. She lifted it to her ear, then pushed the elevator button with her free hand. "Where are you?" she said into the phone. "Good. We're coming out. Can you pick us up out front? We'll drive around the block. Hopefully, the press won't follow and you can take us to our cars."

A ding sounded, and the doors slid open, revealing an empty car. *Thank you.* Still, there'd more than likely be cameras right along with video.

"Elevator is here," Cilla said into her phone. "I'll see you in two minutes."

They stepped into the empty car, and Maddy smacked the button. "Who was that?"

"Phin."

Of all the names Maddy expected to hear, that wasn't one of them, but gosh, it sounded so good. So ... perfect. Phin was here. Making sure she didn't have to schlep to her car with reporters hounding her.

Helping her.

Protecting her.

And, oh, she couldn't go there. Not now, when every inch of her begged for someone to curl into, to let her hide from the world.

"He's here," Maddy said. "Why?"

"Because he's smart. He understands how this works. That law enforcement sometimes leaks information to the press if they think it'll help their case. Phin asked me when we were coming here and anticipated that the press would be outside. He'll pull up, get us to the car and off we go."

"I can't believe he's doing this."

"I can." Cilla shrugged. "He's Phin. That's a good man, right there."

"Sounds like it. I barely know him."

"Well, if I were you, I'd change that."

7

Feeling ballsy, Phin illegally parked in front of FBI headquarters and hopped out to meet Cilla and Maddy at the door.

He bypassed the thirty reporters and cameramen who'd eyed him and clearly decided he wasn't worth questioning.

Good. He wasn't in the mood for any of their nonsense. All he wanted was to get out of here without Zeke throwing a major tantrum and lecturing him on lying low.

He knew all that. Really did. But Maddy? Kinda gettin' screwed here.

And that pissed him off.

Which, on some level surprised him. People got screwed all the damned time and he accepted it. All part of life.

Maddy? She didn't deserve this. Unlike him, she was a straight arrow. A woman passionate about her job, dedicated to doing the right thing. He admired her spunk and her brains and the way every time he got within ten feet of her, he wanted to touch some part of her. Any random part. Just let his hands roam until she was on top of him, her eyes lighting up when he gave her an orgasm that would blow her into orbit.

Jesus. He had to stop.

He ran a hand over his face, shook off thoughts of naked Maddy, and focused on the next few minutes.

Hustling through the door, he found Cilla and Maddy crossing the lobby, Cilla's quick strides causing Maddy to make some serious effort to keep up.

"Hi, Phin," Cilla said. "Thanks for the help."

"No problem."

She peered outside, taking in the crowd. "Eh. Not that bad." She spun back to Maddy. "It'll be quick, but over-whelming. The second we step out, they'll converge and you'll feel like every ounce of oxygen has been sucked away. Fight it. Breathe and stay calm. That's your only job. I'll take care of everything else."

Damn, the woman was good.

Maddy bobbed her head, sending her curls into a frenzy. She may have been agreeing, but her eyes, all wide and spooked, told the tale.

He tugged on one of her curls. "You'll be fine. Cilla's an ace at this and I'll cut a path. We'll be at the car in under a minute." He waggled his eyebrows. "I parked illegally."

When she laughed, he considered it a job well done.

"You two are awesome. Thank you."

"No. Thank *you*," Cilla said. "I live for this."

Phin led the charge to the door while Maddy and Cilla, heads high, stayed just behind him.

Once they hit fresh air, the crowd mobilized, the group of them rushing forward in a solid wall of bodies and cameras. Men and women holding microphones, jockeying for a front row position, all of them forming a circle around them.

"Ms. Carmichael, did you steal the Pierres?"

"Ms. Carmichael, are you a suspect?"

"Back up," Phin hollered, his arms in front of him, tunneling through the crowd and making sure not to push anyone.

All he needed was to knock someone over. The lecture Zeke would level on him would literally turn him to stone. Then, as a brutal reminder to Cruz and Rohan to mind their p's and q's, he'd use Phin as a statue in the entrance to the Annex.

Ha. He'd have to tell Cruz that one.

Right now? Stuff to do. He glanced back, spotted Cilla holding Maddy's arm, dragging her along.

"All right, guys," Cilla said. "Relax. Ms. Carmichael has no comment. This was a casual conversation regarding the theft at the Thompson Center. Ms. Carmichael has made herself available to authorities and will help in any way possible. When we have something to share, I'll let you know. Y'all have a great day now."

The throng of press walked with them, still shouting questions and battling for position, trying to snag the magic shot.

Following Cilla's lead, Maddy kept her head up, eyes straight ahead. She may have been spooked, but she'd aced this assignment.

Just feet ahead of them sat one of the BARS SUVs. A black one they kept in the garage for nighttime jobs.

He opened the front passenger door and Maddy hopped in while Cilla climbed into the back. The gaggle stood beside the vehicle shouting questions and filming even as Phin hustled around the car.

Seconds later, he started the car, filling it with Luke Bryan. Forgot to turn the radio down again. Music still pounding, he hit the gas and pulled from the curb while lowering the volume.

"Well," Cilla said, "I think that went well."

Phin glanced at Maddy. "Have I mentioned she's nuts?"

Cilla barked out a laugh, and then her head appeared between the bucket seats. "Hey. I love my job. Phin, I'm parked in the garage on the corner. Maddy, don't worry about this. When I get through with the feds, it'll look like amateur hour. Just so we're clear, you two can't talk details about our meeting."

That couldn't be good.

He slid a sidelong gaze at Maddy, who angled back to face Cilla. "I have nothing to hide."

"I know. But it's for his protection as much as yours. If he hears anything, he can be called as a trial witness."

Trial? What the fuck had happened in there?

"I'm going to *trial*?" Maddy shrieked.

"Whoa," Phin said.

"Everyone stop talking. Right now. Maddy, I'd love to say you won't go to trial. In good conscience, I can't do that. I don't *think* you will. I'll do everything I can to make sure that doesn't happen."

Maddy sat forward again, sucking in an audible breath, and Phin shot her a glance. He should say something. Anything.

But he knew his brother. And when Ash Blackwell got on a roll, he succeeded.

Nothing of which Maddy needed to know.

Phin made a few random turns, checking his rearview with each one before circling back to the parking garage and climbing to level three.

And ... *dang it.*

"They're here," he said.

Cilla's head popped through the seats again, her view of three reporters and their accompanying cameraman unimpeded.

"Shoot," she said. "I know them. They must have gotten a tip that I was here and found my car. I need to start using another damned garage when visiting the FBI. Let's drive past and make the turn. Let me off by the elevator and I'll walk to my car. Maddy get down. They've probably seen you already, but it couldn't hurt."

A phone—Maddy's—let out a series of rings and dings and various other sounds.

She ignored the phone while Cilla slid to the rear driver's side door.

Phin cruised by the gaggle of reporters, all of them watching, their gazes sharp like the hunters they were. Once clear, he checked the rearview again.

"They're on the move. Cilla, I'll wait until you get into your car and follow you out."

She waved him off. "Thank you, but no. They don't want me. I need you to get Maddy home safely. Maddy, I'll call you tomorrow. I don't think we'll hear from the FBI again this weekend, but you never know. Keep your phone close."

Maddy turned again, facing Cilla. "I will. Thank you again. For everything."

"No problem. Makes my life exciting. Phin, just a suggestion, drive around for a bit. Let the vultures disperse before you take her to her car."

His thoughts exactly.

Phin hit the brakes and checked the mirror again, watching as the small crowd of reporters continued hustling toward them. "Go," he said.

Cilla pushed her door open, jumped out, and rushed to her car. Once he saw that she was safely in her vehicle, he hit the gas again, heading toward the exit, his mind circling back to Cilla's comment about Maddy going to trial.

What could have happened that resulted in that?

And, worse, Ash couldn't have given them a heads-up? Maybe even a hint that they might have a lead?

Beside him, Maddy blew out a breath. "I can't believe this is happening."

"Unfortunately, I can. Whatever it is, the feds are reaching. Ash—Cameron—hasn't said, but they've gotta be under a ton of pressure. Someone's eventually gonna leak that the queen's jewels were boosted along with the Pierres. Nightmare scenario."

He hooked the turn to the street level, stuck his credit card in the machine, waited for the gate to rise, and drove through.

"I was doing my job," Maddy blurted. "Talking to people. How that guy knew where I lived, I have no idea. I ..."

When her voice trailed off, he shot her a look and found her hand raised to her mouth while she stared out the window.

Man, this had to be tearing her up. Phin drove two blocks and parked in a loading zone, leaving the engine running.

He peered over at her, but Maddy looked away, staring out at a café claiming the best ice cream in North Carolina.

"I don't know what happened in there," Phin said, "but your lawyer? She's a beast. She loves battle. The harder, the better."

Maddy finally shifted back to him, her eyes devoid of the spark he'd seen that first night when she'd called him Charlie Charm.

That alone pissed him off and his fingers itched. That

urge to reach for her, slide his hand down her cheek and reassure her that she'd be okay. That he'd help her.

Zeke would kill him. He curled his fingers, holding them in place.

"I looked her up," Maddy said. "She's amazing. Thank you for the referral. I'm worried I can't afford her. What then?"

He shrugged. "When she calls tomorrow, talk to her. From what I know, she'll work with you. This case has everything she craves. It's federal, high-profile, and will get her on national news. At this point, you're doing her a favor. Hell, she should pay *you* for the PR."

Maddy rolled her eyes. "Thanks, but I don't think she believes that right now."

"Well, *I* believe it. I spend a lot of time at social functions. My job requires networking. The people Cilla takes as clients are politicians, CEOs, government officials. This case checks all her boxes."

Finally, she smiled. Maybe his little speech had gotten through.

"Why are you helping me? I'm nobody to you."

"Everyone is somebody. And I have a problem with people in power thinking they can railroad decent people. If you're going against the feds, you need an excellent lawyer. And that's Cilla. It's a win-win for both of you. All I did was make a call. What happened in there that has you so freaked?"

"Cilla just said I shouldn't discuss it with you."

Expert advice from counsel. Too bad she'd left. "If you don't want to talk, that's no problem. But Cilla isn't here. It's you and me and you're spooked, so, you know, if you need to vent? Knock yourself out."

She stared out the window for a long moment, then

peered over at him, her eyes so big he could drive a truck through them. Yep. Spooked.

"I don't want to involve you."

"I'd say it's too late for that."

"Not if I go to trial."

"You're not."

He hoped. Because, really, he still had no clue what went on in that meeting with Ash and his coagent. Walker. Ash seemed to like her. A hard-ass, he'd called her, but they got on okay.

He conjured his best winning smile. "If you go to trial, I'll marry you and I can't be forced to testify."

"Oh, please. This isn't funny."

Sure wasn't. Finally, he gave in and uncurled his fingers. He reached over and touched her wrist. "I know. You can talk to me, though. Okay?"

She peered out the window again, then inched her head back and forth. A surrender. "They have security video from my apartment." She faced him again. "It's that same guy. The one with the neck tattoo? He went inside."

What the hell? Phin gawked. "He broke *in*?"

She met his gaze, made some seriously hard eye contact. "No. He used a key."

What was happening right now? How did Ash not tell him this? His brother needed to learn the art of sharing.

Jesus. Zeke would absolutely, no doubt, kill him for inserting himself into this mess.

The Phin statue seemed like a definite.

"The only thing I can think of," Maddy said, "is someone at the office took them. That's the only time my keys are out of my control. At home, I lock my doors all the time. I'm a single woman and I'm not about to leave myself vulnerable."

Made sense. "Where do you keep your keys?"

"Top right drawer of my desk. Sometimes, I just toss them on the desk if I have to run into a meeting or something."

Behind them, a truck horn blared. Obviously a tourist, since southerners didn't beep at other vehicles. Ever. He checked the mirror. Probably a delivery. He shifted the car into gear and hit the gas, stopping at the traffic light on the corner.

"Do all employees have access to the executive suite?"

"*Noooo*. Only on an as-needed basis. Even then, it's mostly management. Except for President Thompson's nephew, Louis the third. He's in college and interning with us this summer."

"Okay."

"Okay?" Maddy held out her hand. "What does that mean?"

"We need a list of all employees who have access to the executive suite."

"I don't have that. It's an HR thing."

Phin could get it. He thought. Or he'd ask Zeke to call HR. Which would leave Phin out of it and avoid any remote chance of him discussing the list with Maddy and violating the BARS NDA.

Or …

Ash.

Phin had to think on it. Figure it out while he drove. He put the car in gear. "Where to? We need to kill time before I drive you back to your car."

"You don't have to do this."

He checked the light—still red—and looked over at Maddy, locking his gaze on hers and holding his breath for a few seconds because *day-am*, just looking at her destroyed him. Burned right through him and if he didn't get to touch her soon, he'd be nothing but charred bones.

He leaned in, getting close enough that her scent, lilies maybe, filled him. "What if I want to?"

"Well, Charlie Charm, I suppose that would be great. Thank you."

"You're welcome. Now, where are we going?"

Maddy checked her phone. "Would you run me back to my office? I left my laptop and I need it over the weekend. It's after five, so I won't have to face the administrative staff. I can't stand the idea of them looking at me like I'm a thief."

"Then I guess we'll just have to prove them wrong."

8

The front entrance of the Thompson Presidential Center crawled with news vans, cameramen, and reporters. Two networks had even set up tents.

Maddy supposed *they* planned on being here a while.

"Oh my God," she said. "They're here, too."

"I figured," he said, his tone fairly casual.

Was she naïve? She'd never thought so, but somehow, she hadn't expected a mob of reporters camped out in front of the Center.

Yep. Naive.

Phin rolled to a stop at the corner, his attention fixed on the crowd. "How bad do you need your laptop? I can turn on the next block and avoid the reporters."

The crowd had doubled from the courthouse, and sickness rolled in her stomach. Obviously, someone at the FBI continued to leak information to the press.

President Thompson enjoyed PR, but this? One of their employees being questioned regarding the theft of priceless artifacts?

Not good.

"There's an employee entrance around the side. Maybe they're not over there."

"I wouldn't count on it."

Thanks, Mr. Negative. Reporters or not, leaving her laptop all weekend wasn't an option. She pointed out her window. "If you turn right here, we can go to the next block and enter from the rear lot."

Phin turned, cruised to the next street, and pulled into the lot, taking the first available spot. From here, she'd walk to the east side of the building and slip in through the employee entrance.

"How about," Phin said, "I get out and make sure there are no pain-in-the-ass reporters by the door?"

She sat for a second, staring at the pathway leading around the building. Right there. That's where she needed to go. So close. But who knew what waited there?

An entire weekend without her personal computer?

No way. Sure, she could do a lot on her phone, but her life was on that damned computer and the way things were going, she couldn't risk it going missing.

She didn't want to believe someone she worked with would take it, but she wouldn't have believed someone from within the organization would steal her keys and be involved in the exhibit theft either.

And, oh ... The FBI. Every crime show she'd ever watched replayed in her mind. The FBI might seize every-thing in her home and office.

No time for that now. She needed to concentrate on next steps. "Reporters or not, I need my things. I have to go in."

Phin turned the engine off. "Okay. We'll do it like we did at FBI headquarters. If there's a crowd, I'll lead you through."

"I—"

He put up a hand. "Don't argue. We're doing this."

How the heck had she gotten this lucky? Technically, Phin worked for the Thompsons and here he was, helping her. His family couldn't be happy about this.

"Will this get you in trouble?"

He shrugged. "Probably. This isn't about business. What the hell kind of coward would that make me if I sit here while you face reporters? I'm a lot of things. A coward isn't one of them." He unleashed the Charlie Charm smile. "Besides, my mother would skin me if I let you do this alone. I'm more afraid of her than the Thompsons."

A gurgle of laughter burst free, and Maddy took a second to enjoy it. To savor it. To be thankful for those few seconds, thanks to Phin, Mr. Protective, who'd somehow dropped into her life at the exact time she needed extra support.

That had to be a sign, didn't it? That maybe he was ... Nope. She wouldn't do this, wouldn't get ahead of herself, analyzing all the reasons why Phin might be the one.

Not when people might think of her as a criminal.

Good Girl Maddy.

A thief.

The back of her neck throbbed, and she closed her eyes. God, the humiliation.

"Hey." Phin said, tapping her leg and bringing her attention back to him. "You're fine. You've got this. The feds will do their thing, realize you had nothing to do with it, and clear you. It's a process. A painful one, but a process."

Battling her thoughts, she bobbed her head. They'd clear her.

When he said it, she believed it. He had that way about him. Direct and convincing.

"Thank you, Phin. You have no idea."

He lifted his hand, brought it to rest on the side of her head and warmth spread, wrapping around her like a blanket on a cold day.

Later, she'd tell herself it was the human contact she craved. Not an insanely hot guy who'd done nothing but try to protect her.

Not that.

When she didn't move, he eased his hand down. A move so gentle, something in her chest pinged.

Strong, gentle hands.

On her.

She tilted her head, leaning into the gesture, meeting his gaze and holding it for a few seconds while the air conditioner must have conked out because—holy cow—all that slow, controlled heat from his hand turned to an absolute furnace blast.

What if she ...

What?

Leaned in just a wee bit farther? Put herself out there and risked making a move and kissing Phin?

She pictured it, the two of them inching closer and ... and ...

Oh, yes. She could do this.

Brave Maddy.

She craned forward, testing, and he moved closer, his gaze locked on hers.

At least until he sat back, lifting his hand like all that heat had scorched him.

"Phew," he shook his head. "What the fuck am *I* doing? I apologize. I shouldn't have done that. Totally inappropriate."

"Says who?"

"Um, me?"

This was it. Brave Maddy time. "What if I ... liked ... it? You touching me?"

There. Said it. *Brave, brave, brave.* She steeled herself, waiting for him to respond. Waiting for him to say something, anything, that would keep her from expecting too much of him.

"I'd say you should be pissed. But I liked it, too. I just don't want to be *that* guy. Taking advantage of a situation."

Relief mixed with terror sent conflicting signals to her brain. *He's the one. Don't go there.*

It was happening. The spiral. A vision of Phin in a tux at an altar flashed.

She shook her head, the gesture simultaneously pulverizing the image while assuring Phin he wasn't a predator. "You're far from that guy. You've been kind, Phin. That's all. Okay? Whatever that was between us, it felt good. And that's saying something in my current situation. So, thank you. Maybe when we're done with all this, we can ... I don't know ... Explore it?"

He nodded. One solid jerk of his head. He liked that idea.

So did she.

"That'd be good," he said. He pointed out the windshield. "Let's do this before someone spots us."

They exited the SUV, following the brick path around the side of the building where—uh, oh—Maddy halted.

One, two, three people held cameras and another small group of reporters stayed busy on their phones. At least until one woman looked up, spotted Maddy and beelined, bringing the pack with her.

"And so it begins," Phin said, stepping partially in front of her, his long legs eating up the pavement. "Is the door unlocked?"

She dug into the outer pocket of her purse and grabbed her wristband with her keycard. "I have my card."

The female reporter leading the charge shoved her microphone out. "Ms. Carmichael, what did the FBI ask you?"

"Ms. Carmichael," another guy yelled, "what evidence do they have against you?"

Evidence against me? What?

No comment. That's what Cilla had said. No comment. No comment. No comment.

Phin pushed through the crowd. "Coming through. Make a path, people."

"Ms. Carmichael, did you have anything to do with the theft?"

They all screamed at her, each jockeying for position, their voices melding into a *wha, wha, wha* inside her head.

"No comment. No comment. No comment."

How many times did she have to say it?

No. *Comment.*

Two feet from the door, Maddy lifted her keycard, ready to swipe it and breeze on inside.

Swipe.

She pulled on the door.

Nothing.

A red light on the keypad blinked.

For the love of …

She swiped again.

Another red light and panic set in, shooting from her brain, swarming her body like a thousand tiny stabs. *Stabstabstabstab.*

"Try again," Phin said.

Swipe. Once again, instead of the ka-chunk of the lock disengaging, all Maddy received was a red light.

Dammit. Of all the times for her key card to crap out on her.

She spun to Phin. "Front door."

Leading her off the brick path, Phin led her across the grass, where her pumps sunk into the soil, one of them sticking. Her foot came clear out of her shoe and one of the male reporters snatched it, held it up like a prized win.

Oh, come on!

"Seriously," she said. "You're evil enough to hold my shoe hostage?"

Beside her, Phin took one step toward the guy and she whipped her arm out. "Don't bother."

The last thing they needed was the episode making the evening news.

Maddy kicked off her other shoe and made a note of the network's logo on the man's microphone. "Keep 'em both. Even if I intended on commenting, I wouldn't now. And you just took your network off the list of possible exclusives. Great work."

Phin laughed. "Nice."

He grasped her arm, leading her to the front where, just as they cornered the building, another hungry pack waited.

"They're like locusts."

"You're okay," Phin said. "Let's get you inside and I'll go back for your shoes."

She spewed another round of no-comments and did her best to square her shoulders and lift her chin. Almost there.

At the circular door, Phin waved her in, making sure no one followed before entering himself.

The evening guard, Maurice, stood just inside the circular door, his eyes wide. "Maddy. Lord, child, I'm sorry about this. I've been trying to chase them off. They're spooking the visitors." He looked down at her bare feet. "Where are your shoes?"

Maddy kept moving, glancing back to see cameramen lined up along the front windows filming her. Unbelievable. "They're outside. It's not your fault, Maurice."

One reporter banged on the glass, and Maurice headed straight for the door. "That's it. Let me deal with them and I'll be right back."

"While you're upstairs," Phin told her, "I'm going after your shoes."

"Forget it. They're not that expensive."

"It's not the point. That was a crummy move. I want those shoes back."

Men. Funny creatures. "Suit yourself. I'll meet you back here."

Phin nodded and took off after Maurice, throwing himself back into the flock of vultures.

She rode the escalator to the administrative floor, where she once again swiped her key card. Nothing.

A not-so-nice thought peppered her. One door was a fluke.

Two?

That meant a problem with her card. Something that had never happened prior to being interviewed by the FBI.

Somehow that didn't seem a coincidence.

Beyond the glass entry doors, the dimmed lights in reception indicated Aileen had gone home. On a Friday night, she didn't expect anyone to be in there.

She knocked lightly and waited. If necessary, she'd be forced to call security and ask the guard to unlock the executive suite.

After the day she'd had, and the media attention attached to it, the entire staff must know she'd been questioned. Add to that her key card suddenly not working and the gossip mill would be going full steam.

She knocked again.

Nothing.

She pulled her phone from her purse and scrolled her contacts for Frank's number. With any luck, he'd still be in the building.

Two rings in, he picked up. "Maddy?"

"Hi. I'm so sorry to bother you. I need to get my personal laptop out of my office and for some reason, my key isn't working. I think everyone is gone. Are you still here?"

"Uh, no. I left an hour ago. Margaret and I have a dinner."

Great. So, he was probably driving and his wife was listening in via Bluetooth. "I apologize," she said. "I'll see if security can open the door for me."

"I'll call them," he said.

Huh? Why would he call them when she was standing right here? "No. That's okay. I can do it. Go enjoy your dinner."

For a few seconds, silence filled the line. No doubt a by-product of her having multiple conversations with the FBI.

"Maddy, you can't. I'll have to."

"I *can't*? Why?"

"Hold on. I need to pull over."

Maddy's pulse throbbed against the skin at her neck. Call it fatigue, call it stress, call it a damned rotten day, but she was not in the mood for all this wordplay.

"Can you hear me?"

Frank's voice, clearer now, as if he spoke directly into the phone rather than via the car's Bluetooth system. Somehow, it didn't make her feel any better.

"I can hear you."

"Good. I'm sorry to do this over the phone, but while you were with the FBI, we had a meeting."

A meeting. *Excellent.* "And?"

"We didn't expect you back today and planned on waiting until Monday. We're putting you on administrative leave."

Administrative ... wait. What?

She cocked her head, replayed his words in her mind.

"With pay, of course," Frank continued.

"You're *suspending* me?"

"Not *suspending*. Time off. We feel it would be best if you weren't in the office for a bit."

That alone devastated her, and she turned, leaned against the solid wall of glass while her legs decided if they'd keep her upright.

"You can't believe I had something to do with this. Please, Frank. I did nothing wrong. I swear to you."

"We don't believe it."

Liar. If they didn't, she'd have her laptop by now. "It sure sounds like it. Considering I'm locked out of the office and can't even collect my personal belongings. Whatever happened to innocent until proven guilty?"

"*None* of us think you were involved."

"Why am I being suspended, then?"

He drew a long breath, the sound grating on her. *He* was frustrated? Please.

"You're not being *suspended*. Think of it as a paid vacation until the frenzy dies down."

What a load of baloney. "I'd like to speak with President Thompson."

"No, Maddy. He asked me to convey the message. As soon as this gets cleared up, we'll bring you back."

Wasn't that so incredibly generous? But, really, what did

she expect from them? What right, after the FBI had questioned her, did she have to feel betrayed? Still, it stung.

She'd worked so damned hard. Weekends, nights, whatever it took. They'd taken a chance on her and she'd wanted to repay them. After all of that, how could they think...

"Maddy?"

Something in her throat caught, and tears bubbled in her eyes. Dammit. "I'm here," she croaked.

"I'm sorry, Maddy," he said, his voice so matter-of-fact that somehow she doubted he was sorry at all.

"I've given everything I have to this place, Frank. You know it. The Thompsons know it."

And now, after she'd done all she was supposed to, every last thing that had been asked, she wound up persona non grata. *She* was the disappointment?

"They're getting a ton of pushback from the family."

The family. "Meaning Louis Squared?"

Louis Squared. The nickname the staff had given Louis Pierre Senior and Junior. They'd yet to come up with a nickname for Louis III, Junior's son.

"Yes. Obviously, they want the items recovered. Senior is devastated. He designed those pieces for the First Lady. They're worried about the stress and his health."

How was that her fault? If she'd been involved in the theft maybe, but she was innocent.

Frank didn't want to hear that, though. Obviously, none of them did. They wanted a quick resolution and she gave them a handy target.

Fine. She'd prove her innocence, and they'd have to apologize.

She lifted her chin. Forced her mind to focus on the next thirty seconds. She'd hold her tongue, strap on a happy face, and do whatever it took to keep everyone happy. Good Girl Maddy. That was her.

"Just to be clear," she said, "I've done nothing wrong. I guess I'll speak to you when this is all over. If you would, please call security and get me into my office."

RETRIEVING MADDY'S SHOES FROM A PISSED-OFF REPORTER turned out to be more fun than Phin expected. Wasn't every day he could threaten an asshole—and his network—with a lawsuit for stealing a woman's personal property. Why it took suing someone to get anything done, Phin never understood.

What the hell ever happened to kindness? To a little freaking compassion?

Still shaking his head, Phin stood in the lobby of the Thompson Center waiting for Maddy, who'd obviously gotten hung up. How long did it take to retrieve a laptop?

He glanced out the windows where the pack of reporters waited. Not going out that way. There had to be an emergency exit or something.

His phone rang. Zeke's ringtone.

He slid it from his front pocket and punched the screen. "Hey."

"Where are you?"

And, whoopsie, big brother had that I-will-fuck-you-up tone. Probably saw the news, which would put Phin firmly in the doghouse.

Phin glanced up at the escalator, damn near willing Maddy to appear. "Standing in the lobby of the Thompson Center. Maddy is upstairs getting her laptop. The press was waiting when we got here."

"Mom saw you on the news. Arguing with a reporter about a woman's, assuming Maddy's, shoe."

Someone actually filmed that?

"Jesus, Phin. What happened to only helping her get a lawyer? Now you're playing bodyguard?"

"Was I supposed to let her get ambushed after Ash and company interrogated her?"

"Don't even try spinning it, pal. We're being paid to find stolen jewels. You're way outside of scope."

"Then we need to expand the scope."

"Uh, no. The scope stays where it is, but *you* need to get your ass back here. We've got work to do."

Phin took a few steps, aimlessly wandering, the movement helping him align his thoughts. As much as he hated it, Zeke was right. He had responsibilities to his family. Running around with Maddy wouldn't help recover the queen's jewels. But finding the jewels meant clearing Maddy.

"Speaking of work," Phin said. "Can you call Thompson and get a video dump for the executive suite?"

"Sure. And why am I asking for this?"

Tricky territory. His brother had already given him a load of crap for being outside of scope. Now he had to tell him the feds had this guy going into Maddy's apartment?

No. Family or not, Maddy had confided in him. She'd trusted him.

Besides, Ash would probably tell them.

He'd go with that theory. "We should see who's coming and going."

There. Not a lie. Not even a lie by omission.

A brief pause ensued, then a tap-tap-tap sound. Zeke flicking his pen against the desk. "You might be right," he finally said. "Can't hurt. I'll call him. When will you be back?"

Phew. Phin peered up at the escalator again. Nothing. Dammit. "Maddy's car is still at FBI headquarters. Cilla told us to get lost for a while until the reporters cleared out. Once she's home, I'll be back."

Zeke sighed. He might not have liked Phin's plan, but he wouldn't stop him from making sure Maddy stayed safe. None of his brothers would.

"Lay low when you follow her home. Please. The press is camped at her condo."

"Seriously?"

"*That* was also on the news."

Maddy chose that moment to appear at the top of the escalator, briefcase slung over her shoulder and a shopping bag in hand. The glum look on her face wasn't exactly a positive sign. "Here she comes. Gotta go."

Phin disconnected and slipped his phone back into his pocket. He'd have to break the news to Maddy about unwelcome company at her place. Wouldn't that be fun?

She stepped off the escalator and waved at Maurice, standing behind the giant reception desk, his eye on the predators outside.

He came around the desk, shaking his head. "I'm sorry, Maddy."

"Me too, Maurice. Hopefully, I'll see you soon."

Hopefully she'd see him soon? What was that about?

Phin took a few steps, meeting her partway and taking the shopping bag before setting her shoes on the floor. "You okay?"

"Fine," she said in that tight tone women used when they were definitely *not* fine.

She eased her feet into the pumps, holding on to his arm

for balance and twisted fucker that he was, he liked it. The simplicity—and comfort—of her casually reaching for him.

Add that to them agreeing to explore their relationship further when this was all over?

He really liked *that*.

Phinny, Phinny, Phinny.

Shoes in place, she pointed to the entrance. "Let's avoid that mess." She swiveled back to Maurice. "We're parked in the rear lot. Can we go out the employee door?"

"Of course," he said.

Say what now? Why would an employee be asking if she could use the employee exit?

Whatever happened in the time she'd been upstairs, it didn't appear to be good news.

Maddy hauled ass across the lobby, her heels clicking against the marble. Man, the woman could move when she wanted to. Phin caught up, falling in step beside her. "Hey, what's going on?"

"They suspended me."

Come on. She'd gone from being entrusted with hiring BARS to being drop-kicked for something there was no proof she'd even done.

She waved it off. "Well, they're calling it administrative leave. Treat it like a *vacation,* my boss said. A *vacation.*"

He wanted to be shocked. Sure did. He'd been around enough politicians that nothing surprised him anymore. Which didn't say much for his way of life, but whatever.

When protecting their public image, politicians employed enough strategists to make their shit smell like roses. No matter who they took down.

Before they reached the door, he latched on to her elbow, pulling her to a stop. "As crazy as this will sound, this isn't about you."

"*Really?*" She pulled her arm free. "Because it feels like it's about me."

She might rival Zeke with the biting sarcasm. Who could blame her? In a matter of days, her life, her routine, had been pulverized. And from what he'd learned, she liked routine.

"This," he said, "is the Thompson machine doing their thing. You're collateral damage. Which sucks."

A guy appeared at the glass door, cupping his hands against it and peering in. The vultures waiting for their next meal. He spotted them and banged on the glass.

"Let's go," Phin said. "We can talk in the car."

REPEATING THE PLAN FROM THE COURTHOUSE, PHIN USHERED Maddy to the car, the vultures in tow while she threw no-comments around like frisbees. If nothing else, she was getting good at it.

He made a quick left out of the lot, darted down an alley, then hooked another right, followed by a few more random turns before checking his rearview.

No tail. Superb. "We're good. No one followed us."

Beside him, Maddy stared out the passenger window, apparently mesmerized by houses with overrun weeds, sagging gutters, and chipped paint. This street was a truck-stop waitress after an eighteen-hour shift.

Tired with aching joints.

The whole point of Thompson putting his presidential center in this neighborhood. He'd grown up here, under-stood the struggles, and wanted to revive his hometown. Turn that tired truck-stop waitress into a woman of leisure.

"Can I just go home?" Maddy asked, her attention still focused outside.

He paused at a traffic light and she finally looked over at him, her big eyes droopy, which, yeah, irritated him. Grated against his already crabby nerves. From the second he'd met her, she'd had a brightness that bordered on naïve. In his world, naivete got folks stomped on and he'd never allowed himself to be put in that position. Seeing too much sunshine brought rain, and he didn't need the disappointment.

But Maddy? Her relentless idealism had made him feel ... hopeful.

At least until now.

The light changed and Phin cruised along, sticking to the speed limit to avoid unwanted attention from law enforcement. "I hate to pile on, but there's a problem."

She snorted. "Of course."

"Zeke called while you were in your office. They were watching the news. Reporters are at your house."

Maddy's shoulders sagged. "Great." She lifted a hand, let it drop. "What am I supposed to do now? I *have* to go home. It's not as if I have an overnight bag in my trunk."

He didn't want to tell her it wasn't a bad idea. Considering he had one. Always.

"You'll have to face them. Every time you go in or out, you'll have to deal with them. If that's your idea of the comforts of home, knock yourself out. To me? It sounds pretty fucking miserable."

She angled toward him, adjusting the seat belt as she moved. "I agree. But I'm not going to my mother's. She's been calling and texting me all day. I keep telling her I'll call when I'm alone."

Her phone dinged. "Yep! Right on cue. That's my mother. She probably saw everything on the news."

Maddy shot off a text.

"You can call her if you need to. I'll pull over and hop out. Give you some privacy."

"I'll wait until I get to my car." Maddy peered down at her phone, her thumb slowly swiping up and then halting. "Ooh. Cilla called." She tapped, then lifted the phone to her ear. "Maybe she has an update." Holding up a finger, she shifted in her seat again, watching the road ahead. "Hi ... I know ... I'm in Phin's car. They put me on leave."

Maddy jerked the phone from her ear. Probably to minimize Cilla's hollering that came clear through the line.

Phin had to smile. "Told you she was a beast."

"No kidding."

"Do you mind putting her on speaker?"

Maddy punched the screen just as Cilla took a breath.

"Are you done?" Phin asked.

"Honey," she drawled, "I'm not nearly done. I knew these fuckers would do this. I will *crucify* them."

"Um," Maddy said, "thank you? I guess."

Again, Phin smiled. So dang funny.

"No need to thank me," Cilla said. "I live for this. Now, you can't go home."

"I have *nothing* with me but my laptop and the clothes I'm wearing." The words came out in a breathy rush and sounding way too desperate.

"Not a problem," Cilla said. "I can have my assistant meet you somewhere. Give her your key and she'll go to your place and get a few things."

"But—"

"Maddy, if you come out with a suitcase, it'll look like you're running. Not exactly the image we want to project. The reporters are on the sidewalk. If my assistant goes, they won't recognize her and will leave her alone. She'll walk in, fill a duffel and off she goes."

"She's got a point," Phin said.

"Damn right I do. Where are you now?"

"Going to get my car," Maddy said.

"Forget the car, for now. There might still be reporters hanging around the garage. We need to get you set up somewhere."

"I'll go to a hotel."

"No. If they find you, you're toast. They'll swarm the place. Phin, I know it's a lot to ask ..."

He didn't need to be a rocket scientist to know what was coming and his intestines loosened. That statue Zeke would make of him just got to be King Kong's size.

"Cilla—"

"Can you take her to your place?" Cilla, being Cilla, plowed right over him. "Y'all have that insane security."

"No," Maddy said, her voice firmer now. "I can't do that."

"Why?"

Maddy gawked at Phin while hitting the mute button. "She really is nuts." She tapped the button again. "Cilla, I'm not comfortable with that. Phin and his brothers work for the Thompson Center. Plus, I barely know them. I'm not moving into their home."

"Please. People bunk in with strangers all the time. My niece is sixteen and living in France with a host family. You're all adults. You can handle it. Phin, can you make this happen?"

He considered it. Zeke would lose his mind. He'd already told him to distance himself from this situation. Now Phin was supposed to move Maddy in?

Surprise!

But Zeke had moved Liv and Brodie in when necessary. Plus, Phin had withstood his brother's wrath plenty of times. *Plenty.* Zeke would bitch and moan, but he wouldn't turn away someone needing help. Blackwells were suckers that way.

"I'll work it out," Phin said. "There's a guest suite. And I'll get Neuman, Zeke's protégé, to pick up Maddy's car later."

Beside him, Maddy raised her hand. "Hey, does anyone care what I think?"

Phin shrugged. "If you've got a better idea, let's hear it."

She pinned him with a look.

"I don't hear anything," Cilla said. "I guess she doesn't have one. I'll have my assistant call you and set up a meeting place. Glad we got this settled."

9

PHIN HIT THE REMOTE AND THE IRON GATES LEADING TO CHEZ Blackwell eased open. Knowing Zeke had the timing set tightly, he hit the gas and drove through. God forbid he should dawdle. He'd find himself locked out of his own damned house.

"Wow," Maddy said. "Cilla wasn't kidding about the security."

"Sometimes it makes me nuts, but I get it. We did a job a few weeks ago that involved storing a three-million-dollar painting overnight until the client could get here."

"That must have been something to see. After the break-in at the Center, I understand wanting the extra protection. And the jewels weren't even mine. I'm just the hired help."

Phin shook his head as he cruised the long asphalt drive bordered with towering oak, maple, and pine trees. Ahead, the Friary came into view, the setting sun casting an orange glow that gave the place a peaceful, Zen quality.

These were the times he loved living here. Times when he could go out on his balcony and just breathe. Forget all the negativity—the dreams he'd abandoned, the secrets, the idiots who judged him—roaming around in his head and take in the quiet. He wasn't one to meditate, but sitting on that balcony might be the next best thing.

"You're not just the hired help," he said.

"True. Now I'm the suspended hired help accused of theft."

"Not for long." Intending to change the subject, he gestured out the window, "Welcome to Chez Blackwell. Straight ahead is the Friary."

"You call it a friary? Is that a joke or something?"

Considering he and his brothers were far from monks, it probably did seem like a joke. "No kidding. We bought the property a few years ago. It was an abandoned church youth camp at the time, but prior to that, Franciscan monks lived here. The center part is the original building. We added two wings, so we could all have our own suites." He pointed down the road. "There are cabins down that way. We refurbished those and our staff members live there."

"Staff members?"

"The Rios. It's not like they're butlers or whatever. Way too foo-foo for us. But it's a lot of property to maintain, so they help us with it."

He drove to the main entrance of the Friary. His room was on the second floor, but he'd made the instantaneous decision to put Maddy in the first-floor guest suite.

The rationale being if she were far from his room, Zeke wouldn't accuse him of trying to get laid by putting her right next door.

A stroke of brilliance if he'd ever had one.

Phin parked and pointed to the first floor. "Your suite is on the ground level, in back. I'm upstairs. While you're getting settled, I need to talk to Zeke."

This time it was Maddy's turn to smile. "To explain how

you went temporarily insane and decided to bring me, the person your client thinks stole priceless items from him, to your home?"

A woman after his own heart with that sarcastic humor. "Something like that."

If Zeke stuck to the script, he'd hand Phin his ass, get the anger out of his system, and then, being one to always root for the underdog, realize Maddy needed help and they could provide it.

Done.

All Phin had to do was keep his mouth shut and withstand the lecture.

Before he could open the car door, she reached across the console and wrapped her fingers around his forearm. He peered down, then met her gaze and—yow, he liked what he saw.

The killer combo of her hand on him and those soulful blue eyes sent his pulse slamming against his skin. He might have even been sweating.

"Seriously," she said, "if this is a problem. I'll go to a hotel. You've been more than kind and I don't want to cause any issues."

If she kept touching him, she wouldn't be going anywhere. Well, maybe she'd be going *somewhere*. Somewhere that included sheets and a pillow and him on top of her. Or vice versa. He wasn't picky.

"Thanks," he said, "but we're good. We don't turn our backs on people."

Ignoring his side fantasy and his brewing hard-on, he slid from the seat, popped the trunk, and grabbed the small suitcase that Cilla's assistant had retrieved for Maddy. Side by side, they walked the flagstone path leading to the entrance. Once there, Phin pressed his hand against the pad beside the door. The lock disengaged, and he held the door for Maddy. "We'll set you up so you can get in and out."

"Pretty high tech. It's nice not having to worry about keys."

Once inside, he led her through the foyer, pointing out the Great Hall, what some considered a living room, she was welcome to sit in.

He hooked a left, ushering her down the long corridor to a set of double doors. "You're in here. Rohan is next door, and my Grams is on the other side. I'm upstairs. And yes." He laughed. "We're all grown-ass men living with our mother and grandmother. What that says about us, who the hell knows?"

"You don't owe me or anybody else an explanation. The place is enormous. It's not as if you're all sharing a three-bedroom house."

"I still think it's weird, but we needed the space for BARS. We also didn't want our mother and Grams living alone." He opened the unlocked guest suite door and held it for her. "We keep the door unlocked unless someone is here. Once we get you set up, your handprint unlocks it."

Inside, gray-blue walls, a cream sofa, and red-and-white-striped upholstered chairs in the small living area gave the place a homey feel. Maddy glanced around, her gaze locking on the French doors and the mountains beyond. She made a beeline straight for that orange glow of sunset. He knew the feeling. The craving that came with needing to throw doors open and suck in air.

She made no move for the door handle, though. Just stood there. Watching. "This is stunning," she said. "Why would anyone ever want to leave?"

"That's the point. Mom figures if people come to stay, she wants them comfortable."

"Well, she nailed it."

She sure did.

God only knew what Mom had spent on the interior designer, but based on Maddy's reaction, it was money well spent.

Phin made a left into the separate bedroom, tossing the suitcase on the bed. The curtains on the second set of French doors were open, revealing the equally stunning view.

He walked back to the sitting area and found her still by the doors, but this time looking around, checking out the small kitchenette.

"There's no food in the fridge yet, but I'll get that taken care of. There's water, though. And coffee."

Maddy waved him off. "I'm just grateful not to be in a hotel." She pointed to the furnished patio. "Can I sit out there?"

"Absolutely. We arm the house after eleven, so if you're interested in stargazing, call me. I can disarm it for you."

Or I can keep you company.

The room suddenly closed in, the air getting thick enough to smother him. Worse, she just stood there, peering at him with those beautiful eyes that made him think of heat and bare skin and ... sheets. *Tangled* sheets soaked in sweat from a good screwing.

If he kept this up, he might need a cold shower.

Hell, it'd been a good ten years since he'd been forced to try that trick. Typically, if he needed to get laid, he got laid.

No big deal.

That sounded bad even to him, but he was always honest with himself. And women. They knew going in that he wasn't a long-term guy. Why exactly that was, he couldn't be sure. Eventually, he'd like a family. A couple of kids running around. A girl who'd get pissed at him when he scared off boys.

Right now? With his late-night schedule and his sometime hook-ups when he needed to schmooze someone?

Impossible.

Fuck buddies, one woman, Angie, had said. She was the assistant to the chief of staff in the governor's office and called him every couple of weeks when she needed to bust off stress. They'd met at some gala he couldn't even remember and had hit it off. They were a pair. Both hungry for something that didn't include walking down an aisle.

Suddenly, looking at Maddy and her adorable curls, his life didn't seem so great.

Nothing to do about it.

Not with his responsibilities to BARS.

"Okay. I'm ... uh ..." He jerked his thumb to the door. "I'm going now. Call me when you're ready and I'll show you around. I'm gonna check in with my brothers."

He left her to unpack and strode the long hallway back to the Great Hall. All quiet there, so he moved to the kitchen.

Nothing.

Mom and his grandmother might have gone into town for a bite.

Leaving via the front door, he turned left, walking down the drive to the Annex, where he'd most likely find Zeke and his brothers and a barrel of lectures for disappearing all day while they worked their contacts looking for priceless loot.

At the Annex, he pressed his hand against the pad. The door slid open, allowing him access to a vestibule that led to the Theater.

Separating the vestibule and the Theater stood a high stone wall with oversized black metal lettering that said

Blackwell Asset Recovery Services. Who the sign was for, Phin wasn't sure, since they rarely allowed visitors in here, but there you go.

He strode around the wall and found Cruz still at the conference table, laptop in front of him. He glanced up. "Look who's back. We're busting our asses here."

"Remember that when you're tucked in your bed and I'm busting *my* ass schmoozing assholes so you can make a living."

All of them worked hard. They all knew it. Sometimes his family needed a reminder that none of them wanted to do what Phin did. Putting on a suit gave Cruz hives, never mind having to make nice with people.

Cruz, in his own casual way, flipped him the bird and went back to his laptop.

His brother, never one to start a fight, wasn't afraid of one either. He was the sometimes silent-and-deadly type whose protective instincts ran deep. If a brawl needed to be had, he'd fight someone all damn day. Not an ounce of quit in that guy. Over the years, Cruz had probably kicked the crap out of more idiots than Phin, Zeke, Rohan, and Ash combined.

"Phin," Zeke called from his office, "I need a minute."

I'm sure you do.

Rohan, mug in hand, wandered in from the kitchenette. "Good luck. He saw you and Maddy pull in. You got some 'splainin' to do, Lucy."

Rohan, ever the old soul and an *I Love Lucy* fan, channeling Ricky Ricardo. Funny. "I figured."

"Phin!" Zeke hollered, his tone sharp enough to slice a guy in half.

"I'm coming!"

Phin hauled ass, leaving Rohan and Cruz laughing at him. Literally yucking it up.

When he stepped into Zeke's office, his brother sat back in his chair. His body appeared relaxed, but his eyes?

Blazing.

Is it hot in here?

"Shut the door."

Phin waved that off and dropped into a chair. "No need. They might as well hear this. It'll save me from having to say it twice."

"Fine. Why is she here?"

No doubt who the "she" in question was. "Before you start screaming, hear me out. Press was camped out at Maddy's place. She couldn't go home. I thought—"

"How did we get from her not going home to you bringing her here? You realize she's the target of a *federal* investigation."

Zeke's voice took on that tight, controlled vibration that came with trying to not lose his temper.

Phin gave him his best bored look. "I'm not a moron."

There went keeping his mouth shut and withstanding the storm.

"Then stop acting like one. How could you bring her here?"

He shrugged. "Best option."

"How do you figure?"

What? How did he figure? Had Zeke not been paying attention when he watched the news and saw a bunch of reporters circling? Phin cocked his head, studied his brother. "Are you feeling okay?"

"Please," Zeke said, "don't make me kill you."

"Put yourself in her shoes. She didn't want to expose her friends and family to the press, so that option was out. So was going home. You know as well as anyone, with a case this high-profile, the press would hound her night and day. She refused to put the people she cares about in the line of fire. Admirable, if you ask me."

Zeke opened his mouth, but Phin put up a finger. "Before you say it, yes, she could've gone to a hotel. Cilla didn't recommend it. The press would find her there, too."

"Since when does Cilla call the shots? I've never even met her and she's being a pain in the ass."

"What's your point?"

Zeke sat forward and poked his finger at Phin. "You don't think the press will find her here? And then what do we tell our client who is paying us a ton of money to find assets the FBI, and our brother, think Maddy stole?"

"She didn't."

"How do you know?"

Gaze locked on Zeke's, Phin shook his head, ready to launch into a defense, but ... nothing. Aside from Maddy telling him she was innocent, how *did* he know? What proof did he have?

Phin finally sat forward, propping his elbows on his knees while studying his shoes. A nice pair of Ferragamos he'd found online.

After a few seconds, he looked up, faced his brother again. "I understand why you're upset. I don't blame you. You weren't there, Zeke. You didn't see that mob outside FBI headquarters. One of those sons of bitches must have leaked that they were questioning her. And the Thompsons put her on," Phin made air quotes, "temporary leave."

"They move quick. A couple rounds with the FBI and they kick her to the curb?"

"Pretty much. Zero loyalty. I didn't know what else to do. She needed a safe place to stay and we can provide that."

Before Zeke could respond, an idea so superb filled Phin's mind he nearly cried. Should he do it? Should he put his finger on his brother's hot button and pound on that fucker?

In general, no. Except …

"I guess," Phin said, "I could call Reid and see if he'd let her stay at the hotel they built behind the training center. Security there is good."

Phin met his brother's gaze, offering up a smirk because the rock-solid way to irritate any of his brothers would be to suggest asking their Steele cousins for help.

"Good one," Zeke said. "You fucker."

They both knew their mother would *never* allow Maddy to leave their place for the Steeles'. Mom was a Steele and her brother's family owned a massive piece of property on which one of his cousins, a former Green Beret, had built a law-enforcement training center.

Not that they were bad folks. The weird tension that had developed over the years just impeded rational thinking and Phin was bastard enough to use it against his family.

If they plopped Maddy at their cousin's place, all of Steele Ridge would gossip about those "shady" Blackwells.

Plus, Zeke was competitive. He'd never admit the Steeles' security was as good as theirs.

So, yeah, Phin pulled out his grenade launcher and fired it.

"The other thing," Phin said, "is she can help us identify the assets. She set up that exhibit. Handled each piece herself. She probably knows them better than anybody. And, I don't think I need to remind you that you brought Liv and Brodie here last month to protect them."

Zeke rested his head back and stared up at the ceiling.

"Pops, if you're listening, give me strength to get through this day without killing him. That's all I need."

Zeke. Total pisser.

A few seconds passed before Zeke took his gaze from the ceiling and sat forward, resting his elbows on his desk. "It's done now. We can't shove her out the door."

"We could, but it'd be shitty. And, despite what some people think, we're not shitty."

"She's in the guest suite?"

"Yeah. The one by Rohan. I told her to call me when she got settled."

"Have either of you eaten?"

"No. That's next up."

Zeke stood. "Let's go find Mom. Explain what's going on and get you both some dinner. Then we'll update you. Cruz has been backing up Rohan and working the dark web all day."

The dark web. An absolute beehive of illegal bartering. Stolen art and collectibles were no exception. "He's posing as a collector?"

"Yeah. He's weeding through chat rooms."

"Anything with potential?"

"Couple of people said they had the stuff, but when he pressed them on details, they were sketchy."

Scammers weren't unusual after a big heist. People out to make a quick score often posed as the thieves trying to unload goods. They'd either ransom or sell the pieces to inexperienced buyers, receive payment by way of bitcoin, never produce the items, and once again disappear into the bowels of the dark web.

The Blackwells had been in this game way too long to not identify those creeps.

Zeke waved Phin from his chair and strode into the main area where Cruz and Rohan banged away at laptops.

"Oh, good." Rohan cracked, "he's still alive."

Not a statue yet, my man.

"When you're done playing hero," Cruz said, "We could use Maddy. We need details on these pieces. If they have occlusions, number of carats, clarity, etcetera."

"Anything popping?"

"Possibly," Rohan said. "I'm running down the volunteers. I started with the most recent ones and there's a twenty-six-year-old woman who went to high school with a guy Cruz thinks runs with the Vera brothers."

Phin swung his gaze to Cruz. "You think? Or you know?"

"Right now, I think. I found a post from a party on her social media. The pic is her and a group of people she tagged. One guy looked familiar, so I checked his profile, then scrolled through his posts."

"Cruz, love the detail, but cut to the chase. What have you got?"

Cruz clicked something on his laptop, spun it to reveal a photo of four men on a boat holding beers. "The guy in the middle. He's part of the crew that runs with Xavier Vera's son, Cody."

Okay. Now they might be on to something, considering the Vera brothers' recent tendency for reckless thefts. Phin pointed at the photo. "You're thinking the volunteer leaked info to this guy, and he told Cody."

Cruz took the laptop back. "Why not?"

"What does the woman do at the Center?"

"She's a greeter. Stands at the door, hands out maps, answers questions."

"Would a greeter know about security protocols?" Before Cruz started bitching about shooting down his ideas, Phin raised a hand. "I'm not saying she wouldn't. There have to be boundaries."

"I'm sure," Cruz said. "I'm kicking tires here. You asked what's new. That's what's new. Where's Maddy? We'll ask her."

"In her room. I told her I'd call if we needed her."

Phin threw Rohan a glance. Before leaving the house on his way to FBI headquarters, he'd quietly asked Rohan to finish his background research on Maddy.

Now, with her under their roof, he needed her to check out.

Family first. That's how it had to be. Risking his family or their business looking like a bunch of amateurs because he might have more than a professional interest in Maddy didn't compute.

Rohan shoved a folder across the table. "She's clean. Total Girl Scout. Maybe better than a Girl Scout."

Phew. Phin didn't bother looking inside the folder. If Rohan said she was clean, she was clean. He pushed the folder back across the table. He'd learn about Maddy the old-fashioned way.

By talking.

And maybe other things.

"Something happen?" Cruz peered at Phin over the screen of his laptop. "Why are you fired up about Maddy?"

"Maybe," Zeke emerged from his office, "he wants to get laid."

"Don't we all," Rohan deadpanned.

For a second, Phin thought about arguing. Launching into a brutal defense that would shut the whole conversation down.

Eh. Why bother? His brothers weren't blind or stupid.

"I like her," he said. "Sue me."

"Nothing wrong with liking her," Zeke said. "Be careful what you share."

Here we go again. Having temporarily escaped being turned to stone, Phin decided telling Zeke to quit reminding him wouldn't serve him.

Instead, he looked his brother in the eye. "That's why she's in her room."

10

MADDY FOLLOWED PHIN INTO A KITCHEN WITH A MASSIVE island that had to be ten feet long with a waterfall slate countertop. Light gray cabinets ran the length of the room and surrounded a wall oven and a Viking range with another oven.

The chef's kitchen Mom would die for.

A woman, probably Phin's mother, with dark wavy hair streaked with silver, stood behind the island putting something into a drawer while another dark-haired and much older woman sat on a barstool.

"Hey, Mom," Phin said.

She swung her head sideways and upon seeing her son, her lips slipped into a smile that Maddy instantly recognized. Like mother, like son.

"Well," Mrs. Blackwell said, "would you look what the cat dragged in?"

Walking straight to her, Phin kissed her cheek, then moved around the island, offering the same cheek kiss to the seated woman. "Hi, Grams. Did you miss me?"

"You know I always do," she said.

Mrs. Blackwell raised her hands palms-up to Maddy. "And this must be Maddy."

"Yes ma'am," Phin said. "Maddy, this is my mom. Lynette Blackwell."

Calling on her good manners, Maddy marched straight for her, scooting around Phin and holding out her hand. "It's a pleasure to meet you, Mrs. Blackwell. Thank you for opening your home to me."

Mrs. Blackwell clasped her hand, sending a gentle warmth streaming up Maddy's arm.

This house.

So far, everything about it oozed comfort and safety. No wonder Cilla had suggested it. Had her attorney been here? With Phin?

Between the two of them, they'd be the world's most beautiful couple. She could see it. Phin and Cilla storming the Charlotte social scene. Even their slick, no-nonsense personalities fit.

A spurt of jealousy—oh, how she hated that nastiness—flooded her mind. What business was it of hers what Phin and Cilla did on their own time?

"It's Lynette," Mrs. Blackwell said, bringing Maddy from her mind travel. "And this is my mother-in-law, Johona."

Maddy reached across the island. "Good evening, ma'am. I'm Maddy. It's nice to meet you."

"Lovely to meet you, as well. Phin got you settled into the guest room?"

"Yes ma'am. It's perfect. I watched the sunset from the patio. Y'all have amazing sunsets here."

"That we do," Lynette said. "It's one of the things I loved about this place. While you're here, give a holler if there's anything you need. I'm sorry you got dragged into this chaos with the media."

"Thank you. I'm hoping it'll die down and I can get out of your hair. I'm anxious to get back to work."

Phin smacked his hands together. "Mom, I heard tell you made some wicked barbecue for dinner."

"You heard right." She jerked her chin toward the refrigerator. "There's candied sweet potatoes, corn, and that salad you like with the raspberry vinaigrette."

Phin rushed to the fridge, pulling the doors open and grabbing containers. "Maddy, I'm telling you, my mama is aces."

How about that? Phin Blackwell.

Mama's boy.

"Ha," Lynette said. "He didn't feel that way at sixteen when he couldn't stay out of trouble. Bad enough I was a widow raising five boys. I didn't need this one running wild."

"Not my fault you produced a good-looking kid." He set the containers on the island and grinned at Maddy. "I was fighting the girls off with a stick. A stick, I tell you."

"Whatever," Maddy said.

Lynette cracked up. "Good looking and so humble."

Oh, Maddy liked Lynette Blackwell. Not that it mattered when it should be Lynette sizing Maddy up. But Lynette seemed to have an easy confidence Maddy wished for. "My mom didn't have all boys, but she had five, too. There's no job harder than a single parent."

"Are your parents divorced?"

Maddy wished. "No, ma'am. Dad died when I was twelve. Car accident."

Across the island, Johona tsk-tsked. "Dear girl, I'm so sorry."

Lynette shook her head. "Between the two of us, we have

ten kids without a daddy. My husband died when Phin was a junior in high school."

A smacking sound came from behind Maddy. Phin was setting one of the ceramic containers in the microwave. "Let's get this food going," he said, clearly done with the conversation about their dead fathers.

"Maddy," Lynette pointed to a stool, "you sit right there and I'll reheat this. Phin makes everything too hot. Phin, get the girl something to drink."

"I can get it," Maddy said.

Lynette snapped her fingers and pointed again. "Nope. You're a guest here. Phin can make himself useful. We have beer, wine, soft drinks, sweet tea."

"Water is fine. Thank you."

A minute later, Phin set a bottle and glass in front of her, then went to a small refrigerator near what looked like a pantry and retrieved a bottle of beer.

Lynette pointed at the bottle. "Make sure you get a glass. I don't want that bottle on my counter."

"On it."

The woman ran a tight ship. Having grown up in a single-parent home with five kids, Maddy understood chaos would reign supreme without discipline.

The microwave dinged and Lynette retrieved the container, placing it in front of them and handing over a couple of dishes and silverware before putting the next bowl into the microwave.

"I have cornbread, too."

"Oh, my mama. You're the bomb."

Lynette laughed, then popped the top on another bowl sitting on the counter behind her before setting it in front of Maddy.

"Both of you, eat up." She grabbed a crumpled dishtowel

sitting next to the sink and folded it, lining up the edges before hanging it on a drawer handle. She eyed it, moved it a hair to the right, then turned back to them. "Maddy, I hate to be rude, but I have a few things to do yet tonight and I'm straight running on fumes. I'll leave you two. Phin, dishes in the dishwasher, please."

"Yes, ma'am."

"Yes," Maddy said, "We'll be sure to clean up. Thank you again."

Just then, Zeke strolled into the kitchen crossing paths with Lynette, who announced she'd be in her office and then going to bed.

Zeke moved to where Lynette had been standing and snatched a piece of cornbread and a napkin from the holder in front of Maddy. "My God, I love her cornbread. You guys all set in here?"

Phin held up his fork. "Just getting to it. Give us a few to eat."

Zeke nodded. "Find me when you're done." He swung his gaze to his grandmother. "Grams, what kind of trouble are you into?"

"Well, Phin won't let me drive his car, so I suppose none."

"Yeah," Phin said, over a mouthful of food. "That's a hard no."

"You'd deny an old woman?"

He swallowed, washing it down with a swig of his beer. "Grams! You've wrecked four cars and our UTV. I'm sorry. It's not happening. Besides, something happens in that Audi. It's like a demon takes over and suddenly you're doing a hundred. Consider it for your own personal safety that I won't give you the keys."

At that, Zeke laughed. "Good one, little brother."

He walked to the same refrigerator where Phin had gotten his beer, grabbed one of his own and then strode from the room.

"If you hadn't noticed," Phin said, "that was Zeke's not-so-subtle message to hurry up. Cruz and Rohan are working the web and need info on the missing jewels."

Fork midway to her mouth, Maddy paused. "Do they have a lead?"

Please let them have a lead.

Phin shrugged. "Maybe. Maybe not. Can never tell. Could be con artists. That's why they want details. If they're scammers, they'll be able to tell by how much they know about the pieces."

She held the fork up, being careful not to lose a drop of the barbecue sitting on it. "Then eat up, Phin. I want my life back."

DEVOURING THE LAST TWO PIECES OF HIS MAMA'S CORNBREAD left Phin with only an inch—maybe less—of guilt. Chances were his brothers only saved some because Mom told them to. *Thank you, Mom.*

Meal complete, Phin walked Maddy down the flagstone path back to the Annex. Lights blazed in front of the Morton-style office building. In the growing darkness, the black metal roof faded into the mountain backdrop and the blue-gray siding took on a darker hue.

"So," Maddy said. "This is where the magic happens."

"You know it."

He could deny it, play down what they did, but why? There wasn't a lot he was proud of, but BARS? Recovering priceless items? Not a lot of people had the balls to do what they did.

"I like the stone entry."

Phin focused on the bottom third of the building, accented with stone that also covered the vestibule. "My mom wanted as much uniformity with the Friary as we could get. We weren't up for spending boatloads on the office space, so we did the stone, hoping it would tie in."

Hustling a few steps ahead, he opened the outer door for Maddy and then once again pressed his palm against the pad, opening the inner door as well.

Inside the Theater, Zeke, Rohan, and Cruz were still huddled around the large conference table in full research mode. Cruz must have been raking his fingers through his curly hair, which fell well below his ears. Unlike Maddy's, his curls didn't fall in soft rings. His had a maniacal bend. When tired, he'd rifle his hands through his hair and take on a mad-scientist look.

Rohan sat back in his chair, stretching his back while Zeke stood. Both of them looked a lot better than Cruz in the fatigue department, but that inch of guilt over the cornbread suddenly became a mile. He should have been here today, helping his brothers.

He'd make it up to them. Somehow.

"Hello, boys," Phin said. "Sorry we're late."

Phin pulled out a chair for Maddy. She quickly bypassed it, moving to the end of the table near Cruz. She stopped before she reached the whiteboard and pointed. "May I?"

Cruz held out his hand. "Please do. We could use your help."

Photos of the stolen pieces hung on the board, each label indicating whether it came from the Pierre collection or the queen's.

Still in his seat, Cruz pointed. "Let's start with the one on the left. The queen's bracelet."

Maddy swiveled to face him. "Sure. What do you need to know?"

"Everything. Clarity, occlusions, number of carats. Anything we can use to identify the pieces."

"Clarity is easy. All the stones—the Pierres' and the queen's—are flawless."

Cruz let out a low whistle, his fingers banging against his keyboard.

Maddy shifted again, tapping her finger against the photo. "The bracelet has two strands of brilliant diamonds that surround a larger rectangular one."

Still typing, Cruz didn't bother looking up, but Rohan swiveled his chair, his attention now on the board. "How many carats?"

"The center diamond alone is twenty-nine. I'm not sure about these smaller ones along the strands."

She moved to the next photo of a brooch. A flower with a stem, also labeled as part of the queen's collection. The piece showcased a large single diamond surrounded by smaller baguettes in the shape of petals and a stem.

"The center is a pink diamond."

"One of the rarest in the world," Rohan added.

"It is. When we put the exhibit together, Mrs. Thompson told me the diamond was discovered in Tanzania in the forties. There's no provenance on that, though, so we didn't include it in our description."

Cruz finally looked up. "We can use that. Tell us more."

Maddy leaned one hip against the table, her gaze still on the photo. "The diamond was part of a fifty-carat raw one that the queen had broken down into three pieces. The center is now eighteen carats."

More typing from Cruz. "How many total diamonds in the brooch?"

"Between the large diamond and the baguettes? Over two hundred."

"Holy hell," Phin said.

"Phin," Zeke said, "how did you do with the guy in New York?"

Phin peered at Maddy. "I have a contact. A gallery owner in New York. He brokers deals for high-end jewelry and art. He hasn't heard anything about the Pierres."

"What about the queen's collection?"

"He didn't say, and I didn't offer it up. Guessing it's not out there yet about the queen's pieces."

"Maybe they're sitting on them," Rohan said.

Cruz rocked back in his chair. Back and forth, back and forth, back and forth while eyeing the board, his face a stiff mask of concentration. "Ransom grab," he said. "Probably getting ready to make contact."

"That's what I'd do," Phin said. "No reputable auction house or dealer will touch those pieces, never mind buy them."

Maddy leaned back on the table, her body appearing loose and relaxed, and something in Phin's chest lit him up like a summer sunrise.

Dang, he loved seeing her not twisted up and stressed. More of that. That's what she needed. He'd have to figure out a way to make it happen.

She gestured to the photos. "What makes these pieces priceless is the historical value. Even if they're sold on the black market, they'd have to stay hidden. It's not as if the buyer can wear the queen's stolen tiara in public."

"That might be the play," Rohan said. "They make contact and tell the Thompsons they'll save them the embarrassment of the world finding out they failed to keep the queen's pieces secure. They'll return the pieces for a hefty fee."

Maddy's hand shot up like a third-grader with a question. How cute was she? "Just jump in. This is what we do. We spitball."

She nodded. "How much could they even ask? As you said, no reputable collector will buy these pieces."

"They could break them up," Zeke said, "and melt down the metal."

Zeke wandered to the board and picked up one of the markers. He jotted Rory Emlynson's name with a question mark and then below that the words dealer and database. "Where are we with Rory?"

"He's dodging my calls," Phin said. "I'll keep on it."

"All right," Zeke tapped the marker against the board where he'd written "dealer." "Let's contact that company in San Francisco. The one with the stolen art info."

The organization, run by a lawyer, maintained a database of missing art and collectibles back in the '80s. Being a collector, he'd started a spreadsheet for his own use. After years of adding works to it and subsequently getting inquiries from friends and even law enforcement, he saw an opportunity and monetized it. Now, with over half a million entries, the database streamlined investigations and kept collectors, galleries, and museums from the headaches that came with purchasing stolen art.

What he could do for them right now, Phin wasn't sure, since the theft of the queen's pieces hadn't been revealed. "I can call him," Phin said. "What am I looking for?"

"I don't know," Zeke said. "He's a well-known collector. Maybe he's heard something."

Cruz sat forward again, squaring up to his keyboard.

"Let's finish up with these pieces so we know what we're dealing with."

Maddy went back to the whiteboard, rattling off details about the diamond necklace and tiaras belonging to the queen. They worked through the Pierre pieces next with Cruz and Rohan asking question after question.

By the time they reached the last of the seven photos, Phin decided he might blow his brains out from mental fatigue. Details for Cruz, a trained pilot and math wiz, were essential. Phin? He couldn't deal. Too much information sent him into the weeds where he got lost.

And bored.

He checked his watch; 10:30. Maddy had to be fried. "It's late." He peered up at Maddy, still standing at the end of the table. "Are you tired?"

"I'm fine."

"When it comes to women, fine never means fine."

Zeke let out a laugh. "Amen, little brother. Cruz and Rohan, what else do you need from Maddy tonight?"

"I'm set for now," Rohan said.

"Ditto," Cruz added.

Phin stood. "Good, because I'm beat."

"I can keep going," Maddy said.

Phin shook his head. "I know. But trust me on this one. You need to rest. I'll call you if we need something tonight, but rest while you can." He stood and met Zeke's gaze. "I'll walk her to her room. Do you need me to come back?"

"No. Everybody get some shut-eye. Cruz, I'm not kidding. I can't have you down here all night. Tomorrow, we'll prep the Thompsons for the possibility of a ransom request. I'll call Ash and see if the feds have anything we can use."

Maddy gawked, her head lopping forward like a stack of tumbling bricks. "Is the FBI working with you?"

"Not exactly," Phin said. "Our brother isn't stupid. He knows what we can do. If it benefits his investigation, he shares."

"Do you get credit for that?"

Rohan huffed. "Not in this lifetime."

And that irritated the hell out of Phin. Nothing he—or anyone else at this table—could do about it but try to make their client happy.

"Okay," Phin said. "We'll hit it again tomorrow. Who knows, maybe we can piss off our brother by one-upping the feds?"

11

ON THE WAY OUT OF THE ANNEX, ROHAN SCANNED MADDY'S hand, giving her access to the Friary and her room, after which Phin made her test both entry pads to make sure she could get in. Last thing he needed was her going for a walk and not being able to reenter.

Test complete, she stood in the threshold of her room, one hand on the door while he remained firmly in the center of the hallway, hands in his pockets.

Nothing to see here.

Where the hell was Rohan now? Phin needed him to freaking show up because Maddy holding that door open and looking at him with her killer eyes wasn't helping him squash the myriad of sexual fantasies plaguing him.

"So," she said, "I'm going to wind down and sit on the patio. Would you—"

No. No. No. Please don't let her ask...

He'd charmed his way into enough beds to know it was coming. Most times, he didn't have to try all that hard. It just ... happened.

Like sneezing.

"Phin?"

He snapped to, shifted his feet, and searched the hallway. *Come on, man.* When Rohan didn't magically appear, he went back to Maddy. "Uh, sorry."

"I asked if you wanted to come in."

He should walk—no, run—screaming. He was already on thin ice with Zeke. If he stepped into this room? With all the damned security cameras in the common areas? Forget it. Totally screwed.

But it *was* a great night with a sky full of stars. And who said anything would happen? They were both adults capable of controlling themselves. Well, maybe *he* wasn't, but Maddy? Definitely the responsible one.

He slid his gaze to her hand, holding that damned door open.

Walk away.

He checked the hallway again.

Nothing. A sign from the universe, perhaps?

You betcha.

"Sure," he said, wasting no time stepping into the room and flashing a smile. "Can I trust you? I mean, you're not gonna get handsy, are you?"

She burst out laughing, the sound demolishing every ounce of tension locking up his shoulders.

"Somehow, Charlie Charm, I think we'll manage."

He waited just inside the doorway for her to close the door and then didn't move.

She waved her hands, shooing him from the entry. "Come in. It's your house."

"But it's your room."

She studied him for a second. "I guess it is. Thank you. You're a good man, Phin Blackwell."

No, I'm not.

He gestured to the patio doors. "Outside?"

"Yep." She bypassed the seating area, her steps way too springy after the day she'd had, and unlocked the doors, waving him through. "I think there are a million stars tonight. We need a telescope."

"I have one." He stepped outside, taking the high-backed chair on the left, leaving the one closer to the door. "It's in my room. I can bring it down for you tomorrow."

"I'd love that." She sat, sinking into deep cushions and peering out at the darkness. "These chairs are amazing."

"Yeah. Mom drove us crazy. She wanted high-backs with the right amount of curve so you could look up." Phin laughed at the shopping memories. "We must have gone to a hundred stores. One thing about my brothers, they hate shopping. Me? I don't mind, so I drew the short straw each time. She sat in every chair, tipping her head up to see how comfortable they were. If the chair back was too straight, she balked. Too curvy? No good. It was freaking exhausting. Cruz went once and nearly had a breakdown."

"Breakdown or not, it was worth it." She snuggled deeper into the chair, drawing a long breath. "It's beautiful here."

"*That* it is."

"Did you grow up here?"

He shook his head. "Same town. Different house. When the business grew, we found this place. The church camp owners couldn't maintain it."

"That's too bad."

"For them, yeah. For us? Terrific opportunity. Where we're sitting didn't exist. It was only that main part of the house where the kitchen is." Phin pointed to his left. "There's a chapel just down the road. It wasn't in great shape when we moved in, but Mom wanted a quiet place."

"With five boys, I could see why."

"No doubt. She let us design the Annex and she spearheaded the renovations in the chapel. The stained glass is still intact. I think you'd love that. The pews were toast, so she had them refinished and the marble floors polished. Even the statues were cleaned up."

"I'd love to see it. Can I go there tomorrow?"

"Absolutely. We have an unwritten rule. If someone's in there, don't bug 'em. It's our place to be alone if we need it. And all of us living in this house? Believe me, we need it."

She tilted her head up to the stars blanketing the sky in a rainbow of twinkling lights. Nothing compared to a mountain sky.

"Seems to me this whole place is peaceful." She gave up on the stars and peered over at him. "I felt it the minute we came up the driveway."

"Tell my mother that and she'll love you forever. That was the goal. She was career military. Used to people telling her what to do and when. Here, she wanted to relax."

"I love that. You're lucky to have it. I live in 780 square feet with a noisy downstairs neighbor."

Lucky. Huh. He'd been so bent on doing the right thing and fulfilling his responsibilities, he hadn't considered himself lucky. Sure, he appreciated all the open space. The ability to decompress by hopping in his jeep and driving around the property or hoofing down to the chapel. But lucky?

Yeah. Maybe he needed to change his thinking some.

He rested his head back for a second, then turned to her. "This'll sound bad, but I never thought of it as luck. It's just where we live. There are times I feel straight up trapped."

Where did *that* come from? Trapped? Really? Poor baby lived on all this acreage and he was *trapped*?

He broke eye contact and stared straight out, contemplating a swift exit. He'd become a pro at that over the years. "Ignore me. I'm tired. Talking out of my ass."

He made a move to get up and ... crap ... before he could go anywhere, she set her hand on his arm, keeping him in his seat. "Don't go. Please. I like talking."

Not a chance, sister.

Except, it was kinda nice. Particularly with Maddy. Something else he rarely allowed himself. Talking meant intimacy and intimacy meant attachment and attachments meant heartbreak when it ended.

Then again, there hadn't been many women he'd even wanted to have personal conversations with.

It would probably be the end of him, but he sat back.

"Tell me why you feel trapped," Maddy said.

He'd done it this time. Now he had to admit it. Well, he didn't *have* to. But maybe he wanted to.

Say it aloud.

Get rid of it.

"I had a different plan."

"And?" she asked. "What happened?"

"You may not have noticed, but the rest of my brothers aren't exactly schmoozers. Growing up, I watched Ash with people. When you met him he was in fed mode, but he's good. The way he smiles or looks into someone's eyes can sway them. BARS wasn't his dream and he wanted his dream." Phin shrugged. "I don't blame him."

"You took over as resident Charlie Charm?"

"Someone had to." He faced her again. Right about now would be when he typically flashed a smile, cracked a joke, changed the subject, whatever. Tonight? He didn't have it in him. "I have responsibilities to my family."

"What about your responsibility to yourself?"

She tilted her head, and light from inside illuminated her gaze.

This one?

Definitely trouble with all this talking and making him think about things he shouldn't think about. What good would it do?

He shrugged. "As long as everyone is happy, I'm good."

"You know, I get that. I'm always the mediator between the littles and the elders. Even now that we're grown."

"You ran herd on them?"

She nodded. "I did. I enjoyed helping my mom. Plus, I missed my dad and wanted him to be proud. I still try. That's why this thing at work is making me crazy. I mean, how could they think I had anything to do with it?"

Between the two of them, they had serious people-pleasing issues. Probably why she was easy to talk to. Confide in.

Jeez, he'd gone soft.

"Unfortunately," he said. "You're collateral damage. The feds are under pressure. They're kicking every tire. Eventually, they'll realize they're wasting their time. I'd love for us to be the ones to prove it. We'd never get credit for it, but I'd make sure the right people knew."

She shook her head. "I'd *hate* that. Not receiving acknowledgment for my hard work."

"I do hate it. That's why I get pissed at that dickhead Blakely."

She let out another amazing laugh. This one with a snort kicker that made his chest do the weird warming thing.

But, hey, cutest damned snort ever. "Did you just snort?"

"Heck yeah. *You* just called a United States senator a dickhead."

Now it was his turn to laugh. "It's true, isn't it?"

"Absolutely. I've just never heard anyone actually *say* it."

"Well, welcome to the world of Blackwell, where honesty reigns supreme. Even when it's painful."

For a few seconds, she didn't speak. He slid his gaze to her, made eye contact and ... whoa ... felt the pull. The yearning to submerge himself in those blue depths.

Dang it. Shouldn't have looked.

Those eyes might be the devil's best work because here he was, moving closer, a tether pulling him along.

He should fight it. Dig his heels in and ... too late.

PHIN INCHED CLOSER, THE MOVEMENT SUBTLE, MASTERFUL even, yet so very welcome.

When a man looked like Phin, the idea of kissing him, *touching* him, would never be difficult.

Reckless maybe.

It *had* been a rough few days, and he'd been kind. Miraculously so.

And there'd definitely been a lack of that lately.

When he paused, she leaned in, refusing to break the spell and tilting her head, letting him know, without a doubt, she knew what she wanted.

Generally, never a problem with her.

She wanted *the swish*. That glorious flip-floppy feeling in her stomach that occurred when all the goodness in her world briefly united. It had been there during her happiest moments. Museum visits with her dad, the last family Christmas, her college acceptance and graduation, the day her mother got a clean bill of health after a cancer scare.

That swish?

Worse than any drug.

Phin's lips touched hers, softly at first, testing. His breath warm and tasting faintly of the coffee he'd had during the meeting with his brothers.

She didn't mind.

Right now, she didn't mind a lot of things.

More.

That's all she wanted. More of him and the stars and an evening so perfect that her life didn't feel as if it had imploded.

Don't think.

Before her good-girl senses took over, she slipped her hand around his neck, drawing him closer, deepening the kiss until tongues collided and her head did a weird spinny thing that was fairly epic. He brought his hand up, gently running it along her arm, his thumb stroking her skin. *Whoa.* So good.

More, more, more.

She leaned in, her upper body straining for contact and ...

Music blared from next door. Maddy stiffened, the sound an absolute slap to her good-girl side to stay alert. She blinked, then blinked again, clearing the Phin-inflicted haze.

Smokey Robinson.

"Rohan." Phin jerked his thumb over his shoulder. "It's a nice night. He probably opened his door. I'll tell him to lower it."

He lifted one hip and reached into his pocket for his phone. Maddy set her hand on his arm, that spell she didn't want to break sufficiently broken.

Did Rohan see them out here? She peered beyond Phin at the stone wall separating the suites. No. She'd have seen him out there. Maddy patted Phin's arm. "Don't. It's okay."

"Actually, it's not. You're a guest and it's late."

"Please, don't. I ... just don't."

She'd already barged in on them. Now she wanted him to lower his music?

Phin put his phone away. "Suit yourself. He won't have it on long. I think he needs it to wind down. I never asked, but it's a common occurrence."

Settling back into the cushions, Maddy kicked out of her shoes, tucked her legs under her, and bobbed her head to the beat of "I Second That Emotion." "He likes Smokey Robinson?"

"He likes it all. This'll probably lead to Drake or Tammy Wynette. His musical taste is eclectic."

"That's fun. It's like a little surprise each time."

"I never thought of it that way, but yeah. I guess it is."

He stretched his legs in front of him, rested his head back, and they sat quietly for a few seconds before Phin started tapping his fingers against his thigh in perfect time with the music.

"You like this music?" Maddy asked.

"What's not to like?"

"True."

And then, God help her, he started singing. Pitch perfect. How that was even possible with Smokey's falsetto and Phin's not-so-falsetto, Maddy had no clue.

Phin Blackwell. A man of many talents.

Legs still tucked under her, she angled around to face him. "You have a great voice."

"Another of my crazy dreams. I'm more of a country guy. When I was ten, I swore I'd be in Nashville by now." He laughed. "I'd sing into a broom in front of my imaginary audience of fifty thousand people."

"Oh, I think we all did that at some point. Did you really want to be a singer?"

He waved it off. "I don't know. It was a fun fantasy more than anything. I like music, though. Hopping in my jeep, tunes blasting, fresh air. It's a great stress-buster."

"I bet."

"Maybe," he said, "when this mess dies down, we'll go for a drive. I can show you around Steele Ridge."

She nodded. "I'd like that."

Maybe a little too much.

12

AT 9:15 SATURDAY MORNING, PHIN STOPPED IN THE KITCHEN
to grab a cup of Mom's coffee before heading to the Theater.
Mug in one hand, he pressed the other against the pad,
waited for the lock to disengage, and entered the room
where his brothers, including Ash, sat around the conference table.

Phin halted, his coffee splashing over the rim of the
mug, scalding his fingers. "Ow."

Damn, that was hot. He moved the mug to his other
hand and shook out his fingers, thankful he'd managed not
to spill any on his clean clothes.

"Way to make an entrance," Rohan cracked.

Lacking a handy paper towel, he marched to the table,
snatched a napkin from the tray in the center, wiped his
hand and the mug before setting it in front of his normal
chair.

Not a lot surprised Phin anymore, but Ash being here?
Right now? In the middle of a big case?

Stunner.

However, Ash *had* mentioned he'd promised Mom a

visit. He hadn't expected it today. Not with Ash up to his rear in this Thompson Center theft. And, uh, did the guys tell him that Maddy was in residence?

By the tightlipped look, Ash knew.

"Morning," Zeke said. "We were just discussing our visitor. President Thompson called me bright and early."

Yep. Ash knew. Phin took his seat beside Cruz, across from Rohan and Ash.

"Actually," Ash said, his voice flat in that snotty way he sometimes used to his advantage, "we were discussing your *total* lack of judgment regarding your weekend visitor."

Excellent start to a Saturday morning. Phin met Ash's gaze. Part of being the baby of the family meant learning how to stand up to his oldest brother. He wasn't a toddler anymore and as much as he'd looked up to Ash over the years, he refused to be scolded.

"Easy there," Phin said. "Last I heard, you don't get to decide who I invite over."

"It has nothing to do with me deciding and everything to do with you inserting yourself in the middle of a federal investigation."

"In case you forgot, President Thompson hired BARS to recover his assets. Because, hey, the FBI can't seem to get the job done."

Cruz let out a sigh that should have blown the windows out. "Here we go."

"No," Zeke said. "We don't. We're not arguing over this. Our client knows she's here. It's done. You two fighting won't help."

Ash held out his hand. "Did any of you think how this could be a conflict of interest? She's under investigation. We're digging into her financials as we speak and you brought her under Mom's roof? What the hell?"

"Please," Phin said. "Now this is about Mom? That's crap, Ash. This is about you and your career."

The times when Phin actually shocked Ash were few. This was definitely one of them, because big brother's jaw flopped open and a strangling noise erupted.

Bile caught in Phin's throat. The nasty taste of shame. If Ash's shock was a victory, it sure felt like a loss.

"Me?" Ash said. "What do I have to do with it? You brought her here."

"Forget it."

"No. Say what you have to say."

Dammit. Phin should have kept his mouth shut. Too late now. Might as well finish it. Just throw it out there to be exorcised. He met his brother's eye. "I think you're embarrassed. You had to tell your hot shot FBI buddies that your family is harboring a suspect and," in full drama mode, Phin smacked his hand over his chest, "heaven forbid anyone have a questionable thought about Ash Blackwell. Or should I say Cameron Blackwell? You flip between your middle and first name so often, I forget who you are."

Zeke raised his hands. "Whoa. Everybody shut the fuck up. Right now. Phin, you're out of line."

"Bet your ass he is," Ash said.

No argument there. Zinging Ash on using his middle name professionally versus his given name, was a low blow. Phin didn't understand the reasoning, but assumed it had something to do with distancing himself from BARS.

"Ash," Rohan said, "I'd say you're out of line as much as Phin. You haven't been around much and now you're telling us what we should be doing."

"Unbelievable." Ash shook his head and looked over at Phin. "Fine. This *does* put me in a bad spot. I shouldn't even fucking be here at the same time as Maddy. Regardless of what you think, my family comes first, and I needed to make sure you don't have your heads up your asses. You and Zeke called me the other day talking all this bullshit about sharing information. Cooperating with each other. And you know what? I agreed, didn't I?"

Phin paused, thought back on the conversation. "And? What?"

"How much information do you think my superiors are going to give me now? After my boss called me at midnight to ask if there was any truth to the rumor that Maddy Carmichael had moved into my mother's house? My mother's house!" Ash's voice climbed, and he threw his hands up. "And, oh, by the way, President Thompson is a BARS client."

Knowing it was one thing. Hearing Ash hollering about it? Ouch. Had to admit, it created an awkward situation for his older brother.

The bile in Phin's throat tripled.

"We're not doing this," Zeke said. "We've already discussed the conflict of interest. Ash, it's done. She's staying."

"Then you're making a mistake."

Keeping Maddy from being framed was a mistake? "Now you're the all-knowing?" Phin asked, heavy on the sarcasm. "Nothing's really changed around here. I mean, I'm not surprised that Ash is picking the FBI over us."

For a second, everyone froze and for the first time in probably ever, the room went silent. Every bit of oxygen just sucked right out.

Phinny, Phinny, Phinny.

Ash's eyes didn't just widen. Phin could have driven a semi through them. Ten stacked semis.

"Dude," Cruz said. *"Really?"*

Heat filled Phin's face. How many mistakes could he make in one conversation? So much for Mr. Smooth.

Ash had followed his dream, so what? Until last night, until talking with Maddy, Phin had tried, really tried, to bury his jealousy. The truth was, he liked working with his brothers at BARS.

Flexible schedule. Check.

Meeting interesting people. Check.

Nice clothes and good meals. Check, check.

He didn't mind any of it.

He just didn't want to be pigeon-holed.

"I'm sorry," Phin locked eyes with Ash. "I didn't mean it."

"Actually," Ash said, his voice barely audible. "I believe you did. You've just never said it."

He got to his feet, knocked his knuckles against the table. "I'm gonna find Mom and Grams and get some food before I say or do something I'll regret."

"Ash," Phin said, guilt swarming him.

Ash strode by him, throwing his hand up. "Not now. Let me calm down and we'll hash this out. Right now, I wanna kick your ass to California."

Ash left the room and Cruz let out the mother of all heavy breaths. "Nice job, Ace."

AFTER A RESTLESS NIGHT, MADDY WOKE AT DAWN, THREW THE bedroom curtains open to a barely glowing sky, and took full advantage of the patio by watching the sunrise.

Doing nothing had its advantages. Who knew? Typically, if she weren't moving, thinking, being *productive,* she considered it wasted time.

Until now.

Until she took the time to stop and look out over the

mountains surrounding Steele Ridge. Towering trees stood everywhere she could see, their lush green leaves absorbing morning mist while the call of a Carolina Wren cleared Maddy's embattled brain.

Another bird called—tufted titmouse? She wasn't sure. She'd have to look that one up.

Her life was basically being dismantled, and she wanted to research bird calls?

Call it stress management.

Just as she picked up her phone to start said research, her stomach grumbled. She needed fuel and the only way to get it would be to walk to the kitchen.

What was the protocol when crashing in on people? Should she text Phin and ask if she could go to the kitchen? Last night he'd told her to make herself comfortable. And the last thing she wanted was to burden them with making her breakfast.

Having had enough of her stalling, her stomach didn't just grumble, it roared. Time to go.

She slipped out of her pajamas and into leggings and a yoga top she'd bought two weeks earlier. Casual, but cute.

Next came her hair. The absolute horror of morning curls that stuck to her head on one side and frizzed straight up on the other. Mad-scientist-on-steroids hair that she'd temporarily tame with a silk hair tie.

Satisfied that she looked presentable should the hottie known as Phin appear, Maddy quietly left the suite, her sneakered feet falling softly as she moved through the long hallway. As soon as she hit what Phin called the Great Hall, the aroma of something baking assaulted her.

Her stomach's roar eased to a purr.

In spite of her body's demands, she paused for a few seconds by the stone fireplace admiring the antique sword hanging there. Interesting piece that would be lovely to stare at while enjoying a roaring fire.

Growing up, she'd yearned for this setup. Their home didn't have one, so Mom bought a fire pit for the yard, where Maddy spent countless hours missing her father and working through what she'd learned were the stages of grief while Harry Potter transported her to another world.

She tilted her head back, taking in the full breadth of the wide wood planks that climbed to the high ceiling. She set her hand on the stone face and a cool, craggy surface massaged her palm. How she'd love to sit here with Harry and company.

A man's voice, definitely not Phin's, followed by Lynette's came from the kitchen. Thinking back to the night before, Maddy cocked her head, tried to place the voice. Which brother?

"What happened?" Lynette asked.

Rather than eavesdrop, Maddy turned, ready to head back to her room where she'd check the cabinets for a snack.

"Don't worry about it," the man said.

Whoa. Maddy halted at the calm confidence that seemed, from what she'd seen last night, to be a Blackwell family trademark.

"Ash," Lynette said, "whenever one of my sons tells me not to worry, it means I should worry."

That sounded like something her own mother would say.

"I'm going to take a wild guess and say you had a fight with one of your brothers."

A long pause ensued while Maddy stood frozen in the Great Hall.

Spying on her hosts.

Guilt pressed in, but ... Special Agent Blackwell was here. Maybe he had news? Maybe they'd found the jewels?

Could she be that lucky?

She unglued her feet from the floor and took two steps, ready to give Lynette and her son their privacy.

"Mom, it's fine. Phin pissed me off. Not the first time, and it won't be the last. I'll get over it."

"Is it because Maddy is here?"

And, hello. Maddy halted again while another few seconds of silence overtook the room. She should keep walking. Just get the hell out of here.

Except ... they *were* talking about her. Not that it made eavesdropping acceptable, but ...

"I'll take your silence as agreement," Lynette said. "Maddy's presence puts you in a precarious position."

"What's done is done. I'll work it out. But, yeah, Phin screwed up."

Maddy winced. *My fault.* All of it.

"You want him to apologize for trying to help her?"

"I didn't say that. He should have called Zeke and me before bringing her here. She creates a conflict of interest for BARS."

"From what I've heard, she's a decent woman. The press will gobble her up. Pick the flesh right off her bones. You know that. Phin was trying to do the right thing and—"

"Mom—"

"Don't interrupt me. It takes more courage to do the right thing than the popular one. Or worse, nothing at all. I know you know that. I didn't raise my boys to be cowards."

Go, Lynette. In that instant, Maddy decided she might want to be Lynette Blackwell when she grew up. Strong and decisive and unafraid to voice her opinions.

"I'm confused," Special Agent Blackwell said. "He screwed up and you're proud? How's *that* a thing?"

"I'm your mother, that's how. I love my boys and see all sides. Could he have handled it better? Absolutely. But our Phin runs on instinct. Frankly, he learned it from you."

No matter what the reason for Special Agent Blackwell showing up, this was not Maddy's business, and she needed to quit this nasty spying.

She fast-walked out of the room, turned the corner into the hallway and ... *wham* ... crashed into Phin.

He set his hands on her arms to steady her and gave her that amazing Phin smile. "Good morning. Where are you off to in such a hurry?"

"I, um," she shook her head, got her thoughts in order because, yes, she'd just gotten busted spying.

Phin should kick her out on her butt.

Not bothering to disentangle herself from his grasp, she jerked her head toward the kitchen. "Your mom. And brother. I was hungry, but I heard them talking and didn't want to interrupt. It, um, sounded like they were discussing something ... personal."

Phin narrowed his eyes, studied her for a second, then nodded. "Ah. You heard Ash bitching about me."

He knew. How the heck? Was he eavesdropping, too? "How did ... Never mind. I'm so sorry. I'll pack my stuff and go to a hotel. This isn't fair to any of you. I'll be fine."

He squeezed her arms. "Whoa, there, sister. Relax."

"No. It's fine. Really."

"Maddy! The argument wasn't about you."

Of course it was. She'd just heard Ash admit it. She gave him her best you're-lying stare.

"Well," he said, "not totally. I reacted to something he

said and basically accused him of being self-involved. That spiraled into a whole other issue and we had a fight."

"Regarding *me*?"

"No. Something with Ash and me. I was wrong. I'm on my way to apologize."

Good of him, she supposed, to accept responsibility. Another thing she'd add to the list of things she liked about Phin Blackwell. None of it, however, changed the fact that her being in residence created problems.

"Obviously, me being here is not good."

"Stop. Please. There's no reason for you to leave." He hit her with his Charlie Charm smile. "The horse, as they say, has already left the barn."

She mimicked his smile. "Well, CC, I'm putting the horse back in."

"Good one. But, really, it's unnecessary. This is about me and Ash. We're brothers. We fight. We make up. It's all good." Finally, he let go of her. "Let's go into the kitchen, get you breakfast while I swallow *every* ounce of my ego, and apologize to my brother."

And, oh. My. God. First, he'd protected her from the press. Then he'd brought her to his home. Now, he was fighting with his brother for her? Which, really, she didn't want.

At all. And yet, the flutter. The swish. Her drug of choice that created an insanely warm and tickling feeling in her belly.

How she loved that swish.

She stood, allowing it to happen. After the last couple of days, what could be better than allowing herself that tiny bit of euphoria?

No.

Where Phin was concerned, she couldn't get ahead of herself. Couldn't get too attached to him because of the swish. Not with her being the number one target of an FBI investigation.

"Thank you," she said. "I'm causing you grief and you're still helping me."

"Eh, I kinda like having you around." He leaned in, got close to her ear. "I had fun last night. Talking and watching the stars."

She pulled back and met his gaze, watching as the alluring blue turned a hot, stormy gray. Fascinating man.

She rose to her tiptoes, her body begging for the closeness they'd shared last night.

Wait.

Inches from his mouth, she stopped, hit the brakes so hard her body nearly bucked. Talk about a conflict of interest. She'd already caused Phin enough problems. Getting busted sucking face wouldn't help.

It damn near killed her, but she stepped back.

"Later," he whispered.

Heat filled her cheeks, and he let out a quiet laugh. "Maddy, you're burning a hole right through me. I kinda love that about you." He jerked his head toward the kitchen. "Let's get you some food."

She followed Phin to where Lynette stood behind the massive island, her hands casually resting on either side of her. Special Agent Blackwell sat on a barstool directly across from her, a giant plate of food in front of him.

"Are those fresh biscuits?" Phin asked, drawing Lynette and his brother's attention.

"They are." Lynette pointed to the open stools next to her eldest son. "Both of you, sit. I have bacon, eggs, and sausage. Maddy, do you like eggs?"

"Yes, ma'am. Thank you."

Special Agent Blackwell studied her for a few seconds, his face displaying nothing. "Morning," he said.

"Hi," Maddy said, stepping straight into the land of awkward.

Yeesh. What a start to the day.

"Maddy," Lynette said, "how was your night? Sleep okay?"

"I slept great. It's so peaceful here."

At that, Special Agent Blackwell snorted and Maddy prayed the floor would open up and bury her. She half expected Phin's brother to run from the room. Was she even allowed to be in the same room with him?

Lynette glared at him, and he held a hand up. "Sorry." He faced Maddy. "That wasn't aimed at you."

"It's okay—"

"No," Phin said. "It's not."

At which point Lynette turned an icy glare on him, then quickly moved her attention to Maddy. "Sit down and eat. My boys need to step outside and talk before I mess my floor by murdering them."

These people. The way they communicated might either be straight-up crazy or just plain effective.

Maddy clamped her top teeth down, trying and failing to fight a smile.

Phin, Mr. Smooth, shuffled his feet while his brother stared down at his plate.

"Outside," Lynette said. "And don't come back until this nonsense is over. I swear, y'all make me nuts sometimes."

The two men headed for the door while Maddy slid onto the barstool. Lynette picked up a plate, turned to the stove, and started scooping food.

"I'm so sorry," Maddy said. "I hate that they're fighting."

"Honey, with all the testosterone in this house, they're always fighting. It's just a matter of who and over what."

She spun back, slid Maddy a plate piled with enough food to feed King Kong. "Eat up. You must be starving. The jam is homemade. Not by me, but a family member. It's excellent."

"Wow. This looks great. Thank you for your hospitality. This can't be easy, having me here."

"If this is the hardest thing I ever go through, I'd say I'm doing just fine. Around here, we like to help people. And, yes, professionally, having you here takes a bit of explaining, but I wouldn't have it any other way. When people need help, Blackwells step up. My Phin doesn't hesitate to jump into the fray."

"He's a good man."

Lynette nodded. One solid jerk of her head. "Thank you. It's the finest compliment a mother can get."

Maddy imagined it would be.

The only problem was, she might be falling hard for said good man.

13

Outside, morning sunlight blazed, the rays already heating Phin's skin. Summer humidity in North Carolina was no joke and today already felt like a scorcher.

A good ten yards from the house, Phin halted in the grass, shoved his hands in his front pockets just to have something to do with them and spun sideways to face his brother.

"I'm sorry," he said.

There. Done. Oddly enough, not as painful as he'd expected. Probably because he'd been a dickhead and needed to get rid of the guilt.

Ash, being a pain in the ass, held his hand to his ear, lop-sided grin firmly in place.

Ass.

Hole.

Still, Phin laughed.

"Come again?" Ash said. "I'm not sure I heard you right."

He heard.

Phin poked a finger. "Listen, fucker, I'm not saying it

again. It's already vinegar on my tongue. Accept it or we got nothing more to say."

Ash reached out, planted his hand on Phin's chest and shoved, knocking him back a step. "I accept it, moron. I owe you an apology, too. I showed up pissed off and ready to fight. I should've heard you out first."

Phin lifted one shoulder. He'd gotten himself into a pickle with his two oldest brothers, and nothing about it felt right. Not because he'd helped Maddy, no question there. He did what needed to be done.

Going a few rounds with his brothers shouldn't have been the result.

And yet, here they were.

"Zeke ripped into me last night. I fucked this whole thing up. I'm not saying I wouldn't have brought her here, but I didn't think it through."

"You worked on instinct. You've always been good at that."

Whoa. Phin stood for a second, Ash's words looping in his mind. Pressure built in his chest, squeezing against his ribs. Phin tore his gaze from Ash, stared out at the mountain beyond and breathed. In the absence of his father, over the last eleven years, all Phin had wanted was to make Ash, who'd taken on the role of father figure like a champ, proud.

Thinking back on it, Phin had never, not once, admitted it. Blackwell boys didn't give oxygen to emotional nonsense.

No chance.

He drew in the thick morning air, let it douse the fire searing his throat.

What do I need?

Hell if he knew. Might be time to grow the fuck up and figure it out.

After a few seconds, he came back to Ash, the guy who'd

always—always—been there. Whether it was offering advice on navigating teenage hormones or defending him when Mom got pissed, Ash, in Dad's absence, had been the go-to guy.

Phin never thanked him. Or even gave him credit.

He locked his gaze on Ash's. "Who do you think taught me? I spent my childhood watching you and learned way more than schmoozing from you. I'm talking the important stuff that'll keep me a productive member of society and twenty minutes ago, being the asswipe I am, I called you self-centered."

"You were pissed."

"Still a douche move."

"*Ho*-kay." Ash clapped him on the arm. "We're good."

"Thanks. For everything. You've always been there for me."

Ash let out a grunt. "*Really* getting soft here, pal." His voice tightened, took on the rough edge of busted concrete.

Blackwell men. Zero capabilities with emotions.

Clearly pained over the conversation, Ash cleared his throat. "I appreciate that. I do. But I'm the oldest. I did what Dad wanted. You were sixteen when he died. I got lucky. I had him into my twenties. Those last days? Man, that was brutal. He was worried about us and I wanted him to die in peace." Ash stopped, caught his breath, cleared his throat again. "I told him I'd take care of everyone. It made him happy. I've done my best, but it'll never be enough."

What now? Phin fought the urge to react. To let his mouth drop open. Or to fucking fall right off his feet.

His father had always been the strong, hard-nosed one, doing whatever it took to provide and keep his sons in line. Even if his methods might get him arrested nowadays.

Don't start a fight, but I'll kick your ass if you walk away from one.

Then there was the classic, *if you're getting beat, go for the throat.*

That was Dad. In Phin's eyes, he'd been ... a god.

A warrior god.

Now, imagining his warrior god father worried, shifted the ground, right along with Phin's world.

How had he never heard this before? How had he never even considered it could happen?

"You never told me that," Phin said.

Ash shrugged. "Why would I?"

Point there. "Sometimes I feel like I'm chasing a ghost. Maybe we all are. I think he'd be proud of what we've done with the business."

"For sure."

"Anyway," Phin shook his head, clearing the mental clutter, "sorry if I put you in a bind with your bosses."

"I'll work it out. The pressure is on to find the queen's jewels. Everything is setting them off. I'll tell them it was a calculated move on your part to keep Maddy close. They'll buy that."

Oh, Phin wanted to keep her close, but not for the same reason as Ash and that fried him. That the feds—his own damned brother—considered this amazing woman a suspect. Still, he'd play along and keep the peace with Ash. Make Mom happy.

"She's a solid resource," Phin said. "Knows those pieces inside out."

"Good, because with each day, we risk them getting broken up. What leads are you working?"

"I'm heading over to see Rory Emlynson today. He plays golf every Saturday morning." Phin tipped his head back, the sun's rays hitting his cheeks. "It's gonna be hot today. He'll probably head home to clean up. Maybe swim in that over-the-top pool of his."

Ash took a second, apparently pondering Phin's plan, then nodded. "You think he's heard anything?"

"A score this big? Even if he doesn't have a client interested in obtaining any of the pieces, he may have intel on the heist."

"True. Keep me posted. I have to leave this afternoon. Mom won't be happy."

One thing about their mother, she liked her boys close. She gave Ash space to live his life, but wanted way more of him than she got.

"Don't let her get to you," Phin said. "She understands."

"I know. I *hate* disappointing her."

Now it was Phin's turn to clap his brother's arm. "Don't we all, big brother. Let's head in. She's probably got her nose to the glass watching."

They both burst out laughing, which, yeah, considering how the day had started, was kinda nice. It brought Phin back to the early days before Ash had joined the FBI and they'd all sit around drinking beers, inventing imaginative swear words and beating up on each other.

Good stuff, that.

They walked back to the house side by side until Phin stepped ahead, grabbing the door and holding it open. "Elders first."

Striding past, Ash snorted. "Don't make me kick your ass."

"Well," Mom said from her spot behind the island, "sounds as if they've made nice."

"Yes, ma'am," Ash told her.

Phin shut the door behind him, glancing at Maddy, still

finishing her breakfast. That crazy burst in his chest happened, and he took a second, breathed through the fact that he liked seeing her early in the morning.

Total departure for a guy who made early exits.

"Excellent," Mom said. "Now we'll have some peace while Ash is visiting. I want a nice family dinner tonight. No fighting. As much as that might kill y'all."

Whoopsie. With Ash hauling ass out of here, Mom's suddenly cheery mood would tank.

"About that," Ash said.

Mom picked up a skillet sitting on the stove, pausing while she hit Ash with *the* face. The one where she pressed her lips together and didn't bother trying to hide her disappointment. That face? Total killer.

Ash held his hands wide. "I'm sorry. We're in the middle of the …" He cut his eyes to Maddy, then back to Mom. "… a case. As soon as we close it, I'll come out for a long weekend."

Mom set the skillet in the sink, then turned back to Ash. "Fourth of July weekend? The Steeles are doing a barbecue. We're all invited, and I'd like my boys there."

Phin had forgotten about that party. Half of Steele Ridge usually showed up. It was still weeks away, but Phin needed to prep early. Wrap his mind around gossips staring at them, snickering about the sketchy Blackwell brothers. None of those townies knew squat about what they did.

Rumors ran fast and deep and it seemed most, like that weasel Blakely, considered them common thieves.

Hell, BARS had recovered more than $10 million in assets in the last three months. They had nothing to be ashamed of and yet, Phin still felt it. That burn. The sickness tearing his intestines apart.

"As long as this case is wrapped, it's a date." Ash slid his phone from his front pocket. "I'm putting it on my calendar right now."

"Go, Mom," Phin cracked. "You made the calendar."

"Thank you," Mom said. "I hate putting pressure on you. *But* I need to see my son for more than an hour every once in a while."

"Yes ma'am."

Ash headed out of the kitchen and Mom smacked the faucet on, going to work on the skillet with the force of a jackhammer.

"Phin," she said, "what's your plan today?"

"Going into Charlotte to talk to someone."

"The stockbroker?"

His mother. Never missed a trick. "He's more asset management, but yes. That's him."

"Could I ride along?"

This from Maddy, who'd obviously left her good sense on her pillow. Uh, no, she couldn't ride along. She'd stay right here behind the gate where reporters couldn't hound her.

"Not a good idea," Phin said. "You're supposed to be staying out of sight. Eventually, the press will find you. Especially now that the feds know you're here."

"Ash would never leak that," Mom said.

"Ash isn't who I'm worried about." He turned back to Maddy, circled his hand toward her mane of curly hair that she'd regrettably harnessed into a hair tie. "You're easily recognizable."

"Do you have a baseball cap I could borrow? I'll wear sunglasses and stay in the car. Please, I'd like to get out a little."

She hit him with the puppy eyes and ... toast. That's

what he was. Dang it. Why did she have to look at him that way?

He had to be strong here. Not let her get to him. She needed to hunker down. "I won't be gone long. If you stay here, you're free to walk around. Explore the property."

Maddy slid her gaze to Mom, then back again. "I ... um." She faced Mom this time. "This is going to sound bad."

Phin laughed. "If you knew my mother better, you'd know she's almost unoffendable."

"Smart ass," Mom said. "However, he's right. We like truth around here."

"I feel ... stuck," Maddy said. "Not here, but the circumstances. I hate not being able to go places and do my normal things. None of that is available to me."

Mom peeled her gaze from Maddy, and Phin knew he was completely screwed by some weird female bonding.

"Give her a hat and take your Audi."

The one with the tinted windows dark enough to be legal, but still restrict the view inside the car. "Now you're taking her side?"

"Not at all," Mom said. "I *am,* however, trying to see all angles. Just like I did with Ash a few minutes ago."

Touché.

His mother. Total pro.

"I won't leave the car," Maddy added. "I promise."

Appealing to Mom would do no good. She'd already confirmed that by floating the Audi idea. This was him against the two of them.

Mom alone was a force. Add Maddy and her big, pleading eyes? Screwed, screwed, screwed.

Zeke would soil himself, but Zeke wasn't here withstanding the pressure. A man had to be smart enough to know when he was beat.

14

PHIN'S AUDI MIGHT BE MADDY'S DREAM CAR.

She slid into the passenger seat, gently closing the door and settling into the soft leather that somehow seemed custom fit to her body. She inhaled the scent of Phin's soap —something earthy and fresh, like a spring rain shower— lingering in the interior and nearly melted.

Sleek and sporty, with a black finish that gleamed under the sunlight; she imagined sitting behind the wheel, roaring down a deserted highway, and urging the car faster and faster.

Freedom.

That's what she felt in this car. And she wasn't even behind the wheel.

No wonder his grandmother wanted to drive it. Now, so did Maddy.

Beside her, Phin strapped in and fired the engine. "This car," she said. "I think I love it. Maybe even beyond love."

He flashed her the Phin smile. "It's the RS 5 coupe, 444 horsepower, baby. Everyone said I was crazy getting the black because it gets so hot in summer, but seriously? Look at this car. Freaking stunning. Mom calls it my midlife crisis car twenty years too early."

"If it's a midlife crisis, I'm looking forward to it."

"Exactly! Finally, someone gets it. I've got my eye on the R8 next. Right now it's *way* out of the budget."

The R8. Huh. If the RS 5 looked this good, what would the R8 be? When they got back, she'd research it. Play around with designing her own on the company's website. She'd never be able to afford it on her salary, but dreaming never hurt.

Phin cruised down the driveway, turning onto the mountain road. She'd never been a fan of switchbacks, so she rested her head back and closed her eyes.

"Tired?"

She opened her eyes again, stared out the windshield at the lush green hills to the left. "A little. Stress wears me out."

"Stress makes everyone tired. Take a nap."

In this car, it wouldn't be a problem, except ... "That would make me horrible company."

"It would make you *smart* company. When we get back to the house, my brothers are going to be all over us. They'll probably have a million more questions for you. Enjoy the break while you can."

On a normal day, she only had so much energy. The energy bucket she called it. Now? With her life spun upside down, the bucket was already running low and she'd need reserves.

"When you put it that way, it doesn't sound like a bad idea."

"Exactly. Relax. Close your eyes and sleep. I'll wake you up if something happens."

Phin navigated an S curve, not bothering to slow down.

Wow. What a rush. Normally, she'd be pressing her foot into the floorboard or grabbing hold of the door pull.

Now? Her blood hummed, sending little shocks through her limbs. She glanced over at Phin, one hand on the steering wheel, and his gaze fixed on the road. The relaxed focus, combined with his perfectly groomed scruffy not-quite-a-beard stubble that somehow looked stylish rather than unkempt, put him in the running for cover model of the year.

Handsome on another level.

A dangerous level.

At least for her.

She sat back again, closing her eyes because looking at him wasn't helping. Looking at him made her want things she wouldn't get with Phin.

For her, a fun night consisted of watching movies in PJs at home with cartons of takeout. A living room picnic. Somehow, she didn't see Mr. Slick enjoying that life.

She inhaled again, let the clean, earthy scent of the car flood her mind. Breathe. That's all she had to do for the next little while.

Just breathe.

SENSING NO MOVEMENT, MADDY PRIED HER EYELIDS UP, MET blinding sunlight and immediately shut her eyes again.

Where was she?

She took a deep breath to jump-start her foggy brain, braced herself for the assault, and opened her eyes again. In front of her was a tree-lined street with bursts of green leaves offering patches of shade.

Phin had parked at the curb in front of a towering brick home.

She'd done more than nap. She'd gone comatose.

She looked over at him just as he shut down the engine. "We're here?"

"We are."

"And who is it you're going to see?"

"Rory Emlynson. He's a financial planner. Handles a ton of politicians and CEOs. Major wealth management."

"And you think he knows where the jewels are?"

"He's also a collector. Art, cars, anything that makes him look rich. His office is filled with random stuff he's acquired. Rumor has it his latest acquisition is a scepter belonging to George V."

Maddy gawked. Did he just say George V? No wonder they were here. If the man enjoyed collecting sacred British regalia, he might have knowledge of the queen's jewels.

Of the major recent auctions she'd seen, none contained a scepter from George V. "Was it a black-market purchase?"

Phin shrugged. *Shrugged.* As if it wasn't horrifying that a priceless collectible from the British monarchy floated through the black market.

The art world was ripe with backdoor deals and any acquisitions manager or gallery owner knew it. Still, it made her boil.

She peered out her window at the stately mansion big enough for a dozen people. Clearly, the man had money to burn. Or simply wanted to look like he did. Neither would surprise her. So many in the art world were broke, living beyond their means just so they could keep their social status.

"So," she said, gaze still on the house, "you're thinking maybe he's heard something about the jewels being available?"

"For a guy like him, this heist is catnip. He's made a side job of using his contacts to broker deals."

She swung back to Phin. "He's the middleman."

"Yes. He never touches the stuff. All he's doing is connecting people. As if that justifies dealing in stolen masterpieces. It's ridiculous."

"And he's never been caught?"

"He's discreet enough that law enforcement leaves him alone. He's on Ash's radar." Phin gestured to the house. "I'm not sure he's home, but he's been ducking my calls for two days. You stay here. Windows up. With all that press, I'm sure he's seen you on the news."

Remembering her Good Girl Maddy promise, she raised her right hand. "I won't budge. Good luck."

PHIN WALKED TO THE FRONT DOOR, HIS PACE CASUAL, unrushed. Just a guy visiting his buddy. A good thing too, because the humidity was enough that sweat already beaded on his upper lip. He gave it a swipe just as he reached the door. No point looking like a slob.

As houses went, this was nice. He supposed. Too high-brow for his taste, but these big-time finance guys, at least in Phin's opinion, wanted everything over-the-top.

And not necessarily because they liked it. Rory Emlynson was one of them. He drove a Rolls because no one else on his block had one. Did the guy even *like* that car?

At least when Phin made a major purchase, he enjoyed it.

People.

Complicated.

He rang the doorbell and, since this wasn't exactly a

stealth mission, lifted his head to the overhead camera and smiled. A few seconds in, the front door opened.

Phin had met Rory's wife, a blonde with skin stretched tight over high cheekbones—she needed to ease up on the visits to her plastic surgeon—a few times at events. Now she stood eyeballing his jeans and pressed white T-shirt, her green eyes oozing annoyance.

"Can I *help* you? There's no soliciting in this neighborhood."

Seriously? That's how she answers her door? He peered down at his Magnanni low-top sneakers. What about this get-up said homeless? He nearly laughed.

"Mrs. Emlynson, I'm Phin Blackwell. We met at Congresswoman Anderson's charity ball in March. I'm a friend of Rory's. I can promise you, I'm not selling anything."

"Oh," she said, her red lips forming a perfect oval. "I'm so sorry. We have the help constantly ringing the bell."

The *help*? What. The fuck? Who talked like this?

He might hate this woman.

"I could see where *that* might be a problem," he said, heavy on sarcasm.

"You really have no idea."

She was right about that. Phin cleared his throat and stifled a sigh. "I was hoping to catch Rory after his round. Is he home?"

Knowing the man's schedule added to Phin's credibility and might earn him some points.

"He'll be here any second."

When she failed to invite him in, he considered his next move. She was probably alone. Why would she let him in?

Even if he knew her husband, he could be a freaking ax murderer.

Plus, no way he'd leave Maddy outside alone.

He jerked his thumb over his shoulder. "I'll wait out here."

Before she got the door closed, a glistening white Range Rover pulled into the curving driveway.

Phin hustled to the three-car side garage before Rory could pull in, close the door, and duck him.

The stained door glided up in silence and Rory eased the SUV inside, killing the engine. He slid from the vehicle, offering a toothy smile tighter than his wife's most recent facelift.

"Phin." He exited the garage, moving into the sunlight with an extended hand. "This is a surprise."

I'm sure it is.

Phin glanced to the curb where Maddy kept to her word and sat in the car, windows up. He'd left the engine running, AC on, so she wouldn't bake.

"I was in the neighborhood."

Rory rolled his eyes. "No, you weren't."

"When you ignored my calls, I figured I'd try the direct approach."

"It's been a busy couple of days. I forgot to call you back."

Liar. "Not a problem. I won't keep you. What have you heard about this Thompson Center heist?"

"Not much."

"How much is not much?"

Rory hit the button on his key fob, raising the SUV's tailgate. "I heard they hired BARS to locate the pieces. That true?"

Telling Rory he'd heard wrong might be a possibility, but why bother? Phin's face had been all over the news last night when he'd walked Maddy from FBI headquarters and the Thompson Center. That shoe clip had probably already gone viral.

Jesus, Phin.

He put it out of his mind, focused on Rory lifting his clubs from the vehicle. "You heard right," Phin said. "We'd appreciate any info. Obviously, we'd make it worth your while."

Being the hound he was, Rory considered that. "I don't want money."

Well, there was a shocker. Maybe the guy wasn't as shallow as Phin had thought. "I'm listening."

Rory set the clubs on the ground and sat on the edge of the SUV's cargo area, folding his arms. "I have a client interested in one of the queen's pieces."

And *whoa*. Phin tilted his head, organized his thoughts. The theft of the queen's pieces hadn't been released to the public, only the Pierres. But Rory knew. Which meant chatter somewhere.

Playing dumb wouldn't hurt.

"The queen's pieces?"

Rory laughed. One of those fake salesperson laughs Phin had heard at way too many functions not to recognize.

"Don't play me, Phin. If BARS is involved, y'all know the pieces from the queen's collection were lifted along with the Pierres. We can waste each other's time or we can work together. Your call."

"Have you made contact with someone who knows—or has—something?"

This time, Rory chuckled, yet another patronizing sound that rubbed right up against Phin's already charred nerves. The fight with Ash had drained him and he wasn't up for condescension. But he'd stand here and deal with this arrogant ass because he had a job to do. "Rory, call me crazy, but you seem to find this humorous. What's funny?"

"You want me to give up my information when we both know you wouldn't do that."

Well, *that* was true. Certain things Phin couldn't deny. "Working together," he said. "What would that entail?"

He circled a hand. "I'm spitballing here. My client has an interest in one of the queen's pieces. He doesn't care which. He's not that deep. I'm happy to work my contacts, but if I get you something that leads to recovering the collection, you'll have to convince the powers-that-be to let me have one of the pieces."

"That's a huge freaking ask, Rory."

"That depends on how bad Thompson wants the pieces back."

"What's in it for you?"

He shrugged. "My client will compensate me. It's a good deal, Phin. I get paid, the Thompsons save face, BARS gets the glory. Everyone wins."

BARS gets the glory. If only *that* were true. Phin angled back, checking on Maddy, still tucked in the car.

Phin shook his head. "I can't do that."

"Sure you can. If they want the collection back, they'll be willing to give up one small piece."

Nothing about these items could be described as small. Selling this idea to the Thompsons would be impossible. They'd have to admit to Granny they'd let one of her priceless jewels go. Plus, with the feds involved, not to mention Ash, Phin wasn't sure how they'd make it work.

And it wouldn't clear Maddy. With one piece still missing, she'd never shake free of suspicion. BARS or no BARS, he couldn't stomach her life being destroyed.

Frying rays sizzled against the back of his neck and

drops of sweat trickled into his shirt. By the time he got home, he'd need another shower and fresh clothes.

He itched to lift his hand, to wipe the sweat, but no. He kept his hands at his sides, having a simple conversation with a guy devoid of a moral compass.

What else was new?

Business was business. He couldn't worry about the scumbags of the world when he had a job to do.

He met Rory's eye and nodded. "Let me see what I can do."

FROM HER SPOT IN THE PASSENGER SEAT, MADDY KEPT HER head down, but tilted enough to spy on Phin and the financial planner/lowlife.

Too bad they couldn't have outfitted Phin with a microphone so she could listen in.

Not that he would have done it. Or maybe he would have. She didn't know him well enough to be sure.

Phin broke away from Rory, his face a full sheet of bland. He strode along the driveway, in no particular hurry. If he'd looked her way, he'd hidden it well by not turning his head. This was just a guy on a sunny day walking back to his car.

An expert at emotional subterfuge.

Something she'd never mastered and, really, had no reason to want to. Mom always said she'd make a horrid poker player.

Aside from two brief phone calls assuring Mom all would be fine, Maddy had avoided her family. Humiliation did that. Good Girl Maddy might be in colossal trouble and the last thing she'd wanted was to tarnish their name.

Was it fair to shut her family out? No. But if she stayed away, maybe the press would leave them alone.

Wishful thinking, perhaps, but she could only process so much and she'd been busy pondering the ramifications of FBI interrogations. In her mind, the questions led to handcuffs and trials. Orange scrubs and plastic shoes. Group showers.

Prison.

A vision of her trading cigarettes for phone time popped into her brain. Could prisoners even swap phone time?

Swelling panic filled her just as Phin opened the door, yanking her free from the mental rabbit hole she'd dived into.

He slid into his seat, bringing that Phin smile and an equally warm blast of air. So much better than prison thoughts.

In silence, he buckled his seat belt and checked his rearview.

Seriously? He wasn't going to tell her anything?

No, sir.

"Well," she said, "how'd it go?"

He shifted the car into gear and pulled from the curb. "He wants to make a deal."

Her spine stiffened, bolting her upright and giving her lower back relief from her slouched position. "He knows where the pieces are?"

Could it be that easy? Phin calling some shady guy he knew and—bam—they found the pieces?

He eased the car to a stop at the corner, checked for traffic, and made the turn. "I don't think so. He's cagey."

"Then what kind of deal does he want?"

"Call it a hypothetical. He has a client interested in securing one of the queen's pieces. And, before you ask, yes, apparently the word is out on the black market that the queen's collection was stolen. The thieves are probably trying to unload the stuff. Quietly."

"Which piece do they want?"

Phin shook his head. "Doesn't matter. According to Rory, his guy isn't that deep. He just wants *something.*"

Why? Why? Why? People. Sometimes they made no sense. "It's not as if he can show it off. He'll have to keep it locked in a safe." She held up a hand. "Trust me, I'm not naïve. I've been working in the art world long enough to know this happens all the time, but I'll never understand owning a flawless piece and not being able to share it."

"It's not about sharing it. It's about knowing they have it. They sit in a private vault in their basement with a thousand-dollar bottle of wine and stare at their illegally obtained art. It's a power trip."

"It's a *stupid* power trip."

Phin glanced at her. "Aren't they all?"

He brought his attention back to the road, where they cruised along just a tick over the speed limit. Could he not speed up? Just a little? Get them back to the house where she could stretch her legs and breathe fresh mountain air. Maybe visit the chapel he'd told her about last night, where she'd lay down her worries inside its doors.

She shifted in her seat, studied his profile. His perfect nose. The angle of his jaw. Phin Blackwell. Total stunner.

She wouldn't mind seeing him naked. *Oh, bad girl. Bad, bad, Maddy.*

Imagining Phin naked sure beat contemplating prison swaps.

These crazy thoughts. Maddening.

Even more maddening, in her opinion, was the underground world of stolen art and she'd be smart to keep her focus on that.

Not Phin.

Definitely not Phin.

"Explain to me," she said, "how hiding makes someone feel powerful. Shouldn't it be the other way around?"

"I like that about you. That you want to understand the other side. You don't just jump into an argument."

She shrugged. "I'm a curious person."

"My job, as you saw at Kayla's, requires me to go to events and mingle with people. Most of them have way more money than anyone would ever need. Some give it away."

"And the others?"

"They spend it. Giant houses, boats, whatever they can think of. Money creates a hierarchy. The more you have, the more power you wield."

Nothing new there. That'd been the way since ... well ... always. "I get *that*. How does hiding art make them feel powerful?"

He paused for a second, seeming to gather his thoughts while he navigated the merge onto Route 74 and finally pressed the gas, darting into the left lane.

"It's sort of a self-fulfilling prophecy," he said. "Take my buddy Senator Blakely. I could see him hiding art. He'll do whatever it takes to make himself feel in charge. To be 'the man.' Talk down to people, kill important legislation simply because he can. Doesn't matter that it hurts people. *He* thinks it makes him strong when all it makes him is an asshole. He's operated this way for years and it's escalating. The more press he gets, the more damage he does."

"He needs the spotlight. It's all about the high it gives him."

"Yes. It's the same with stolen art. They lock a painting

in a vault and it gives them that high because they have something no one else does. Even if nobody knows they have it."

Maddy shook her head, peered out the windshield as Phin blew past a stream of slower cars. "It's really astonishing that people operate this way."

"Eh. Spend enough time with them and you learn how they think."

"That's why you're the face of BARS. You connect with people."

"That's what I'm told. I figure out what makes them tick. Kinda like Rory Emlynson. I met him at some gala. We talked about art and his clients and just random crap. Four months later, he called me. A client was having an issue with a gallery that had borrowed his forty-million-dollar Basquiat."

Now, this sounded fascinating. "What was the issue?"

He looked over at her and smiled. "They refused to give it back."

"Yikes."

Phin snorted. "Sometimes, you're so damned funny, Maddy."

And, ooh, didn't that make her female radar ping. Phin Blackwell, super-stud, thought she was *funny*. Not pretty, not sexy, not *attractive*.

Funny? Really?

She'd show him funny.

Right after she got him naked.

"I'm going to assume," she said, "he didn't call the police because he couldn't verify its provenance."

In the legitimate art world, provenance was everything. Reputable museums, collectors and galleries wouldn't touch a piece without knowing who owned it and when. The risk of losing an investment when the FBI knocked on the door looking for a stolen painting was too great.

"I don't know," Phin said. "Rory's client had a receipt showing he'd purchased it from someone on the west coast and had a written agreement with the gallery outlining the terms of the loan. When it came time to give it back, the gallery suddenly couldn't find it. Rory asked if we could help. Zeke looked over the paperwork, did some research, and we determined the guy was telling the truth. The gallery had a reputation for being shady like that. We got the painting back."

"How? Or can't you tell me?"

He shrugged. "We took it."

Maddy let out a long, highly unattractive snort. "Oh, right. You just walked into the gallery and *took* it? Why weren't you arrested?"

He glanced over at her again, then immediately brought his attention back to the road. "For returning a painting to its owner? Who's gonna call the cops?" Phin shook his head. "No one is opening *that* door. Imagine all the other stolen stuff the gallery owner had borrowed and refused to give back."

This might be her problem. Too honest. Too willing to hope humans would do the right thing.

Maybe she *was* naïve. In this case, she'd accept it.

She rolled one hand. "So, BARS is a modern-day Robin Hood."

"Oh, hell no. We don't steal from the rich to give to the poor. BARS is paid to do a job and we do it. We're careful, though. If there's a question about ownership, we don't take the job. In Rory's case, his client had the receipt and the gallery agreement. It belonged to him."

"Makes sense."

"Sure does. You haven't answered my question."

"Which question?"

"About the Thompsons. How likely are they to make a deal?"

Oh. That. Yeesh. Talk about going down a rabbit hole. Or maybe she'd wanted to forget Phin had even asked her. Somehow, she didn't want to view the Thompsons, who'd fought for human rights and nonviolence, as people who'd make black market deals.

"I'm not sure," she said. "What specifically are we talking about? President Thompson is getting tremendous pressure from his brother. Their father is in his eighties and losing these pieces has devastated him. And then there's Mrs. Thompson's grandmother."

"The Queen of England."

"Crazy, right? I can't wrap my mind around the idea that they'd be willing to sacrifice one of her pieces. How would *that* impact family relations? Never mind the US-England relationship. She allowed us to showcase those pieces, and we lost them."

"Not a good look."

No kidding there. He may have been the one in office, but his wife had helped get him there. Everything was about the look.

Maddy blew out a breath. "I don't know. If they're desperate enough, maybe. Obviously, I'm out of the loop. Considering they think I'm the mastermind behind this heist."

"It's nonsense. Don't worry about it." He held up his free hand. "I know it's easy for me to say, but the feds are reaching. They need it to look like they're on to something. Unfortunately, you're the sacrificial lamb. They're looking at all the employees just like we are. If they add enough pressure, they're hoping someone involved will cave."

Well, it sure as hell wouldn't be her because she wasn't involved. Even being targeted in the matter was insulting. At some point, she'd have to deal with the fallout of obsessively giving three years of her life to a job only to be accused of stealing.

Not now.

She focused on Phin and his perfect face and all the goodness found there. "Have *you* found any suspicious employees?"

"Rohan is on that. We have to vet them, then figure out who their family and friends are. It's tedious work."

In Phin speak, the answer to her question would be a hard no. Or maybe he was intentionally being vague. She *was* an outsider.

She faced front again, resting her head back and watching the mountain in the distance grow closer. "What now?"

"We go back to the house, update my brothers, and call President Thompson. See how willing they'd be to make a deal."

15

"Houston," Zeke said, "we have a problem."

For privacy, Phin popped his earbud in and took Zeke off the Audi's Bluetooth. "What's up?"

"Company outside the gate. Where are you?"

Company? What did that mean? "On my way back from the meeting with Rory. We're twenty minutes out. Who's there?"

"The question should be, who's *not* here?"

Phin bit down, grinding his back teeth. Who knew his brother had a flare for drama?

"As of two minutes ago," Zeke said, "we have reporters, cameras, and satellite trucks. All sitting at the foot of our driveway."

For a few long seconds, Phin's mind froze. How the hell …?

Feds leaked it.

Again.

"Swear to God," Phin said, "someone needs to plug the holes in that building before it effing sinks."

As a precaution, he eased up on the gas pedal, shifting to the right lane in anticipation of his upcoming exit. He kept his eyes on the road, refusing to acknowledge Maddy in the passenger seat beside him, even though he could feel her gaze boring through him.

"It may not have been the feds," Zeke said.

Of course it was. They were all about pressure points and squeezing them. Invading privacy? Major pressure point. "Who else?"

"I don't know, Phin. All I know is we have attention I'd rather not have."

Barely noon, and Phin had managed to piss off both Ash and Zeke. Maybe by 2:00 he could add Cruz and Rohan to the fun.

He shook it off. Besides, when was the last time Cruz got mad at him? "Are they blocking the road?"

No doubt, his brother sat at his desk or the conference table with the security images on screen. "Eh, we could make a case."

"What's happening?"

Maddy's voice cut in, holding a sharp urgency that Phin hated on her behalf. He finally slid her a glance. "Company outside the gate. Don't worry. We'll take care of it." Phin went back to Zeke, his mind already moving ahead to the call he'd put in to Maggie Kingston. Not only the sheriff, but a relative of his Steele cousins. "I'll call Maggie. See if she can send a deputy up. If they're creating a safety issue, she can chase 'em off."

"Already on it. I left her a voice mail before I called you. I didn't want you surprised when you pulled up."

"Appreciate it. I'll come in the back way. If they don't see us, maybe they'll bolt."

"Let's hope."

"Zeke?"

"Yeah?"

Phin kept his gaze straight ahead. He needed to apologize. He'd caused this mess and now his privacy-obsessed family had reporters camped out in front of the house. But saying it in front of Maddy? Who already had a serious case of the guilts? *Family first.* "I'm ... uh."

"Don't you dare fucking apologize," Zeke said. "We decided to let Maddy stay. That's on all of us."

Relief surged, the tension inside Phin deflating like a ripped tire. Zeke could have torn him a new one. Had every right to.

But no. He'd given him a pass.

Family first.

Damned straight.

Phin clicked off, concentrated on the road. They didn't use the back entrance to the property much. Mainly because it was a pain in the ass driving all the way around on a winding mountain road and then bumping and bouncing along what amounted to a dirt path.

And him in his Audi. His suspension might be toast after this.

Sensing Maddy's attention, he glanced sideways, found her staring at him, her eyes filled with all sorts of questions.

"I'm so sorry. Your family must hate me."

That statement, Phin could immediately shoot down. He shook his head. "Not at all. Zeke is pissed, but not at you. He called the sheriff—she's a cousin to our cousins on their mom's side—to clear them off the road. They're creating a safety hazard."

"Will that work?"

"It's as good an idea as any."

"Do you think the FBI told them?"

The sign for the Steele Ridge exit loomed and Phin flipped his blinker on. "Maybe. Probably." He waved it off. "Seems logical. They want you uncomfortable. Uncomfortable people say things they wouldn't normally say."

"Good to know," she said.

Had to love this woman. No screaming. No histrionics. No drama.

Phin cruised onto the exit ramp and slowed for the stop sign ahead. "We'll get to the house from the backside of the property. The entrance is tucked off the road a bit. Unless you're looking for it, you roll right by."

"Once we get back, I'm leaving. I'm not putting your family through this."

Here we go again. He hooked a right at the stop sign and stifled one of Cruz's trademark sighs. This whole concept of her leaving aggravated him. "Where will you go that provides the security of our place? Plus, it's too late. They know you're there. Might as well ride it out."

"It's not fair to y'all."

"It's not fair to you, either."

"But it's *my* problem," she said, her voice a tad pissy. "*Not* yours."

It's my problem now, sweetheart.

He didn't dare say it. Maddy had yet to show him a glimpse of a tantrum, but something told him that when it happened, it was epic. As much as he wouldn't mind seeing her let loose, he wasn't that guy. The one who created chaos for the fun of it.

In ten minutes, they'd be back at the house and he'd see what they could find out about how these reporters knew Maddy was in residence.

He'd start with Ash.

A few hours ago, they'd had that whole brotherly-love-kumbaya-moment and now? *Now* the feds unleashed a bunch of reporters on them and Ash hadn't even sent a warning.

Apparently, his brother had forgotten the famous Blackwell family-first motto.

He'd have to give him a reminder.

AFTER ARRIVING HOME AND LEAVING MADDY AT HER SUITE'S door, Phin entered the Theater, where his brothers gathered around the conference table, watching on the big screen as Sheriff Maggie did her thing with the reporters.

"I am *pissed*!" Phin announced.

Cruz angled back, gave him his I-don't-give-a-crap face, then went back to the screen. "About anything in particular?"

Was he kidding? The feds had unleashed the media on their home, a place where they guarded privacy like it was one of the queen's priceless tiaras and Cruz wasn't upset?

"Our brother is bending us over this table and you don't think I should," Phin waved his arms—Broadway at its best, "you know, be upset about that?"

Keeping his gaze on the monitor, Cruz shrugged. "I think you're emotional about something you shouldn't be emotional about."

What the ...? "Did someone hit you with a two-by-four?"

At that, Cruz laughed. "I love that line. It's business. You take it personally."

Phin made eye contact with Rohan. "Have I gone insane? Is this happening?"

"It's happening. Gotta say, I agree with Cruz."

"Great. Another one."

Rohan held up a finger. "Hold up. Ash may not have known Maddy's location was leaked. The feds are probably keeping him on a need-to-know status. Hell, probably the only reason he hasn't been drop-kicked from this case is us. They want to use us."

That made sense. Why wouldn't the feds ride their coattails?

It sucked eggs that Ash had to be in the middle of it. The whole goddamned situation aggravated Phin. Ignited that churn inside him.

Phin grunted. "You're right. We're the lowlifes they need. Why not keep us around?"

"Holy shit with the drama, Phin," Zeke said.

"Drama my ass. I go to these events in my six-hundred-dollar shoes and deal with assholes treating me like dog crap they stepped in."

Cruz raised one hand, sliding his forefinger over his thumb. The world's tiniest violin. "Wah, wah…"

"*Fuck* you, Cruz."

Finally, Cruz met his eye. The bored look again. "If you wanna go, we'll go. Burn off some stress. It's been a while since I kicked your ass."

Phin would be an imbecile—a lesson he'd learned *years* ago—to take on Cruz. The guy got a partial college ride on his wrestling chops and had, more times than Phin liked to admit, pinned him in warp speed. Humiliating, that.

Right now, though, with his blood reaching epic heat levels, he might be able to pummel his brother.

Anything to get rid of this … this … *sewage* … rolling inside him.

All of it. Causing his family trouble, getting himself on the news, Ash being pissed at him, the FBI.

Maddy being a suspect.

And staying under their roof.

Thinking too much. That's what this was. A spiraling mess screwing with his mind. He curled his hands into fists, rested them on the table and leaned in, letting all his weight flow into his arms, his knuckles taking the brunt of the punishment against the hard table.

Phinny, Phinny, Phinny.

Goddammit, he couldn't keep doing this. Letting people and situations get to him. Making him feel shameful.

Unworthy.

Jesus. *I need to go.*

Just get out.

He pushed off the table, spun, and headed for the door. "I gotta go."

"Hey," Zeke said. "We still got reporters out there."

Nowhere to run. Story of his life. He shook his head, picked up his pace, pushing through the vestibule door and then the outer one. Desperate for air, he sucked in a hot breath.

Summer in North Carolina.

He stopped, turned back, contemplated going back inside. To cool air and his brothers, who would offer the strange comfort of riding him endlessly about being soft.

One step was all it would take. One step back to the door and Zeke's over-the-top security.

To BARS.

He turned again, marching along the path to the side door of the Friary.

MADDY REACHED PHIN'S DOOR, LIFTED HER HAND TO KNOCK, and a phone started ringing. Not from inside. Behind her.

She turned just as Phin hit the top step, his tall, fit frame filling the space and igniting a starburst inside her. Heat streamed and her body, even from six feet away, yearned for something. Something that included Phin losing his clothes.

The man had a way.

He pulled the phone from his pocket, silenced it, and shoved it back before looking up and spotting her.

The set of his jaw and hardness in his eyes, nearly knocked her back a step.

"Whoa. Are you mad at me?"

He moved closer.

When he reached her, she stepped aside. He shoved his palm against the pad next to his door and a red light blinked. "Goddammit."

He tried the door again, this time leaving his hand a second longer, and the lock disengaged. "Finally," he muttered.

"Phin, please. Talk to me. Did I do something?"

He smacked at the door handle and pushed the door open. "Guess what? Not everything is about you."

"Hey!"

Great comeback to a scorching insult, but, well, she couldn't think of anything else. A few seconds ago, she'd been considering the idea of Phin naked. Kinda challenging to shift gears that fast.

He shoved the door open and kept one hand on it, holding it for her as he crossed the threshold.

When she didn't move from the hallway, he glanced over his shoulder.

"Are you coming in? I'm assuming since you're here, you want something."

And *wow*. "Gee, Phin, who knew *you* could be such an ass?"

For some reason, that made him laugh.

"I'm not kidding," she said, "I have issues, believe me, I'm aware, but man-oh-man, you take passive aggressive to new heights."

He spun back, his eyes wider than dinner plates. "Are you nuts?"

Actually, this might be the most sane she'd ever felt. "You should ask yourself that."

He propped his hands on his hips and craned his head toward her, clearly shocked that Good Girl Maddy actually had a spine.

"What the hell, Maddy?"

She stepped inside, stalking by him and then whirling back, jabbing her fingers into her chest. "Seems to me, of the two of us, I'm the more self-aware. I mean, yes, I'm a pleaser. To a fault. I know that. I'm working on it. Trying not to apologize all the damned time. Trying to make sure people don't walk all over me because I'm the good one. Good Girl Maddy. That's me. And, let me tell you, after the last couple of days? I'm about filled. *Up.* I am fucking *choking* on my need to make people happy. I *know* that about myself, Phin. Understand it on a visceral level. You? Complete denial."

His mouth hung open. Total shock.

Good.

"Denial?" he said, his tone harsher than he'd ever used with her.

Good. Whatever this was between them, he needed to know they were equals. Despite his apparent protective instincts, she had a say in her life.

"Yes," she shot back. "Denial. Whether it's not living the life you'd expected—you said yourself you feel trapped—or being around people like Senator Blakely who make you feel crummy, you, my friend, are not happy."

Whoa. She'd just said that. Out loud. *Buh-bye, Good Girl Maddy.*

Instinct kicking in, she opened her mouth, ready to apologize. To plead her case.

No.

She clamped her lips shut. Wrong? Maybe so, but he'd been rude to her first, which, news flash, wasn't exactly a mature attitude.

So what? For once, she'd be reckless.

If she'd stepped over a line, so be it. He could tell her to fuck off. Which he probably would, forthwith. Tout de suite.

"Oh, please." Phin waved her off with both hands. "Happy. I love how people throw that word around like it actually means something. Is anyone *happy*? There's always more to want. Does that make us *un*happy or ambitious? Why does wanting more mean I'm unhappy?"

"Wanting more isn't the problem. Not going after it is. That's the damned difference. Clearly, you're mad about something. If whatever happened in the time between us getting back and now isn't my fault, don't take it out on me."

She made a move toward the door, striding past him, head high. Before she got there, his hand clamped on her wrist, halting her.

She peered down at his hand, then slowly drew her gaze up, meeting his eye before she blasted him for putting his hands on her. Immediately, he let go, held his hands up in surrender.

"I'm sorry," he said.

"For?"

"Grabbing you. Acting like a toddler. All of it."

She folded her arms across her chest, forcing herself not to be tempted to touch him. "All I wanted was a box of tissues. That's why I came up here."

He dropped his chin to his chest, shaking his head. "I'm sorry. You walked into me having a meltdown. No excuse for being nasty to you."

And, oh, the tips of her fingers itched. She tapped them against her biceps, keeping them busy so she didn't get the harebrained idea of doing something. Something like touching Phin. *Tap-tap. Tap-tap.* "What happened?"

He let out a huff that may have been a laugh but didn't quite make it. "Honestly, I'm not sure. It started out with me being pissed at Ash because he was here this morning and we had that great talk. Then we came back to reporters outside, and he didn't even give us a warning."

She uncrossed her arms, holding up her hands. Classic halt signal. "Not to throw your words back at you, but it's not about you. It's about me and this crazy situation."

Fingers on fire, she finally reached for him, loosely clasping his forearms. "I know you don't want to hear this, but I really should go. Being here is causing y'all way too much trouble. I'm a grown woman and can take care of myself."

Phin's phone rang again. Bon Jovi's "Wanted Dead or Alive."

By now, she knew it to be Zeke's assigned ringtone. Something she found amusing in a way only a sibling could.

"Zeke," she said. "You should answer that."

He dug the phone from his pocket and swiped. "No. I shouldn't."

Oh boy. Obviously, something had happened between Phin and his brother. Or brothers? Who knew?

A few seconds later, Bon Jovi filled the room again. A different version of the same song.

"Now he's texting."

Phin grunted and tapped the screen. He read the text, his eyebrows hiking up.

"Everything okay?"

Phone still in his hand, he lifted his head. "Can we finish this later? Thompson just got a ransom call."

16

PHIN FOUND HIS BROTHERS STILL STANDING AROUND THE conference table, as they'd been when he stormed out just minutes earlier.

What the hell could he even say after that? *Sorry, I'm a baby?*

"Call just came in," Zeke said. "Thompson said he tried to reach you."

The call that he'd ignored on his way to his suite. Should he have done it? No. But, he was smart enough to know at that moment he wasn't in the headspace to talk to a former President of the United States.

All he needed was one damned minute to get his head together. One damned minute to figure out who and what he was pissed at. He wasn't even sure he knew anymore.

"Yeah, sorry. I was in the john."

Somehow, the excuse seemed better than admitting to his brothers that he was totally freaking losing his mind.

Phin pushed his shoulders back, focused on the job. "What do we know? Where did this call come from?"

"Apparently, Louis Pierre—Junior—put out a reward. An eleven-million-dollar one."

Phin nearly wet himself over the eleven-mil bomb. "Hello, daddy. The feds agreed to that?"

"No. Never got to the feds. Thompson shot the idea down. Louis did it anyway. Quietly put the word out. Now, Thompson got a call about the reward. He's calling it a ransom demand. Either way, someone wants to get paid. Whoever called knew there was money in play and wants it."

"Tell you what," Cruz said, "the guy is good at working on the down low. I haven't found any chatter about a reward."

"It's gotta be out there somewhere if Thompson got a call. The feds must be livid," Rohan said.

"They don't know yet. Thompson notified us first."

Oh, hell. Ash would love that. "Is he not telling the feds?" Phin asked.

Zeke lifted one shoulder. "Don't know. Not our problem. We need to call him back ASAP. I didn't want to get too deep into it until you got here. Is it a coincidence you just met with Rory and now we have a ransom call?"

Excellent point. One that Phin had pondered on the walk back to the Annex. They all took their usual seats at the table and Phin filled them in on his meeting.

When he finished, Zeke sat back, clasping his hands behind his head.

"Do you think Rory's involved in this ransom/reward request?"

It had to be Rory. Had to be. "If it's a coincidence, it's a damned convenient one. He knew the queen's pieces were boosted. That hasn't been released."

Phin swung to Cruz. "Have you found anything on the queen's collection?"

"Zippo. It's all about the Pierres. It could be out there and I haven't found it yet."

Doubtful. Cruz had a knack for dealing with lowlifes online. Somehow, he slipped into that greasy underbelly and let it go the minute he shut down his laptop. Phin had always admired that. His ability to turn ugliness off.

Zeke tapped his phone's screen a few times, then turned the volume up and set it down. "By the way, Thompson agreed to send us the video you wanted from the executive suite."

Alrighty then. Loads of progress today. "Great. When we get it, I'll take a look."

"For?" This from Cruz.

The sound of a phone ringing filled the room and Thompson immediately picked up, cutting off Cruz's inquiry. "Hello?"

"Sir," Zeke said, "I have Rohan, Cruz, and Phin on the line. Thank you for your patience while I assembled the team."

"Hey, guys. Louis called me about ten minutes ago. He took it upon himself, after being advised not to, to offer a reward. I've been holding him off, but my father is antsy. That makes Louis panic. All that being said, we'd like to put an end to this situation as quickly as possible."

Phin sat forward in his seat, rested his elbows on the table. "Sir, it's Phin. Do you know how he put this reward out? Who he talked to?"

"He told me he spoke to a couple of dealers he trusts. I'm told they have connections on the black market."

In which case, one of those dealers could have reached

out to Rory. "That's not unusual. I spoke to someone this morning who has similar contacts."

"The good news," Cruz said, "is they've kept it quiet. We haven't seen anything online regarding a reward or the queen's collection."

But Rory knew. Phin chose not to add that little factoid. Wouldn't serve anything at this point.

"It won't stay that way," Zeke said. "Now that it's out there, we should move quickly. What did Louis say regarding this reward?"

"Reward, my ass. I'm calling it a ransom. One of his contacts called him. This contact, he wouldn't tell me who, says he knows where the jewels are hidden."

Zeke exchanged a look with Phin, who rolled his bottom lip out and gave a noncommittal shrug. Could be something. Could be bullshit. He held his hand to Zeke, the I've-got-this signal. "Sir, Phin again. Do we know which pieces?"

"Louis said it's the Pierres and the queen's collection."

That made two people, Rory and whoever Louis spoke to, who knew the queen's pieces were in play.

"Gentlemen," Thompson said, his voice low and direct, "what's your gut reaction? Do you think whoever we're dealing with actually knows where the pieces are?"

Phin exchanged another look with Zeke, holding his hand for Zeke to take that one. "Sir, I like to have proof and we're not even close to that. What else did Louis say? How is this reward supposed to be handled?"

"Wire transfer. But there's a catch."

Of course there was. Catches always made Phin think scam. Then again, dealing in the black market, nothing was easy. "Louis said," Thompson continued, "the person knows the location, but it's a secure area. He can't get in."

Well, that's a problem. Zeke held his hands up, giving each of them the WTF face. Phin waved it off. Wouldn't be the first time they busted into a secure building. Still, it was a pain in the ass that came with a lot of risk. The main one being the legal headaches and possible jail time.

In this case, they had a former President of the United States on their side. That alone was a bonus.

Phin glanced at Cruz, who wore one hell of a big-ass smile. This was right up his alley. The guy lived for action. The more adrenaline, the better.

Cruz sat forward. "Sir, we'd need to know what we're dealing with in terms of the location. Security, floor plan, that sort of thing."

"If I'm understanding," Thompson said, "you're saying you'd be willing to breach the area?"

"That's correct," Zeke said so matter-of-factly that Phin had to question all of their decisions. Did anyone find it shocking that they had no issues—none—with breaking and entering?

And risking prison time.

Apparently not because now Rohan leaned closer to the phone. "Sir, this is Rohan. How would you like us to handle contacting this person?"

"Louis is getting another call from him in an hour. I'll get instructions then."

Zeke poked the screen. "We're on mute."

Phin jumped right in. "We need Louis out of this. If he offered a reward after Thompson nixed it, he's too much of a loose cannon. Lucky for us, this wackadoo reward idea got us some movement."

"We don't know that yet," Rohan said.

Phin nodded, conceding the point. Zeke unmuted the phone. "Sir, I'd like to suggest we ask Louis to step aside. In our experience, it's best to work directly with the dealer."

"I agree," Thompson said. "Too many cooks in the kitchen, and Louis doesn't know what the hell he's doing. You'll have more experience with this. Tell me how you want it done and we'll do it."

"We'll give you a phone number," Zeke jerked his chin at Cruz, who was already out of his chair and moving to the storage closet where they kept a stash of prepaid phones. "It's a burner phone. Have Louis give his contact the number and tell them to call us. We'll set up a meeting to vet the information. If this is legitimate, we'll plan to recover the jewels. Is that agreeable?"

"Absolutely. Thank you. I prefer to keep the FBI out of it. At least for now. It won't make me popular, but Louis said his contact is adamant. No law enforcement. Are you comfortable with that?"

Considering their brother was one of the lead agents on this case? Hell, no, they weren't comfortable.

Phin raised his eyebrows, prayed for the floor to swallow him so he wouldn't have to experience Ash's wrath when he found out about this.

"You're our client," Zeke said. "We're fine with however you'd like to handle it."

Cruz reentered the room, burner phone in hand. Zeke took it, located the label they'd attached to the front of the box with the number. "Sir, do you have a pen handy? I have that number for you."

"I'm ready."

While Zeke read him the number, Phin glanced at Cruz, then moved to Rohan, who was probably already considering all the things that could go sideways.

His brothers. Funny bunch.

"Let us know," Phin said, "after Louis makes contact."

"I'll call you. Stand by."

They disconnected, and Phin let out a long whistle. "Talk about a development."

"Yeah." Zeke set the phone down, tapped his fingers on it. "Could be nothing. If word is out that Louis is desperate enough, they might be playing him."

"For sure," Phin said. "We should set up a meeting with whoever this is. In person. Someplace public. A lot of people. While that's happening, I'll call Rory. See what he knows."

"Agreed," Rohan said. "Let's look at this guy, see what kind of proof he has. If we think it's legit, we can make a deal."

FIFTEEN MINUTES AFTER PHIN HAD LEFT HER, MADDY wandered into the kitchen in search of a snack. Or maybe a sandwich, since they hadn't stopped for lunch.

On the unlit stove sat a Dutch oven, the cover failing to contain the aroma of slow-cooked meat and rich spices that sent Maddy's system into some sort of euphoria. If she spent too much time in this house, she'd gain weight. Lots of it.

All she'd wanted to do since she stepped foot on the property was eat. At least that's how it seemed.

Taped to the side of the island was a note from Lynette. Maddy paused, admired the neat, no-nonsense script informing the reader—or readers—that she and Johona had decided on an impromptu trip into town for shopping and an early dinner, but everyone, including Maddy, should eat.

These people. So kind.

Maddy had never been big on shopping and searching for items she probably didn't need. All that precious time wasted. She was more of an I-need-it-and-will-order-it person. Her newly gained popularity with the press had more or less eliminated the option of a casual stroll around a quaint little town.

She'd done nothing wrong and now, unless she wanted to be hounded, she couldn't even go out for a meal.

Stressing over it wouldn't help. She'd have to suck it up and trust that she'd be vindicated.

That's all.

Leaving Lynette's note in place, Maddy moved to the stove and lifted the cover from the pot. Beef stew. Meat and vegetables, all uniformly cut, rose almost to the top. Clearly, Phin and his brothers hadn't made it from their offices.

She closed her eyes, let the spices tickle her senses. Her tummy waved a white flag. Begging for mercy.

Food. *Amazing* food that Maddy's body nearly swooned over.

She pulled a bowl from the stack on the counter and using the ladle from the spoon rest, helped herself before grabbing silverware and a dinner roll from the basket Lynette had set behind the bowls.

Rather than sit at the giant table alone, she opted for the island, settling in to savor Lynette's cooking. Living alone, Maddy didn't bother with cooking much and her own mother was ... well ... not a gourmet chef. But she tried. Always.

The first spoonful of Lynette's stew hit Maddy's tongue in epic fashion. The truth was, she should have popped it in the microwave, but even lukewarm the savory meat nearly melted on her tongue.

"There you are."

She swallowed and spun her stool to find Phin and Cruz heading toward her. "Hi. Sorry. I was hungry." She pointed to the note. "Your mom left food."

"Nice," Cruz said, already lifting the lid off the pot. "Stew. She makes *the* best stew."

Maddy waved her spoon. "I just found that out. Good thing you got here when you did, or I might eat all of it."

"Dude." Phin pointed to the pot while he read Lynette's note. "Hook me up there. Mom and Grams went into town."

While Cruz doled out food, Phin slid onto the stool beside Maddy. "I tried your cell. You didn't answer."

She sat straight. Her phone. Had she ...

For whatever reason, she patted her pockets, knowing full well she wouldn't find it. In the middle of a crisis and she forgot her phone?

"I'm sorry. I must have left it in my room."

"Don't worry about it."

"Did you need something?"

Cruz passed the first bowl of stew to Phin. "Your brain."

"Actually," Phin said, "your eyes. I can't give you too many details, but Thompson has a lead on the jewels."

She dropped the spoon, sending it clattering into her bowl. "What lead? Do you think it's the real thing?"

Phin held up a hand. "We have to vet it. Sorry. I shouldn't have gotten your hopes up. We're setting up a meeting for tomorrow at noon to feel it out."

"Thus," Cruz said, not bothering to sit and digging into his meal from the opposite side of the island, "the meeting."

Calm. She'd have to stay calm and not expect too much. Wasn't that always her problem? Expecting things to go a certain way and then being disappointed. Her standards, her mother would say, were too high. She put thoughts of her mother—and her avoidance of said mother—out of her mind. When this was over, she'd apologize and explain. Right now, she couldn't talk about it. About the embarrassment and shame she'd brought to her family by being a suspect in a jewelry heist.

She focused on Phin and this possible lead. "How can I help?"

"This person," Phin said, "claims he knows where the jewels are and has photos. The plan is to meet in town. There's a sidewalk sale this weekend. That's where our mom went tonight. They've closed off Main Street to vehicles. The restaurants are setting up outside food stations and dining, so it'll be busy. "

Maddy thought of all the movies she'd seen where kidnappers have their victims hold up newspapers as proof of life. Did people even read newspapers anymore? What would the guy do? Show them an online article with a pic of the missing jewels?

"You want me to go with you?"

"Uh, no."

Cruz shoved a monster-sized spoonful of food in his mouth, chewed once and swallowed. Lord, the man ate like a dinosaur.

He pointed his spoon at Phin. "Little brother here is gonna wear a camera so you'll be able to see what he sees."

As fascinating as this whole James Bond mission sounded, without seeing the pieces, she couldn't be sure of anything. "That won't work. I need to see the actual jewels. Pictures might be Photoshopped."

Phin shook his head. "The real thing isn't an option. If you want to come, you'll stay in the car with Zeke. You'll be able to watch on a tablet. All we need you to do is tell us if the photos he has look like the actual pieces. If so, we'll figure out our next move."

· · ·

AT 11:53 SUNDAY MORNING, MADDY SAT IN THE PASSENGER seat of the same black SUV she'd driven in with Phin on Friday. This time, Zeke sat behind the wheel. After dropping Phin off a block away, they'd parked in a lot behind a place Zeke called the Triple B. From what Maddy could see, it appeared to be a bar and grill with an adjoining coffee shop.

So far, Maddy had seen little of Steele Ridge—only what she'd glimpsed on its quaint side streets on the drive in. Something about the old-fashioned, small-town charm left Maddy, the one who hated shopping, daydreaming of wandering the stores, grabbing a coffee, and chatting with locals.

"Shit," Zeke said.

Maddy glanced at Zeke, who was studying the tablet propped between them.

If things went according to plan, Phin would meet with whoever this person was, be shown evidence that he knew where the jewels were, and Maddy and Zeke would witness all of it, seeing what Phin saw so Maddy could identify the pieces.

On screen, Phin—according to the funky camera embedded in his sunglasses—spoke to an older woman with gray hair teased to perfection and straight out of the seventies.

Why Zeke would be worried about her, Maddy hadn't a clue. She certainly didn't look like an art thief. "Who is it?"

"Mrs. Royce. The town battle-ax. It's not her, so to speak. Should have anticipated this."

What in the heck was he babbling about? "I don't understand."

That made him laugh. One of those huffing, sarcastic ones. "Most times, I don't understand either." He waved it off. "We don't come into town much. It's not our thing."

She considered that for a moment, then glanced at the screen where a second person clapped Phin on the shoulder and moved on. Ah. *Charlie Charm.* "He draws attention just by being here."

"Yep." He grabbed his phone from the cupholder, tapped the screen and a ringing sound filled the vehicle.

"What's up?"

Male voice. Sounded like Cruz.

Zeke glanced around the parking lot, then went back to the tablet's screen, where Phin continued chatting with the town battle-ax. "You seeing this?"

"You betcha. Guess we should have chosen another location. Brother, we just made a rookie mistake."

"Someone needs to save him."

Just that fast, the solution came to her and Maddy reached for the door handle, ready to jump out. Before she got the door open, Zeke clasped her arm, his fingers firm, but not squeezing.

"Hold on there," he said. "Where are *you* going?"

"You just said someone needs to save him. It can't be a Blackwell." She gestured to the screen with her free hand. "Case in point. If one of you shows up, you'll both be sucked into the vortex. I'm a stranger. I'll pretend I'm his date and pull him away."

"Eh," Cruz said. "Not a bad idea."

As complements went, it wasn't a doozie, but she'd take it. "Why, thank you, Cruz."

"But—"

"No buts. I have sunglasses on. No one will recognize me. And I doubt reporters are expecting me to be here."

Counting on Zeke not wanting to cause a scene, Maddy grabbed her purse from the floor, yanked on the door handle and hopped out, hurrying across the parking lot toward the side street.

Zeke wouldn't follow. Would he? She glanced back to where he still sat in the SUV. Drawing any attention wouldn't help their mission, so chances of him yelling for her or running after her were nil.

And she wasn't about to lose this potential opportunity to find the missing jewels and clear her name.

Music blared from the front side of the building, so she hustled along, reaching the sidewalk. A child screamed just as Maddy turned left to where a barrier had been set up to block Main Street from vehicle traffic.

She knew, from conversations on the way over here, that Phin was to meet the person in front of the Triple B. Shouldn't be that hard to find him. Steele Ridge wasn't that big.

And Phin? With the movie-star good looks? Hard to miss. Exactly why they were in this predicament.

She glanced behind her again. No Zeke. She sidestepped the barrier, joining the crush on Main Street where open-air tents blocked the sun's rays. To her left, a line extended out the door of a bakery, the sweet aroma of fresh-baked cookies drawing a crowd.

If all went well, after the meeting, she'd stop and buy Lynette some cookies as a thank-you.

Her phone chirped. She slid it from her back pocket. Zeke. Checking on her.

She put her thumbs to work.

Still looking. Total madhouse.

What she hadn't expected when she jumped from the SUV was that Phin could be lost in the crowd.

Zeke: He's in front of La Belle Style. Two doors down from the B.

Two teenagers pushed around Maddy, giving her the hairy eyeball for blocking the way.

All around her, people bobbed and weaved, crowding the sidewalk and the street.

No Phin.

A group of tables for people to sit and dine had been placed in the road in front of the Triple B. She wandered by them, searching the area beyond for the orange baseball cap Phin wore. Not too many of those around here.

A flash caught her eye.

There.

In front of a clothing boutique a few doors down. Phin clearly hadn't made it that far once he'd stepped onto Main Street.

The gray-haired older woman continued chatting him up, monopolizing his time. Maddy would have to rectify that. Business to conduct. She was the FBI's number one target in a priceless jewelry heist and this old woman was in the way.

Time to break this up.

Maddy kept moving, not too fast, not too slow. Isn't that what she'd seen in all the undercover cop shows? Look *natural.*

As if any of this was natural.

Maddy kept her gaze pinned to Phin, who stood at least a foot taller than the woman and could easily see over her. If he'd just lift his head, he'd see Maddy coming.

Come on. Look up.

Nothing.

Of course.

In another ten feet, she'd be there. He had to see her coming. Had to.

Look up.

She almost laughed. Could nothing go her way this week?

Fine. She'd take care of it herself.

"Phin," she called, holding her hand up. "Hi."

Following the sound of her voice, he lifted his head, peering right over the top of the woman's head. "Uh," Phin said. "Hi."

The older woman turned, eyeing Maddy. "Well, hello."

"Maddy," Phin said, recovering fast, "this is Mrs. Royce. She lives here in town. Mrs. Royce, this is my friend, Maddy."

Following Phin's lead, Maddy stuck her hand out, offered her version of a hopefully genuine smile. "So nice to meet you."

Mrs. Royce puckered her lips, gave Maddy a not-so-casual once-over. "Are you new here in town? Or just visiting?"

"Visiting," Phin said. "We're meeting a friend for lunch."

"Speaking of which, we should get moving." Maddy made a show of checking her watch. "I hate being late. So rude."

Mrs. Royce nodded. "Oh, my dear, I completely understand. You young folks go on ahead now."

After saying goodbye to the woman, Phin led Maddy back toward the group of tables in the street. If they were lucky enough to snag one, crowd noise would prevent anyone from eavesdropping on their conversation.

"What," Phin said, his voice a low growl, "are you doing here?"

"Rescuing you from the locals."

"Last I checked, I didn't need rescuing. I can't believe Zeke let you out here."

She pulled her arm free, smiled at a woman pushing a

stroller through the pack. "He didn't *let* me do anything. You were hung up with Mrs. Royce. I didn't think it would be wise for one of your brothers to come out here. Then you'd *all* be recognized and distracted. Nobody knows me. I'm the logical choice."

"Hey," a man said from behind them. "Is there a jewelry store in town?"

Jewelry. The code word. Phin halted. Maddy right along with him. The two of them turned to see a young guy, maybe midtwenties.

With a neck tattoo.

17

Upon hearing the code word, Phin turned, hands at his sides in case he needed them.

Facing the man, Phin sized him up. Maybe five foot nine, five foot ten at the most. Short, dark hair.

And a prominent neck tattoo.

This was their guy.

The one from the Center. The one who'd visited Maddy's apartment not just once but twice and had a key.

Phin drew a silent breath, forcing his brain into a calm, controlled state. Busting this guy in two for freaking Maddy out wouldn't get them priceless jewels.

Plus, Maddy stood right beside him, in front of the person who had made her look like a criminal mastermind.

That alone fried him.

He peeled his gaze from Neck Tattoo, glancing at Maddy, her eyes boring into the guy.

She should have stayed in the damned truck. She wore her heart on her sleeve like no other. At this rate, she might beat him to busting this guy up.

Nothing he could do about it except hope she didn't let

her emotions rule. Not that he'd blame her for it, because he himself was currently riding the struggle bus on that front. But they had a job to do and losing her temper had no place in it.

He turned back to Neck Tattoo. Obviously, he wasn't as dumb as Phin thought, because he made a production out of looking everywhere but at Maddy.

Coward. He'd turned the woman's life upside down and didn't have the balls to look her in the eye.

"Phin!" a female voice broke through.

Not another one.

Phin angled back, spotted his extremely pregnant cousin Micki and her fiancé Gage Barber working through the crowd. Only Micki, a badass hacker currently teaching cyber warfare classes at her brother Reid's law enforcement training center and—rumor had it—moonlighting for the CIA, could find a black maternity shirt emblazoned with a white skull.

Micki and Gage darted, as much as an eight-months-pregnant woman could, between a group of teenagers pushing and shoving, one of them plowing right into Micki.

"Hey," Gage said, his voice dangerously low. "Lady with a baby, here. Knock it off before I bust some heads."

Phin leaned down, got close to Maddy's ear. "This is my cousin Micki and her fiancé."

He stood tall again, plastering a smile on his face.

Normally, he enjoyed seeing Micki. She'd left town right after high school, moving to Vegas and working for some shady fixer. For years, she'd been the black sheep of the Steele family. A gossip-fueling enigma, like the Blackwells, and he considered her a kindred spirit.

Micki understood him. All of his brothers, really. They'd

never discussed it, but she knew the weight of being the bad egg.

She marched straight for him, a smile lighting her face. Jesus, the last thing he needed was her and Gage, a freaking former Green Beret with a monster hero complex, in the middle of this.

Between Mrs. Royce and Gage, a public meeting was an epic fail. Fail or not, it was his mess to get out of.

He'd like to step away from Neck Tattoo, but he wasn't about to leave Maddy with him. But, if he suddenly grabbed Maddy's hand and dragged her with him to meet Micki, he'd be introducing a woman to a family member, which, in this town?

Major news.

If he wasn't careful, by dinner, the rumor mill would have him engaged.

To Maddy.

And why wasn't *that* an altogether horrible thought?

He shook off thoughts of Maddy in a skin-tight wedding dress that showed off her curves and held his arms wide for his cousin. "Hey, you," he said, carefully wrapping her in a hug.

He held on for a second, giving her a gentle squeeze and putting his mouth next to her ear. "I'm in the middle of something, here. Can I call you later?"

She returned the hug and stepped back, nodding.

Phin turned to Gage, held his hand out. "Good to see you."

Shoulders brutally pinned back—military habits, hard to break—he grasped Phin's hand, gave it a solid pump. "You too."

"Oh." Micki set her hand on her belly.

Gage whipped his head around. "What? You okay?"

"Gotta pee! Right now. Stupid bladder. Phin, I'll call you later."

Good old, Micki.

She took off through the crowd, Gage hauling ass after her, and Phin met Maddy's gaze. Dodged a bullet there.

With them gone, Phin brought his attention back to Neck Tattoo. "Too many people here. Let's step away from the crowd."

Phin jerked his thumb over his shoulder toward La Belle Style, the boutique owned by his cousin Reid's wife. "Let's walk to the side street. We'll talk there."

Phin grasped Maddy's hand, leading her past La Belle Style to the police barricades at the end of the block. They hooked a left. Bumper-to-bumper parked cars lined both sides. Phin crossed the street, moving to the sidewalk and stopping halfway down at the rear of a black Camaro with rims that cost more than three of Phin's best suits.

The guy stopped, folded his arms, and leaned against the car. Just a group of friends shooting the shit.

Phin positioned himself between Neck Tattoo and Maddy and left his back to the street. Totally fucking vulnerable.

Not good. This entire meet was turning into a class A screwup and Phin's skin itched.

He shifted, giving himself at least a partial view of the street and anyone who might be sneaking up on him.

"Let's make this fast," he told Neck Tattoo. "What have you got?"

"He must have a lot," Maddy said. "Considering he was one of them that stole the collections."

Jesus. Now he had to deal with her mouthing off. He shot her a look, but all it got him was an icy stare. Maddy choosing today to become defiant.

Excellent.

"*Both* collections," Neck Tattoo said, Phin now noticing his accent.

Cajun maybe. Definitely not North Carolina.

"I know where they are," NT said, "but I can't get to them alone."

"Why?" Phin asked.

"They're stored in my boss's warehouse. Security is a problem."

"How do you know they're there?"

He shrugged. "I put 'em there."

"You got in once. Why can't you get in again?"

"They were expecting us that night. Security is tight. Two armed guards plus cameras. The guard opened the gates for us and then unlocked the bay doors so we could drive in."

"Who's us?"

Neck Tattoo shrugged. "Nice try."

"Let me get this straight. You want the reward, but can't produce the jewels. Why do you deserve a reward?"

"Because a former president wants his stuff back. Dude, I can walk away. No problem there."

"Then why are you here?"

The idiot smiled. "This score sets me up for life."

Beside him, Maddy flinched, and Phin shot her a look. She kept her gaze on Neck Tattoo and her fingers drumming at her sides. Probably to keep them busy so she didn't sock the guy.

"Where is this warehouse?"

Neck Tattoo slipped his phone out of his pocket, tapped the screen a few times and held it up. On screen was a photo of what looked like a commercial warehouse surrounded by an iron fence.

Wouldn't be the first time they'd cut through iron. But if security was that good, they'd have to find the cameras' blind spots. Good luck doing all that in such a short time.

"Okay," Phin said. "What about inside?"

"Climate controlled. The jewels are inside a safe."

This just kept getting better and better. "You got the combination?"

"If I had that, I wouldn't need you. I'd pay off one of the guards and steal 'em back myself."

"How do I know you're not lying?"

"I took pictures before we left." He grinned. "In case I needed them."

Phin snorted. A real stand-up guy, this one. "You work for the Veras?"

"I work for whoever is hiring."

Mr. Loyal. Phin gestured to the phone. "Show me the pictures."

Neck Tattoo swiped at the screen and held the phone up again. "Scroll left."

Phin reached for Maddy, bringing her closer for a better view of a photo, revealing the inside of a safe outfitted with velvet-lined shelves. He swiped again, zoomed in on one shelf. A diamond tiara sat on a stand. He glanced down at Maddy, and she nodded.

"It's from the queen's collection."

Phin swiped again. Brooch.

Maddy's eyebrows hitched. "That looks like the pink diamond brooch. It's stunning and hard to mistake."

Another swipe led them to a triple-strand diamond necklace, also from the queen's collection. Photo after photo revealed all seven items and Phin nearly crapped himself.

So close.

Now they had to recover them.

The sound of an engine broke through the distant crowd noise. A minivan cruised along, probably a family looking for parking. The van slowed to a crawl.

Phin froze for a second, watching, forcing his brain to engage. White minivan. Dodge logo. Knocking engine. Older vehicle.

His itchy skin fired again.

Just a family. Just a family. Just a family.

But what if it wasn't?

Not taking any chances because, holy hell, his body was on fire, every nerve ending sizzling as he sidestepped, body blocking Maddy from the street. Taking a cue from Phin, Neck Tattoo moved two steps to his right, separating himself from Phin and Maddy.

Even better.

The van's driver gunned the engine, the vehicle lurching forward, picking up speed. The passenger window came down, the guy sitting there lifting his right arm.

Gun.

No, no, no, no.

Phin spun, locked his gaze on Maddy. She must have seen something on his face because her eyes bugged out and her cheeks turned the grayish-green hue of death.

He shoved her. Just hauled off and pushed her. "Get down!"

Boom-boom-boom. Three quick shots rang out and Phin leaped, plowing into a still upright Maddy who'd bucked backward, teetering.

Cement sidewalk. If she hit her head? Toast. Major head trauma.

Boom-boom-boom. More shots, one of them whizzing right past his ear, lighting every nerve on fire. They'd die on the street.

Maddy.

He lifted his arms, wrapping his hands around her skull as her feet came out from under her and the two of them careened to the ground.

"Oofff!"

She hit the sidewalk. The backs of his hands scraped against cement, his fingers curling into her hair, cradling her head.

The van roared by, tires squealing. A sudden wailing scream erupted. Maddy. The piercing shriek shredded Phin's ears. Was she hit?

She continued howling, drowning out any sound beyond them.

They had to move. Fucking sitting ducks. And where was the van?

Phin swung his head left, peeping between the cars. No shooter that he could see. Didn't mean anything since his view was limited. What he could see was Neck Tattoo face-down beside him.

Phin's pulse slammed, blurring his vision while Maddy continued screaming.

They had to move. Had to.

"Maddy!" he said, his voice way harsher than he'd wanted, but he needed her focused.

She stopped screaming. Just shut up. That fast. Good.

He set his hands on either side of her head, pushing off of her, taking in her face and the surrounding sidewalk. No blood. "Are you hit?"

"I don't ... think so."

"I don't know where the van is," he said. "We need to crawl to the street so I can see."

And pray the shooter took off. With Main Street packed, they had to have bolted.

A horn blared, and Phin rolled off Maddy, looking over his shoulder. Black SUV. Zeke.

Phin hopped to his feet, clasped Maddy's arms, and dragged her to her feet. "Zeke is here. Get in the car."

He ripped open the rear door, shoved Maddy inside to safety.

Behind the wheel, Zeke focused on Phin. "Either of you hit?"

"No." Phin shoved Maddy in. "Get down. On the floor."

He slammed the door, then opened the front passenger one, ready to jump in. Neck Tattoo still lay unmoving on the sidewalk.

Sirens blared.

Close.

The firehouse was just a couple blocks away.

"I called 911," Zeke said. "You can't help him. Get in!"

Leaving the door open, he hustled to Neck Tattoo, felt for a pulse. Weak but there.

His phone sat on the ground beside him.

Evidence.

Seconds. That's all it had been since Phin swiped that screen. The phone may not have gone to sleep yet.

If ever there was a time to break the law …

"Phin!" Zeke hollered. "Get the fuck in!"

No more thinking. Thinking never got him anywhere good. He scooped up the phone, did what his brother told him, and got in. Zeke hit the gas. Up ahead, a sheriff's cruiser flew around the corner, followed by an ambulance, a fire truck, and two more squads.

"Ambulance coming around the corner. Is he dead?"

"He had a pulse. Not much, but there."

Hands trembling from the adrenaline rush, Phin peered down at a photo of a diamond bracelet.

He'd done it. Grabbed the phone in time. He swiped up, found the settings icon, tapped.

"What the hell are you doing?" Zeke roared.

"Changing the password."

"You're tampering with evidence!"

As if he didn't know?

"Shut up a second."

He finished changing the password, dropped the phone in his lap, and held his hands up. Done. Jesus, how much time could that get him?

"It has pictures," Maddy croaked from her spot on the floor. "The phone. There are pictures of where the jewels are."

18

"MS. CARMICHAEL?"

Maddy lifted her head and stared up at a woman with honey-brown hair tied in a ponytail. She wore a uniform, a gun holstered at her waist.

"This is water," the woman said.

Maddy accepted the cup, guzzled its contents like she'd been stranded in the desert for a week. The icy blast cleared the fog in her brain and she lowered the cup, holding it with both hands, battling the jitters consuming her.

The woman set her hand on Maddy's shoulder. "You're probably in shock. Do you need a doctor?"

Maddy shook her head. "I'm ... okay."

And she was. Still alive and unhurt. Physically, at least.

She peered around the table where Phin, Zeke, Cruz, and Rohan also sat.

Zeke had driven them here. To the sheriff's station, where they'd waited in this conference room, mostly in silence, for an hour.

Maddy glanced back at the woman, still standing beside her. She lifted the cup. "Thank you."

"More?"

"No." Maddy set the cup on the table. "I'm good."

The officer held out her hand. "I'm Sheriff Maggie Kingston."

Oh. Wow.

A female sheriff. The one who'd chased the reporters from in front of the Blackwell property. How cool was that?

Maddy shook her hand. "Hi. I'm sorry, I thought ... Never mind."

Sheriff Kingston moved to the end of the table, sitting in front of a pen and pad, her posture erect.

Purposeful.

Controlled.

"All right." She picked up the pen. "Who wants to explain to me why some guy talking to Phin got shot during a sidewalk sale? You realize, I'm sure, Grif, your cousin and the town manager, is going to lose his mind."

"Maggie," Zeke said, "I'm sorry. There's an explanation."

"There better be, or Phin may wind up behind bars."

"Oh my God," Maddy said, whipping her head back and forth. "No. He was just ..."

Beside her, Phin cleared his throat. "I've got this."

In other words, shut up.

Yelling from the outer room sounded, and Sheriff Kingston shook her head. "Terrific," she muttered.

"Fuck," Zeke said.

"Excellent," Cruz said.

"This should be good," Rohan said.

Phin sighed.

The door flew open and Special Agent Blackwell stood there, shoulders squared, eyes like lasers locking on each of his brothers. "What did you do?"

Before anyone could answer, he stepped into the room,

swinging the door closed behind him. "Seriously!" He stalked to the far wall, paced the length of it and turned back. "What in holy *fuck* did you do?"

Sheriff Kingston pointed at him. "Calm down and take a seat before I lock all of you in a cell."

Special Agent Blackwell whipped around to face her. "Maggie, I need a minute with my brothers."

"Not when a shooting has just happened in my town, you don't. Are you here in an official capacity?"

"No."

"Then you're here visiting on a day when your brother meets with a man who's been shot and may die?"

Her tone, that sort of flattened sarcasm, let everyone—at least in Maddy's opinion—know that Sheriff Kingston wasn't in the mood for games. Who could blame her?

When Special Agent Blackwell didn't respond, Sheriff Kingston cut her eyes to Zeke. "Since Cam isn't talking, how about you clue me in?" She sat forward, rested her elbows on the table. "I'm serious. I have no problem throwing all of your asses in jail."

Second threat for a stint behind bars.

Phin rocked back in his chair, angling it to face the sheriff. "Maggie," he said, "we can't discuss it. We have an NDA."

Her mouth flopped open. "An *NDA*. That's what you have to say?" She cocked her head. "I don't think the guy who just bled all over my street would be satisfied with that answer. I don't give a rat's ass about your NDA. Start talking."

Special Agent Blackwell ran his hands over his face. "What a mess."

Phin jerked his chin at Zeke. "If we don't tell her, she'll make our lives hell." He faced Maggie again. "Here's the deal—"

"Phin," Special Agent Blackwell warned. "Don't."

"No. If you've got a problem with this, leave the room."

Special Agent Blackwell turned a hard glare on him, his eyes nearly black with fury. Phin didn't seem fazed.

Wasting time sitting around a table wouldn't help them find the jewels.

And, as far as Maddy knew, he still had Neck Tattoo's phone in his pocket.

The sooner they got out of here, the sooner they'd get on with figuring out where the jewels were.

Special Agent Blackwell shook his head, but leaned against the whiteboard.

Phin turned back to Sheriff Kingston. "The Thompson Center has hired BARS to help recover their stolen jewels."

For a moment, she simply stared at him, taking in the information. "I see," she finally said, obviously not needing to be briefed on the case. "This man you were meeting with, what's his name?"

"We don't know."

She eyed him for a few seconds and he held his hands out. "I'm not lying. Literally, we didn't get that far. Maddy and I met him in front of the B, but it was too crowded. We moved off of Main Street to talk."

Sheriff Kingston put up her hands. "You're going to need to start at the beginning. If you don't know who he is, how did you set up a meeting?"

Another round of yelling sounded from the outer hallway. Another man.

Active place.

"Oh, for God's sake." Sheriff Kingston pushed out of her chair, walked to the door, and threw it open.

A mammoth, insanely jacked guy appeared in the doorway.

"Great," Special Agent Blackwell said. "This nightmare won't end."

The guy angled around Sheriff Kingston, his enormous presence filling the room. "Y'all are involved in this?"

Clearly, they were acquainted.

"Reid," Sheriff Kingston said, "get out. I can't talk to you right now."

The guy ignored the sheriff and pointed at Phin. "Mrs. Royce said she saw you with the victim."

"Reid!" Sheriff Kingston said, her voice firm. "Out!"

"No, Mags," he said. "In case you forgot, my very pregnant wife owns a shop half a block from where this guy got popped. It appears my cousins were involved and I want to know what the fuck happened."

Wait. Cousins? Maddy shifted her gaze to Phin. He ignored her, keeping his focus on the Superman lookalike.

Sheriff Kingston shoved Phin's cousin, backing him up a full two steps out the door. An impressive display since he was basically a walking mountain.

"Wait outside," she told him. "The Steeles have created their fair share of drama in this town. Now get out."

You go, girl.

Maddy swiveled her chair to Phin, grabbing his attention. "Wow."

Phin snorted. "She's a tank. She'd kick any of our asses." Then he stood up and headed to the door. "Zeke, finish filling Maggie in."

Zeke peered up at him. "Where are *you* going?"

"I'm gonna talk to Reid. Calm the big man down."

"NDA," Zeke said.

Phin lifted one finger, made an imaginary check mark. "Check."

On his way by, Special Agent Blackwell met his eye. "Federal investigation."

"Check, check. If I'm not back in ten, he's killed me."

THIS WOULDN'T EXACTLY BE A BARREL OF MONKEYS.

On his best day, Reid Steele was a pain in the ass. Loud, opinionated, unfiltered. All of it wrapped in a six foot three body that had served him well as a Green Beret until a career-ending knee injury.

Now, he was back in Steele Ridge and had brought Gage, his former teammate and friend, onboard to help him run a law enforcement training center. Rumor had it that Jonah, Reid's billionaire brother, had made Reid a partner after buying the property. Only right since he'd put in the sweat equity on the project.

One thing about Reid, he didn't pull his punches. If he had questions about Blackwell family secrets, he—as just evidenced—went to the source. None of this small-town gossip shit.

Reid pushed through the sheriff's station's main entrance with Phin on his heels. He turned right, heading to the parking lot where his pickup sat gleaming in the sun. They reached the lot and Reid turned, crossing his arms over his chest.

Waiting.

Out of all his brothers, why was Phin the one trying to talk his cousin down?

Because he could. Phin had the patience for a guy like Reid. A guy notorious for peppering you with unrelenting questions that would no doubt become offensive.

The trick with Reid was for Phin to make it clear he

wasn't intimidated. Not an easy feat considering Reid's massiveness.

Mirroring Reid's wide-legged stance, Phin crossed his arms. "Are you gonna listen? Because if all you wanna do is scream, I don't have time."

Reid gave him a vicious glare. "I'm here, aren't I?"

Yeah, he was. And maybe he had a right to be. Brynne, Reid's wife, was weeks from delivering twins and given the foot traffic on Main Street, had probably been in her shop, half a block away.

Fuck the NDA.

Fuck the feds.

The guy had a right to answers.

Phin held his hand up, thumb and forefinger pinched together. "See this?"

Reid gave him his classic what-the-fuck? face and Phin used his free hand to point to the imaginary document between his fingers. "It's an NDA. I need you to sign it."

"Did you receive a head injury during this shooting?"

Phin laughed. Had to. Reid had used his own version of Phin's two-by-four line on him. "No. But Zeke will go nuts on me if I tell you anything, and don't get me started on Ash. So, you're going to sign my pretend NDA and if you violate it and get me in hot water with my brothers, I will hunt you down and kill you. You're bigger and stronger, but I know how to use a gun."

"Dude," Reid said, pretending to sign the invisible NDA. "I definitely think you got a head injury today."

When Reid finished signing, Phin dropped his hands. "The Thompson Center hired us."

Reid gawked, his mouth literally falling open. "The former president? That Thompson Center?"

Was there any other? "Yes."

"Well, well. Y'all have hit the big time."

Insult number one. Patience, patience. "We've been working our asses off the last couple of years. Anyway, the Thompsons."

Phin gave Reid the shortened version of their work on behalf of the Thompsons, casually leaving out the queen's collection. Some things his cousin didn't need to know.

"The guy who got shot," Reid said. "You think he's doing a side deal?"

"I was vetting him. Trying to see if he's legit."

"And is he?"

"If he survives, yeah, I think he is."

"How do you know?"

Phin wouldn't expand on the guy's phone in his pocket. He pointed to his neck. "He has a prominent tattoo on his neck. Easily identifiable. He was on security footage from the night of the heist. He told us he knows where the jewels are stashed, but needs help getting in."

"Who shot him?"

Phin shrugged. "My guess? He runs with a Vera crew. The Veras are known for big heists. They're ballsy, I'll give you that. They have no concern—zero—for historical value. They steal the stuff and either break it up or try to sell it on the black market. When this guy contacted Thompson, we figured it'd be safe to meet him in an open, busy area for a conversation. Obviously, if we'd thought it would be danger-ous, we wouldn't have exposed innocent people. I apologize for that. For endangering your wife and children."

Reid lifted his hands, scrubbing them over his face and then dropping them back to his sides as if they held the world's weight.

"You Blackwells."

Phin cocked his head—*patience, patience*—ready to lay into his cousin.

Clearly sensing Phin's reaction, Reid shook his head. "That came out wrong. Y'all frustrate me with all your secrets and cloak-and-dagger crap. We live in the same damned town. We're family. Why didn't you call me?"

Call him? Had he not been listening? "Um, NDA? And why would I call you?"

"Dude! I would have signed your fucking NDA and let you use the training center for a meeting. It would have been a lot safer than the middle of town. What the hell did I ever do to you that would make you not trust me? I just don't get that."

Not trust him?

What now?

Phin considered it a second. Tried to wrap his mind around the idea. Sure, he and his brothers kept to themselves. That was their dad's doing. Don't get too close to people. Don't share your business. That's what he'd tell them. He probably didn't mean family, but a message like that? Delivered repeatedly, it tends to evolve. It starts with random strangers, then it spreads, permeating a household.

Had they meant to isolate themselves? No. It happened. Like cancer spreading to healthy cells. In this case, family.

Phin blew out a hard breath, pressed his palms into his forehead and squeezed his eyes shut while it all came into focus. No wonder people thought they were shady. When faced with nothing but, as Reid said, cloak-and-dagger crap, what would they think?

All these years of rampant gossip could have been avoided. By keeping to themselves, by hiding from people and not getting close to outsiders, they'd unwittingly created the thing that Phin hated most.

Shame.

Maybe Phin and his brothers needed to make changes. Forget the secrecy and bring their Steele cousins into the loop. Hell, with the power the Steeles wielded in this town, it could change small-town minds and Phin wouldn't feel like every time he went to the post office, people snickered.

He dropped his hands, met his cousin's eye. "God help me for saying this because I'm fairly sure I'll hear about it for the next fifty years, but you're right."

"Whoa." Reid held his hands up. "Come again?"

Phin laughed. Yeah, fifty years was a long time. "Fuck you."

"No. Fuck *you*."

The sound of an engine drew their gazes to the street where a tricked-out minivan stormed into the lot and came to a skidding halt.

Somehow, Grif, his hot-shot sports agent cousin and Steele Ridge town manager, made a minivan look cool.

"You're screwed now," Reid said. "I haven't seen him drive like that since I hid his favorite Ferragamos."

Leaving the engine running, Grif jumped out of the van, leaving the door open. He poked his finger at Phin. *Jab, jab, jab.* "What the hell?" he hollered.

Now Phin would have to go through this whole episode again. Dammit.

"Go inside," Reid said. "I got this."

Now that sounded like a brilliant plan. "You sure?"

"Wouldn't be the first time I cleaned up a mess. Go. When I calm him down, he'll be in. Be ready."

Thankful for the intervention, Phin peeled off, hustling

to the door that would lead him back inside to his family and Maddy.

"And Phin?"

At the door, he paused, facing Reid. "Yeah?"

"Next time, call me. Doesn't matter what it is. I'll help you. Got it?"

"Got it," he said. "And thank you."

19

"HE'S DEAD," PHIN SAID.

Maddy sat back, her body slumping into the curve of Phin's sofa. After being questioned, Maddy and the Blackwells were sent home and told to stay put in case there were further questions. Ash, being one of the agents assigned to the Thompson theft, had remained with Sheriff Kingston and they'd yet to hear from him.

Not wanting Maddy to be alone, Phin invited her up to his suite. Now, he sat across from her in a black upholstered chair, his elbows resting on his knees, his gaze on hers.

For a few seconds, he didn't speak. Somehow understanding she needed to absorb this news. *Horrific* news that a man they'd been speaking to just a few hours ago had died.

Murdered, while standing right next to her.

"Maddy?"

She shook her head, battling another round of shock. "I'm ... I ..."

What? What could there possibly be to say? The man

had died, and maybe he wasn't exactly a stellar citizen, but someone must have loved him.

Phin touched her knee, jolting her from her thoughts. "Ash just called and told us. You okay?"

Was she okay? Compared to what? The dead guy?

She focused on Phin's eyes and how the afternoon sunlight streaming through the open curtains brought out the dark speckles in his irises.

Getting ornery with Phin wouldn't help. His only infraction had been caring about her. What kind of bitch did it make her to be irritated with him?

She squeezed her eyes closed. These thoughts. Too much. Stress. That's all this was. She opened her eyes again. "I'm okay. I'm sorry you and your family got involved in this."

"I'm not. It's important work. And, whatever you're thinking, it's not our fault he lived the life he did. Did he deserve to die that way?" He shrugged. "I don't know. But, make no mistake, he was not a good guy. The only thing I feel bad about is putting you through it and it happening in town. That was an epic fail on our part."

She scooted to the edge of the sofa cushion. "Hey, none of that. You thought it was a meeting. A *conversation*. None of us could have anticipated what happened. What now?"

"Probably more questions from Maggie. It's a homicide and she'll need every detail we can remember. As far as finding the jewels, we have his phone. Well, the feds have it. I didn't want to keep it from Ash, so we backed it up to an external hard drive and gave it to him."

"You backed it up? Wow."

"It might help us. Cruz, Rohan, and Zeke are going through everything."

"Won't Maggie need it?"

"Ash said he'd take care of Maggie. The phone has evidence regarding an FBI investigation. They'll probably get warrants to search his house."

"What's his name?"

"Brendan Eckert. He didn't have any ID on him, but they ran his prints. He's in the system. A career thief."

Did she know that name? Had she run across it anywhere? No. Not that she recalled. "Do you think there's anything on the phone that can help us? The photos he showed you. Will you be able to figure out where the jewels are?"

"I don't know. It's a warehouse with an iron fence. It could be anywhere in the Charlotte area. Cruz and Rohan are playing with the images, seeing if there's anything distinguishable. Maybe in the background or something. There might be metadata they can grab." He shrugged. "We'll see."

All of this work to find stolen jewels. Yes, they'd be paid a hefty fee, she knew that for sure, but they'd gone beyond their job to help her. Phin specifically.

She held his gaze for a minute, soaking in every inch of his face. The long, straight nose, the bit of stubble over carved cheekbones. Perfection. Phin perfection anyway. "Thank you."

"For what?"

"Everything. Helping me. Giving me a place to hide from reporters. All of it. You've done so much, including battling with your brothers, for me. You're a good man, Phin Blackwell."

"It was the right thing to do. And, as for my brothers, it's not a normal day around here if we're not fighting."

The warm gush of a smile made it to her face. Phin did that to her. Made her happy.

She wanted him. Quite badly. Wanted to feel his hands

on her. His lips on her. Maybe it was the trauma of the day, the stress of the last week or maybe she just needed the connection.

"You know," she said, "don't take this in a weird way."

What was she doing? Jumping in like this.

Again.

"Maybe take it weird. I don't know. All I know is that someone shot at us this afternoon and we could be in a morgue right now."

She closed her eyes, thought of beaches and sunny skies and the crash of the ocean. Anything to get the memory of Brendan Eckert on the pavement from her mind. She opened her eyes, found Phin staring at her with his electric gaze she'd never forget. "I'm doing it again."

"What?"

She let out a strangled laugh. "That thing I do. I fall hard for certain men. Thinking I see in them what I want. What makes me feel good and warm and ... *safe*. It's like an addiction, this love thing. I *love* to be in a relationship. But every time I think it's going great, it somehow doesn't work out and I question—*question, question, question*—my choices. It's a brutal cycle that tears me up."

His eyebrows hiked up a fraction. A barely noticeable move—oh, Phin was so good at masking his feelings—that let her know she might be freaking him out. Scaring him off before they even got anywhere.

Good. At least she'd know now. Before it got worse for her.

"Um," he flashed that Phin smile, rolled his hand in front of him, "just making sure you're thinking straight here." He threw up his hands. "Not that, you know, this doesn't all sound amazing to me because it does. Really amazing. We gotta make sure, though. That you're not feeling something only because of what happened today. That would be bad. For me. Really bad. So, I want to make sure."

Make sure? Hello? Had she not been clear? "Phin?"

"Yeah?"

"What the hell are you talking about? I'm basically throwing myself at you. What is it you need confirmation on?"

"I need to be sure this is what you want. That your wires aren't crossed. Because I'm about to bang the hell out of you."

20

WHAT WAS HAPPENING?

Phin Blackwell, asshole supreme, totally taking advantage of a woman in a vulnerable state.

With his mother right downstairs.

Oh, man. He needed to get that thought out of his mind.

Maddy's head lopped forward. "You want to bang the hell out of me?"

Uh, yeah. "Wow, Maddy. Don't sound so shocked. The question should be why *wouldn't* I want to? Especially after telling me you're throwing yourself at me. Way to send a guy to his knees."

Ach. Bad choice of words because now his thoughts went there. Him on his knees. In front of a naked Maddy.

Oooh—eeee.

He blew out a hard breath, wiped sweat beading on his upper lip. Christ, that sun coming through his windows was hot.

Apparently reading his mind, Maddy got to her feet, standing in front of the sofa and leaning over, bringing her lips dangerously close to his. "On your knees, huh?"

Oh, yeah. She wanted to play.

He inched closer, felt her breath on his lips, and met her eye. "Yep. And you're naked."

She kissed him. Just whammo, let him have it. Tongue and all and Phin's body did the *I'm-getting-laid* happy dance, sending a massive blood rush ricocheting in all directions.

Dang, he loved the happy dance.

Except ... trauma. Today, they'd watched a man get murdered.

He backed away, put his hands up. "Hold on."

"No."

She made a move to kiss him again, and he laughed, backing away. "Seriously, are you good? Because I'll make you come in ways you never imagined. Multiple times. But, honest to God, Maddy, if you wake up tomorrow and regret it, I'll be devastated."

Since when did women devastate him? And since when had he gone soft?

What. The. Fuck?

She straightened, standing over him and peering down. Yep. He'd done it. Gave her enough reason to think he was a pansy psycho getting way too attached way too early. Now she'd leave. Run like hell from the idiot who'd blown a perfectly amazing moment.

She held her hand out and he peered up at her, drilling her with a look because he needed to know. Needed to hear it.

"Phin," she said, "between the two of us, we're thinking way too hard. I'm fine. You're fine. I'm not concussed. I have more clarity than I've felt in a really long time. So, shut up and take me to bed."

Alrighty then. Talking over.

He popped to his feet, took her hand, and nearly

sprinted to his bedroom where, hey, at least he'd made the bed this morning. Even if he'd left his dirty laundry basket out, clothes strewn over the top.

Behind him, Maddy giggled. Giggled. And what a great sound that was coming from the ultra-mature Maddy.

He pushed the bedroom door open. When he'd left that morning, he'd thrown the curtains open and now the view of the mountain filled his vision.

First time.

It hit him at that exact moment. The view, the laundry, the bed.

First time.

Not just with Maddy. Bringing a woman here. To his home. To his bed. Something he never shared.

He shook it off. Thinking too much. Just like she'd said.

He let go of her hand, closed and locked the door behind them in case one of his brothers walked in. He moved the laundry basket. "Sorry. I wasn't ... uh ... expecting company."

She waved it off. "It's okay."

He needed to get himself together. He'd done this a million times. Well, maybe not a million, but a lot. His body basically operating on rote. Knowing exactly when to lean in, where to touch, how to move. Over and over, time and time again, he'd performed. A freaking circus act.

That was him.

"Stop thinking," she said. "I can feel you thinking."

He turned back, nearly bumping into her. Her wild, looping curls fell over her shoulders and he tugged.

"Can I tell you, I've had some fantastic fantasies about your hair." He slipped his hand into the mass, burying himself in the softness. "God, it's so soft."

Tilting her head, she rested against his fingers. "I love that you like it. Some days, I hate it. Total frizz-fest."

Oh, he liked it. He'd like it even more spread across his pillow. Keeping his hand in place, he dipped his head, let his lips glide over hers.

Slow. He wanted slow. Wanted to shut his goddamned brain off, give his body a minute to decompress. To relax and enjoy this woman who'd turned out to be a major surprise.

The one who might, if she hadn't done it already, upend his life.

She worked her hands under his T-shirt, lifting the hem, dragging her fingers up his torso, and he fought the urge to let loose. To crush her against him and invade her mouth with his tongue.

A million times he'd done this. Why was this time such a battle? Such a freaking war with his own body?

Maddy helped him out by taking charge darting her tongue into his mouth, then sliding it out again and sending his body into all sorts of havoc.

Her fingers climbed higher, the soft tips moving over his skin and nipples and he got so hard his mind zonked. He let out a moan, and she inched back, grinning at him.

He might love her.

Phinny, Phinny, Phinny.

He helped her lift his shirt off and she explored his chest, her fingers gliding over his pecs, his biceps, his abs that he damned near killed himself for.

Fucking sit-ups suddenly seemed worth it.

"I knew it," she said. "I knew you'd be stunning."

All part of the job.

He dove in again, kissing her hard, inching her to the bed until her legs hit it and she fell back, her eyes wide with shock. She burst out laughing and the sound bounced off the walls like a thousand—a million—fucking angels singing.

Laughter. In his space. Another thing that had been missing.

Oh yeah. If she'd let him, he just might love her.

Still laughing, Maddy sat up. Every second of being near Phin felt easy.

Good.

Right.

"You make everything fun," she told him.

He offered a shy smile. Not the flashing, player one. This one was the anti-CC one with a bit of boyishness. "Let's hope the trend continues."

From the second she'd met him, he'd been charming and flirty and fun. Now, when he looked at her, when he looked right into her eyes, he somehow made her believe she'd be okay.

Always.

Go figure. Brainiac Maddy and a player.

He peered down at her sleeveless shirt and jeans, waved a finger at them. "You have way too many clothes on."

She kicked off her sandals. "Better?"

"Those are shoes. Not clothes. You'll have to try harder."

"Scandalous!"

He leaned in, trapping her between his arms, and kissed her again, gently nipping her bottom lip and tugging. "How competitive are you?"

"Not much."

"So, if I challenged you to a race—who can get naked faster—it wouldn't rev you up?"

"Go!" She ripped her shirt over her head, clocking Phin on the forehead in the process and knocking him back a full step.

"Oh my God!" She hopped up, put her hands on his cheeks, holding his head in place so she could survey the damage. A red spot. Nothing bad.

"I'm so sorry." She went up on tiptoes and kissed the spot, letting her lips linger. "I'm so, so sorry."

He brought his arms around her, pulling her close and patting her rear. "I'm fine. All good."

He dipped his head, trailing kisses along her neck, sliding her bra strap down her shoulder while sliding his hands up her back and—whoopsie—bra unhooked.

Way too good at that.

But she didn't want to think about that. About how much practice he'd had with other women. *Not helping, Maddy.*

She shrugged out of the bra, a pretty satin one she'd bought last month as a treat to herself because it made her feel feminine. Sexy.

When around Phin, that's what she liked to feel, so she'd given it overtime the last few days.

She tossed the bra on the floor, and her fingers found the clasp of his jeans. She popped the button and dealt with the zipper before he stepped back and toed out of his loafers. Waiting while he kicked out of his jeans and removed his socks, she plopped on the bed, slid out of her own jeans and tossed them next to the bra.

Phin pointed at her underwear. A plain white pair with satin edges she instantly regretted wearing today.

"Pretty," he said.

"Plain," she said.

"*Understated.* And pretty."

"Oh, CC, where have you been all my life?"

He hooked his fingers into her underwear, shoved them down. "Funny. I was thinking the same thing."

She stood in front of him, completely naked and vulnerable and he made no effort, zippo, to hide his visual exploration of her body. He placed his hand on her hip, the warmth sending tiny shock waves straight to her already sensitized nipples. He brought her closer, skin to skin, and she wrapped her arms around his waist, sliding her fingers into the waistband of his boxer-briefs.

"These need to go."

"Amen, sister."

She worked them down, over his thighs, squatting to pull them off, his erection right there.

On her way back up, she grabbed hold of him, felt the heat of said erection, and imagined him on top of her, all that Phin goodness just for her. "I like that I do this to you. It's an amazing feeling."

He blew out a hard breath. "Jeez, Maddy. You're killing me. You're amazing. Everything about you. I love it. Before tomorrow morning, I'm doing it."

"What?"

"My fantasy. You'll be naked with me on my knees."

And, wowie, wow, wow, she wouldn't argue over that one.

He kissed her again, stroking his lips against hers and doing that tugging thing she suddenly discovered she liked.

She backed up a step, this time slowly, anticipating the bed behind her. When they reached it, she lowered herself, scooting backward and pulling the comforter back. She patted the spot beside her and he crawled across the bed, stopping at his bedside table and digging in the drawer for a second before retrieving a condom.

He did his thing with the condom, then stretched out beside her, the two of them nestled on the king-sized mattress.

Propping on one elbow, he smiled down at her, letting his gaze and his hand wander down her body, his fingers warming her as he went. She scooted closer, wanting that skin against skin again, wanting to feel her breasts against his chest.

After the day they'd had, the week they'd had, they deserved this. A few minutes to feel ... relief.

Rolling to her back, she brought him with her, his weight pushing her into the mattress. Safe. Protected.

Phin propped himself on his elbows. "I don't want to rush."

"We're not," she said. "I want to know what you feel like."

She opened her legs and his erection pressed against the inside of her thigh. She let out a gasp at the size of him. "Oh, boy!" she said, making him laugh.

Then he shifted, and she adjusted her hips, her body nearly purring with anticipation before ... yes ... he slid into her, the invasion at first a shock. A burst of heat and fullness and ... So good. One fluid stroke so perfect it made her think her body was made for his.

He worked his way deeper, gently moving, finding a rhythm with her, two bodies figuring it out. Exploring.

"I knew it," he said, his breath hot on her ear. "I knew I'd love being inside you."

She lifted her hips, pumping with him, increasing the urgency, letting the heat build, climbing, climbing, climbing. Her mind spun, and she closed her eyes, enjoying the light show as the squeeze of an oncoming orgasm nearly paralyzed her.

Opening her eyes again, she found Phin's, the two of them holding each other's gaze as their hips pumped and pumped.

Boom!

Her mind and body exploded, all of it happening at once. She cried out, letting go, embracing the chaotic whirl as she clamped her hands over Phin's rear and forced her hips to keep going. To keep pumping. To help him over that fantastic edge.

His body went rigid, his movements quickening. Faster, faster, faster. The headboard banging against the wall so hard that if this kept up, they'd go right through. Thank goodness his suite was at the end of the building.

He plunged, one last time, the force of him banging the headboard again as he gritted his teeth and ...

Gave in.

MADDY FELL ASLEEP IN HIS BED.

Refusing to move, Phin stared up at a sliver of moonlight that had bullied its way through the curtains and illuminated the ceiling.

He'd been this way for a while. Afraid to move or make a sound. If he did, she'd wake up and then what? Hell if he knew what to do with a woman snoozing in his bed. Typically, they were busy doing other things. And not in his own damned house.

Casual conversation? *Gee, honey, how was your day? Aside from getting shot at.*

Maybe he'd suggest a 2:00 a.m. snack, hustle out of bed, and completely avoid his intimacy inadequacies.

Phin Blackwell. Relationship failure. Probably because he never had one worth changing for.

One thing was for sure, he couldn't stay here all night with his mind whirling. Times like this, when he couldn't shut his brain down, he left his bed and found something to occupy him. That's what he needed. Stick to his routine of being productive. None of this pansy shit.

Time to grow a pair.

Slowly, he rolled to his side, easing the comforter off and getting his feet to the floor. Behind him, Maddy made a sound, a soft sigh that tripped his mind back to the orgasm he'd given her. The first one. *Heh, heh, heh.* The one before he'd fulfilled his fantasy of being on his knees in front of her. No one could ever say he wasn't a man of his word.

Heh, heh.

Heh.

More of Maddy. That's what he needed. Immediately, his body stirred. If she woke up, maybe he'd lure her into a replay.

He glanced back, pausing for a second to take in the moonlight casting over the gentle slope of her cheek and nose.

Beautiful.

Tempted, he lifted his hand, intent on running his fingers over her face, her delicate skin and sumptuous mouth. Anywhere just to *feel* her. To be close.

He halted. Fought every instinct urging him to wake her up.

Rest.

It looked good on her. After the week she'd had, he didn't have the heart to rob her of sleep.

Setting his hands on either side of him, he carefully got to his feet and waited. Maddy let out another soft breath and he stole a glance over his shoulder. Still asleep.

He slipped on the shorts and T-shirt he'd thrown across

the chair next to his bed, grabbed his phone from the night-stand and made his way to the living room, checking his messages as he went. Nothing urgent.

His laptop sat on the bistro table near the kitchen. His normal workspace when not in his office downstairs. After filling a water bottle and downing half, he settled in to check his e-mail. News updates, retail sales, various trade journals and—whoa. E-mail from Gerald Thompson sent at 10:05 p.m.

He clicked on it. Thompson had e-mailed Zeke, with Phin cc'd, informing them he'd put the requested security footage into a shared folder.

The executive suite video. Had to be. That was the only thing Phin had requested. He pulled up the folder, found the footage, and settled in for a long night.

An hour in, Phin decided it might be easier to head to the Annex, choose a .45 from the weapons vault, and blow his brains out. This kind of stuff, this sitting around analyz-ing, was more Cruz and Rohan's speed. He tapped the mouse, checked the time; 3:06.

Still no movement from Maddy. She'd let out one of her soft sighs a half hour earlier, but other than that, not a peep.

On his laptop screen, a young guy—late teens, early twenties maybe?—wearing dress pants and an oxford shirt, sans tie, entered the executive suite. Whoa. Who was this now? Phin sat straight, watching as the guy moved through the hallway toward Thompson's office.

Hang on.

Phin recognized him. He thought. Pausing the video, he clicked over to the Internet and searched for Louis Pierre III, finding a series of photos. Grandfather, son, grandson. All with the name Louis Pierre. The third image in the row showed all three of them at a recent charity function.

Yep. Louis Pierre III was the kid on the video.

Phin's momentary excitement crashed like a falling log. Maddy had told him Louis III was interning at the Thompson Center as an executive staff assistant. Of course, he had access to the executive suite.

He went back to the video, hit play, and took a gulp of water, his gaze still on the screen where Louis III, now known as Louis Three for short, strode past Maddy's office.

When he paused and glanced into the conference room, Phin sat a little straighter, his brain synapses firing as the kid retreated a few steps.

To Maddy's office.

He peeked in, swinging his head left and right.

Phin set his water bottle down just as the kid ducked into Maddy's office. Before Phin got too far ahead of himself, he considered options. They'd hired Louis Three as an assistant. Maddy could have sent him for something. Who knew?

Seconds later, Louis entered the hallway again and ...

"Hello, young buck." Phin tapped his mouse, pausing the video.

Dangling from Louis's previously empty right hand?

Keys.

—————

21

Laptop in hand, Phin hauled ass into the Theater.

Cruz, being a notorious night owl during an active case, sat in his normal spot at the conference table, pounding away on his computer.

His brother flicked his gaze over the top of the screen. "What are you doing up?"

"Couldn't sleep. I found something. I think. I don't know. Maybe."

"You're babbling." Cruz sat back held his hands wide. "And you don't babble. What is it?"

"When Maddy was questioned by the feds, they showed her a video. Neck Tattoo guy at her apartment. He had a key."

Cruz's jaw dropped and anticipating the vicious tongue-lashing he was about to receive for not clueing his brothers in on that little development, Phin held his hands up. "I know."

"Then why didn't you tell us?"

An excellent question Phin had no response to. A sour taste filled his mouth. "I ... uh."

When was the last time he, of all people, was speechless?

Fatigue. That's what this was. Total lack of mental and physical rest.

"Forget it," Cruz said, clearly sensing Phin's impending self-flagellation and giving him a reprieve. "We'll deal with it later. What have you got?"

Cruz. Always willing to give a guy a chance to make things right. Had to love him.

Phin set the laptop on the table, opened it, and entered his password. He brought up the video and spun the laptop. "Thompson sent security footage from the executive suite. I couldn't sleep, so I started going through it."

"You got a hit?"

"Maybe. Thompson's nephew—Louis Three—is interning as an executive assistant." Phin pointed at the laptop. "Watch."

Cruz tapped the mouse pad. "This him?"

"Yep."

A minute later, Cruz sat back and let out a whistle. "We're assuming those are Maddy's keys?"

"He didn't have them in his hand when he walked in. At first, I figured eh, no big deal. Maybe Maddy told him to grab them for her or whatever."

"Did you ask her?"

"It's the middle of the night. I'm not waking her up for that."

He'd also rather not mention exactly where specifically she snoozed.

Phin pointed at the laptop. "Did you see how he walked by, looked inside, kept going and then turned back? He made sure she wasn't in there."

"Suspicious, for sure." Cruz sat forward. "Let's get Zeke down here."

His phone lay next to his laptop on the table, and he tapped it. A ringing sound filled the quiet air, and then abruptly stopped.

"Three-thirty?" Zeke said, his voice carrying the jagged edge of sleep. "This better be good."

"It is. I'm in the Theater with Phin. He has a possible lead."

"Give me five."

Poking at the screen, Cruz sat back, propped his feet up. "I didn't get into you holding out on us. No sense pissing him off when he's half asleep. We'll tell him when he gets here. Now, do you wanna explain what you're doing up at this hour?"

Finally, Phin slid out a chair and dropped into it. "I guess you're the only one allowed to work at night?"

"Not at all. But it's my thing. My *pattern*. You? You sleep."

"Sometimes I can't."

Cruz rolled one hand. "Exactly my point. I know you, little brother. Are you losing it over the shooting?"

Phin shook his head, let out a huff. Cruz, as big of a heart as he had, lacked a sensitivity chip. "*Losing* it? Did you seriously just say that to me?"

"Yeah. If you are, it's normal. I'd be freaked."

Could it be the shooting—and not Maddy sleeping in his bed—tripping him up? "Maybe."

"There's no gray area here. You either are or you aren't. Which is it?"

Phin tilted his head one way, then the other, thinking it through.

Across from him, Cruz put his feet on the floor and

leaned in, knocking on the table. "Listen up. Whatever is going on with you, just say it. Get it out."

"I fucked up."

"Now we're getting somewhere. Is this about that mess with Ash?"

"No. It's ... uh ... Maddy." When the words wouldn't spill from his trap, Phin rolled a hand. As if *that* would help him. "I ..."

"You fucked her."

Freaking Cruz. "No!"

He didn't *fuck* her. *Fucking* was ... impersonal. A means to an end. Something you did with strangers. A quick, meaningless release.

A hook-up.

Definitely not what he did with Maddy.

Cruz held up two hands. "Okay, fine. I get it. Whatever you want to call it, you had sex with her."

"Yeah."

Cruz lowered his hands. "And was it, you know, *casual*?"

"I don't think so."

"For her? Or you?"

Phin scrunched his nose, once again considering the question. "Both?"

"I see."

He sees? What the hell did that mean? "Listen, Dr. Phil, are you going to help me or not?"

His brother laughed. "Would love to, but I'm still trying to figure out what you want me to do. I mean, are you happy about this?"

Yes.

No.

Shit.

"I like her. A lot. I'm comfortable with her. She's amazing. And *kind*. Do you even get how rare that is? Particularly with the company I keep. She has no motives. She doesn't use people."

"I *don't* know that, but you've spent time with her, so if you say so, I believe you."

"I say so. And Zeke is going to lose his mind. She didn't steal those pieces. I know it."

"Yeah. I'm not buying that, either. She's a Girl Scout leader. We clear her and you two live happily ever after." Cruz smacked his hands together. "Good talk."

Phin gawked. "That's your solution? I'm drowning and you're waving goodbye?"

At that, Cruz laughed and sat back again, rocking in his chair. "I'd like to. Believe me. I don't know what to say. You like her. You're comfortable with her. What are you afraid of?"

Afraid. There was that damned word again. But the bigger one, the one that got Phin's attention? Comfortable.

Comfort meant intimacy. Caring.

Taking the schmoozer mask off and letting her know him, know the hurt buried down deep that he'd refused to give oxygen until now. Until Maddy got him all kinds of stirred up.

Thoughts of social events, parties, *women,* invaded his mind. How the hell would he do his job? He wasn't even sure he could operate without using his looks to move women along.

Another nasty little secret.

What had he let himself become?

All this time, he'd done the job, didn't think too hard, and all was fine. Fine, fine, fine.

Except, Maddy.

With her, he could hit pause and live in the moment.

Something he'd never done. Pausing meant time to think. And thinking? For him?

Not good.

Thinking meant obsessing over things he couldn't change. Like becoming a man whore in order to do his job and fulfill his responsibilities to his family.

My fault.

"I'm basically a man whore," he said. "We know that, right?"

Cruz's jaw dropped. "Fuck is this now? Are you high?"

"Stone-cold sober. We don't talk about it, but come on, it's not beneath me to use sex to get information. Some-times, it's necessary."

"That doesn't make you a *man whore.*"

Phin waved it off. "That's not the problem. Crazy as *that* sounds."

A somewhat funny gagging sound came from Cruz who smacked himself on the head with both hands. "What are we *talking* about?"

How to explain this? Phin let out a breath. "I'm willing to use sex to get what we need. I never force it, but, hey, if there's a mutual spark, and it happens," he shrugged, "it happens. Consenting adults. No commitment. Until Maddy came along. Now, my thinking is all screwed up. I'm analyzing too much. Getting comfortable with a woman—with Maddy, the Girl Scout leader—means revealing myself and I'm not exactly proud of who I've become."

There. Said it. Oddly enough, it felt like someone had lifted a building off him, all the weight suddenly gone and letting him breathe. "Until Maddy, I did the job and didn't think too hard. Thinking, for me, is a downward spiral that leads to the fact that it's all my fault."

"I'm so confused. *What's* your fault?"

"I could have gone into politics. I chose BARS instead. My ego lets me pretend my anger is with BARS, but really, it's me I'm angry at."

"Why are you angry about BARS?"

The question came from behind him. From Zeke.

Phin spun, spotted his brother standing by the wall separating the entry and the open area. He couldn't have been there long. Cruz would have spotted him and said something.

"Well," Cruz said, "welcome to the fun."

22

"It's *not* BARS," Phin said, still facing Zeke. "That's what I said. Since when do you eavesdrop?"

Zeke walked to the table, took his seat at the end. "You guys called me. If you didn't want me to hear, you shouldn't have been talking."

"Phin fucked Maddy," Cruz offered and Phin nearly launched himself across the table to beat the ever-loving crap out of his brother.

Before he could set Cruz straight, Zeke drilled him with a look. "You fucked Maddy?"

If the two of them didn't stop using that word, there'd be a homicide tonight at Chez Blackwell.

How did this conversation spin so far out of control? "I didn't *fuck* her!"

"My apologies," Cruz said, half laughing. "Would you prefer we call it making love?"

Phin pointed a steady finger at him. "Keep it up and I'll lay you out."

"Both of you," Zeke said, "shut the fuck up. Phin, please tell me you didn't sleep with her."

"He slept with her. Now he's freaking out about some personal crisis that makes absolutely no sense. To me anyway. And I'm not exactly dumb."

Zeke shifted back to Phin. Gave him the here-comes-a-lecture face. "You're thinking too much, aren't you? I've talked to you about this. It's not healthy. What's this personal crisis?"

"He thinks he's a man whore—his words, not mine—because he bangs women at fundraisers."

Enough. How much humiliation did he need to endure?

Phin got to his feet. "You are *such* an asshole."

"You're not a man whore," Zeke said, his tone so flat he might as well have been reading a grocery list. "Why would you say that?"

"It's true." Phin met Zeke's eye. "When I need to get information, sometimes I'll go there." He cleared his throat. "You know. With women."

"And?"

Phin snorted. "Fellas, I gotta say, if we're all okay with me trading sex for information, we've got enormous problems."

"First of all," Cruz sat forward, his big shoulders seeming to widen, "you're not doing that. You make it sound transactional."

"Isn't it?"

"Hell no," Cruz said. "We all do things to move a case forward. I sit here in the middle of the night having conversations with scumbags who make my skin crawl. Last week, I forwarded to Ash a conversation I had with a collector who's into child porn."

Phin knew this. Intellectually, he understood it. Hearing it, though? Having Cruz confirm it, twisted Phin's stomach.

"Dude," Cruz continued, "sometimes we do things we despise. I don't know if it's right or wrong, but I know for sure it doesn't make you a man whore. And, can I just say, I should kill you for making me say man whore?"

"He's right," Zeke said. "That being said, *no one* expects you to use sex as a tool. When it comes to Maddy, I'm not blind. I see you like her."

"I do."

"And I don't think I have to remind you that you can't share certain things."

The sacred NDA. Phin gave him a hard look. "You keep pounding on the NDA. I'm not violating it. I wouldn't. And fuck you for questioning my loyalty."

Zeke gawked. "When have I *ever* questioned your loyalty? Are you high?"

"I asked the same thing," Cruz added.

"And I'll tell you the same thing I told Cruz. No. I'm not high. I'm about as clearheaded as I've been since Ash went to the feds. I gave up my career aspirations to be here."

"No one forced you."

"Right. And who the hell was gonna do it? Cruz? I think we've just seen that he's the king of inappropriate."

"Damn straight," Cruz said. "No argument there."

Zeke shot him a look. "You're not helping." He came back to Phin. "So ... what? You want out? Is that what you're telling me?"

"No."

Tipping his head back, Zeke stared up at the ceiling. "Nearly four a.m., I'm tired. Help me not murder him."

Cruz laughed and sat back again, propping his feet on the table to enjoy the show.

"Zeke," Phin said, "I'm not trying to make you insane. Yeah, I think too much, but this last week? Watching Maddy lose the job —"

"She didn't lose it."

"Fine. Watching her be put on leave when she loves that job. You saw it. That first day when we toured the space, you saw her passion. She comes alive talking about the exhibits. I don't have that. I don't hate what I do for BARS. For the most part, I enjoy the work. The recoveries. Working with my family. The schedule. But I'm not passionate about it. I don't wake up excited every morning, and that's gotta change."

"I agree. How do we make that happen for you?"

If Cruz was the brother always willing to offer a pass, Zeke was the solution-finder. Always. No matter what it meant for him personally, he'd figure out a way to help.

"I don't know. I have room in my schedule to work for BARS and do something that makes me feel ..." He paused, searching for the word. For that one thing he needed. "Inspired."

"Okay. Obviously, we'll need to talk to Rohan about this." He jerked his chin at Cruz. "I'm gonna assume you're okay with him possibly working part-time for BARS?"

"I'm good. We've got Neuman almost up to speed, so that helps. We need Phin working his contacts. Everything else we can handle on our own."

"Thank you," Phin said.

Cruz met his eye. "For wanting you to be satisfied? No one in this house should thank anyone for that. We all deserve it. No question."

"Figure out what you want," Zeke said. "I'll support it. As long as you can give BARS some time for business development and working your contacts, we're good. Life's too fucking short, Phin. Now, what did you call me down here for?"

Back to business. Thank God. Phin pointed at his laptop

still sitting in front of Cruz, who shoved it close enough for Phin to cue up the video.

He slid it to Zeke and hit play. "Take a look."

Seconds later, Zeke tapped the mouse pad and peered up at Phin. "Who is he?"

"Thompson's nephew. Louis Three. Thompson hired him as an intern in the executive suite. Don't scream at me for what I'm about to say. I should have told you. That's on me. I apologize."

Zeke whirled a finger. "Get on with it."

Excellent. No lecture. Maybe he should wake Zeke up in the middle of the night more often if it got him off the hook so easily.

Phin nodded. "When the feds questioned Maddy, they showed her a video of one perp—the now very dead one—entering her apartment. He had a key."

To his credit, Zeke sat still, taking in the information, while a muscle in his jaw jumped. Big brother was definitely pissed.

"Oh-*kay*. That's why you wanted the additional security footage?"

"Yeah. She freaked—for good reason—that this guy had her key. She said she leaves her keys in her desk drawer all day. We figured someone swiped them." He pointed at the laptop. "I found this right before we called you down here."

Zeke shifted to Cruz. "Do we have anything on the nephew?"

"I don't. Rohan is checking out employees."

"Let's not wake him up. There's nothing we can do now, anyway. First thing, we'll call Thompson. See if we can run over there and show him this. Maybe the nephew will be working and we can ask why he stole Maddy's keys."

· · ·

Maddy rolled over, sliding her hand across the mattress in search of Phin and all that luscious warmth she wanted a whole lot more of.

Empty space.

She opened her eyes, let them adjust to the bit of artificial light sneaking under the closed door.

She rolled to her back, shook off her brain fog and reached for her phone on the nightstand, the movement lighting up the screen.

3:57.

And no Phin.

A night owl. Or early riser. Something she most definitely was not. But she wouldn't go there. Wouldn't start making mental notes, analyzing every aspect of the relationship—if it was a relationship—and picking it apart.

For once, she'd force herself to take it slow. To not fall too hard, too soon.

For now, she'd focus on finding Phin. Dressed in the T-shirt he'd given her to sleep in, she walked to the door, her feet sinking into the deep fibers of the area rug.

To avoid possibly waking him up if he'd fallen asleep on the sofa, she carefully eased the door open and peeped into the living room.

No Phin.

Huh. He liked to work at the bistro table. He'd mentioned that. She left the bedroom, checked the table.

Nothing. A quick search yielded an empty bathroom and balcony and no note.

Phin was gone.

At least he trusted her, but who did that? Left her in his own bed without at least letting her know?

Don't analyze.

There were at least a hundred reasons he'd leave. The

first being he knew she was exhausted and didn't want to wake her. Which, eh-hem, makes him a nice guy.

But what now? Should she go back to bed? The one that wasn't hers. Or return to the guest suite?

Phone still in hand, she found Phin's name in her contacts. Before she could tap the icon to call, the apparently unlocked entry door came open and Phin stepped inside looking seriously sexy, with his hair poking in odd directions and a jaw covered with dark stubble. The wrinkled T-shirt and shorts only added to the just-rolled-out-of-bed look. Only Phin could make it all look ... inviting.

"Hi." She held up the phone. "I was just calling you."

"Hi, yourself."

His gaze slid to his T-shirt and held there for a second, his eyes narrowing while he pursed those amazing lips that had taken her on one heck of a ride a few hours ago.

Too bad she couldn't read minds because the way he was looking at her might be regret.

Might also be yearning.

Time would tell. "I just got up." She conjured a hopefully playful smile. "I thought you left me."

Smile or not, the minute the words left her mouth, she hated herself. Hated what probably sounded like paranoia. Or desperation.

He turned back, gesturing to the door. "I had a meeting with Zeke and Cruz."

"At four in the morning? Is everything okay?"

Because, really? When they'd gone to sleep, he hadn't been too concerned with work. Now, after two rounds of extremely amazing sex, he suddenly had a meeting?

Or was he avoiding her?

"Yeah," he said. "We ... uh ..." He waved it off.

Avoiding her. Excellent. Maybe all last night had been

was two people finding a soft place to land after a traumatic experience. If that were the case, better to know sooner than later. Even if it did sting.

She lifted her chin. Pointed to the bedroom. "I'll get dressed and head back to the guest suite. Give you your space."

"*My* space? Is that what you want?"

"No. But I think it's what you want."

His eyebrows shot up. "Excuse me? I've barely said two dozen words. How did you get to that assumption?"

Uh-oh. Chill bumps shot up her arms. She'd screwed up. Already. "I got up in the middle of the night. You were gone. Not even a note. I thought you ..." What was she doing? Besides making a fool of herself. "Forget it."

"Maddy, I just told you I had a meeting with Zeke and Cruz. We don't work normal hours. We work when we work. I woke up and couldn't get back to sleep, so I came out here to check my e-mail and found the executive suite footage we asked for."

The burn of humiliation scorched her cheeks. He'd been nothing but kind and she'd automatically thought the worst. It had to stop. "Did you find something?"

"Maybe." He held up his hands. "But I'm sorry. I can't talk about it. Zeke's pain-in-the-ass NDA."

Uh-huh. He'd literally licked every inch—*every* inch—of her and he couldn't tell her what was on that video? As if she'd tell someone? Good for him for being a team player, but really? How insulting that he didn't trust her.

"I see," she said, the last word coming out way sharper than she'd intended.

He lifted his hand to his forehead and squeezed. "Please don't do this to me. There will be things I can't share. You know that."

Yes. She did know. However, if the roles were reversed, had Phin been the one tormenting himself over being a suspected thief, and she could relieve his mind, she'd do it. She'd trust him.

And, hey, she might be a tad pissed about that. She fought the urge to cross her arms—terrible body language there. Instead, she kept her hands at her sides, fingers relaxed. "You've been clear about the NDA. I guess I'm confused. I've shared everything with you. Even when my lawyer told me not to, I *trusted* you."

"This has nothing to do with trust."

"Doesn't it?"

"No. This is about loyalty to my family. We have a business that runs on confidentiality. Right now, I can't tell you what I met with Zeke and Cruz about. Tomorrow? Maybe."

Maybe. How very generous of him. "I guess that's that, then."

He pulled a face. The are-you-kidding? one. "Now you're pissed at me," he said.

Statement, not a question.

"I'm not pissed." Yes, she was. "Look at it from my side. I woke up, and you were gone. I thought—"

"Yeah. I know what you thought."

"I wasn't done speaking. You left and then you came back and can't tell me what you met with your brothers about. I'll admit, after what we went through yesterday and the night we just had together, the fact that you don't feel *comfortable* confiding in me ... I don't know," she flapped her arms, "stings. I guess."

"Well, how about next time you give me half a chance to explain before jumping to the conclusion I was walking out on you. Or that you don't think I'm *comfortable*. After last night, what would make you think I'd bolt? I let you sleep in my own damned bed! If I didn't want you there, trust me, you wouldn't have been there."

He turned, walked into the galley kitchen, whipped open the fridge, grabbed a carton of orange juice, and held it up. "You want something?"

Phin Blackwell—super-schmoozer—running from an argument.

Fascinating.

"I'm good," she said. "I like a level of honesty in my relationships."

He set the carton down and held up a finger. "Honesty or intimacy? They're two different things. I've never *not* been honest with you. So, think about what you're saying to me."

"Intimacy. Yes. Better word. I love our conversations, that's all. I'd like to know you better. To know—"

"Everything."

Yes. And why not? She deserved that. A man who'd share his life with her. "What's wrong with me wanting to learn your hopes and desires? What you want from life. If that's everything, then yes, I guess that's what I want."

"In the first *week*? I've spent most of my adult life keeping secrets and you want me to flip a switch and become someone I have no idea how to be."

"That's not what I want."

He tipped his head back and snorted. "Sure seems like it, babe."

If he thought he was frustrated, he should jump to her side. She shook her head, fought the urge to scream because, you know what?

This sucked.

She drew a hard breath, dragging air into her nose and holding it a second. *Get it together, here.* What she didn't want to be was a hysterical female. Rational Maddy. That was her. Even when it killed her.

She released the breath, counted to five, and battled the slowly building tornado inside. "What it seems like to me," she said in her rational Maddy voice, "is that you have information that could give me,"—she pinched her thumb and index finger together—"a *smidge* of hope that I'll be cleared of this mess, and you won't do it. Everyone thinks I'm a thief. Worse, I've dragged your family into the middle of it. I'm literally trapped in your house. Can't go outside the gates or the press will hound me and you have no idea how horrible that feels. To know I brought this to your very private family. All I want is to go *home*. And to see my mom and my siblings. To feel like my life hasn't been flipped upside down. I can't do *any* of that."

Yikes. That was way louder than she'd intended.

Too bad.

He could help her. Could give her something to hang on to. He could look into her eyes and tell her they'd be okay. *She'd* be okay.

And he wouldn't do it.

And here she was, right where she said she wouldn't let herself go. Falling too hard too fast and expecting things from him he couldn't deliver.

Way to go, Maddy. Fist bump to you, sister.

She raised her hands. "Let's stop. I'm exhausted and probably asking too much of you. I'll get dressed and go back to my—" Not hers. No. "To the guest suite. After I get some rest, I'll figure out a plan."

He lifted his hands, his own exhaustion shown by his puffy eyes. "What the hell does that mean? A plan for what?"

"That's the problem, Phin. I don't know."

She headed for the bedroom, Phin hot on her heels. "Maddy, hang on a second. Yesterday was tough. We're both strung out and tired. Can we please ..."

She spun back, halting him. "Please what?"

"I don't know. Hit pause? Get some sleep and talk about this when we're fresh."

Excellent idea. "That's what I'm doing. I'm leaving. I'm giving us both space."

He cocked his head, studying her, his gaze moving over her face, and even now, all churned up and angry, she wanted him. Wanted him touching her. Kissing her. Making her feel that amazing heat that came with him. Always.

Dammit.

"There's that word again," he said. "Space. That's what you want, not me."

Did she? She didn't know. But this, this internal mayhem, wasn't working.

She waited a beat, the hesitation bringing his gaze back to hers and locking on. "Yes," she said. "That's what I want."

He stepped back as if she'd struck him. As if the mighty Phin Blackwell, conqueror of men and women alike, couldn't believe it.

"Well," he said, holding his arms wide, his face solid stone. "No one is forcing you to stay. If you want to go, then go."

23

THE SOUND OF A KNOCK ON HIS DOOR ROUSED PHIN FROM what couldn't be considered sleep. It was more like a war between conscious and not. He forced his eyes open, battling the grit that might as well have been glue trying to keep them closed.

Sunlight sliced between the curtains, the glare damned painful. Jesus, he was tired. Physically and emotionally strung out.

No wonder he didn't like to think too much. Between he and Maddy almost getting shot and trying not to piss off his brothers, all this emotional nonsense exhausted him.

The knock sounded again. "Phin?"

Zeke's voice.

Instantly awake, Phin rolled out of bed, adjusted his basketball shorts, grabbed a T-shirt and slid it on as he hustled to the door. "Coming!"

He swung the door open and Zeke, freshly showered and looking way more rested than Phin, stepped in. "Sorry I woke you. I tried your cell."

His cell? How did he not hear it? He glanced around, spotted it on the coffee table, and picked it up. Dead.

Christ almighty. When was the last time he'd let that happen? Refusing to admit his carelessness, he tucked the phone in his pocket. "Sorry. Didn't hear it. What's up?"

"I talked to Thompson. He knows about Brendan Eckert dying. Now, we're heading to the Center to show him the video you found."

Okay. That was worth waking him up for. He needed to get showered and dressed ASAP. "Does he know what's on it?"

"No. I told him we wanted his take on a few things. Figured we'd show it to him cold."

"Smart move. He's a politician. Any warning gives him time to prep. This way, you get his initial gut reaction. Plus, if you tell him why we're coming, the first thing he'll do is pull the footage himself or call the kid."

"That's what I was thinking."

Phin nodded and started toward his bedroom to pull fresh clothes from his closet. "Give me fifteen to shower and I'll meet you downstairs."

"No."

He stopped walking, stared right through the bedroom doorway for a second, then angled back. "No, what?"

"No, you're not coming." Before Phin could muster an argument, Zeke's hands shot up. "After what happened with you and Maddy yesterday, I'm not taking a chance. It's too dangerous. That shooter might be ready to eliminate witnesses."

Tired or not, Phin had to keep his cool. Yelling never got him anywhere. He slowly turned, choosing his words as he moved. "If they were after us, they'd have gotten us yesterday."

"You don't know that."

"I've been involved in this case from the start. Every step. Now you're freezing me out?"

Zeke folded his arms, spread his feet, and pushed his shoulders back. The I'm-in-charge stance. "You and Maddy will be safe here. Mom won't have to worry and neither will I. It's one meeting. We can video you in, if you want."

What he wanted was to go to this goddamned meeting, see what was what with Louis Three and find those damned jewels. Maybe then he and Maddy could get back on track. Whatever that track might be.

But Zeke was dug in. The posture? Dead giveaway.

"I guess I'm staying here then."

Zeke nodded. "Rohan and Cruz will come with me. We'll call you as soon as we're done."

"Thanks for that."

"Come on. It's not a punishment. It's for your safety. And Maddy's."

"Yeah. I get it."

Not really, but Zeke could be headstrong and when he got like this, arguing wouldn't help.

And, hey, Phinny boy, you can take a nap.

"Good," Zeke said. "Please stay in the house until we get back."

What. The fuck? Were they toddlers now? Not allowed to play outside. "Uh, negative. When did I become your prisoner?"

The smart-ass comment earned him a massive eye roll. Yes, he was working Zeke's last nerve. Couldn't help it. Nothing. *Nothing* seemed to go his way.

A load of cement settled onto his shoulders, the weight pressing in on him. *So fucking tired.*

"Knock it off with the drama," Zeke said. "I want the two

of you safe until we get back. Then we'll figure out next steps. Okay?"

Phin looked back, peering into the bedroom where he'd spent half the night in paradise with Maddy.

Somehow, that great night had turned into purgatory. "Whatever, Zeke. Go to your meeting."

"Look at me."

What the ...? Phin lifted his head, met his brother's gaze, ready to blast him. Phin may have been the youngest, but he was way too old for orders.

"Tell me," Zeke said before Phin got a word out, "you will stay inside."

"Now you think I'm *lying*? Yes, I'll stay inside. Happy?"

"Not even close." He turned, headed for the door. "Get some food and rest. We'll huddle up when we get back."

HALF AN HOUR LATER, AFTER A SHOWER THAT DID NOTHING TO lighten his mood, Phin strode into the kitchen to find pancakes, sausage, bacon, and biscuits sitting in the warming oven.

His mother. Godsend.

He plugged his phone cord into the socket on the side of the island, checked that it was charging, grabbed coffee, and then piled a plate high before sitting at the counter. With the amount of food in front of him, he'd have to hit the gym. Not a bad idea, actually. Bust off calories and stress and maybe he'd fall asleep afterward. Get some rest, as Zeke had suggested.

Stabbing at the pancakes, he shoved a forkful in his mouth, barely chewing before swallowing. His interest in food right now was about fuel and not flavor. The quicker he got out of here, the less chance he had of running into Maddy.

Yes, he was still pissed about their fight. How the hell did everything go sideways so fast?

Women.

This was why he didn't like emotional entanglements. Too much trouble.

And aggravation.

"Morning."

He swiveled, found Maddy standing at the kitchen entrance. She wore black leggings and a white top and had pulled her hair into a ponytail. That might be the biggest tragedy so far today. He loved that mane of hair. Loved having his hands in it.

Immediately, his mind drifted back to hours earlier. Her head on his chest, the two of them laughing about her morning frizz horror stories.

Then he remembered he was pissed at her.

"Morning."

Phin pointed his fork toward the warmer. "My mom made breakfast. Can I make you a plate?"

His mother hadn't raised them to be inhospitable. Even if he was mad.

"I'll do it. Thank you."

She entered the kitchen, her gaze glued to the wall. Bypassing him, she moved to the oven.

He stabbed at another hunk of pancakes, pretending the woman on the other side of the island was an apparition. Better yet, he'd pretend she wasn't even there.

She wanted space. She'd get it. No problem there.

But even he, in the midst of his freeze out, had to admit this sucked. He enjoyed Maddy. Loved her smile and her drive and her passion.

Her idealism and kindness.

In short, she gave him hope for humanity.

Suddenly, his idea of a cold war didn't seem worth it. What the hell were they doing?

He lifted his head, watched her stack a couple of pancakes and bacon, and then slide over to the fridge for butter. She took her time, getting a precise amount on the knife and carefully spreading it across the entire top of the pancake, hitting the edges.

Maddy. So freaking cute.

And someone he might not be able to live without.

I'm so screwed.

"I wanted to be a senator," he blurted.

Butter knife in hand, she looked over at him. "Pardon?"

Once again, he mind-traveled back to last night and the fun they'd had. The care they'd taken with each other while having said fun.

He cleared his throat. "When we were fighting, you said you wanted me to tell you my hopes and desires. Growing up, before I came to work for BARS, that was my dream. To be a senator. To make positive change. To help people. That's why Senator Blakely irritates me. He's been in office thirty years and it's not about his constituents. It's about his ego and power and making sure people kiss his puny ass. I hate that."

Her mouth dropped open, and his body froze. What was he doing? Should have kept his damned mouth shut. This was what *talking* got him. Regrets.

Him, a senator. Who'd believe it?

Using his fork, he pointed at the knife still in Maddy's hand. "If you intend to stab me, grab something sharper."

Her dark brows drew together, squeezing the skin

between them. Then she looked down at the knife aimed right at him and burst out laughing.

She set the knife down. "I could totally see you as a senator. You're great with people."

Relief hit him like a twenty-foot wave, knocking him off balance. She didn't think he was ... what? An idiot? A fool?

Maddy rested her hands on the island, focusing on him rather than her food. "So, do it. Why not?"

"Um, besides the illegal breaking and entering we do when executing recoveries?"

She waved that off. "Spin-control. You, of all people, would make it work."

"My time for that is gone. I've made peace with it. Besides, after spending time with guys like Blakely, do I really want that? Some of them are straight-up toxic. I talked to Zeke though. This morning, in fact, about doing something else part-time. Something for me."

She blinked, then blinked again. "Wow. That's big."

Massive understatement there. "You inspired me."

The look she gave him, all wide-eyed horror, made him laugh.

"Me?" she said. "The one currently under federal investigation?"

"Yes. You. That day we came to the Thompson Center. Seeing you talk about the exhibits and your passion for the work, I don't have that." His half-eaten meal, which he had no desire to finish, sat in front of him. He pushed the plate away and peered across the island, holding her gaze while he sorted out the right words. "Look, Maddy, I don't know what happens when this case is over. I'll never be a chatterbox, and I've got huge hang-ups, but I love spending time with you."

"Phin—"

"Wait. You wanted me to talk. I'm talking. Hear me out. Okay?"

She nodded. "Sorry for interrupting."

"With the crew I live with, I'm used to it. The idea of being a senator, I've never told anyone that. Ever. In this family, we don't share our business. It's not a criticism or complaint, it's how we've been raised. Stay tough and keep your mouth shut. I've felt like I failed myself. That I didn't have it in me to chase my dream. For you, that might seem like simple conversation. Me? It's sharing a secret I've held since before puberty. You accused me of not trusting you. Well, I just told you something I've never spoken of. Sharing my feelings isn't easy. You need to know that."

Finally, she reached across the island, grasping his hand. "Thank you for telling me. It's a gift, really. You're right; to me, it *is* conversation. Now I understand why it's hard for you."

"*Brutally* hard. But I hate fighting with you. It makes me miserable. And strung out."

"Me too. I picked up my phone a dozen times this morning, but I didn't think you'd want to talk."

"Honestly, I didn't. Until I saw you standing there and all I could think about was how happy I was last night. Then I knew I wanted to try. You have to meet me halfway, though."

She bobbed her head. "Absolutely. I don't expect—" She shook her head. "I don't want you to think you always have to give in. That my expectations are more than you can do. I can't stand the idea of making you feel that way. I do need to be clued in, so I know I'm hitting a hot button. This morning, I thought you didn't trust me. Now I know it's hard for you to express certain things."

"Thank you, sweet baby Jesus!"

She rolled her eyes, smacked his hand, and grabbed her

plate, probably to warm the food that was no doubt cold by now.

She popped the plate in the microwave, pushed a couple of buttons, and faced him again. "How about we take it slow? When all this craziness ends, we'll go on our first official date. We're a bit out of order with the whole multiple orgasms last night, but hey, whatever."

"As long as being out of order doesn't mean we can't do more of the multiple orgasms, I'm on board."

The microwave dinged, and she retrieved the plate, carrying it around and setting it down beside him.

Then she smacked her hand over the back of his neck and hit him with a lip-lock that had him rethinking his workout and a nap. Her tongue darted into his mouth, exploring, gliding in and out, in and out and oh, this woman. He'd never get enough of the whole good-girl, bad-girl fantasy.

He backed up an inch, lifted his hands to her cheeks. "I'm crazy about you. I'm all torn up."

She kissed him again. A quick one this time that made his brewing erection pulse.

She sat next to him, a sly grin on her face. Clearly, she understood the condition she'd left him in.

"Sorry, big boy. I'm starving." She picked up her fork, but leaned over, getting close to his ear. "After we eat, maybe we can continue doing things out of order."

Oh, yeah, they could.

"And I'm crazy about you, too." She went back to her food, breaking off a dainty piece of pancake. "Now, what did Zeke say about you doing something you're passionate about?"

"He was surprisingly calm. As long as I can work part-time for BARS, he's fine with it."

She picked up the pitcher of maple syrup and drenched her pancakes. After the time and precision she'd taken with the butter, this was a puzzle. How the hell did she eat it with so much syrup?

A lot to learn.

"You know," she said, "why don't you talk to Kayla? Maybe you can work for her part-time. You go to political functions, anyway. You could double-dip."

He snorted. "Double-dip?"

"Hey, buddy, don't pooh-pooh it. You'd make connections for BARS while convincing the Senator Blakelys of the world to pass whatever bill Kayla is pushing. It's a win-win."

He swiveled to face her. "You know, you might be on to something there."

"There's no might about it. I'm definitely on to something."

Before he could respond, his phone rattled against the counter. Of course. Just when he wanted a second to process Maddy's not-so-crazy idea, his phone interrupts. He glanced at the screen—*hello*—and tapped.

"Rory, what can I do for you?"

24

PHIN HELD THE PHONE TO HIS EAR AND STARED STRAIGHT ahead, not even glancing at Maddy. He didn't need the distraction of whatever that citrusy scent of her shampoo was. All he knew was he liked it.

"Hey," Rory said. "Got a lead for you."

A lead. Excellent. "I'm listening."

"I received a call early this morning. A contact of mine is in touch with someone who knows where the Thompson jewels are. Including the queen's collection."

Now he needed privacy. Yes, they'd just had a blowout over him not sharing, but this?

Not only was it BARS business, she might get her hopes up, and this situation was already emotionally charged. He didn't need to light a match next to it.

He swiveled, got to his feet, and squeezed Maddy's arm. "I need to take this outside."

"No problem," she said, her voice a tad too chirpy, but they'd agreed to meet halfway.

With BARS, this was halfway.

He strode to the back door and stepped outside into the late morning heat and humidity that doused him.

A bird swooped low, darting by him, heading for the cover of distant trees. With this heat, who could blame him?

"If I'm understanding," he said into his phone, "you've got a guy who has a guy. How are we supposed to vet this?"

"You trust me, that's how."

Good luck there, pal. Interesting timing since he'd just had the big trust convo with Maddy. "No offense, Rory. I don't trust anyone."

Except, apparently, Maddy. Her he trusted. Phinny, Phinny, Phinny. *Focus.*

"I've got proof," Rory said.

"What kind?"

"Brendan Eckert."

Phin stared off into the thick trees where his bird friend had disappeared.

Brendan Eckert. The name of the guy who got blown away on the street yesterday hadn't been released yet. The only reason Phin knew was Ash.

If Rory knew, someone who knew Eckert must have told him.

"Brendan Eckert?"

Playing dumb sometimes netted excellent returns. Plus, he'd learned long ago that people like Rory need to hear themselves talk. Call it ego, call it needing to fill space, call it whatever, as long as Phin got what he wanted.

"Yes," Rory said. "I'm sure you know him, given he died right in front of you. My contact works for the Veras. He was part of the original job. Brendan Eckert went rogue. You know that since he was trying to make a deal with you. Vera found out about it and ... Well, you were there and don't need the details."

He definitely didn't, when there was a homicide investigation going on. It was all hearsay anyway, but he'd give Maggie a heads-up. Let her know to put heat on the Veras.

"Who's this coming forward now, then?" Phin asked. "Why, after almost getting my ass shot yesterday, would I take a chance again?"

"He's scared."

"With good reason."

"My guy says Vera panicked. Called him after the Eckert shooting and told him to move the jewels. He wasn't sure how much Eckert had told you."

Zeke may have been right about the danger. And here Phin was standing in the open after he'd promised to stay inside.

Then again, if someone had bypassed the security and was hiding in the trees, Phin would be dead by now.

Definitely not among the unliving. He took a few steps to his right, peeked back toward the trees, just in case. "Vera knows who I am?"

"Not sure. He knows Eckert was meeting with someone. My guy is shitting the bed. He and Vera are the only ones who know where the jewels are. The feds are gonna figure out Eckert worked for Vera. It's only a matter of time before Vera gets arrested. My guy, too."

"He's bolting and needs cash."

"Precisely. He wants the eleven mil Louis Pierre promised Eckert. If you're interested, you'll have to move fast. He'll be gone by tomorrow."

Which meant they'd have to recover the jewels today. And with no time to prepare.

Phin tipped his head back, stared up at an impossibly blue sky. They had nothing. No schematics of the target building, no intel on security, nothing.

They'd be flying blind.

"Tomorrow? Jesus, Rory."

"That's the deal, Phin. I'll get you a meeting location and call you back."

Like hell. "After yesterday, *I'll* get the location. It'll be somewhere safe, but I'll control the environment. Call you back."

Phin disconnected and, further risking getting shot by the imaginary boogeyman in the trees, took a second to get organized.

Updating his brothers came first. But, knowing them, they'd insist on coming back for planning. A total waste of time considering they'd nailed Louis Three on stealing Maddy's keys.

If the kid was somehow involved, they needed answers from him.

Divide and conquer. That's what had to happen. Inside, Maddy no doubt watched him through the window. The minute he stepped inside, she'd be on him.

"Get a plan together, Phinny boy," he muttered.

Plan first. Then, he'd call Zeke, inform him of said plan and not offer any options. Or, better yet, maybe he wouldn't call Zeke and just do the meeting.

Easier to beg forgiveness than seek permission.

Dividing and conquering was one thing, going to a meeting alone? Was he that stupid?

No.

Which meant he needed help. And a plan. He tapped his phone against his free hand.

Meeting place.

Somewhere safe and guaranteed not to have a replay of yesterday. Hell, the only place that gave him that kind of confidence was their own house, and there was no way he'd do that. No way.

A niggling thought streamed, his brain zeroing-in on his conversation with Reid the day before.

Dude! I would have signed your damned NDA and let you use the training center for a meeting.

He must really be tired if he was considering asking his cousin for help. Phin shook his head, somehow hoping he'd knock those words straight out of his mind.

Not only would Zeke kill him and make him that statue after all, if Phin wasn't willing to do the meeting here, it wasn't fair to ask Reid. Not when his mother and pregnant wife lived on the same property.

He offered.

Phin got moving, pacing the yard, getting some blood flow going to clear his thoughts. Reid never did anything without confidence. And, yes, he had offered.

Wouldn't hurt to at least explore the idea. Then, if Phin didn't like it, for whatever reason, he'd can it.

An exploratory conversation. That's all.

Phin swiped at his phone, found his cousin's name in his contact list. Two rings in, Reid picked up.

"What's up?" he said, by way of greeting.

"Hey."

"Y'all okay?"

"We're good. I ... uh ..."

An image of Brendan Eckert's body filled his mind. This wasn't right.

Not after what happened yesterday. Not after he wouldn't be willing to have a meeting at his own home. Phin waved a hand. "Forget it. Never mind."

"Phin, if you hang up on me, I'll tie you to my bumper

and drag your ass over gravel. Mess up that pretty face some."

He'd probably do it, too. Still, Phin laughed. "You're an asshole."

"I'm a busy asshole. What do you need?"

"Nothing. I changed my mind."

"Why?"

Because it's not right. Because it'd make me a helluva hypocrite. "Some things I won't ask family to do."

"I'll ask again. What do you need?"

Goddamned Reid. Stubborn as the day was long. Phin started pacing again, burning off some energy. "I need to set up a meeting. Somewhere I can control the environment. The only place I can think of is our house. Which I'm not willing to do. I'm also not willing to ask you to do that. I'll figure something else out and everyone stays safe. Let me go. Got shit to do."

"Just hold on. Let me think a minute. This meeting? Who's it with?"

Phin relayed only the need-to-know information. His brothers on their way to a separate meeting, Phin flying solo, their contact ready to bolt, possibly doing a recovery that very day.

"It's one guy?" Reid asked.

"Yes. I'll insist on it."

"And Zeke is okay with you having this meeting?"

Phin hesitated. "He doesn't know, and probably not."

Reid whistled. "You're brave."

"Or stupid. Sometimes they're one and the same."

"True. Let me help you. We can work through it."

We? Phin let out a breath he'd apparently been holding, relief swarming him. Not alone. He'd known it, but with Zeke and his brothers gone, that nasty thought had wormed its way into the back of his psyche.

Now he had an ally from the strangest of places. Considering the Blackwell-Steele relationship had been distant over the years.

"If we do it right," Reid said, "I don't have a problem with you having the meeting here."

"When I was thinking about doing it at our place, my plan was to blindfold him. Even then, it was risky. Once we took the blindfold off—unless we have this meeting in a closet—he'd see our workspace. I can't risk that. If you have an office with no windows, we could make it work. I blindfold him until we get him into that office. He won't even see where we are. When the meeting is done, blindfold goes back on and we drive him to his car."

"I have an office that'll work."

Yeah. Phin liked this. He needed to keep his mind sharp. Not distracted wondering if he'd fucked up by bringing the guy to their home. "I swear to you, I'll make sure everyone stays safe. I've got this."

"With the arsenal I have here, this schmuck would be crazy to try anything. He's probably nuts anyway attempting this deal, but whatever. Not my problem. Meeting here will keep you from getting your ass shot off. *Again.*"

Good old Reid. Couldn't resist that one jab. Although Phin deserved it.

"Thank you," Phin said. "I didn't—"

"Shut the fuck up, Mary. Let's do this."

WHAT SEEMED LIKE AN HOUR LATER, PHIN STRODE THROUGH the back door, his long, lean frame loose, arms at his sides, his pace steady, but unhurried.

If he was upset, one would never know it from his body language.

Maddy knew.

Plus, his face told the tale. Even in the short time she'd known him, she'd learned enough, studied him enough, to recognize his mood shifts. The smile that flashed a little too bright. The slightly raised eyebrows that feigned interest.

All of it a smokescreen to hide what was really going on.

She finished rinsing her plate and set it in the dishwasher along with her silverware and wiped her hands dry on the dishtowel, hanging it exactly how Lynette had left it on the oven handle.

Phin picked up the plate with his half-eaten meal and dumped the contents in the trash.

"You were out there awhile," Maddy said. "Everything all right?"

"Yeah." He rinsed the plate and carefully placed it behind hers in the dishwasher. "The first call was Rory, the guy I met with on Saturday."

Using his foot, he closed the dishwasher—his mother would probably kill him for that—and dried his hands on the towel.

She resisted the urge to straighten it and concentrated on the more important matter of Rory. "Did he have news?"

"Maybe. Someone else has come forward looking to collect the reward."

The ever-present blast of hope shot straight from her gut and she reminded herself not to expect too much. After all, she'd felt hopeful the day before and that got them barely escaping a bullet—or six. "One of the thieves?"

"He claims the guy was part of the heist. He didn't say in what context. However, the guy knows where the jewels are. *Says* he moved them last night. After Eckert got shot. His boss was afraid Eckert told us where they were and wanted them moved."

Maddy tried to wrap her mind around the idea of this person double-crossing his boss when someone else who'd attempted the same thing was now in a morgue. The thought terrified her, sent her pancakes tumbling in her stomach. She shook her head. "I don't understand why he'd risk it after what happened to Brendan Eckert."

"He's freaking out now, that's why. Afraid the Veras will take him out because he knows where the jewels are."

"No honor among thieves, I suppose."

"Anyway, I called Reid. He's gonna let us use his training center for a meeting. I called Rory. We're set for eleven."

Wait. *What?* "Eleven? This *morning*? Your brothers agreed to that?"

"No. They're on their way to meet with Thompson."

"Did something happen?"

For a few seconds, Phin hesitated and she put her hand up. "You don't have to tell me."

"I shouldn't, but I will. It's the reason I left the suite this morning. I was reviewing security video from the Center. I found Louis Three sneaking into your office. He walked out with keys in his hand."

Keys. Maybe hers? "Mine?"

Phin shrugged. "That's why the guys went to meet with Thompson. To see why he was poking around in your office."

Louis III? Or as Phin called him, Louis Three. It had to be a mistake. Or maybe he just held his own keys. Why would he steal her keys? That made no sense.

Phin boosted himself off the counter, waving her to follow him. "Rory's guy wants to get it done, collect his reward, and bolt."

Double-timing her steps, Maddy fought the pressure from her suddenly weak bladder. "But your brothers. We can't go alone."

He halted, shifting sideways to face her. "*We're* not. You're staying here. I'll make sure the Rios are around and I'll get Clay—the guy who picked up your car for us—to come over. He's Zeke's protégé." He gently grasped her forearms, running his hands up and down. "I promise you'll be safe here."

Oh, please. After everything they'd been through, if he intended to treat her like a helpless female, he had a surprise coming. She slid her arms free. "Don't do that."

"What?"

"Patronize me. "

His eyebrows came together. "Huh?"

"And that pacifying tone? You're treating me like a toddler."

A strangling sound erupted, and his eyes bugged out. "Whoa. Take it easy. I nearly got you shot yesterday. So, you know," he circled a hand in the air, "forgive me if I prefer not to have a replay."

"Me almost getting shot was not your fault. I put myself into that situation and I would do it again. Forget this macho thing you've got going. My freedom is on the line. I'm done with everyone dictating my fate. Even if I can't contribute to this meeting, I'm not staying here."

Phin backed up a step. "Well, then we have a problem, because you're not coming with me."

Huh. It appeared they were about to have their second fight of the day. She cocked her head, fought her rising temper and—yow. She needed a flipping bathroom pronto. "So that's it? You think you can tell me where I can't go?

News alert, Phin, I'm a grown-ass woman and my car is outside. You won't force me to stay here."

"That's true," he said, his tone lacking any of the patronizing softness of seconds ago. "However, you're a highly intelligent woman and understand the danger. At least I hope so after what happened yesterday. I'm not willing to risk you, Maddy. I won't apologize for that. It's bad enough I have to go. Please, just stay here."

When she didn't respond, he obviously took it as agreement because he jerked his head once, turned and headed toward the main staircase leading to the second floor.

"I have to prep for this meeting," he called over his shoulder. "Wish me luck."

25

As soon as Phin opened the Friary's front door, Maddy ducked behind her car's steering wheel. If he wouldn't let her ride with him, she'd drive herself.

Hot wind blew through the open driver's-side window. To avoid him noticing her until the last possible second, she'd started the engine, lowered the windows for a cross breeze, then shut the car off.

The black SUV sat in front of the Friary. When he fired it up, she waited a few seconds before peeping over her steering wheel to where he headed down the driveway. She bolted upright, quickly started her car, and shifted it into gear. The AC blasted hot air, so she left the windows open until things cooled a bit and then eased her foot off the brake, following him down the driveway.

A hundred yards in, Phin's brake lights flashed. Busted. Not altogether a surprise. She stopped, shifting the car back to park.

He hopped out of the SUV, left the door open and charged toward her.

Here we go. Fight number three.

And judging by the rock-hard planes of Phin's face, it might be a doozy.

She gripped the wheel, squeezing until her knuckles turned white. Good Girl Maddy was becoming an ace at starting trouble.

Somehow, she didn't mind. If this was what standing up for herself brought, so be it. At least she wouldn't be stifled by the constant need to please everyone.

Phin stopped at the door, placing his hands on it as if that would keep her from driving off.

"Maddy, *what* are you doing?"

She grinned up at him. "You know what I'm doing."

"It looks like you're following me. After I asked you to stay here. Where it's *safe*."

"You didn't ask, you told. Whatever. It's beside the point. I'm not staying here alone while y'all figure this out. If I can't go with you, I'll go to the Thompson Center. This is *my* life and someone is setting me up. If it's Louis's son—and that would be an epic tragedy—I want to look him in the eye and get answers."

He drew a hard breath, sucking the hot summer air through his nose. Yes, she was aggravating him. Couldn't be helped. Not with so much at stake.

He slammed his eyes closed for a second, exhaled, and opened his eyes again, focusing on her for what felt like ten years.

"Please," he said, "don't do this. I'm trying to keep you safe."

And, oh, the way he said it. All desperate and caring and ... protective. That wispy flutter tickled her. *The swish.* Total killer when she'd been searching for it for so long.

But she couldn't just sit here and be a victim. Not anymore. She set her hands over his. "Please understand. If someone were wrecking your life, wouldn't you want to be involved?"

"Maddy—"

She tore her gaze from his, stared out her windshield at the rear bumper of the SUV. "We're not doing this," she said, sitting taller. "Either I'm going with *you* or I'm going to the Thompson Center. You choose."

Finally, she looked back at him, found his crystal blue eyes turning a stormy gray. Irritated with her. Too bad.

A week ago, she'd have folded under the pressure. Given in just to keep the peace.

Yay, me.

He continued staring at her for a good ten seconds that might as well have been a year. "I can't believe you're doing this."

"Believe it."

"And there's nothing I can say to you, including reminding you a man died yesterday, to convince you to stay here?"

That reminder she didn't need. Then again, Phin-the-schmoozer knew how to push just the right buttons. She couldn't let him do it. No, sir. "One way or the other, I'm leaving here."

He shook his head, let out a stream of creative swear words that singed her ears. "You're killing me, Maddy."

She wouldn't apologize. Not for taking control of her life. "I know. It's unfortunate. But I'm sure you understand, at least on some level, what it feels like to not be in control of your own life."

His eyes softened, that stormy gray fading.

Bull's-eye.

He pointed to the side of the driveway. "Park your car there for now."

"You're letting me come with you?"

"That's what you want, isn't it?"

She nodded. "That's what I want."

"Will you at least not sit in the meeting with me? Or will you argue about that, too?"

"Full disclosure? I'll argue about that, too. I get that you want to keep me safe. But you're not seeing me as an asset. I'm the one who's seen these pieces up close. I've also seen the thieves. If this person you're meeting with is saying he was involved, I'll recognize him. I can help you figure out if he's the real deal. Tell me I'm wrong."

"You're not wrong."

She nodded and shifted the car into gear. "Good. Then let's go and maybe I'll get my life back."

ON THE DRIVE TO PICK UP RORY'S CONTACT, PHIN INFORMED Maddy that her tagging along would give him the opportunity to sit in the back with the, as he put it, *asshole* they'd be meeting with and keep him in line.

Sound reasoning, in Maddy's opinion. And having a task kept her mind occupied.

Phin drove into an abandoned strip mall twenty minutes outside of Steele Ridge and pulled to the rear where a blue Toyota was backed into one of the empty parking spaces.

Phin came to a stop just as the Toyota's driver opened the door. "I'll sit in the back with him," he told Maddy. "You okay driving?"

"I'm fine. My mom had a Suburban I learned to drive on."

She reached for the door handle to switch places with him.

"Wait," Phin said. "Do me a favor and climb over. I need

to make sure he's not carrying. I don't want you near him until I do that."

Good point. "Will do," she said.

Phin hopped out and the Toyota's driver, a man wearing cargo shorts and a faded black T-shirt, slid from the vehicle. He stood for a second, eyeing the SUV.

Wait one second. Was that him?

Standing in front of her was the guy from the Center, the one she'd met on her walk-through and found cute. The one the FBI, on their first round of questioning, had video of her speaking with.

That slimy *bastard*.

Fiery anger tore up her windpipe and her jaw flopped open. "Son of a bitch."

Outside, Phin stood a few feet from the guy, gesturing to the Toyota. The guy nodded and turned, placing his hands against the side of the car so Phin could pat him down. Then they repeated the exercise, this time with the slimy bastard patting Phin down.

When the guy pointed at Maddy, Phin shook his head, probably telling him he had a better chance of seeing God than putting a hand on her.

He and his buddies had set her up. Part of her wished she had a gun. Not that she had the nerve to shoot him, but …

I'm better than this.

Yes. She was.

Phin started toward the SUV, nudging his chin at her.

Driver's seat.

Crap.

She needed to get her head out of her rear, put her anger aside, and stick to the plan. She unhooked the seat belt and climbed over just as the rear doors came open, Phin getting in on the rear driver's side.

Once the doors shut, Maddy swiveled—couldn't help it—looking the guy dead in the eye.

For a few seconds, the only sound in the car was the hum of the AC. Everything else seemed to freeze, a sudden tension thickening the air as his eyes grew wider.

"I know you," he said.

"You *fucker*," she said. *Whoa! Go, me.* "I'm the one whose life you're wrecking."

"Blindfold," Phin said before the conversation could go on any further.

The guy held out a hand for the scrap of fabric.

"Nice try." Phin whirled his finger. "Turn and I'll do it. We're doubling up so you can't see. Try anything and I'll leave your ass on the side of the road. Got it?"

"Dude, I'm just trying to get out of the country. I need this done."

Frustrated with her loss of control—did she seriously just call this guy a fucker?—Maddy swung back, wrapping her fingers around the wheel hard enough to crush it. At some point, hopefully, she'd laugh about her rare use of the F word.

Totally worth it. Ooh, she'd like to wallop this guy. *Fucker, fucker, fucker.*

Maddy checked the rearview, watching as Phin finished tying the blindfold.

"You're good," he told their passenger. "Buckle up."

The guy did as instructed, with Phin helping him secure the belt. As soon as they were all strapped in, Maddy shifted the car into gear.

"How do I know," the fucker said, "you're not driving me straight to the feds?"

"No talking," Phin said. "As for the feds, we're both flying blind. You could be setting us up. The only thing I have confidence in is Rory being a greedy S.O.B. who wants a payday."

He sat forward, handing Maddy his phone. "Address is loaded, sound is off. If you miss a turn, I'll let you know."

As much experience as she'd had in Mom's Suburban, she'd never driven it on mountain roads. That alone gave her the twitches.

She could do it. If it ended this nightmare, she'd get it done.

PHIN SAT IN THE BACKSEAT, STARING STRAIGHT AHEAD, HIS gaze a constant sweep, checking on their passenger, who'd barely moved an inch since buckling in.

Good. After the morning Phin had had, his patience wasn't exactly hefty. Kicking someone's ass for a juicy stress release wouldn't be a hardship.

"It's coming up on the right," he told Maddy.

"Got it."

Maddy rounded the curve leading to the Steeles' sprawling 20,000-acre property, formerly known as Tupelo Hill. Jonah, the youngest of the Steele clan—nicknamed the baby billionaire after he'd designed and sold a viral video game—had purchased this property a few years back. Initially intended to be a sports complex for the community, the property had fallen into disrepair when the town had gone bust and scrapped the plans.

Enter Jonah Steele and his fat pockets. After major renovations, Phin's Aunt Joan moved into the main house and Reid converted the abandoned sports complex into a law enforcement training center that now brought major revenue to not only the Steeles, but the town as well.

Maddy pulled to the gate, and Phin lowered his window for the camera. A few seconds later, the gate slid open, revealing a long curving driveway. Maddy pulled through and Phin unbuckled. He sat forward, sticking his hand between the bucket seats and pointing to the glass-fronted building to the right. "Follow the driveway to that building. There's a small lot in front. Park at the curb near the door."

To their left, acres and acres of green grass and oak trees surrounded Aunt Joan's gleaming white house. For today, they'd steer clear, but maybe, when this was over, Phin might pay a call to his aunt and uncle. Finally, try to open up and build on the relationship.

He brought his attention back to their passenger, sitting stock-still in his seat. At least he followed instructions.

Pulling into the lot, Maddy eased to a stop at the building entrance and parked. The last time Phin had been in the training center was on Reid's wedding day. He, Zeke, and Ash had walked down from the main house to run the obstacle course.

The front door opened and Reid—in all his hugeness— appeared. He wore flip-flops, cargo shorts and a T-shirt tight enough for the world to see his insanely jacked torso. Superman in flip-flops.

Later, Phin would harass him about it and risk his own ass-kicking. It'd be worth it.

"Stay in the car," Phin told their guest before hopping out.

Maddy killed the engine and slid out as well.

"Hey." Reid strode from his spot and the door swung closed.

He met them at the curb and realizing Maddy and Reid hadn't been introduced the day prior, Phin did the honors.

"Maddy, this is my cousin Reid. Reid, Maddy. She works for the Thompsons."

"Pleasure, ma'am. Sorry about what happened yesterday. I hope you're all right."

"I'm fine," she said. "Ready for this to be over. But thank you."

Reid nodded and came back to Phin. "Here's the deal. We'll walk him through the front and down the hall. There's an empty office at the back of the building. Gage is upstairs if we need him. Y'all set?"

"Let's do it."

Phin walked to the SUV's rear door and opened it, helping their still-blindfolded contact out. What he didn't need was this guy tripping on the curb, taking a header and winding up with a brain injury.

A vision of the statue Zeke would turn him into streamed in his mind, the guilt over breaking his word to his brother in every fucking way possible, floating right behind.

He locked his hand around the guy's biceps—they didn't even know his name—and halted him. "Curb. Step up."

Once inside the glass-enclosed lobby, Reid made sure the door behind them latched shut and Phin glanced at the two leather chairs, sofa, and coffee table with a crystal sculpture on top that glittered under the sun's rays.

According to the rumor mill, Brynne had broken the bank on decorating the lobby area and Reid blew an artery.

Good for her.

The big man marched them down a long corridor, the soles of their shoes squeaking against the pristine floors. The sound hit him a certain way. An annoying way that scraped against his eardrums.

He focused on the hallway, the back of Reid's head. Anything but that damned squeaking.

Fatigue. That's all this was.

And guilt.

Reid made a right and stopped in front of a door at the rear of the building. He pushed it open and waved them in.

Inside, a generic metal desk sat in the center of the small office, the top empty except for a desk phone. Two equally bland chrome guest chairs were situated in front of it and the light gray walls stood bare. Zero personalization.

And definitely no windows.

Phin led the guy—*let's call him Bob*—through the doorway, with Maddy bringing up the rear.

"I'll be out here if you need something," Reid said, closing the door.

Time to get the show on the road.

Phin removed the blindfold, tossing it on the desk, and gave Bob a second to adjust to the harsh overhead lighting. He directed him to one of the chairs. Not wanting Maddy any closer to him than necessary, Phin took the chair beside Bob, leaving the desk chair for Maddy.

"Let's make this quick," Phin said. "What have you got?"

"Hold on," Bob said, giving Phin a hard look that nearly made him laugh.

Please. He'd take this weasel in three seconds.

Maybe less.

"I'm not talking," Bob said, "until I know I'm gonna get paid. I want half upfront. The other half when the job is done."

"You're dreaming. You get nothing until those jewels are returned."

"Then no deal."

Phin shrugged, got to his feet, and scooped the blindfold

off the desk. "I'm not the one trying to get out of Dodge by tomorrow morning. On your feet. I don't have time for this."

Bob's gaze shot to Maddy.

"You're better off with me," Phin said. "She'll throw you to a mountain lion."

"He's right," Maddy said. "If I were you, I'd start talking."

"Just ... wait." Bob patted air with both hands, then lowered them. "What guarantees do I have that you won't take the jewels and screw me over?"

"Guarantees? Dude, you're in the wrong damn business. You could send us to a location where there's an army of guys waiting to blow us away. The only reason we're here is that Rory is a greedy prick. That greed makes me believe you're legit."

"I am," Bob said.

"Then consider me your get-out-of-jail-free card. You tell me where the jewels are and if we find them, we'll wire $11 million to the account of your choosing. Pretty simple."

Clearing this deal with Thompson might have been an excellent option, but ... whoopsie. Too late now.

Besides, Louis had offered the reward. It was out there and Phin rolled with it.

"That's what Brendan thought," Bob said.

True 'dat. "Why do you think we're meeting here?"

Apparently satisfied that Phin wouldn't hose him, Bob nodded. "I got a call yesterday. From Xavier Vera."

The head honcho himself. Interesting. Phin tossed the blindfold back on the desk and sat. "You work directly for him? Or part of a crew?"

"There's one guy between me and Mr. Vera. I worked my way up. Started with petty theft. I was good at that, so as the jobs got bigger, I got more chances. Now? I'm involved in all the big stuff. Nothing like this. Ever. This? Huge mistake."

Blah, blah, blah. Bored with Bob's sudden remorse, Phin rolled his hand. "You got a call yesterday. Before or after Eckert died?"

"After. Mr. Vera called me himself. That never happens. There's a hierarchy. He calls my boss and then my boss calls me. Anyway, Mr. Vera said he needed my help. I couldn't believe it. I mean, I'm thinking I'm getting in good with them if he's calling me directly."

Biting down, Phin fought a smart-ass comment about Bob climbing the corporate ladder. "What did he want?"

"He said Brendan sold us out. Tried to make a deal for the jewels and collect the reward. That he needed them moved."

Leaning forward on her elbows, Maddy drew their gazes. "Did you know where they were?"

"They keep a bunch of warehouses. They spread the stuff around in case someone gets pinched. That way, they don't lose everything. Brendan knew where the jewels were. After the job, Mr. Vera told him where to take them. When he got shot, Mr. Vera called me. Told me to move everything."

Made sense to Phin. Move the merchandise before the feds show up and raid the place. "You're thinking the Veras shot Brendan?"

Bob shrugged. "Aren't you?"

He sure was. And now Phin, Maddy, and probably Phin's entire family were on this maniac's radar. "How did the Veras know Brendan was meeting with us?"

"Who knows? A job this big? They probably bugged his place. Mr. Vera told me which warehouse the jewels were in. I was to go right over there, get everything, and move it to another location. Which I did. I mean, I was freaking the fuck out. Brendan was dead and now they were telling me to move the stuff. I figured if I said no, I'd be toast."

Bob shook his head, lifted his hands to his face, pressing his palms into his eye sockets. "Total goat fuck. The whole operation. I knew it would bring too much heat."

Phin blew right by that. He needed to vet this intel. "Where did you move the jewels from? Describe it."

Bob dropped his hands, gawking at Phin. "What the hell does that matter? They aren't there anymore."

"Brendan showed us photos. Making sure you're not lying."

Bob gave an eye roll that had Phin curling his fingers. Just one pop. That's all he'd need and this idiot would go lights-out.

Focus.

He uncurled his fist, the movement not lost on Bob.

"It's a warehouse," Bob blurted. "One of those commercial types. Like a distribution center. Giant iron fence around the perimeter. Front and rear entrance. Guard at the front gate. Another guard inside."

Based on the photos Phin had seen the day before, the intel was solid. "Where's the new location?"

"Another warehouse, east side of Charlotte. Smaller building this time. Still two guards, though. All the buildings have the same basic setup. Two entrances. Guard in front. Guard in back."

Not surprised, Phin nodded. "How big is the place?"

"Pretty big. I can draw a map. The jewels are locked in a safe in the office."

"The map better be spot-on," Phin said. "I'm trying to not get me or one of my brothers killed. The faster we get in, the faster we get out. Once we have the stuff and we're safely out, we'll wire you the money and you can go off to wherever it is you intend to continue your thieving ways."

Silence filled the room. Phin kept his gaze on Bob while he considered his options.

Not that he had any.

Finally, he nodded. "All right. But you better not be setting me up. Even from behind bars, I'll find a way to kill you fuckers."

"Hey!" Maddy poked her finger. "Watch it. After you set me up, you're the last person who should be making threats."

As much as he loved seeing her get feisty, they needed to stay on point. He stood. "Nobody is screwing anyone." Phin picked up the blindfold again. "I'll take you back to your car. Give me a couple hours to work out details. But plan on doing this tonight."

"I have a question," Maddy said.

Phin knew her silence after he'd blown over her last comment had been too good to be true. Now he swung his head to her, offering his best what-the-hell? face. She ignored him, her gaze on Bob.

"Someone at the Thompson Center," she said, "gave you information. Who is it?"

"That's extra."

Apparently discovering his balls again, he grinned widely enough that Phin might pop him after all.

Phin glanced back at Maddy. If they intended to clear her, they needed to know who had tipped off the Veras about the security. Given they'd found footage of Louis Three stealing Maddy's keys, Bob might confirm his involvement.

Phin did the thing he'd become really good at. He took a flyer. "You'll get an extra hundred grand—call it a bonus—

for telling us who it is. But," Phin put up a finger, "it has to check out. You're not just gonna give us a name and we pay you. Once the intel is verified, we'll wire the money."

Bob faced Phin again, let out a long sigh.

Who the hell was he kidding? They all knew he'd take the deal. Still, Phin gave him his moment to earn his Oscar nomination.

"The Veras," Bob said, "didn't do this job on their own. Rumor among the crews is they were hired."

Made sense. The Veras were known for over-the-top jobs, but this one? Way too high-profile. The seriously curious part of this? Who hated Thompson enough to humiliate him this way? Could've been any number of his political rivals, but why now? Why, when the man was out of office and clearly not running for any other, would someone do this?

"Who hired them?"

"I don't know for sure. I told you it was a rumor."

"Oh, come on!" Maddy said, clearly losing her patience. "What was the rumor?"

Bob slid a sideways glance at Maddy, then came back to Phin. "The kid. Thompson's nephew."

26

THERE IT WAS.

The confirmation they needed. For whatever reason, President Thompson's nephew had been involved in the theft at the Thompson Center. Stealing Maddy's keys was one thing. It wasn't beyond her that a young, privileged kid with opportunities most would never imagine could be convinced to do that.

But actually hiring the Vera brothers, apparent criminal masterminds?

Come.

On.

A bizarre mix of relief and bewilderment washed over Maddy, her head dipping forward a fraction before she caught herself.

This was what she'd wanted. To find the person responsible and clear her name. Now it seemed they had a start, but the idea of President Thompson's own nephew, someone the man had given precious time and knowledge to, being involved?

A niggling thought bugged her. Louis Three hadn't even

graduated from college yet. Age didn't matter with money and a person's want of it, but Louis?

"Thompson's nephew," Maddy said. "How would he even know how to pull that off?"

The man shrugged. "That's the rumor."

Maddy looked up at Phin, still on his feet, blindfold in hand. Perhaps his experience, his insight into how people ticked, might offer clarity. "I don't understand that," she said. "It's not as if he needs the money. His father gives him whatever he wants. President Thompson has been good to him. *Really* good. How could he do this?"

For a second, Phin stared down at her, his gaze direct. No pity. No poor-sweet-Maddy. "I don't know," he said.

At least she wasn't the only one perplexed. Maddy went back to the creep. "What else did you hear?"

"That's it. Guys talk all the time."

Phin lifted his hand, gesturing for the man to stand. "We'll get into the who and why later. Right now, we need the jewels back. Let's hit it."

THE SECOND THEIR CONTACT PULLED OUT OF THE PARKING LOT Maddy and Phin switched places, passing each other in silence at the rear bumper before she hopped into the passenger seat.

She swiveled sideways to face him.

"Louis!" she said, still gobsmacked. "That's ... wild."

"Eh. Nothing shocks me anymore."

Should she do it? Get her hopes up that she'd be cleared as early as today?

No. Not with the way the last few days had gone. Until she heard from the FBI that she was no longer a suspect, she wouldn't get sucked in.

She held up her hand, palm out. "He said it was a rumor. And rumors aren't necessarily accurate. If true at all. *And,*" she flapped her outstretched hand, "if Louis hired the Veras to steal the pieces, why do they still have them? They should have turned them over to him by now. I don't understand any of this. I think he's lying."

"It's possible. Believe me, there's plenty of gossip floating around Steele Ridge about my family and most isn't even close to the truth. Same could have happened here."

He reached across the console, set his hand on her arm, and squeezed, the warmth settling her embattled thoughts.

"This is where it gets hard," he said. "Adrenaline flows and you want to jump ahead five steps. We can't. We need to take it one step at a time. Okay?"

She knew this. Had experienced it herself during the weeks leading up to the opening of the Thompson Center. And every time they unveiled a new exhibit.

The pressure she put on herself was immense and the mental bedlam often wore her to a nub.

She leaned closer to him and he met her halfway. She rested her forehead against his shoulder, the swish in her belly reminding her to be grateful Phin Blackwell had come into her life.

Where they'd wind up as a couple, she couldn't know, but he'd helped her. Literally saved her life yesterday. For that alone, she wasn't sure how to repay him.

For now, she'd get her mind right. Do as he said and focus on one step at a time.

She sat straight, lifted her chin. "One step at a time," she said. "I can do that. Where to now?"

"The Thompson Center."

Whoa. She didn't see that one coming. Were they just going to walk in and accuse Louis Three of theft?

"I know," Phin said. "It's nuts. If my brothers are still there, they can stall until we get there and we'll talk to Thompson about this new information."

BEFORE HITTING THE ROAD—HE'D NEED EVERY WORKING BRAIN cell for this conversation—Phin hit the button on the steering wheel, directing the Bluetooth to call Zeke.

"Hey," Zeke said, his voice booming in the quiet car. "Y'all all right?"

Just peachy. Phin lowered the volume. With the yelling that would ensue, they'd hear Zeke from five miles away. "We're good. You still at the Center?"

"Yeah. Thompson ran long with the mayor this morning. We showed him the video. To say he's stunned is an understatement."

"I'm sure. Is Louis Three there?"

"No. Thompson went back to his office to call Louis Junior. He doesn't wanna talk to Three without the kid's father there."

"Makes sense. So, Thompson's not there with you?"

"No. Just me, Cruz and Rohan cooling our jets."

Excellent. "Good. We have a *development*." Before his brother could answer, Phin charged ahead. "I got a call from Rory. One of Eckert's buddies wants to make a deal on the collection. Vera had him move everything last night. Now he wants out and wants Louis's eleven mil to get him there. Maddy and I just met with him and—"

"Hold it. You did what?"

"Before you yell, y'all can't be in two places at once and the guy was gonna bolt. He's already told me he'll be gone by tomorrow. Zeke, we could have the entire collection back by tonight."

"Well, she-it," Cruz said. "Little brother's been busy."

Damned straight.

"Shut it," Zeke told him. "Phin, we don't know who the hell this guy is. And after yesterday, after you said you'd stay inside, you took this meeting alone? Wait, no. Not alone. You took *Maddy*. Someone fucking kill me. Please."

As if Phin was an idiot who hadn't considered it could've been a setup? "Dude, I took care of it. The location was secure."

"Where was this location?"

This from Rohan, probably administering CPR to Zeke.

If Cruz thought the idea of Phin going rogue for a meeting was fun, he'd love this one. Phin sat a little taller, closed his eyes for a second.

Mr. Smooth. That was him. The guy who'd wined and dined and sweet-talked his way through hundreds of events.

He opened his eyes. "I called Reid. He let us use the training center."

Silence descended like a falling guillotine.

Was that Phin's head that just rolled?

"You really are trying to kill me," Zeke finally said. "I mean, *Reid*?"

"Yes. *Reid*. Think about it. His security rivals ours. We blindfolded the guy, took him to a windowless office, and made the deal. Fellas, we might do a recovery later today."

"What deal? What are you *talking* about?"

Big brother might be losing it here. Might be? Phin had known that the Reid thing would drive him bonkers. He'd done it anyway. And had no regrets. As much as his brothers hated it, everyone was safe.

"Zeke, I know you're pissed, but you need to set that aside for two minutes and listen. The guy we met says it was a contracted job for the Veras. Rumor amongst the Vera crews is that Louis Three hired them."

Cruz let out one of his signature whistles. "That makes for a tough Sunday dinner."

Beside Phin, Maddy snorted and he shot her a look.

"What?" She shrugged. "He's funny."

Irritated with the lot of them, Phin rolled his eyes. "We're on our way to you now. After we talk to Thompson, we need to huddle up."

"Ya think?" Zeke said. "Do you know—and I'm talking a solid address—where the stuff is?"

"According to the dude we met with, it's in a warehouse on the east side of Charlotte. I don't have the address yet. He's giving us a map and exact details on the location. I don't want us going in blind. It's not ideal prep, but this afternoon we'll come up with a plan and tonight, we roll."

MADDY HELD HER BREATH AS SHE PUSHED THROUGH THE circular door—the visitor's entrance—to the Thompson Center.

For over two years, she'd loved coming to work. Being entrusted with thousands upon thousands of items belonging to a former president and given the opportunity to tell a story with those items.

The historical significance alone mesmerized her, never mind her role in preserving it.

How, in a matter of days, had she gone from being a valued team member to one under suspicion?

As much as her logical self understood the need to put her on leave, her emotional self, the one wanting everyone satisfied, recognized the sting of betrayal. That nasty bite plunging into her and spreading venom.

Could she ever walk in here, no matter what entrance, and not think about being accused of stealing?

Once through the door, she waited for Phin, right behind her. He stepped free of the door, his hand immediately going to his hair to straighten it. The move was done with such ease she imagined he did it by rote. A habit. Part of his super-schmoozer persona.

So much to learn.

He set his hand on her back, sliding it slowly to the base of her spine. A soft flutter—the swish—tickled her belly, and she paused for a second, taking it in.

Phin Blackwell.

The bright spot of this experience.

He leaned in, bringing his mouth close to her ear, his warm breath cascading over her skin. Just last night, in bed, he'd done that. Telling her all the things he'd intended on doing to her and ... *ooh-eee*. Her cheeks flamed.

Phin Blackwell.

Bright spot.

"Hey," he whispered. "I know this is tough, but if all goes well, we'll have answers soon. I need you to stay focused."

Not exactly the dirty talk her mind had looped back to, but enough to get her locked in again.

She nodded. "It's all so confusing. We're about to walk up there and accuse Louis. He's a good kid."

"That good kid may have set you up."

"I trusted these people."

"I know," he said. "I'm sorry. Sometimes people are shitty."

A simple, yet devastating statement. Louis had everything. *Two* parents who loved him, private school educations, and an uncle who—oh, yeah—happened to be the former president of the United States mentoring him. How many people received that abundance?

Not her.

The inequity of it baffled her. She'd lost her father and then clawed for every opportunity. Good Girl Maddy did everything expected of her. Subjected herself to unrelenting pressure to ensure everyone in her world was happy. Happy, happy, happy.

This was her reward for all that work?

Focus. Phin was right. Soon they'd have answers.

"Hello, Ms. Maddy." She swung her head, spotted Percy, the security guard, coming toward her, one hand extended.

Putting scheming college students from her mind, she strode to him, clasping his hand. "Hi, Percy. Have you missed me?"

"You know we have. Place just isn't the same without your smiling face. Are you back to work?"

How, after all this, could things ever be the same?

That alone sent a punch to her chest. Later. She'd deal with it later.

"No. Just here ..." *To accuse President Thompson's nephew of setting me up.* She cleared her throat. "Sorry. Just here for a meeting."

Phin appeared at her side, nodding a greeting at Percy. "There's Zeke."

She swung her head around, spotted Zeke coming off the escalator, waving them forward. She took one step, then halted. All guests were required to have a pass prior to visiting the executive suite. Given her current status of administrative leave, she was technically someone smack in the middle of a gray area.

Not quite an employee, but more than a guest.

Maddy looked back at Percy. "Do we need guest passes?"

He waved a hand. "You're fine."

"I don't want to get you in trouble. It's okay to give us a pass."

His kind eyes drooped. "I'm not giving you, of all people, a guest pass. Y'all go on up."

Bubbling tears threatened, and she peered at the floor, blinking them away before meeting Percy's gaze again. "Thank you."

"We should go," Phin said, drawing Maddy's attention.

She followed him to the escalator where Zeke stood.

"Junior and Three just got here," Zeke said. "Everyone's in the conference room. Thompson asked us to step outside so he could show them the video in private. Rohan and Cruz are in the hallway."

"Does President Thompson know I'm here?"

"I told him." He held his hand for Maddy to precede him on the escalator. "Not sure he wanted the complication, but you have the right to face this kid."

They rode the escalators up, up, up while Maddy's heart slammed against her ribs. In the next few minutes, the truth might come out.

Vindication.

As satisfied as she'd be, if Louis Three was involved, the Thompsons would suffer enormous emotional and political fallout. On a national and maybe even global scale. Absolute catnip for President Thompson's enemies.

All created by his own nephew.

When this was over, Maddy intended to find her mother and siblings and wrap them in a group hug. Hold them so darned tight, she might not want to let go. She simply could not imagine a betrayal like this from them.

At the executive suite door, Zeke swiped a keycard. More than likely Aileen's.

Phin and Zeke headed straight down the hallway toward Rohan and Cruz, who lingered in front of her office. Two Secret Service agents stood across from them just outside the conference room.

Maddy paused and Aileen rose from her seat, coming around the desk and extending her arms.

Was Aileen about to hug her?

They'd been friendly and shared a mutual respect, but hugging? That was new.

She stepped right up and wrapped her arms around the much shorter Maddy, giving a light squeeze.

"Something crazy is going on," Aileen whispered, her voice a jittery rumble.

This hug, Maddy decided, wasn't a greeting.

Aileen was freaking out. And she didn't know the half—the quarter—of it.

Everything might change, and Maddy couldn't even warn her. Instead, she returned the hug, gently patting Aileen's back. "It's okay. I think it'll all be over soon and things will go back to normal."

Whatever normal would be after this mess.

Maddy backed away from the hug, gripping Aileen's forearms. "You okay?"

She lifted her chin, gave a tight smile that was anything but okay. Still, she tried.

"I'm good," she said. "Heading out to lunch, so if you're not here when I get back, it was great to see you. I miss you. I hope you're back soon."

The last week played in Maddy's mind. In six days, she'd gone from being the Thompsons' messenger and hiring BARS, to being questioned by the FBI, losing the trust of her employer, and falling hard for Phin.

And Aileen had just told her what she'd yearned to hear

from her bosses. That they missed her. Wanted her back.

All Maddy could do was nod. Bob her head like one of those cheap dolls from baseball games.

"Ditto," she finally managed.

She hurried away, pulling herself together while walking toward Phin and his brothers, all looming in the hallway with the two Secret Service agents. The testosterone level in the suite might be at epic heights with this bunch.

Four feet from her closed office, she stopped. Just inside that door were her belongings. Certificates and photos and the crystal paperweight of the American flag the Thompsons had given her in recognition of her hard work the day the Center opened.

Now it all seemed a blur. A different Maddy.

A light throb thumped at her temples, and she peeled her gaze from the door, leaning against the wall beside Phin. "This sucks."

"Absolutely," he said.

Voices sounded from behind the conference room door and the light throb went to an all-out pounding. Right inside that door, Louis Three could be lying. Making up some story about why he took Maddy's keys.

Prior to meeting with the jerk who worked for the Veras, she didn't believe it. Now, all she knew was he'd stolen them. He'd gone into *her* office, opened *her* desk, and took them.

And that pissed her off.

Big time.

Enough.

She stepped between Phin and Zeke. "Pardon me. I'm going in."

One of the Secret Service agents shot her a look, but didn't move.

"Whoa—" Phin held up his hands. "Not a good idea."

She gripped the handle, let the cool metal bring her thoughts to sharper focus. "Actually, I think it's an excellent idea."

She pushed the door open and stepped inside.

27

"WHAT IN THE HELL?" LOUIS JUNIOR HOLLERED, HIS EYEBROWS hiked nearly to his hairline. "This is a *private* meeting."

"Too bad," Maddy said. "My reputation is wrecked and I want answers."

President Thompson sat in his normal spot at the head of the table. Louis Junior, dressed in his typical CEO suit and tie with pocket square, sat to his right with an empty chair between them. Louis Three, directly to President Thompson's left, stared across the table at her like she'd lost her mind. Maybe she had.

The door came open and one of the Secret Service agents poked his head in.

"We're fine," President Thompson said. "Thank you."

The agent retreated and closed the door. Maddy pointed at Three. "Did you steal my keys and copy them?"

The whites of his eyes became dinner plates. "I ... uh ..." He faced his father. "Dad?"

Oh, puh-lease. Daddy couldn't help him this time. "Hey," Maddy said, her voice sharp. "Don't look at him."

Junior swiveled his chair to face her. "How dare you speak to my son that way?"

How dare she? Seriously? When she was the one being accused? When she was the one sitting through FBI interrogations and having her home violated by strange men who could have walked in on her and done all sorts of horrible things?

How dare *she*?

White-hot rage spewed like acid from her brain, eating away at her, tearing up her insides.

Speaking of the FBI. Anticipating needing to make a call, she dug her phone from her pocket.

Answers. She needed answers.

And she'd get them.

"How dare *you*!" She jabbed a finger at Louis Junior. "How dare *he*? Do you have any idea what I've been through?" Not expecting an answer, she turned to Three. "There's a rumor out there that you're behind this theft. That you hired people—the Vera brothers—to steal from your uncle. Unless you tell me otherwise, I'm about to call the FBI."

"Maddy, please."

This from President Thompson, who sat back in his seat, one arm on the armrest like this was a normal day at the office. Maybe for a former president it was.

"Maddy."

She spun back. Phin now stood two feet from her, his brothers behind him, lined up against the interior wall, looking like soldiers holding the fort. The two Secret Service agents had also joined them, both of them moving behind Maddy to flank President Thompson.

"No, Phin," Maddy said. "I'm done." She turned back to President Thompson. "Please what? Please allow myself to go down for something I didn't do? To save you the humilia-tion? What about *my* humiliation?" She slammed her hand against her chest, her fingers smacking the bare skin above her V-neck shirt. "My professional reputation? Frankly, I deserve better. So Louis, start talking or I'm calling the FBI."

The kid's head whipped back and forth and he turned to his father again. "Dad! Please."

"Relax, son. There's nothing she can do."

Dream on, pal. "Oh," she scoffed, "there's *plenty* I can do." She pretended to dial because, really, she'd have to Google the number for the FBI, but they didn't know that. It wasn't as if she had Ash Blackwell in her contacts.

She brought the phone to her ear, feigned listening for the ring on the opposite end, then held her finger up. "Spe-cial Agent Blackwell, please," she said into the phone.

Louis Junior, his face twisting, leaped from his chair, sending it careening backward, crashing against the wall beside Maddy.

He whirled on her. "Hang up. Right now."

Fast on his feet, Phin slid in front of Maddy, pointing at Louis. "Sit down."

When Phin's brothers stepped up next to her, forming her own little cocoon, Maddy went on tiptoes, peering over Phin's shoulder to where he and Louis were in the middle of one heck of a staredown.

Eventually, Louis's gaze shot left and right to the men at Phin's sides. Way overmatched, he'd apparently regained his good sense, reclaimed his chair, and took his seat again.

President Thompson sat forward, pulling closer to the table. "Everyone, take a breath."

"It wasn't me," Louis Three blurted. "I swear. It wasn't me."

Maddy put her hands out and pushed, squeezing

between Phin and Cruz, leaving her behind Louis Junior's chair. "Then why did you steal my keys?"

The kid turned to his father again. "Dad! *Please!*"

His father looked across at him, the two exchanging some kind of silent message. "Son," he said. "Calm *down*."

That tone. Like the jagged edge of a thousand tiny razors. She didn't know Louis Pierre Junior well, hardly at all, but he'd always been professional. Stoic and serious, but never intimidating. That voice?

Scary.

Louis Pierre. *Ohmygod.*

They were both Louis Pierre.

Could ...?

No.

Maddy gasped and all heads in the room turned. Louis Junior swiveled his chair around, fully facing her.

"It was you," she said.

"You come in here to accuse my son of stealing from my brother and now you're talking some other gibberish nonsense?"

"You knew," she said quietly as it all came back to her. "You sat through every planning meeting. The security, how shift changes worked, who did rounds and when. About the windows not being shatterproof above the first floor. You knew my routine. How I walked the building after lunch every day."

She stopped, took a breath. Inhaled the woodsy scent of Louis's probably outrageously expensive cologne that somehow sharpened her senses.

"You did it," she said. "You set me up."

Louis stood and straightened the cuffs on his suit jacket as if having someone accuse him of a crime was an everyday occurrence.

Maybe in his world it was, but she wanted answers and he wasn't leaving until she got them. Even if she had to lie down in front of the door.

She backed up a step, huddling closer to the wall near the door.

"I won't sit here and listen to this nonsense." He finished messing with his cuffs and peered at his brother, still seated. "We're leaving."

Um, no. You're not.

Maddy slid an inch closer to the door.

As usual, President Thompson's face remained neutral, his thoughts and emotions hidden behind a politically hardened mask. "Louis," he said, "you're not going anywhere."

"You don't tell me what to do. I'm not one of your fucking minions."

The Secret Service agent to Thompson's right, apparently offended, shot a dark look at Junior just as Thompson's mask crumbled, revealing flushing cheeks.

"My *minions*? Have you lost your mind? When have I ever treated you that way?"

"How about right now?"

"I'm trying to figure out what the hell is going on!"

The room fell silent. Not even Phin dared to speak.

Finally, Louis shook his head. "This is ridiculous. We're leaving."

"No."

Thompson sounded like her mom when the elders became teenagers and constantly rebelled.

"Don't make me call security to aid these fine gentlemen in keeping you here," he said.

Security. Wow.

Maddy glanced down at the floor, at Louis's perfectly

shined dress shoes—Italian, no doubt. Would he try it? Bolt to the door before security could even get here?

Possibly.

Well, she'd take care of that right now.

While Louis and President Thompson continued their pissing match, arguing over who had the right to do what, Maddy got busy on her phone and poked at the Center's security app.

The one that allowed senior staff to lock the executive suite's shatterproof entry doors in case of an active shooter or some other threat to a former president. Unlike her keycard, the app was controlled by the security department and not HR. With any luck, the head of security hadn't yet paused her access.

An image of a bright red lock appeared on her screen. *Yes.*

Tap-tap.

Done.

She cleared her throat, drawing all eyes in her direction. She offered Louis a smile à la Phin. "Maybe you missed it in all of our meetings, but we have excellent security measures in place to protect your brother." She held up her phone, revealing the bright red lock on the screen. "We're locked in."

Louis stood still for a second, his dark brown eyes going black, the heat behind them firing missiles that should have blasted Maddy through the wall.

Her knees wobbled and Good Girl Maddy begged her to make nice. To smooth it over. To make everyone see reason and talk it out.

Fuck off, Good Girl Maddy.

So what if she'd pissed Louis off? This was her life. Her career. The reputation she'd worked so hard for.

She locked her knees, lifted her chin.

"No one leaves until I get the truth," she said. "I want my life back."

Louis's jaw dropped. Apparently, she'd shocked him.

Good.

"Guess what, sweetheart," he took a step toward her, "you don't tell me what to do."

His right hand moved under his suit coat, and he took another step.

Hands. What's he doing?

To her right, Phin moved closer. "Maddy," he said.

Too late.

Louis lunged, grabbed hold of her arm, jerking her toward him with his left hand.

"Gun!" Phin yelled.

Gun? What gun? Her stomach cramped, and panic exploded like a charging army.

In his right hand, Louis held a giant black gun. He swept it left and right, pulling her tighter against him.

The back of her head bumped his chest and—*ow*—the man had an iron grip.

Louis swung the gun left to right again, keeping the Blackwell men and the Secret Service agents at bay. The agents had drawn their weapons, repositioning themselves to block Louis's view of President Thompson. They pointed their weapons at Louis, who shifted, putting his back to the wall.

"Everyone," Louis said, "back up."

"Louis!" Thompson said from behind the agents. "Are you insane?"

Yeah, clearly. What sane person takes a room full of people hostage? No one Maddy knew.

At least not until today.

"Mr. Pierre." Phin's voice, its low, steady resonance, broke through Maddy's whirling thoughts.

Phin held his hands out, palm up. "Please," he said, "put the gun down."

If a prowling panther could talk, he'd be Phin in this moment. All calm confidence, controlled energy and ... power. He'd get them out of this. Somehow. She knew it. Felt it in the pit of her stomach where the long sought-after swishy feeling did its thing.

Swish, swish, swish.

The arm around her neck tightened. *Oh, God.* Pressure built in her throat—*no air*—and she gagged.

"Sir," one of the agents said, "put the gun down."

Dragging Maddy with him, Louis sidestepped toward the door, the movement loosening the choke hold enough that Maddy sucked in a breath, allowing all that glorious oxygen to fill her brain.

Room. She had room. She dipped her chin, shielding her throat from that tightening move in case he tried it again.

"Once I get outside," Louis told Phin, "I'll let her go. Back away from the door!"

What the hell did he not understand about being locked in?

"Louis," Thompson said, "what have you done? Forget that. What are you *doing*?"

Hands still outstretched, Phin took a tiny step forward. "Let her go."

"Stop!" Louis said. "Right there."

Phin halted and his brothers sidled up beside him. A united front. A dangerous looking one.

"No problem," Phin said. "Lower the gun and let's talk this out."

"Sir!" the agent repeated, his voice sharper as he took a step closer. "Gun down. Right now."

Louis jerked the gun at Phin. "Back up. Away from the door. Son," he said to Louis Three, "figure out how to open those doors. The dingbat receptionist has to have a code. I'll shoot our way out of here if I have to."

Holy cow. The man had indeed gone insane.

Maddy inched her head around, made eye contact with the Secret Service agents, all of them obviously thinking the same thing.

"You can't," she said. "The glass is bulletproof. If you shoot, who knows what'll happen? The shot might ricochet and hit someone. Maybe your son."

Louis Three pushed out of his chair. One agent angled toward him and he froze. Just stood there, exchanging a pained look with his father.

Now.

Maddy lifted her foot and—*stomp!*—drove her sneaker into Louis's foot. Why oh why hadn't she worn wooden-heeled shoes today? That would have really done some damage. Maybe broken a few bones.

"Ow!"

Her rubber sole cushioned the blow, but the impact knocked him off balance. A juicy jolt of adrenaline plowed into her limbs.

Wham! Wham! Wham!

She stomped again. Again and again and again.

Gun.

It moved into her sight line and she looked down, spotted him raising his arm higher, pointing straight at Phin.

No, no, no.

She flung her right hand out, connecting with Louis's

and shoving his arm sideways, forcing his hold to loosen again just …

A.

Smidge.

Maddy stomped again.

Go.

She lunged, breaking free of his grip, and clawed for the pistol still in his hand.

Boom!

A thundering shot rang out. The bullet hit the table, sending a hunk of wood flying.

All at once, shouts filled the air and everyone leaped, all of them scrambling and closing in on her and Louis.

Phin pounced, shoving Maddy with enough force to knock her straight into a charging Secret Service agent.

He caught her, somehow keeping her—and himself—upright as the other agent guarded President Thompson, whose path to the doorway was blocked.

More yelling, all of it from behind her. She swung back, rage fueling her, sending her blood rocketing because that, that, that…*fucker*… Louis had held her at gunpoint.

Phin, his face red with the same fury scalding Maddy, slammed Louis against the wall, gripped his wrist and banged it. Hard. Three times.

Whap, whap, whap.

The gun tumbled free, falling to the floor. Cruz, closest to Phin, scooped it up as Zeke and Rohan moved in, ready to assist Phin.

He didn't need the help and went to work on Louis, pummeling his gut with three quick punches.

Ouch.

The older man slumped over, his body falling into Phin as let out a groan.

Obviously, taking no chances, Phin stepped back and let the man fall to his knees.

"Down!" Phin yelled. "On your stomach!"

Movement.

Maddy swung her head. Louis Three. Rushing Phin, his gaze fixed on his target.

And, oh, that was *not* happening. She'd had enough of these Pierres.

Before Zeke and Rohan could beat her to him, she launched herself at Louis Three, throwing her weight against the much taller young man. They careened into one of the rolling chairs and—shoot—Maddy's feet tangled with his. The chair flew backward, smacking against the wall, leaving Louis nothing to break his fall.

Going down now.

Maddy braced herself, tried to focus on not stiffening and rolling through the landing. He landed on his side, his elbow taking a hit when Maddy crashed on top of him.

"Oooff!" he said.

Cruz pointed the gun at Louis Three while extending his free hand to Maddy. "Don't move," he told Louis. "I'm done fucking around."

28

"Ash is on his way," Zeke said, tucking his phone into the front pocket of his jeans.

Phin stood in the conference room, staring down at Louis Junior and Three, both on the floor, backs to the wall and hands zip-tied behind them.

"Security is on their way up," Maddy said from her spot near the door.

President Thompson sat in his spot at the end of the table, still guarded by the two Secret Service agents.

"Please unlock the suite," Thompson said.

A few taps later, Maddy held up her phone. "Done."

After what Thompson had put her through? That whole administrative leave thing? Phin would have told him to shove it.

But he supposed that's why he enjoyed Maddy. She didn't hold grudges.

A minute later, two security guards entered, both of them stopping short at the sight of the president's brother and nephew zip-tied.

President Thompson stood, approaching the guards. "Gentlemen, the FBI is en route. We need to keep my brother and nephew secure until they arrive." Thompson peered at Phin, then at Zeke. "A word, please?"

Whatever this was, Thompson didn't want an audience. Zeke and Phin followed him and the two agents to the closest office—ironically, Maddy's. The agents remained in the hallway when Thompson closed the door, ensuring complete privacy from the cameras.

Thompson didn't bother sitting. He stood behind the door, leaning against it with his normally gelled-into-submission hair falling across his forehead. This might be as close to disheveled as Phin had ever seen him.

He held out his hands. "Do you know where the jewels are?"

Phin nodded. "Yes. But, sir, the clock is clicking. When the FBI gets here, everything hits the fan. The jewels will disappear again. We have to act quickly."

"Meaning, you need to get a jump on the FBI?"

"Precisely," Zeke said.

They gave Thompson a second, maybe two. This was a man accustomed to deciding on missile strikes and collateral damage. Human carnage.

This decision shouldn't take long.

"Go," he said. "If there's fallout with the FBI, I'll deal with it. I promise you that. Just get the jewels back."

Phin nodded. "You got it, sir."

"HERE'S THE MAP BOB DREW FOR US," PHIN SAID. "HE JUST texted it to me along with photos of the interior of the warehouse and the location of the jewels."

He stood at the end of the Annex's conference table, his brothers beside him. Two images—one an interior rendition, one an exterior—of their target location filled the wall screen.

Phin pointed to an X that Bob had marked at the rear exterior of the building. "There's a guard stationed at this gate. Delivery bay is behind it. Once we get in the gate, we drive straight ahead to the bay. We have photos of where the jewels are. There's so much stuff in there, the Veras took to marking the rows and subsections of those rows."

Stepping closer to the screen, Zeke shook his head. "The feds'll go crazy cataloguing all that evidence."

Based on what Bob had described, Phin couldn't guess how long it might take. He was just glad he didn't have to do that tedious work.

"We're looking for an office behind row one." Phin pointed to another X at the top of the screen. "It's on the front, east side of the building. The jewels are locked in a safe. We have the combination."

"Assuming the stuff is still there and the combination's not changed."

This from Rohan. Mr. Mary Sunshine.

Ignoring his brother, Phin pointed to an X near the bottom of the map. "This is the other entrance at the rear. There's another guard stationed there. Video monitoring is done from within the gate houses. The guards can see interior and exterior footage. Nobody inside at this location. Just cameras. So, we need a distraction in front. Keep that guy occupied while we talk our way into the back."

Cruz cocked his head. "Delivery truck."

Last year, thinking a truck would come in handy for moving larger items, they'd purchased a used step van when a local company went bust.

It turned out to be a solid investment. They'd already posed—multiple times—as uniformed delivery guys to gain access to airports, distribution centers, storage facilities, and even private residences.

"Exactly," Phin said. "We'll throw a piece of furniture in the back. Act like we're delivering it. Bob claims there's all kinds of items stored in the warehouse. A piece of furniture wouldn't shock anyone. All we need is to get beyond the gate. Then our diversion at the front escalates and guard number two has to see what the hell's going on."

"And if he doesn't go?" Mary Sunshine again.

As much as Mr. Dark Side Rohan sometimes irritated the crap out of Phin, he'd saved their asses countless times. They now depended on him to find holes in their plans.

Still standing in front of the screen, Zeke shrugged. "We detain him. One of us keeps watch while Phin goes in and finds the jewels. If we do it right, we'll be in and out in minutes."

"Just like when they broke into the Thompson Center."

They all swung to Maddy, quietly sitting at the table. Preoccupied with planning, Phin had forgotten she was even there. Now she had their attention. Particularly his.

She'd pulled her wild hair into a loose ponytail, but a few tendrils broke free, framing her face.

That crazy, happy feeling surged and Phin fought to refocus his mind on priceless jewels.

But, dang, he loved looking at her.

"I'll go with you," she said.

Had she been ingesting hallucinogens after her ordeal earlier? "Uh, no," Phin shot before his good sense kicked in and made him shut his mouth.

Maddy tilted her head, drilling him with a look, and he put his hands up. "Sorry. That came out too quick. I'm not telling you what to do." Yeah, he was. "This is dangerous. You've been around gunfire twice in the last two days. The guards are armed. Someone could get hurt."

A long pause ensued. Finally, she sat back, casually folding her hands over her belly. "All right. You all go in and possibly grab the wrong items. Or," she mused, "maybe not all of them. That's a definite possibility, since none of you have ever actually seen these pieces."

"Maddy—"

She threw her hand up. "I get it. I'm an amateur. It's *dangerous*. I don't know what I'm doing, blah, blah. Save your breath. What it all comes down to is that I'm the only one in this room who knows these pieces intimately. We all know that as soon as Ash and Walker get Louis Junior talking, it's over. The FBI will lock down every building associated with the Veras. They may be working on warrants as we speak."

"*If* Louis talks," Rohan said.

Maddy met his gaze. "Oh, he'll talk. President Thompson refuses to travel with him because he constantly complains at five-star hotels. Gentlemen, Louis isn't built for prison. As soon as he admits his part in this heist, the FBI will arrest anyone involved, including members of the Vera family."

"And then they move the jewels," Cruz said. "Gotta give it to her. She's right."

"I hate it," Zeke admitted. "However, it's not a bad idea to bring her. She can identify all the pieces and we're done."

What?

The one obsessed with security, with *safety,* wanted to put Maddy in the middle of an op they'd had no time—zero —to plan and practice? Normally, they'd be erecting walls in the shoot house out back and running the plan over and over and over while Grams and Mom timed them from the catwalk above.

Now Zeke decided to go rogue?

"Absolutely not," Phin said. "We'll do the camera thing again."

"Right," Maddy said. "Because that worked out so well the first time."

Phin whirled back to her, gritted his teeth. "You're not coming. If anything happens to you, I'll lose my mind. Not doing it."

She pushed out of her chair, tenting her fingers on the table, but otherwise not moving. Just stood there, her gaze pinned to his. "I appreciate you wanting to protect me. Protecting me also means getting these jewels back and clearing my name. We're partway there with Louis pulling that gun today. Obviously, he's hiding something. We don't know the details yet, but they'll come. Right now, we need to get these collections back. And we need to do it fast, before they're gone forever."

She'd actually talked them into bringing her along.

Yay, me.

But, holy cow, getting stuffed into the upper part of an armoire they'd borrowed from one of the Friary's guest suites, and bumping along in the back of a delivery truck, wasn't exactly what she'd had in mind. Not to mention the darkness and heat and sweat dripping from every one of her pores.

Maddy needed fresh air.

Pronto.

And light.

And room to move because—yowzer—hot stabs darted down her cramping legs.

And, and, and ...

Her mind. Chaos. She closed her eyes and drew hot air into her nose, exhaling slowly while locking her thoughts on the plan and finding the jewels.

Getting her life back.

She lifted her phone to check the time. The screen lit up the interior of the armoire, nearly blinding her. She slammed her eyes closed again, tried again and again until they adjusted.

Phin had told her, barring traffic, it would be forty-five minutes.

Getting close.

After much discussion, the guys decided Zeke riding up front would be safest in case things went kooky, and they had to detain the guard. Fine with Maddy. She'd be zero help with that part of the operation.

As a result, they'd anchored the armoire to the truck wall. For additional safety, Phin tied a rope around it, trapping her inside. She'd never been claustrophobic, but the idea of someone crashing into them and her being stuck inside this thing made her lungs clog.

She lowered her phone, concentrated on the mission. A buzz zipped along just under her skin. By the time this was over, maybe she'd be cleared. No more sitting around waiting for everyone else to decide her fate. That alone was a win.

"Pulling up to the gate," Phin muttered, his voice streaming through the listening device in her ear.

The plan was for Cruz and Rohan to pull up in a gray sedan Maddy had never seen before and stop midway between the front gate and the end of the fence. Once Phin got to the rear gate where all deliveries were made, Rohan would hop out and run along the front fence throwing what they called flash bangs—a device that created loud noise and flashes of light—over it. If all went well, they'd create general mayhem and draw the rear guard to the front.

"We're in place," Cruz said. "On your signal, we'll roll."

The truck eased to a stop and surrounded by darkness, Maddy rested her head back.

Waiting.

A few more minutes, that's all it should be. Long enough to get inside, grab the jewels and go.

She shifted, trying to stretch her legs and battle the cramps.

"Hey, guy," Phin's voice came through her earpiece. "Got a delivery for Xavier Vera."

Silence descended. Maddy froze. What was happening? Had she lost the connection?

"Hang on," another male voice—presumably the guard —finally said.

Maddy let out a breath. She had to relax. Not freak out at every slight plan variation. A minute later, the pfft-pfft-pfft of papers shuffling filled her ear. *Please, let this work.*

"I don't have a delivery tonight," the guard said. "You sure it's this location?"

Pfft-pfft-pfft.

"Dude," Phin said, "I don't know what to tell you. I got an order right here. Take a look."

Before leaving, Phin had loaded a clipboard with fake paperwork, adding an order to the top for the delivery of an antique armoire. Should she be concerned that the man was such an accomplished liar?

More paper shuffling. "It's an armoire," the guard said.

"Dammit. I hate when this happens. I got nothing on my schedule for this."

"Well, I can't sit here all night. The order is right there. Let us drop it off and you can figure out the paper trail later."

Yes. Excellent idea. Maddy waited an almost intolerable few seconds. And, worse, this entire experience added undue pressure on her bladder.

Her mind drifted back to summer road trips. All of them packed into the Suburban. Dad driving, her mother in the passenger seat, reminding her she should have gone potty before they left the house.

"Open up," the guard finally said. "Let me look."

A long sigh sounded. Probably Rohan or Cruz, but Maddy was too busy trying not to urinate in Lynette's armoire to think too hard about it.

Her pulse slammed, the buzz from a few minutes ago turning to an all-out assault. What if he opened the armoire?

Gee, honey, how'd you get inside there?

The master schmoozer would have his work cut out for him on that one.

A sudden, clackety-clack—the metal door rolling up— lit her skin on fire. She flinched and her bladder rebelled against the movement.

Please, please, please.

Instinctively, she drew her legs in tighter, wrapping her arms around them.

So not cut out for this.

"There it is," Phin said. "Antique armoire. Let's get it unloaded. I have a pick-up clear across town and my dead-line is tight. If I miss it, my ass is toast."

More silence.

Could whatever angels might be in the vicinity please help a girl out? Between her bladder, the heat, and the confined space, she wasn't sure she'd even be able to walk when she got out of this thing.

"Awright," the guard said, "when I open the gate, pull to the first bay. I don't know where they want this, but we'll get it inside and the day shift guy can figure it out."

Thank you.

Maddy blew out a hard breath and rolled her shoulders.

The truck inched forward, barely a crawl, but the still open rear door rattled against the rails when Phin hit a bump.

Whoa. Maddy's body tipped sideways against the doors held in place by ropes that kept her from spilling out.

The truck halted again, a second later going in reverse.

Backing into the bay?

Phin had said it was just beyond the gate.

When the vehicle stopped, Maddy's chest tightened, the pressure pushing, pushing, pushing against her ribs. Lord, she needed to get out.

Soon.

Fresh air. Room to move.

Soon.

Here we go...

"You gonna open that bay door for us?"

Phin's voice again, obviously cueing Cruz and Rohan.

"Yeah," the answer came. "Give me a sec."

"Sure thing. I'll get these ramps set. You got a hand truck inside, or should we use ours?"

"There's one inside the door."

A few seconds passed and then... "Blow it," Phin whispered so softly Maddy almost missed it.

Boom!

Maddy lurched up, her spine going ramrod straight. Phin had warned her the flash bangs might startle her.

Boom!

A radio squawked. The guard's?

"Ed?" The guard's voice came through Maddy's earbud. "What was that?"

Boom!

Wow. Rohan and Cruz were making the most of those flash bangs.

"Ed! What's happening?"

More silence.

"What the hell's going on?" Zeke asked.

Boom!

"I gotta check this out," the guard said. "Get this unloaded. Leave it on the dock and we'll bring it in."

Hell no.

They needed that bay door open and this guy taking off before unlocking it was a big fat nada. Just their damned luck the guy would have his key in the lock, but hadn't opened it before Phin's Johnny-on-the-spot brothers started throwing flash bangs.

Beside him, Zeke angled back, scanning the area near the back entry door.

Boom!

Phin flinched. Even knowing it was coming, those flash bangs still rocked him. The guard right along with him. The guard took off, his utility belt—complete with handcuffs, weapon, and a bunch of keys—jangling as he ran toward a parked white SUV beside the building.

"There's a door back here," Zeke said. "My lock-picking tools are in the truck."

Ah, big brother, the expert lock-picker. Phin was already in motion, climbing into the truck and bypassing the metal ramp they'd used to load the armoire.

"We gotta be fast," he called to Zeke. "With all those flash bangs, someone probably already called the cops."

Tires squealed from outside the truck. Probably the guard Phin just spoke to, roaring to the east end of the building where Cruz and Rohan were having a freaking field day.

Phin hit the button on his ear bud. "Heads up, boys. Guard coming your way."

"Got it," Cruz said. "What's your status?"

"Bay is locked. There's an entry door. Zeke is on it."

"Well, tell him to hurry the fuck up."

Ignoring his brother, Phin clicked off and went to work on the bungee cords and rope. Maddy'd been in there a while and he found himself rushing, tugging too hard on the ropes he himself had knotted. What the hell was he thinking, tying them so tight?

A woman he cared about—a lot—not falling out, that's what.

"Maddy, you okay?"

"Yes. I need to stretch. What's happening?"

His fingers slipped on the last knot. The one on the thick rope holding the armoire closed.

Dang it. *Come on, man. Get it together.*

He stopped. Lifted his hands and took a breath.

Focus. Slow down.

Rushing never got him anywhere good.

Trying again, he concentrated on unlooping one end and ... bingo. The rope fell to the floor.

He ripped the armoire doors open and a sweat-soaked Maddy swung her legs out.

"Oh my God," she said, using the upper part of her short-sleeved shirt to blot her face. "I'm cramping up."

Great. They didn't have time for that. He gripped her forearms, steadying her as she kicked her legs out, trying to restore the circulation. His fingers sunk into damp skin and he locked his gaze on her flushed cheeks.

What had they been thinking, shoving her in there?

"I'm sorry we did this to you."

"Hey, I insisted on coming."

"Still."

He shook his head. No time for this. Later, he'd figure out a way to make it up to her. "Can you walk? We have to move fast. The guard I talked to went to help his buddy up front. Cruz and Rohan won't be able to hold them off long."

"I heard. Is Zeke good at lock-picking?"

"The best."

Maddy nodded and broke free of his grasp, reaching back for the duffel they'd stuffed in the armoire with her. "Let's go. Before I wet myself."

Seriously?

He led her to the rear step, hopping down and swinging back to give her a hand down. His T-shirt caught on his waist holder and Maddy's eyes bulged at the sight of the nine millimeter tucked there.

Yes. He was carrying. Maybe he should have mentioned that, but they always carried on recoveries and he damned sure wasn't used to explaining their operating procedures.

He held his hand to her. "Gotta go."

Dragging her gaze from his weapon, she grabbed hold and leaped, sticking the landing on what had to be wobbly legs.

"Do you seriously have to piss?"

"Yes. Why do you have a gun?"

"Standard procedure. Just in case."

Whether the answer satisfied her, he didn't know, but she fell into step beside him, running to catch up with Zeke already at the rear entrance. By the time they got there, he'd slid his tension wrench into the lock with his left hand and inserted the pick with his right, raking back and forth, moving the pins up and down.

"Almost there," he said.

"Good. We have things to do."

Zeke snorted and removed the wrench. Rotating the pick, he hit the lever and—*voila*—open door.

He waved them inside. "What are you waiting for?"

"That is so cool!" Maddy said, following Phin inside. "Total badass."

Had to love her enthusiasm.

Straight ahead, two forklifts sat idle in what had to be an 80,000-square-foot warehouse. If they'd had more prep time, Phin would have known the exact number. Yet another reminder of how hastily they'd pulled this operation together.

Zeke paused in front of a row marked with a white sign displaying a giant red six at the top. He swung his head left, then right, getting his bearings among the rows and rows— twelve to be exact—of stuffed shelves that stretched clear to the two-story ceiling.

"Wow," Maddy said, her voice breathy and filled with wonder. "All this stuff. Is it all stolen?"

"No idea," Phin said. "Make a right," he told Zeke.

Based on their map, the office would be at the front of the building to the right.

"Let's move." Phin burst into a run, heading to the east

side of the building. As he went, he hit the button on his earbud. "Status?"

"About to head back to the car. You about done?"

"We need a few minutes."

Translation: We've barely started.

"Christ on a cracker, Phin." This from Cruz, clearly pissy. "You getting your nails done or what? We'll distract them. Hurry the fuck up!"

Phin hit the button again and hooked a left, tearing down row one.

Boxes and boxes lined the row. Some cardboard, some plastic and rubber. God only knew what kind of stolen goods they contained. If they'd had more time, he'd have taken a peek.

They reached the front of the building and Zeke pointed. "There."

A set of metal stairs led to a platform with a glass-walled office and what looked like a crappy clapboard door. "If the door is locked, we're kicking it in."

Phin led the charge, hitting the narrow stairs at a dead run and sprinting to the top where he gripped the door-knob, gave it a turn, and pushed it open.

Finally, a break.

Stale, musty air hit him like a punch and he held his breath a second, watching dust particles fly.

He scanned the back wall.

Metal filing cabinet. There.

According to Bob, the safe would be next to it.

Cornering the desk, he cut it too close and banged his hip. *Ow*, but ... yes!

On the floor sat a rectangular safe, more tall than wide. He eyeballed it, estimating it at about two and a half feet high.

"Combination is twelve, thirty-two, eighteen, four," Zeke blurted.

Phin squatted, quickly spun the dial, and tried the lever. Nothing.

He dipped his head, forced his mind to order. *Breathe. Work the problem.*

"Try again," Maddy said. "Maybe you missed a number."

Lifting his head, he zeroed in on the dial, spun it again, making sure to hit each digit exactly. He tried the lever again. No dice.

"Well, I didn't miss a number that time."

Fuck it.

Phin reached in, grabbed the safe from the bottom, planted his feet and ... heaved. The safe however, went nowhere.

How much did the damned thing weigh? He scooted sideways, giving Zeke room to squeeze in behind the desk. "It's gotta be over three hundred pounds. Help me."

They both squatted. Phin leaned in, throwing some weight into pushing the top of the safe sideways. Zeke took hold and Phin gripped the bottom.

"On three, we lift," Phin said. "One, two, three."

Upsy-daisy. They pushed up, bringing the safe with them.

"The hand truck!" Maddy said from her spot in front of the desk. "Downstairs. I'll get it."

Phin shot a look over his shoulder. "Be careful. Just get it to the bottom of the stairs. We'll carry this down."

If it didn't possibly contain priceless jewels, he'd toss the safe over the rail.

A click sounded in Phin's ear. "Your guard is getting back in the SUV," Rohan huffed, his voice breathy.

Running.

"We gotta haul ass," Zeke said.

Moving together, they worked their way around the desk to the door, where they stepped onto the metal landing of the staircase. "I'll go first," Phin said. "One step at a time."

"Got it."

One by one, they descended the stairs, checking their footing—step, step, step—each time and going way slower than Phin would have liked.

His chest thumped, his pounding pulse begging him to go faster, and his mind went to war with his body. One of them tumbling ass over elbow would turn this into a total shitshow.

Step.

Step.

Step.

"I'm here," Maddy said. "Got the hand truck."

They reached the bottom, Maddy swung in with the hand truck, and they lowered the safe.

"Hello?"

Everyone froze and Phin's internal war went to DEFCON one.

The guard.

Phin shot his hand out, grabbing hold of Maddy. "We need to split up. Maddy, stay with me."

Zeke took off, sprinting along the back of the rows while Phin and Maddy pushed the hand truck down aisle two.

"Hello?" Zeke called out, hopefully drawing the guard in his direction.

Five feet from the end of the row, they stopped, inching their way forward. Phin peeked around the edge.

"Where the hell are you?" Guard's voice again.

"Oh, hey," Zeke said from somewhere to their right. "We

didn't want to leave the piece outside. Side door was open, so we brought it in for you."

Good one.

"The door was *not* open," the guard said. "Where's your buddy?"

29

Trapped was all Maddy could think.

And she was damned sick of it.

She peered at Phin, in front of her, peeping around the end of the row. They needed to get this safe out of here. How they would do that with the guard somewhere near the door they'd come through, she wasn't quite sure.

If she didn't pee her pants, it would be a miracle.

Diversion.

Phin hadn't specifically said that's what Zeke was doing, but it didn't take a genius to figure it out.

It also didn't take a genius to figure out another diversion might help.

She tugged on Phin's shirt. *Tug, tug. Tug, tug.* He glanced over his shoulder and she moved in closer, getting right next to his ear.

"I'll head back toward the office and distract him. Maybe he'll come looking for me and you can wheel the safe out to the truck."

"No. Stay with me."

Sorry, hon. Can't do it.

She retreated. One step that had Phin spinning toward her, shooting his left hand out. She dodged it, leaping clear of his reach and whirling back, charging down the row.

She could do this.

Just run down to row ... which one? She'd have to go farther down than the one adjacent to the door they'd come in. Row six. That's where Zeke had stopped when they first entered the rear of the building. She needed to at least get to seven. Hopefully, lure the guard away from the entrance so Phin could get out the door.

Sprinting back down the row, she hit the turn at full speed—her full speed anyway—and shot a look up, double-checking the next row number. Three.

No Zeke.

Heaven help her, she had no clue what she was doing. And now she was alone.

Winging it.

So not built for this.

At row four, she stopped, catching her breath for a quick second. She closed her eyes, exhaled, and ...

"Help!" she wailed, the effort shredding her vocal cords. "Someone, please! Help!"

Moving fast, she darted across, stealing a glance left, where Zeke stood squared off with the guard.

"Stop!"

Guard's voice. Definitely not Zeke's deeper tone.

Maddy kicked to her next gear, hauling past row five and then six. One more.

If she could draw the guard away from where they entered at row six, and then lure him to the opposite end of row seven, Phin had a shot to sneak out unnoticed.

"Stop!"

The guard again. Closer, but still at the rear of the building where they entered.

At that end, he'd see Phin taking the safe out.

"Help!" she screamed again, still moving toward the far corner of the building. "Please! Help me!"

Someone give her an Oscar. Although, with the amount of terror pounding her, she wasn't altogether faking her fear.

"Please! He's at this end. Help me!"

The guard. Where was he?

She kept moving. Passing row eight and glancing back. Soon, she'd run out of room. *Where is he? Where is he?*

"Hey!"

She skidded to a stop, her hands flying in the air.

The guard stood in front of her, smack in the middle of the space separating rows ten and eleven.

And pointing a rifle at her.

Fuming, Phin peeped from behind the cover of boxes and —*shit*—spotted the guard, booking it in Maddy's direction.

When this was over, he'd murder her. The woman had broken the most important rule. The one about not going rogue.

The guard turned, disappearing from view, Phin swung the hand truck in front of him and bolted.

Zeke appeared, holding out his arms in a WTF? gesture. By the looks of him, he might beat Phin to homicide.

Phin hustled up to him. "Load this up and go. She's totally off-script. I'm gonna kill her."

"I'm not leaving you."

"Yeah, you are. Rohan and Cruz can get us." Phin jabbed a finger at the hand truck sitting beside them. "Get the safe out of here."

It took barely a second for rational Zeke to strap in. At this point, Phin's working theory of priceless jewels being stored in the safe took priority. Thus, they were balls to the wall, doing whatever it took to get the safe out, crack it open, and hopefully find their quarry.

"I hate flying blind." Zeke grunted, grabbed the hand truck, and headed for the door just yards away. "We'll be back for you."

"I know. Go."

"Help!"

Maddy again. Still at the front of the building, but closer to the far corner. Away from Phin.

And then it all made sense. Maddening, brilliant woman attempting to draw the guard from the door where the truck was parked. All so Phin and Zeke could smuggle the safe out.

Hauling ass, he stormed by the next row, glancing to the opposite end as he went. No Maddy.

Next row.

No Maddy.

Where the hell was she?

Row after row and no Maddy.

"Please!" Maddy yelled. "Put the gun down. I need *help*!"

And whoa. Did the guard *draw* on her? If that asshole pointed a gun at Maddy, he'd pound the fucking daylights out of him.

Phin kept running. Despite the pumping AC, annoying sweat beaded on the sides of his face and the back of his neck, dripping down his spine.

Row nine. No Maddy. He had to be getting close. He hauled by row ten, swung his head right and ...

Maddy.

Hooking the turn late, he plowed into a stack of boxes

that didn't budge. Not one inch. Not half an inch. Whatever was in those suckers had weight.

He pushed off, righted himself, and focused on Maddy at the end of the row, her hands in the air, but no guard in sight. Probably blocked by the end cap.

But, in front of her? Or behind.

Zeke was right. Flying blind. It'd be a miracle if they got out of this.

And he'd been short on miracles this week.

If the guard showed himself, Phin had a target to pounce on.

"Kelly!" Phin yelled, not about to use her real name.

The guard swung around the end cap, automatic rifle raised and aimed in Phin's direction.

Phin halted, ripped his gun from his holster and pointed it at the guard. "Gun down!"

Classic standoff.

Helluva way to die.

"No!" Maddy said.

Beading sweat grew to a waterfall, all of it pouring down his face and neck, spilling into the collar of his shirt. He ignored the urge to wipe it away, concentrating on the guard.

Would this guy shoot him?

Given that he worked for the Veras, probably.

A flash of movement drew his gaze right. Maddy. Arms extended, body in midair, diving toward the guard.

"No!" The word tore from him like jagged glass carving his throat.

His feet moved, pounding against the hard concrete as Maddy crashed into the guard, knocking him sideways against the stacked boxes. A round of shots went off, one of them—*ping!*—ricocheting off one of the shelf's steel supports and whizzing by Phin's shoulder.

Jesus! His heart banged, the pressure damn near fracturing his ribs.

Maddy.

Terror mounted inside. A tsunami, sending his brain into full-on fight-or-flight mode.

Get the gun.

Pistol trained on the guard, now facedown on the floor with an unmoving Maddy sprawled on top of him, Phin rushed them.

Jesus, Jesus, Jesus. He'd done this to her. Agreed to bring her along. She had no damned business here, and it was his fault.

If she was dead, he'd never forgive himself.

"Maddy!"

Used her real name. *Think, moron.*

Gun trained on the guard, he reached her, still motionless. He touched her with his free hand and—whoa!

She sprang up, hands swinging. He leaped back, lowering the gun in case she walloped him. Relief dropped on him so hard he nearly buckled.

"Honey," he said, trying like hell to keep his voice steady. "You're safe now. Are you hit?"

No blood. Not that he could see. Excellent.

She stared at him, her gaze all wide-eyed and clearly spooked. Had she even heard him?

"Hey!" he said, his voice sharp enough to slice through a tree. "Look at me!"

She blinked once. Then again. *Come on, Maddy.* Snap out of it.

Quickly, he checked the guard, still down, then came back to Maddy. "Are. You. *Hit?*"

"Hit?" She sucked in a hard breath, her shoulders pinning back and—bam—something must have registered. Her gaze was still on him, but this time? Total focus.

"Maddy, are you hit?"

"No. Oh, my God!"

Still on his belly, the guard lifted his head. Phin aimed straight at his skull. "Don't move. We don't want to hurt you."

Overhead light glinted off the guard's utility belt. Metal. Handcuffs.

"Honey," Phin said, refusing to use Maddy's name again. "Get his handcuffs. On his belt. And his keys."

She bobbed her head, tentatively shuffled closer, bent down, and lifted the cuffs and keys.

"Good." Phin nudged his chin at the guard. "You. Push your weapons away from you. The rifle and the sidearm."

Phin waited while the guard slowly unstrapped the rifle and slid it across the cement floor. Next came his sidearm.

"On your feet." He peered at Maddy. "Give him the cuffs and come by me."

Her hand trembled, the chain rattling as she handed them off.

Phin kept his weapon on the guard. "Cuff yourself to that rail. Do it."

Once the guy got hooked on, Phin nudged his chin again. "Tug on it."

All good. This guy wasn't going anywhere.

Still, Phin wouldn't take any chances. He took a step, moving backward while eyeing the guard. "We're getting out of here," he said to Maddy, who fell in step with him.

He pressed the button on his ear bud. "We're coming out," he said. "And Maddy needs a bathroom."

"Oh, man," Cruz said. "You scared me. We'll grab you at the gate."

. . .

After hopping into the backseat of the nothing-special, gray sedan BARS kept on hand in case they needed a nondescript, blendable vehicle, Phin dialed Zeke, putting the phone on speaker.

"Everybody safe?" Zeke asked.

"We're good. In the car with Cruz and Rohan. Where are you?"

"Looking for a quiet place to pull over so we can crack this safe open."

Being prepared, thanks to Rohan-king-of-doom, they'd brought a drill, extra titanium drill bits, a borescope, a mini-vacuum, and of course, a generator in case they needed electricity.

"The condo?"

"I thought of it, but it's thirty minutes from here. Thinking we find an abandoned building, pull into the lot, and do our thing."

"If you have a problem," Rohan said, "we could be stuck there awhile drawing attention."

"Hold on," Maddy said, her thumbs flying over her own phone's screen. "Zeke, if you're not too far from us, we're only fifteen minutes from the Thompson Center's storage facility. It has a security guard. If my key card still worked, I'd have access, but I don't. President Thompson could tell the guard to let us in."

"Is it big enough for us to work in?"

"For sure. It's a small warehouse. It doesn't have bay doors like the one we just left, but you could pull up front and take the safe inside."

Cruz stopped for a light on the busy thoroughfare and eyed Maddy in the rearview. "Where am I going?"

"Make a left."

"I'll call Thompson," Phin said. "I'll explain the situation and see if he'll let us use it. Maddy, send Zeke the address. Bro, we'll meet you there. I'll call you back."

In full get-'er-done mode, Phin hung up on Zeke and dialed Thompson.

"Phin," Thompson said, picking up on the first ring. "How's it going?"

"Good, sir. We've secured a safe that, based on the intel from Vera's guy, we believe has the jewels in it."

Thompson let out a breath. "Excellent."

"Unfortunately, the combination we have didn't work. It's not a problem. Zeke can crack it open, but we're two hours from our place and don't want to spend time driving. I'm aware the Thompson Center has a warehouse near our location." He wouldn't say how he knew this, but it also didn't take a rocket scientist to figure it out. "To save time, if you'll allow it, we'd like to swing in there and open the safe."

Don't ask if Maddy is with me.

If he did, what could Phin say? Technically, until the feds cleared her, Maddy was still a suspect.

Total pickle.

"Do it," Thompson said. "I'll have the guard let you in."

Phin held up his fist, pumping it. How he loved decisive people.

"If you don't hear from me," Thompson said, "assume it's set. Do you need anything else?"

"No, sir. We have everything. Thank you. I'll call you as soon as the safe is open."

Twenty minutes later, after admitting them into the one-story warehouse on a main drag near the airport, the guard closed and locked the door behind his visitors, then shuttered himself into his office.

Zeke, with Cruz in tow, wheeled the safe into an open area near the door. A lack of windows left only overhead track lighting to illuminate the air-conditioned building, which Phin supposed was better for the artifacts. At least they could control the environment.

Behind them, random boxes and storage containers were stacked on shelves. To the right sat a car. An old Datsun 280Z straight out of the seventies.

Gearhead Cruz, wandered over, circling it while he examined tires and taillights and then the T-top.

"What's with the car?" he asked Maddy.

"It was President Thompson's when he was in college. He's saved it all these years. He's still deciding if he wants it in the Center or not."

Maddy brought her attention back to Zeke, who'd slid the hand truck from beneath the safe and was on his knees, unpacking a drill from its case.

Maddy stood, head cocked, watching Zeke lay out his tools. "How does this work?"

Pointing at the thick titanium drill bit, Phin said, "He has to drill a hole in the top so he can see the lock inside. If he misjudges, he'll need another hole. And he has to avoid the relockers."

Maddy swung her head up. "What's that?"

Safety glasses on, Zeke picked up the drill. "An additional security device. If I breach it, it triggers the auxiliary lock and we're screwed. Even if we had the combination, the safe won't open."

"Oh my God." Maddy put her hands out. "Should we be doing this, considering what we think is in there?"

An excellent question that, with anyone else manning the drill, might be worth considering.

"Zeke," Phin said, "how many times have you hit a relocker?"

Zeke pressed the trigger, sending the bit whirling. "Once. When I was learning. Swore it would never happen again."

Phin held out his hand. "There you go. Between practicing and actual jobs, he's done this literally hundreds of times."

Zeke got to his feet, bending over the safe, estimating where to drill based on the position of the dial. He set the drill in place, hit the trigger, then leaned in, pushing down with both hands for leverage.

The warehouse filled with a *bzzzzzing* noise as the drill ground into steel, the hard titanium bit slowly plowing through.

A minute later, he removed it, set the drill down, then cleared debris from the hole with his vacuum.

Hole cleared, Phin picked up the borescope, squatted next to Zeke and handed it off. Zeke placed the handheld monitor on top of the safe while he fed the bendy tubelike wire into the hole.

Phin then picked up the monitor, held it while Zeke checked the screen. "There's the relocker. I didn't go far enough back. Dammit. Need a second hole."

Once again, he picked up the drill, but changed out the bit for a longer one and went through the same routine again. Drill, vacuum, scope.

"Bingo," he said while Phin held the monitor. "There's the wheel pack."

One hand on the scope, Zeke turned the safe's dial with the other, watching the monitor as he went.

Microinch by microinch, Zeke adjusted the scope. "There's the opening for the fence. Got it."

Phin had watched him do this plenty of times, but still didn't know—nor did he give a rat's ass—what a fence was.

Zeke spun the dial again.

"There," he said, "someone write this down."

Maddy grabbed the pen and pad Zeke had pulled from his duffel. "Ready."

"Forty-eight."

He spun the dial again. Spin, spin, spin.

"Seventeen."

Maddy jotted the number, waited for the next.

"Nine."

Spin, spin, spin.

Eyes glued to the monitor, a noise came from Zeke's throat. "Come on," he muttered as he adjusted the scope again.

Knees barking from squatting, Phin was reminded he had no patience for complications.

"There," Zeke said, jerking his head. "Twenty-eight."

He let go of the scope and sat back on his haunches, rolling his shoulders before reaching for the dial again.

Phin stood, stretching his legs and Zeke peered up at Maddy. "Read that back to me. Please."

"Forty-eight."

He spun the dial left a few times and then to the right a few times more to clear it before spinning counterclockwise to forty-eight.

They continued the process with Maddy reading each digit and Zeke working the dial.

After the last number, he reached for the safe handle, gave it a twist and—boom—opened it.

. . .

TRANSFIXED, MADDY STOOD, WATCHING ZEKE PULL OPEN THE safe door.

Holy smokes, he'd just done that. Broken into a safe. Right in front of her.

How did people learn to do this stuff? Was there some master class for safecracking?

She wasn't sure if she should be horrified or wildly impressed. Maybe a bit of both.

Was there anything these men couldn't do?

Phin bent low, peering inside the safe before standing again. He pointed at the safe. "Take a look."

Stepping up, Maddy peeped in and her pulse picked up, thumping against her skin. Velvet bags in assorted colors sat stacked on top of each other in a tumbled mess.

Whether the transport had left them thrown about or the thieves just didn't care to store them properly, Maddy couldn't know.

Please don't let them be damaged.

She looked back at Phin, then to Zeke as she gestured to the contents. "May I?"

"Sure," Zeke said.

She lifted one of the bags, working open the drawstring and peeking inside.

Diamond necklace. She blew out a breath, forced herself to take it one step at a time because it might not be *the* diamond necklace.

Gloves.

Gently, she set the bag on top of the safe. "Don't touch that. Please. I need to grab gloves. There's some on the shelf."

She jogged the ten yards to the shelves near the front door where she'd stored everything from cotton gloves to plastic bags and clips. Each pair of gloves had been secured in a sealed freezer bag, ensuring their cleanliness. When it came to handling the jewels, she donned a clean pair each time to avoid any transfer of dirt or skin oil.

At the sink, the one she'd requested be installed and utilized prior to touching any artifacts, she gave her hands a good scrub

Grabbing one of the bags, she ran back to Phin and his brothers, all of whom gathered around the open safe, hands in pockets.

"Do you wash your hands each time?" Rohan asked.

"Without question. Skin has natural salts, moisture, and oils that can damage artifacts." She pulled a fresh set of gloves from the bag. "Gloves too. For jewelry, I use cotton. Other items, I can use nitrile."

She lifted the velvet bag, reached in, and gently wrapped her fingers around the necklace, carefully withdrawing it, making sure it didn't snag and wind up somehow tumbling to the floor.

"Wow," Phin said, his voice breathy and full of the wonder Maddy felt each time she'd touched one of the pieces. "Stunning."

"It is." She held it up for them all to see. "Gentlemen, this is the triple-strand diamond necklace."

"One down," Rohan said. "What else is in there?"

Maddy placed the necklace back in the bag and gently set it on top of the safe. "I'll need to wrap these better before we take them. Something with cushioning. I'll look through the supplies we have here. I may have jewelry cases."

Next, she pulled a blue velvet pouch—at least the thieves had taken care to store them individually—from the safe, repeating the same routine.

"Tiara," she said, her heart skipping.

She wouldn't get too excited. Not yet. After she'd been

through each bag, if all seven items were here, she'd celebrate.

Two tiaras and two brooches later, Maddy raised a double-strand diamond bracelet, the large center diamond nearly winking at her.

"The last of the queen's collection," she said, her eyes filling with moisture.

Relief mixed with joy and crashed in on her. They'd done it.

Recovered all the missing pieces. She'd be cleared. She knew it. Felt it right down to her bones. All because of Phin and his brothers.

She blinked her tears away, met each man's gaze for a few short seconds before finally landing on Phin.

"Thank you," she told him. "I'm so grateful."

Despite his brothers surrounding them, Phin nodded, stepped forward, and wrapped his arms around her, kissing the top of her head.

"We should be thanking you. We did this together."

Together.

Yes, she supposed they did.

"Not to be the one to break up this little lovefest," Cruz said, smacking his hands together. "But let's get this stuff to the feds."

ALREADY EXHAUSTED FROM AN EVENTFUL DAY, MADDY accompanied Phin, Zeke, Rohan, and Cruz to FBI headquarters.

Her preference would have been to go home with Phin, grab dinner, and settle in for a quiet night. All this excitement?

Too much.

The adrenaline surges alone were enough to wear her thin.

Her quiet night would have to wait. *Almost there.* First, the FBI had summoned them to a meeting. They wanted an explanation for activities that included her riding shotgun on the recovery of priceless jewels belonging to the Queen of England.

Just another day.

They stepped up to the X-ray machine where, on the other side, Special Agent Blackwell stood waiting.

Based on his tight lips, locked jaw, and the dark shadows under his eyes, Maddy wasn't sure if this was a fatigued Special Agent Blackwell or a furious one.

Probably both.

She peered up at Phin, waiting patiently beside her to be ushered through the checkpoint. "Your brother looks mad."

"Eh. Wouldn't be the first time. He'll survive."

Phin held up the duffel bag containing the priceless jewels and Special Agent Blackwell nodded before wandering over to the guard. They spoke briefly. Special Agent Blackwell pointed at Phin and the duffel and the man nodded.

"Sir," he said to Phin, "place the bag on the belt and step through."

Doing as directed, Phin waited for the bag to enter the machine before moving.

Phin had already warned her that BARS would receive no credit for their role in this recovery.

The idealist in her found it a travesty. The Blackwells had risked their own lives to recover priceless artifacts and the FBI would enjoy the accolades?

So unfair.

The guard waved her through the machine.

Press.

Ooh, they'd been trying to reach her for days. Maybe she'd leak the details of the recovery? Give them a good juicy story praising BARS.

Could she get in trouble for that?

A week ago, Good Girl Maddy would've been terrified. Now? After what Phin and his family had done for her?

Bad Girl Maddy found the idea massively appealing.

Special Agent Blackwell took two steps toward them, lifted the bag from the belt and … wait … held it out to Phin. He halted, his head literally snapping back as he stared at his brother.

At some point, Maddy would laugh about it. Phin, the master schmoozer, stymied.

"Take it," Special Agent Blackwell said. "You did the work."

After a rough start, Maddy might grow to admire Ash Blackwell.

Or maybe, even if the FBI froze BARS out, Special Agent Blackwell intended to let whatever late-working coworkers remained in the building see his brothers carrying a bag, the contents of which possibly being the stolen jewels.

"Huh." Phin took the bag and clucked his tongue. "You feds. Always with the surprises."

At that, Special Agent Blackwell laughed. "I'm still pissed at you." He made eye contact with each of them, including Maddy. "All of you. You shouldn't have gone rogue on us."

"Sorry, bro," Phin said. "You guys have too much red tape. By the time you secured a warrant, these pieces would've been in the wind."

Special Agent Blackwell lifted one shoulder. "Possibly." He pointed at the duffel. "Is that everything?"

"Yes," Maddy said. "I packed them myself."

"Good." Special Agent Blackwell headed toward the elevator bank. "Follow me. Thompson is upstairs."

Maddy had figured as much. The bigger question, though concerned his brother. "What about Louis?"

Special Agent Blackwell nodded. "Him too. He's talking with his lawyer now. We're hoping he'll cooperate and tell us what he did. The kid is here as well. Waiting on a lawyer."

Cooperate.

She could only hope. His cooperating might mean clearing her and ending this nightmare.

Don't.

She couldn't go there. Couldn't let herself believe it.

Yet.

"Well." She stopped at the elevator, watched Special Agent Blackwell poke the button. "That would be great, but after the last few days, I'm not counting on anything."

"Smart," Zeke said. "If not a tad pessimistic."

"Welcome to the club," Cruz cracked.

A phone rang and Special Agent Blackwell patted his front pockets, dragging his device out. "I need to take this. Give me a sec."

He walked a few feet away as the elevator doors opened and several people, carrying an assortment of briefcases and backpacks, stepped out, obviously leaving for the day. The guys all backed up a few steps, clearing the area in front of the elevator while Maddy stood off to the side. The elevator doors closed and she shot a look at Special Agent Blackwell, still talking on his phone. Once again, she waited on someone else while her career—her livelihood—hung in the balance.

Waiting, waiting, waiting.

With Phin and his brothers still a few feet away, she took

a second to enjoy some brief solitude. She leaned against the wall, rested her head back, and closed her eyes. Soon. All of it would be done. She simply had to stay patient and let the system work.

Having a former president involved should move things along. She hoped.

"You okay?"

Phin's voice.

She peeled her eyes open, found him standing in front of her.

"I'm good."

Liar.

Good Girl Maddy butting in again. Wanting everything to be a-okay.

"Actually," she said, "I'm tired. And sick of waiting for all the pieces to come together. I want this over. Now."

"You should be tired. We're almost done. I promise you that. Okay?"

Phin. Such a good guy. She reached for him, clasping his forearm. "You know I'm crazy about you, right?"

He flashed that magic Phin smile. "Ditto. After this, we're going on a date. A lot of dates, if I have anything to say about it."

Special Agent Blackwell chose that moment to return, his call apparently finished.

"Development," he said.

"Oh. Goody," Phin cracked.

"Hold it!" someone yelled.

They all turned to where Cilla stood at the X-ray machine, gathering her briefcase and purse from the belt. Maddy had called her on the way over, giving her a rushed version of the events.

At which point, Cilla had instructed her to keep her mouth shut until she arrived. *Okey-dokey.*

Crossing the lobby, she jogged toward them. An enviable feat considering her sky-high heels and navy dress that fit too well not to be tailored to her lean body.

"Oh. Goody," Special Agent Blackwell said, mimicking Phin.

Cruz broke away from Zeke and Rohan, his gaze fixed on a charging Cilla.

"And who might this be?" Cruz wanted to know.

"My lawyer," Maddy told him. "Careful, she may eat you alive."

"Special Agent Blackwell," Cilla's eyes shot darts at the oldest of the Blackwell bunch. "What did I say about all communication with my client going through me? Was I not clear enough?"

"Ha!" Cruz swung to Phin. "Anyone who talks to Ash that way? Just so you know, I might be in love."

Maddy snorted. Cruz. So funny.

Cilla, however, must have been in her badass lawyer zone because she remained totally unaffected. Had she even heard him? Didn't seem like it.

For his part, Special Agent Blackwell kept his attention on Cilla. "I've barely said two words to her. Now that you're here, Louis—Junior—wants to speak with Maddy." He swung his head to her. "Are you up for that?"

Maddy gawked. Couldn't help it. What the heck? *"Me?"*

He held up the phone still in his hand. "That was Walker. The lawyer told her he'd like a word with you in private. Supposedly, he's ready to talk, but won't say anything until he sees you."

This was it. Time for him to come clean. She felt sure. Why else would he want to see her?

"She's not going in there alone," Cilla said.

"No chance." Phin faced her. "And I'm not turning caveman on you. It's just common sense. The guy held a gun to you. Not happening."

Cilla held up a finger, her barely-there pink polish catching the light. "I want him handcuffed and chained to something so he can't get to her."

"Absolutely," Special Agent Blackwell said. "He won't be able to touch her."

Maddy bobbed her head. "I'll stay near the door. That way, if he moves, I'll leave."

"Hang on," Phin said. "You *want* to do this?"

Of course she did. Looking the man in the eye or better still, making *him* look *her* in the eye only added to her anticipation. After what he'd done, she couldn't imagine a better ending to the chaos.

"I absolutely do. The man tried to wreck my life. I want him to look at me and suffer through giving me an explanation."

"I like it," Cruz held up a fist. "Go, Maddy."

Phin gave him the hairy eyeball. "You're not helping."

Ignoring them, Maddy took two steps and pressed the elevator button. "Let's do this. I'm ready."

More than ready.

30

MADDY WAITED FOR SPECIAL AGENT BLACKWELL TO OPEN THE door to the interview room, ironically, the same one she'd been questioned in, before stepping inside.

Frigid, air-conditioned air enveloped her, puckering her skin. So damned cold.

Against the far wall, Louis sat with his cuffed hands resting on the table. A long chain stretched over the edge and she thought back to her earlier visit to this room. She'd failed to notice it, but there must have been a hook attached to the wall to shackle prisoners.

Probably better that she hadn't had that little detail in her mind when being questioned. Now, though, the extra bit of security allowed her to focus on the conversation.

Besides, Special Agent Blackwell had promised he'd be in the hallway. All she needed to do was holler.

"Maddy," he said from his spot in the doorway, "I'll be right outside. With your lawyer."

"No recordings," Louis said. "That was the deal."

"We agreed to it for this part only. Once Maddy leaves, everything gets recorded. Understood?"

Louis nodded, and Special Agent Blackwell met her eye. "He's got ten minutes."

The door closed with a quiet click that boomed in the confined space. Realizing she still had her back to Louis, she whirled around, leaning against the wall to the right of the door.

"You can sit," he said.

She folded her arms, crossed one foot over the other. "I prefer to stand. The view is good."

"Me in handcuffs?"

"Absolutely. You tried to ruin me."

"Not intentionally."

That earned him an award-worthy eye roll. "Please. You don't *accidentally* frame someone. Tell me why you did it. That's the only reason I agreed to this meeting."

"My lawyer is finalizing the deal, but I already told them I'd confess. I felt ... obligated, I suppose, to talk to you first."

That was something. Maybe the man wasn't a total loss. "You owe me at least that."

The damage he'd done to her would change her forever. After this, she wasn't sure she could even go back to the Thompson Center. They'd thought—or believed on some level it could be possible—that she'd stolen from them. Otherwise, they'd have let her stay.

That alone devastated her. How could she go back to work as if nothing had changed?

"The plan," Louis said, "was to take the Pierre jewels. Only my father's."

"Why?"

He let out a forced, huffing laugh. "Gerry is my half brother. You know that."

Maddy nodded. "Of course. He was a teenager when he came into your life."

"I ..." He shook his head, stared down at his cuffed hands, studying them. "I ... well, resented, I suppose is the word, him. And my father. All I ever wanted was my father's time. He had little of it for me or my mother, but had it for other people. Obviously."

"That had to be difficult."

"It was. I didn't want to know Gerry. He was the symbol of all the reasons my dad didn't have time for me. My father would set up weekends and dinners and such, but we never really bonded."

"Understandable."

"We're different people. Different hobbies. He's a book-worm. I'm not. I liked to watch sports, he didn't. Zero in common." He shook it off. "My mother, she's dead now, was a good wife. Excellent mother. My father, although a good provider and genius designer, got cocky. Fame went to his head. He had affairs. I don't know how many, but I heard the rumors. And saw the press clippings."

A part of her, the Good Girl Maddy part, ached for him. Having lost her father, she knew that yearning. That want. Louis's father may have been alive, but he'd checked out emotionally.

"Y'all never talked about it? The hurt he was causing."

"Heavens no. We were exemplary at masking the obvious. At least until Gerry showed up. He'd found his birth certificate with Dad's name on it and wanted to meet his biological father. Dad was off on a buying trip, so Mom spoke to him and then called Gerry's mother. A few weeks later, instant brother. A paternity test confirmed it."

Poor Mrs. Pierre. Not only the betrayal, but to have the young man unexpectedly turn up at her door?

Devastating.

"Your mother stayed with him?"

"She did. She later told me life was easier as Mrs. Louis Pierre."

He looked down at his shackled hands again, let out a sound. A cross between a grunt and sigh. Disgust, no doubt.

"She liked her life," he continued. "They kept the situation with Gerry as quiet as possible, but how do you explain an instant teenager? Dad finally admitted it publicly and once the scandal waned, we got back to some sort of normalcy. As I said, Gerry would spend some weekends with us. My mother insisted on it. His circumstances, she told me, were not his fault. He deserved a father as much as anyone."

"She sounds like an amazing woman."

"She was. I was furious with my father for blowing up our lives. As we got older, the good news was that Gerry had no interest in the family business. Politics was his game. He stayed in his lane and I stayed in mine." He met Maddy's eye again. "We were in an oddly good place."

"So, what happened? Why steal from the Center?"

He pressed his index finger against the table, rattling the chains, the clanking sound grating against Maddy's stretched nerves.

"I'm the CEO of Pierre." he poked at the table this time, clanging the chains again, but seemingly unfazed by it. "A twelve-billion-dollar company. Twelve *billion* dollars. It was worth half that when I took over. And somehow, I play second fiddle to my bastard brother."

Bastard brother? Ouch. Maddy put up a hand. "Hey, that's not fair. The man became a president."

"Not only did he become president, he married the Queen of England's granddaughter. Unbelievable. I'm the legitimate heir, busting my ass running my father's business, and all people, including my father, can talk about is what

Gerry has done for the brand. Gerry. What about what I've done? Gerry has his wife wear a necklace, and he's the hero. Like Dad, all that fame and attention went to his head. He needed to be knocked off his perch."

Knocked ... what? *That's* what this was about? His brother's ego?

Madness.

"So," she said, still trying to wrap her mind around it, "you stole your company's own jewels because you wanted to make your brother look bad?"

"I know it sounds ... misguided."

It sounded a lot worse than that. "Ya think?"

He gave her a hard look. As if *she* were the nutty one.

"I saw it as my opportunity to be the hero. I hired the Veras to steal the Pierre pieces. They were not to touch the queen's collection. The plan was to keep the pieces hidden, and then I'd set it up so my investigator would locate them. For once, *I'd* be the hero."

All of this because he wanted attention. The glory that came with being a so-called hero. Pride. Always dangerous.

Maddy cocked her head, tried to see the humanity in this man who'd caused so much trouble. "Your plan didn't work out, I guess."

"When they took the queen's collection, I lost my mind. The Pierres were one thing. That I could control. The queen's collection took this to another level. I was trying to negotiate a deal with the Veras for *all* the pieces when they hadn't even given me *my* pieces yet."

Shock assailed her, heating her skin and warding off that damned cold air. "They double-crossed you?"

Misery hollowed out his cheeks, and he dipped his head. "Should have seen it coming."

"Or, hey, maybe not have done it at all?"

He shrugged, giving her the victory that hardly felt like a win.

She waved it off. "How did I become your target?"

"I panicked. In my initial meetings with the Veras, I told them everything. Security protocols. Staff habits. They needed anything I could provide. I knew you walked the building every day."

The hits just kept on coming. They had used her dedication to her job against her. She dug her heel into the floor, forced herself to be still while her mind whaled on her. A fool. Good Girl Maddy, so easy to pin a crime on.

No. Nuh-huh. She wouldn't berate herself for this. For being a decent person. She lifted her chin, pushed her shoulders back. "You gave them information they could frame me with. You really are a horrible man."

Again, he peered down at his cuffed wrists. "It was their idea to be seen on video with you. When they stole the queen's pieces and refused to turn them over, you were the obvious way out. I asked Louis to grab your keys. That was his only involvement. He knew nothing about this."

"You expect me to believe that? Really?"

"He didn't. I thought if I had the key to your home, it would give me negotiating power. I could give them the key. If one man on the security video went to your house, it would look like you were involved and take more pressure off of them. One morning, I was talking to Louis. He mentioned that you had a tour that day. I knew you'd be out of your office, so I told Louis I had talked to you. That I needed a few other Pierre pieces back that were on loan to the Center and locked in storage. When I told him I needed the key, he didn't question it. He took your keys and gave them to me. I had copies made."

"You gave the keys to my home to the Veras."

Maddy locked her jaw shut, biting down hard enough to snap her back teeth. The vile nerve of this self-centered narcissist. She hoped they sent him to the worst prison available. Good Girl Maddy tsk-tsked.

Screw off, Good Girl Maddy.

"I panicked," Louis said. "They were supposed to turn over the Pierres in exchange. They didn't."

Maddy scoffed. "There's a shock. For a smart man, you've failed yourself and your family miserably."

A knock sounded and a second later, the door opened. Special Agent Blackwell stood there, one hand still on the knob, his gaze on Louis. "Time's up." He glanced at Maddy. "You good?"

Good? Hardly. She pushed off the wall and paused before turning to the door. "Whatever happens to you, I hope you find a way to be free of your demons. I pity you. I'll also forgive you. Maybe not today, but I won't continue wasting my energy over this."

"You *forgave* him?"

A physically and mentally whupped Phin stood in an FBI conference room staring at what appeared to be an equally exhausted Maddy. Puffy eyes, slumped shoulders, wild hair. The whole bit.

Before walking into FBI headquarters, she'd complained of a headache, popped two ibuprofen, and relieved her curly hair of its tie. Thanks to the moisture outside, all those curls had exploded into a ball of frizz.

She might be the most beautiful thing he'd ever seen.

Add to that the fact that she could forgive someone who'd framed her.

"I told him I would, but not today," she said. "What kind

of imbecile would I be to carry all that anger around? I refuse to give that man any more of my energy. Now, he's in the hands of Lady Justice. She can deal with him."

He stepped closer, got right into her space, and cupped his hands over her cheeks. "I think you're amazing."

Her face lit up. She ripped off a wide, toothy smile. He might have to marry her.

"Well, Phin Blackwell, I think you're pretty darned special, too."

The door came open and Ash stuck his head in. "Whoopsie."

Ash needed to work on his timing. Phin lowered his hands and stepped back. "Have I mentioned you have a timing issue?"

His brother laughed. "No. But I'll take it under advisement. Sorry to interrupt. You two good in here?"

"Yeah," Phin said. "Where are Zeke, Cruz, and Rohan?"

"Zeke and Rohan are finishing up their statements. I just saw Cruz chasing after Cilla. Imagine *that* combination? She's currently harassing my boss about a statement to the press regarding Maddy's vital cooperation in solving this case."

"Cruz and Cilla." Phin ran a hand down his face. "That might tax me."

"Please," Ash said. "They'd murder each other in a day." He shifted to Maddy, holding her gaze for a few long seconds. "I apologize for what we put you through. If it's worth anything, I was having trouble believing you were involved. We had to ... well."

She waved him off. "You were doing your job."

Yeah, Phin needed this woman in his life. Her ability to see through the haze, to maintain a rational and uncynical mind, gave him hope.

A reason to believe even assholes had potential.

"Sometimes," Ash said, "the job sucks."

"Sure does," Phin added, taking a cue from Maddy and suppressing the full weight of his sarcasm.

Still, she shot him a look. "Hey," he said. "Baby steps. I could have droned on about them harassing an innocent woman. In my mind, I gave him a pass."

Ash let out a snort and Phin waggled his eyebrows at him.

"Y'all are nuts," Maddy said. "Anyway, as long as the FBI clears me, I'm happy."

Ash stepped inside, shutting the door behind him and coming closer to Phin and Maddy. If Phin knew his brother at all, he had some intel for them.

"You didn't hear this from me," Ash said, "but based on what I heard from Louis, you'll be free of this soon."

Maddy cocked her head. "Will they make an announcement? I mean, will they actually say I wasn't involved?" Before Ash could answer, she put a hand up. "I'm not being a jerk. Actually, maybe I am, but this could wreck my career. Who would hire a curator previously suspected of art theft?"

"I understand. Let me see what I can do. Plus, you know ... *Cilla*. Between the two of us, maybe we can accomplish something."

This was the Ash that Phin worshipped. The one who strategized. The one who made things right when protocol screamed foul.

Fuck protocol.

Phin reached up, grabbed his brother, and yanked him closer, bear-hugging him. If he'd had the balls, he might have even kissed him on the cheek. A loud, smacking one.

"Dude," Ash said, arms still at his sides. "Is this necessary?"

Phin laughed and added a back slap to the hug. "Hell yeah it is. Before you know it, the whole building'll be talking about Cam Blackwell going soft."

"My ass," Ash said, lifting his arms and returning the hug.

"Aww, y'all are *killing* me right now."

They both stepped back and turned to Maddy, whose face had basically collapsed as she fought back tears and flapped her hands in front of her face.

"I *hate* crying," she said. "I really do. So tired. Strung out. And I miss my family." She ran her hands over her face, dropped them. "I want to see my family."

Phin left Ash in the dust and this time pulled Maddy into his arms, kissing the side of her head. "Your car is still at our place, but after we're done here, I'll take you to your mom's. Okay? I'll drop you off and pick you up when you're ready. Press might still be on you, but we'll figure it out."

She pressed her cheek against his chest and squeezed closer, her body crushed against his, and there it was. That punch, that eruption inside him that made him ...

Happy.

Content.

Both of which hadn't happened in a long time.

If ever.

"Maddy," he said, his voice splintering with some kind of crazy emotion he wasn't sure he minded. "We really need to go on a date because I'm falling in love with you."

"Whoa," Ash said from behind him. "I am *out.*"

Phin didn't bother looking. The click of the door shutting told him his brother had turned tail and run. Who could blame him? When the hell had Phin ever uttered the word "love" about a woman?

Talk about going soft.

Maddy arched back, staring up at him with her eyes that made him think of a Caribbean beach and lounge chairs and tropical sun and fruity-ass drinks he'd hate but would drink anyway because that's what you did in the Caribbean.

He wanted it. All of it.

With Maddy.

"A date." She peered up at him. "I'd like that. Maybe a picnic. Just us and quiet. When it's quiet I don't have to think about anything but you and how much you've done for me and how I've been waiting my whole life for you and how I think I love you, too."

Yeah. This was the good stuff.

He kissed her. Long and slow until his body hummed and the little brain considered a list of naughty things they could do on an FBI conference room table.

Stepping back, he held up two hands. "We'll need to hit pause on this before my pants get really uncomfortable."

Maddy's gaze shot straight to his crotch, and they both cracked up.

"To be continued?" she asked.

"Without a doubt. Let's find my brothers so we can get the hell out of here."

On Tuesday evening, freshly showered after spending the night before with her family and staying over, she strolled into the Friary's kitchen, where the rich scent of spices lingered in the air.

As he'd promised, Phin had scooped her up at Mom's and sat through the equivalent of an FBI interrogation. Phin, bless him, patiently answered every question until Maddy put an end to the entire thing and hustled him out of the house just before lunchtime.

They'd returned to the Blackwell estate, where they spent the afternoon cruising around the property in a jeep that was apparently Phin's. Still so much to learn.

And, yes, he'd treated her to a picnic with sandwiches thick as bricks and the best potato salad Maddy may have ever tasted.

The day had been nothing short of stunning and now she'd been invited to a Blackwell family dinner.

How lucky was she?

Pretty darned lucky. Even her stomach knew it because it let out a roar. Whatever Lynette had simmering, her body wanted it.

She loved spending time with Phin, but tonight she'd go back to her apartment. She had to. Phin had promised to change the locks and, as grateful as she was to his family for giving her shelter, she wanted to reclaim her space.

And her life.

The Blackwell men—including Ash—sat at the island with Grams while Lynette busied herself with several pots on the stove.

"There she is," Phin said. "There's Maddy."

A round of hellos came from everyone, and Phin slid off his stool, gesturing her toward it. "Sit."

He grabbed a glass from a cabinet, poured her what looked like sweet tea from a pitcher on the island and placed it in front of the stool he'd just vacated.

"Thank you," she said, waving him back to the stool while she stood beside it at the end of the island. "You sit. I'll stand. Maybe your mom will let me help her."

"Not in this lifetime," Lynette said. "You're our guest. Stand if you like, but you're not working. Besides, you've had a rough week. You deserve a rest."

Rest, she'd had. "I slept *twelve* hours last night. Can you believe it?"

"I can. You must've needed it."

Lynette went back to stirring the contents of one of the pots, and Zeke held up a hand from his spot at the opposite end of the island. "Since everyone is here, I'll update y'all. I heard from Thompson earlier."

Oh, now this would be interesting.

"He said," Zeke continued, "Louis is cooperating fully. The Veras are going down in huge numbers. The feds used Louis's phone records to locate one guy involved in the heist. He's singing like a second soprano. Storage facilities, organization hierarchy, all of it. The feds raided three warehouses today, including the one we hit yesterday. It's a literal gold mine. Thompson said it's one of the biggest recoveries the FBI art crime team has done."

"Good," Phin said. "What about the guy we met with? He hasn't contacted me about the reward/ransom yet."

"Don't know. They haven't found him. I'm guessing he heard Louis got pinched and he ran."

Maddy held up her glass. "All of this is thanks to BARS."

"And to you." Returning the gesture, Cruz held up his glass. "To BARS, to Maddy, and to family. Cheers."

They all clinked their glasses, their voices ringing out in hearty cheers and the swish in Maddy's belly went haywire, tickling the underside of her flesh and bringing a burst of joy up into her chest.

This family. So good.

And, hopefully, she'd be part of it.

She met Phin's gaze, grinning like a kid on Christmas morning. He set his hand over hers and squeezed.

So good.

She turned back to Zeke. "I'm glad the Thompsons are getting closure on this. I feel terrible for them."

Ash shook his head. "They should feel terrible for *you*."

"They do," Zeke said, leaning forward and meeting Maddy's eye. "He told me that today. I know he's a politician, but he sounded sincere. I think they have genuine affection for you. He said he'd call you tonight. He wants you back ASAP."

They wanted her back. Two weeks ago, simply hearing those words would have sent her to a state of euphoria. A former president and First Lady wanted her.

What greater compliment could there be?

How about the one where they supported her when the FBI suspected her of theft?

Maddy took a sip of her tea and set the glass down, running her finger along the side where condensation dripped.

She had decisions to make. And soon.

"You know," she said, still running her finger up and down, up and down, up and down. "I believe he's sincere. I just ..."

She lifted her gaze to Phin, then to his mother.

These people had helped her. Had given her security when she needed it. Oddly, no matter what happened between her and Phin, she'd always feel connected.

"You just what?" Phin asked.

"I can't believe I'm about to say this, but I'm not sure I can go back there. It's strange. I know they care about me, but they put me on leave. I understand it, but it also feels like they didn't stick by me. Not the way you all did. Is it wrong to feel that way?"

"Honey," Lynette said, "you can't help what you feel. All you can do is follow your instincts. You have every right to be disappointed in them."

Buoyed by Lynette's approval, Maddy sat a little

straighter. "Thank you, Lynette. That means a lot to me."

"So," Phin said, "what do you wanna do? Quit? Just walk away?"

Yes, actually, she thought she might.

Good Girl Maddy would, for once, do what she wanted, rather than what others expected.

You go, girl.

"I haven't fully decided yet," she told Phin. "But I might. I want to work where I'll be appreciated. I know that sounds naïve —"

"It's not," Rohan said. "It's admirable. Frankly, you deserve that."

"I can reach out to Kayla," Phin said. "She's got a ton of contacts in the art world."

"If you have any interest in consulting," Zeke said, "BARS could use you. Liv is coming on board full-time, but I'd like to have more support for her during busy times."

Consulting?

For *BARS*?

What would *that* entail?

If it meant going on recoveries, like she'd done yesterday, forget it. She didn't have the fortitude for that.

Phin's face lit up. "You'd kick ass as a consultant. It pays big bucks. You'd have time to get your PhD."

During their first meeting, she'd mentioned she'd wanted to add her PhD to what he called the wall of Maddy. If she could manage enough consulting hours, she'd be able to double up on her classes. Not do the part-time thing that would take forever.

Her PhD.

Wow.

She leaned in, swung her head to the end of the island, where Zeke waited for some kind of response. "I'd like to discuss this further with you. Let me know when is convenient."

"I'm around tomorrow afternoon if you want to kick it around."

She smacked her hand on the island. "Tomorrow it is."

"Nice," Phin said, setting his hand on her shoulder and giving her an affectionate squeeze before turning back to his family. "And, um, speaking of Kayla, I have news."

"Can we skip talking about *that* woman at dinner?" Ash asked.

Lynette pointed her wooden spoon at him. "Watch it."

"Yes, ma'am."

She set the spoon down and faced Phin. "Is this about our conversation? You working for her?"

Clearly, in Maddy's absence, Phin had discussed with his mother the idea of working part-time for Kayla.

Phin nodded. "I talked to her this morning." He glanced at Maddy. "Before I came to get you. I didn't want to say anything until I heard from her. She called me thirty minutes ago."

THIS WAS IT.

Time for him to speak up and walk his own path while still fulfilling his responsibilities to his family.

Whether he could pull it off remained to be seen, but he wanted to try. He owed it to himself.

To his family.

If he could be happy, he'd be a better version of himself and probably more useful to BARS.

He met his mother's gaze, then each of his brothers. By the time he got to Maddy, she was already nodding, spurring him on.

Gently coaxing him.

Eventually, he'd marry her. Sure as he was standing here, he knew it.

In front of his entire family, he leaned over, kissed her quick, just a peck on the lips that left his mom and Grams wide-eyed and his brothers clearing their throats.

They'd have to get used to this Phin. The one who brought a woman home and freaking kissed her in front of them.

"Kayla," he said, "is on board with me working for her. She has concerns about me doing both. More from a time perspective than anything else. Lobbying, like BARS, isn't a nine-to-five job. We agreed to a trial run to see if it'll work."

"Wait," Ash said. "You're working for Kayla Krowne? What'd I miss?"

Phin gave Ash the synopsis of his conversations with the fam, explaining his yearning to do more in politics. Of all people, Ash would understand his desire to grow.

"I didn't know you felt this way," Ash said.

Phin shrugged. "Nobody did. After you went to the FBI, I didn't want to—" No. He wouldn't make this about Ash. "I should have spoken up right then. Said I wanted a career in politics. Maybe hold public office. I didn't, and that's my fault. It's on me. Now, it's time. I'm no good to y'all if I'm unsatisfied and losing patience with people like Blakely." He glanced over at Maddy. "Sometimes, someone comes along and makes you see that."

Lynette pointed her spoon at Phin. "Kayla Krowne is lucky to have my boy."

His mother. Always a hard-ass. He snorted. "Thanks, Mom."

As confident as Mom sounded, they'd have to see how transferable Phin's schmoozing skills were to shaping policy.

The challenge of it, the potential of doing something new and meaningful, filled him. Left him ... excited.

Hopeful.

He drew a long breath, held it, and let it fly again. Finally, he'd done something for himself.

"Your contacts alone," Maddy added, "would help her. Together, you'd get a lot done. Real change, Phin, and that's amazing."

"She said the same thing. I'm meeting with her on Friday to work out details."

Zeke leaned in, offered a smile that stretched wide. "Even if, down deep, I hate it, I'm glad this is falling into place. I want you happy. Are you happy?"

That word again. Was he?

He glanced at Maddy, thought about their picnic earlier that day, the time they'd spent together over the last week talking and making love and ... laughing.

Happy.

"Yeah," he said. "I am."

"Good," Zeke said. "Then I think we need to do the family toast. Everyone, glasses up."

They all lifted their glasses and Phin met Maddy's gaze. "You heard the man. We're doing the family toast. Lift your glass. You'll love this. After Cruz does his bit, you say 'no exceptions.'"

Beaming up at him, she did as instructed and lifted her glass.

"Family first." Zeke said, holding up his beer.

"Through blood," Phin said.

"Through hate," Rohan said.

"Through fear," Cruz said.

"No exceptions," they all said in unison.

ACKNOWLEDGMENTS

As odd as this will sound, thank you to the Blackwell brothers, who just wouldn't go away. The last couple of years brought changes that left me wondering if this series would happen, but the pesky Blackwell men (and Tracey!) kept us on track.

To Tracey Devlyn, thank you for always being the voice of reason and for a friendship that has changed my life. I am forever grateful for your wisdom and inability to give up. We did it, girlfriend!

Thank you, thank you, thank you to Kristen Weber for challenging me in ways I didn't necessarily want to be challenged. Your efforts helped me bring Maddy and Phin's relationship to another level and I'm enormously grateful.

Thanks to our eagle-eyed copy editor Martha Trachtenberg who, as I write this, has not yet received the manuscript, but will more than likely leave the pages bloody. You, too, leave me exhausted, but I wouldn't trade it. Your talent is exceptional.

Thanks to Stuart Bache for making our vision a reality by designing fantastic covers for *Flash Point* and *Smoke Screen*.

Milton Grasle, you once again saved me from writing myself into a corner. Thank you for always being there.

To Team Steele Ridge, Sandy Modesitt, Leiha Mann, and Heather Machel, thank you for all that you do. Maureen Downey and Tessa Russ, thank you for keeping me organized when shoulder surgery derailed my writing schedule. I'm so grateful for all of you.

Thanks also to Liz Semkiu and Sandy Modesitt for doing an early read of *Smoke Screen* and offering feedback.

As always, thank you to my guys, who make my world a beautiful place. Whether it's at a baseball game or just sitting around making each other laugh, because of you, I'm reminded daily how lucky I am. I love you.

ABOUT ADRIENNE GIORDANO

 **Adrienne Giordano** is a *USA Today* bestselling author of over forty romantic suspense and mystery novels. She is a Jersey girl at heart, but now lives in the Midwest with her ultimate supporter of a husband, sports-obsessed son and Elliot, a snuggle-happy rescue. Having grown up near the ocean, Adrienne enjoys paddle-boarding, a nice float in a kayak and lounging on the beach with a good book. For more information on Adrienne's books, please visit www.AdrienneGiordano.com. Adrienne can also be found on Facebook at http://www.facebook.com/AdrienneGiordanoAuthor, Twitter at http://twitter.com/AdriennGiordano and Goodreads at http://www.goodreads.com/AdrienneGiordano.

Don't miss a new release! Sign up for Adrienne's new release newsletter!

Made in United States
Orlando, FL
01 September 2023

36613097R00243